Shadow of a Thief

Also by Norman Green

Sick Like That

The Last Gig

Dead Cat Bounce

Way Past Legal

The Angel of Montague Street

Shooting Dr. Jack

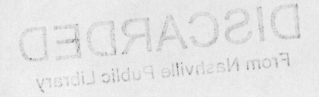

Shadow of a Thief

A Thriller

NORMAN GREEN

WITNESS
IMPULSE

An Imprint of HarperCollinsPublishers

Excerpt from *The Last Gig* copyright © 2008 by Norman Green.

Digital Edition OCTOBER 2017 ISBN: 978-0-06-267278-0
Print Edition ISBN: 978-0-06-267279-7

Cover photograph © M. Shcherbyna / Shutterstock

FIRST EDITION

17 18 19 20 21   LSC   10 9 8 7 6 5 4 3 2 1

For Christine

The knower and the known are one. Simple people
imagine that they should see God as if he stood
there and they here. This is not so.

MEISTER ECKHART

Step Eleven

So who am I, my friend, and who are you
How can I understand this world, this life
or even just myself, what do I do
to find my place in all this noise and strife
I know I haven't listened all that well
or even thought to ask until too late
for what is right for me I cannot tell
am I this dumb or is it just my fate
But I am really lost, I'm screwed this time
alone, I'll always make the poorest choice
unless you help me, I will never find
my way. And so I try to hear your voice
But even now, I know I'm faithless, still
afraid that you won't speak, afraid you will

D. E. KELLOGG

Prologue

THE SAFEST TIME *to walk lower Manhattan's Avenue D, in Corey Jackson's opinion, was early in the morning. Early in the morning, chances were, the ghouls who ruled the projects at night would be passed out somewhere, not roaming around looking for entertainment the way they were now. Half an hour to midnight, Avenue D, a white kid from South Carolina with his African girlfriend, even the cops would tell you that you were asking for it, and for no good reason. But at the tender age of twenty-three Corey already knew enough about women to know that there were some arguments you weren't gonna win. "Babe," he said. "Babe, where the hell are we going?"*

"This way," she said, and she kept on walking.

Corey could not wait to get back to Batesburg.

Two more semesters, that's what he kept telling himself, two more semesters and he would be a real teacher, with the degree to prove it, and that would allow him to move out of the purgatory otherwise known as New York City. A degree would give him a leg up, a toehold in the middle class, a degree and a job teaching high school science and he just might be the first of the Batesburg Jacksons not to live in a trailer since the damn things were invented . . . It sounded like a good plan, it had always sounded good, and sometimes you had to take a shot, but you never knew when you were gonna hit a pothole somewhere. You never knew when you were gonna wind up walking down a sidewalk in a neighborhood where you and everybody else knew you didn't belong.

You never knew when you were gonna fall in love, or with whom.

She was Nigerian. Her name was Aniri and she was the most beautiful person Corey had ever known, surely the sweetest, the kindest, the sexiest, the most wonderful thing God had ever put legs under. Okay, sure, she was black and he was white and that might be viewed as a problem by some, particularly by his never-been-north-of-the-Mason-Dixon-line mother, but either she would adapt and accept Aniri or she wouldn't, and Corey was okay with that. And nobody in Batesburg was ever going to hear that she once worked as a call girl. And okay, Aniri didn't have a green card but Corey was sure that he could find a work-around for that; hell, people did it all the time. No, the real problem was that Aniri was, essentially, owned and operated by the escort service that occupied the top two floors of the Hotel Los Paraíso on Tenth Street. Corey was no push-over and he was not without courage, but he knew when he was in over his head. The men who ran the escort service were out of his weight class and, even after months of racking his brain, he still had no idea how to pry Aniri out of their clutches.

Aniri, though, had a plan, and that was why they were walk-ing south on Avenue D at eleven-thirty on this particular Thursday night. "Babe," Corey said. "Are you sure about this? A witch doctor? If my grandmother could see me now . . ."

Aniri whirled to face him. "Corey Jackson, you have no idea how hard this is for me! It's costing me two thousand dollars to see this guy!"

"Two thousand bucks! Now I know you're crazy!"

Aniri grabbed a handful of his shirt. Corey could feel her trembling. She pulled him close and hissed in his face. "Corey, this could be my only chance. Now we're going to go see this man, and I want you to keep your trap shut. When your mouth opens the only sounds I want to hear are 'Yes sir' and 'Yes ma'am.' If the word 'witch' or 'doctor' comes out of you I will kill you myself. I need this, Corey. We need this. You know I don't ask you for a lot . . ."

It was true. "But Babe, those guys in Los P are Chinese. They probably don't even believe in this shit . . ."

"They believe in pain! And we are going to bring them some."

He had never seen her this adamant before, or this scared. She released her grip on his shirt and tried to pat out the wrinkles she'd made. "Okay, baby," he said. "I'll do this. For you."

"Do it for us," she told him, and she popped the collar on his jacket, even though she knew he hated it. "And try not to look like you're from South Carolina, just for an hour or two."

He sighed. "Yeah. Sure." At the next corner, they turned off the well-lit avenue and into the relative gloom of Eighth Street. They were almost to the end of the block, steps from Avenue C when Aniri stopped in front of a tiny storefront. It was painted a dull, powdery red but the door was black. There was a display of dust-covered African masks in the single window. Aniri pushed open the door, bells jangled, and they entered.

There was a woman behind a tiny counter and she murmured something in Yoruba, Corey knew it was Yoruba because Aniri murmured something back, her fear clouding her voice.

There was a skull on a shelf nearby. It looked like a human skull, and if it was a reproduction, it was damned accurate. The lower jaw was missing. Two of the molars on one side had been implants, they stood away from the bone on tiny steel studs. *This can't be real,* Corey thought, and he inched closer, peering.

"Don't touch anything!" Aniri whispered harshly.

Corey Jackson put his hands in his pockets and began to pray.

MONEY CHANGED HANDS.

Aniri counted out twenty crisp Ben Franklins. Corey tried not to think about how much Aniri paid and in what currency in order to earn each of those bills. There was another murmured conversation, and then Aniri removed her watch and handed it to the woman before turning to Corey. "Give me your watch, baby. And your cell. We can't take anything mechanical out there with us."

"Out where?" Corey handed her his watch and fished around in his coat pocket for his phone. He preferred to keep it clipped to his belt but Aniri would yell at him and call him a nerd when he did that.

"Shh. This is an earth ceremony."

"Oh great, an earth ceremony. Does that mean like the alleyway out back?"

"Coreeee . . . Please?"

He didn't know if she knew it but he was powerless over her, he would do anything to get her to love him back. The woman behind the counter took the phone and the watches, put them in an old cigar box and stuck the box up on the shelf, next to the skull. "Please wait here," she said softly. She opened a door behind the counter and went out. Corey looked at Aniri as the door closed. "Life with you," he said, "is many things, but never dull."

She locked her pale brown eyes on his. "Someday in South Carolina," she said, "what a great story this will be."

"Right now," he told her, "I can't even picture what South Carolina looks like."

THE WOMAN CAME back, beckoned them to the door. Aniri went first, Corey followed. The door shut behind them with a click. Three wooden steps down and they stood in the dirt of a courtyard. There was an arbor made of greenish pressure-treated lumber shielding them from the night sky. There was a large silver-colored tray on the ground in the very middle of the courtyard, with a plastic Clorox bottle and a paper bag next to it. A man sat in the corner. He wore a dark blue pin-striped suit, a crisp light blue shirt, a dark tie fastened with a gold pin, black penny loafers, no socks, dark glasses. He looked to be no older than Corey.

Corey stared.

"You were expecting maybe feathers?" The voice was pure Brooklyn, USA. "And a grass skirt. With a bone in my nose. Please, have a seat."

Aniri went from standing to sitting in one graceful movement. Corey did the best he could.

The guy in the suit looked at Corey. "You gotta have questions," he said. "Am I right? I know you gotta."

"I'm not allowed," Corey said. Aniri stared at him, her lips pursed. "I promised."

The guy looked at Aniri and laughed. "Things we do for the ladies." He fished a thin, plastic-tipped cigar out of an inside pocket, stuck it in his mouth and lit it with a plastic lighter. "How about I ask the questions."

"Shouldn't we, ahh . . ." Corey glanced at Aniri. "Shouldn't we be telling you about the, ahhh, situation we, ahhh . . ."

"No. I don't need to know nothing about any of that."

"Now I'm really confused."

"The Arisha is gonna speak to her tonight, not to me."

"Why not?"

"I am only the Babalao." He leaned forward, cigar in his teeth, picked up the Clorox bottle. It was filled with white sand, and he poured it onto the silver tray. "I know that don't tell you a hell of a lot. You ever hear of the I Ching?"

The acrid smell of the Babalao's cigar was starting to burn Corey's eyes. "Yeah. Pennies and nickels. It's the Taoist book of divination. You toss the coins, and then from the pattern they make, there's supposed to be a corresponding verse in the book. Superstition, really, is all it is. There isn't a shred of evidence, scientific or otherwise . . ." He looked over at Aniri and stopped talking.

"Yeah," the Babalao said. "Figured we'd come to that. The problem with Americans is that most of us don't know what we don't know." He upended the paper bag. A bunch of wrinkled brown balls poured out, along with what looked like a desiccated chicken foot. He picked up the chicken foot and began raking the sand with it. "You a religious guy, my brother? You believe in God? Don't worry about Aniri, you can answer."

Corey wanted to say no but he couldn't. Hadn't he been praying, just moments ago? The Babalao continued raking until he had the sand spread out over the tray to his satisfaction. He picked up one of the balls, rolled it in his fingers, held it out over the tray, and dropped it. "Easier question," he said. "Why did that dried goat testicle just hit the sand?"

"What the fuck? A goat's testicle? Seriously? And a chicken's foot?"

"It's a betel nut," the Babalao said. "Sorry, man, I couldn't resist. And why a betel nut? What could I tell you. Why do Catholic priests *wear dresses? Who knows? It's just the way it's done. Lug nuts would prolly work just as good. But why did it hit the sand when I let go of it?"*

"Because you dropped it. Gravity . . ."

"Which is what?"

"Gravity is one of the four fundamental forces . . ." Corey's voice faded as his conviction waned.

"There are five fundamental forces in the universe, by the way, not four. Think, now." The Babalao leaned back, puffed on his cigar, picked up two more balls. "You stick your finger in a socket, right, you feel it. Electricity is made of stuff, and we know what it is, even if we can't see it."

"Electrons," Corey said, and then he racked his brain. Gravity, electromagnetism, the weak atomic force, the strong atomic force. That made four . . .

"So they say." The Babalao leaned forward, dropped the two balls in the sand. "Something just pulled those down. Something is holding them down right now. Some kinda force. So what's it made of? Gravitons?"

"No." Corey shook his head. "I've heard that argument and it's complete bull, it doesn't even work in a quantum environment. No such thing as gravitons. We don't know . . ."

The Babalao finished his sentence for him. "How power works. Or force, if you like that word better. We can measure it. We know how to use it. But we don't really know all that much about it." He continued dropping his betel nuts until they were all in the sand. He leaned forward again, handed his cigar to Aniri. "Inhale," he said. "And hold it."

The tip glowed as she complied, and she handed the cigar back to the Babalao, who passed it to Corey. "Inhale," he said. "And hold it."

Corey knew this was his last chance to back out, but if he did he would spend the rest of his life wondering whatever happened to the first woman he'd ever really loved. He could hear the cigar burn and pop as he inhaled.

His ears began to ring.

"Would you like to see," the Babalao asked him, "how power works?"

Corey stared at him.

"Exhale," the Babalao said to Aniri. "Blow it out." He turned to Corey. "Exhale. Blow it out."

Corey exhaled, feeling light-headed.

"The fifth fundamental force in the universe," the Babalao said. "Would you like to feel it? Ideally, there should be nothing between you and the earth."

"No shoes," Corey said. He sat still but his mind reeled.

"No nothing," the Babalao said.

You ain't scaring me, Corey thought, and he clambered to his feet and began to strip. Aniri, her eyes wide in disbelief, did the same. Jesus, Corey thought dimly, she's as beautiful as Eve or any woman since. God, I love this woman . . . And then they were sitting again, bare skin on dirt, and the Babalao passed the cigar to Aniri. "Inhale." And then it was Corey's turn. "Inhale." The edges of his world began to blur and then his field of vision began to narrow. He heard the Babalao's voice, sensed him up close. "I am the guardian," the Babalao said. "I am the keeper of secrets . . ."

And then Corey's world went black.

Chapter One

THERE ARE STILL some lonely places in the world, if you go looking.

IN SOME CIRCLES it's known as a geographical cure; it's the notion that you can walk away from your problems, that you can relocate yourself to some new place and in the process become new yourself. The consensus is that it's a sucker's bet, that it leaves you lost and alone and still dealing with all the same old shit, but man, is it ever a seductive idea, and if it's a trap, it's one I've fallen into more than once. And sometimes, just for maybe a day or so, it really feels like it's working . . .

I stood where the inrushing waves reached up to my knees and I worked the long rod, flinging the heavy lure out into the verge of the sea, feeling the weight on the end of the line, reeling it back in slowly, waiting for the twitch, the hit that almost never comes, repeating the process over and again. I had come to love the feel of the cold wind, the weak sun, the unending surf, the rod like a living thing in my hands. More than that I loved how my mind seemed to empty, how for that one moment I could just be, nothing more than now, no past, no future, and not another soul in sight. There was something eternal about the way the hard, thin orange sunrise veiled itself in a cold northern haze while the chill breeze stole through my ragged flannel shirt with a pickpocket's touch, feeling for warmth.

It wasn't the end of the world, that's what the locals said, but you could see it from there. I never had a good reason for choosing that particular stretch of the Maine coast, any other spot should have done just as well and sometimes I thought about heading farther north, farther away from other people, but I hadn't done it. For four hundred and thirty-one days I stayed, four hundred and thirty-one days without any of the chemical assistants that had been propping me up for most of my life; it was my longest stretch of abstinence since my teens. I was only substituting one compulsion for another and I knew that, but it seemed to work. The shadows that haunted me were not far away, though, they were as close as the nearest pharmacy, and if there were no drugstores, a bottle of Johnny Dark would awaken the dragon just as easily, so I stayed close to that one spot where I felt like I was safe, knee-deep in salt water. With the rod in my hands, I couldn't pick up anything else, that's what I told myself, and if it wasn't quite the life that I'd been intended for, what could I do? I waited, wondering if I might see some kind of a sign, but all I got was the crunch of wave on rock as the universe went about its business without a sidelong glance. I still couldn't escape the conviction that I'd missed the boat, that there was something else that I was supposed to be doing, but I couldn't picture what it could be or how the hell I could ever get to it without falling back into my old addictions. Faith dies hard, though, and even when you can't believe in a damn thing anymore, you still hope.

All I really knew for sure was that I had grown sick of the man I had become, tired of the daily con I had to run on myself just to get my ass up and out the door in the morning. You never really know yourself, you don't know who you really are until that day comes when you've finally had enough. One year and some months prior my day had come and I'd walked away, washed up a while later on that forlorn and deserted stretch of coastline. And no matter how deeply I ached for some kind of connection to something greater and deeper than the inside of my own skull, there are too many alternate explanations for that sort of phenomenon, mostly involving medication and the reasons I haven't been taking it. So like a man who has settled for order instead of law, eventually I gave up on peace and contented myself with what moments of quiet I could find.

But even that was too good to last.

I sensed the man before I actually saw him; it was a kind of sourness in my stomach, similar to the aftereffects of something I shouldn't have eaten. I've never been sure how that works, exactly. A survivor's reflex, perhaps, the residue of a life spent in harm's way, an awareness of sound pitched too low to register in the conscious mind but there regardless, and the reptile mind deep inside took note and reached for the alarm button.

I had learned to trust my intuitions.

The intruder struggled with his balance as he navigated the steep gray ledges back over my right shoulder. He made no effort to conceal his approach. He was an older guy, and heavy, dressed up in a suit and tie. Some guys wear a suit and tie everywhere because that's who they are, they got nothing else going. This one had a familiar face: Anyone who ever channel-surfed in the middle of the night would probably recognize him. Or even better, early Sunday morning, sometimes you could catch the guy on several different cable channels at the same time. He had snow-white hair, it was cut a little long and he combed it back with a touch of pomade. His jowls made you think of your grandfather or maybe your favorite uncle, and his suit would not have looked out of place on Daniel Webster or Henry Clay, four buttons on the jacket, wide flowing tie so as not to look like Colonel Sanders. They always shot him from below so that, onscreen, he seemed like he was up a little higher than you, and he liked to hold his Bible open in his right hand, it was a big book with floppy covers so it could lie there like some silent movie goddess at the end of her death scene, a snake-bitten Cleopatra all tragic and limp while you looked up at him preaching sin and redemption, come back to Jesus, brothers and sisters, He has always loved you, come back to God, let us help you, the pitch buried so deep in his schtick you hardly ever felt the fingers reaching into your pocket, he was one of the best around. I had not seen him in person in fifteen years.

The day was not shaping up the way I'd pictured it.

The good Reverend McClendon, come all the way north to see me. He was one of several stepfathers who'd cycled through my life. He'd been the first, the one with the longest tenure, and I had no fond memories of him. He'd been too midwestern for my tastes, too self-righteous, judgmental, abusive, arrogant, violent on occasion, too confident in his own opinions. Told me more than once that I was Lucifer's disciple, and would never amount to much.

Nice enough guy, apart from that.

I looked away, out over the endless ocean, trying to take it all in, to wrap it up somehow, stow it away in a back pocket so that when the day came that I needed it, I could take it out just to remind myself that moments like this were still possible.

I wondered, just for a second, how the son of a bitch found me.

A marauding bluefish chose that moment to hit my lure. I knew it was a blue because it telegraphed its fury right through the forty-odd yards of monofilament. A striper will just pull, not much more than a sullen weight on the end of your line; catching one is more or less like winching in an old boot, but some creatures are overendowed with fire and spirit and a blue is one of those, a blue will fight you right up to his last gasp. This one actually came up and tail-walked across the surface, it looked like it was about an eight-or ten-pounder but it fought like a pissed-off welterweight. It took another ten minutes before I finally landed it. I backed out of the waves, dragging it up the beach behind me. It was tired enough for me to get a foot on it. I took the hook out of its mouth with a pair of rusty needle-nose pliers. You have to watch the teeth, a blue can hit you like a meat cleaver, this one had chewed the braided steel leader all to hell. I got it loose, finally, took my foot off it, meaning to chuck it back into the ocean, but it must have felt the wave coming, a couple of spastic flips of its tail and it was back in the water and gone.

You wonder what you'll do when it's your turn, will you fight when the fisherman comes for you or will you close your eyes and wait for the knife.

"Was that your dinner," the preacher said.

I wondered if I just rebaited the hook and waded back out there, would the guy get the hint? But my life is rarely that simple. "Reverend McClendon," I said. "You got some fucking nerve."

"Saul Fowler," the reverend said. "Nice to see you, too. Last report, you was living the life in a penthouse in Zurich. I thought maybe you'd finally gotten your act together. How the hell do you go from a high-zoot burg like that, two girlfriends and a Porsche to a place like this?"

"You walk out the front door, turn left, and keep going."

"You look like shit," McClendon said. "Are you okay?"

"I was fine until you got here."

"Beautiful place," he said, staring out at the sunrise, undeterred. "Shelter Island. Bit of a misnomer, though, especially for a man like yourself." His eyes flicked from the horizon back to me. "You weren't all that hard to find. You're living in a Winnebago? Does that thing even run?"

"What the fuck do you want from me?" I cleared my throat and spat into the ocean. "How may we here at Black Sheep Enterprises not be of assistance?"

"There's a loaded question," McClendon said, and the air went out of him. "For starters, I want to show you a picture of my daughter."

"I didn't know you had one."

"I don't," he said, and for a second McClendon looked like just one more guy who'd gotten slapped around by time and consequence. "But I did." He pulled a smart phone out of his coat pocket, fiddled with it for a moment and then handed it to me. She was part Asian, straight black hair, with McClendon's bright blue eyes. "Very pretty," I said.

"She was," he said. "Emphasis on past tense." His voice cracked, he seemed right on the edge of losing control. "Her name was Melanie Wing."

"What happened to her?"

McClendon squared himself up. It may have been a cold way

to look at it, but I knew McClendon well enough to wonder how much of what I was looking at was the reverend's real reaction and how much was just for show. "Six months ago," McClendon said, "the cops fished her out of the water just off Staten Island. New York City. Most of her, anyway. Someone riding the Staten Island Ferry spotted her body floating by; if they hadn't she'd have been swept out to sea and we'd never have found out what happened to her. We'd have never known." He took back his phone, banished his daughter's image with a swipe of a finger. "The cops keep telling me it's an open case. They're working on it. But you and I both know that after all this time, house money says they ain't catching the guy." He stared out across the gray ocean and hitched his coat up around himself.

"Sorry to hear it," I told him.

"It gets worse," he said, not looking at me. "She might have been your half sister."

"What? Are you kidding?"

"You knew your father left your mother just after she came up pregnant with you," he said. "It was because he hadn't touched her in over a year. You weren't his. Your mother could be hard to live with, you know."

"Yeah, no shit. Are you serious? It was you?"

"I'm not saying it was me, Saul." He backed away from that in a hurry. "There was more than one candidate. I mean, your mother, she got around. I tried to make it work with her, but like I said, she could be difficult."

I looked up at the sky. I didn't know what the hell difference it made, really, whether the sperm donor had been McClendon or some other anonymous asshole. But God, if you're up there, I have to say this: You're just like Mike Tyson, or maybe Bill Clinton, because just when I'm starting to like you, you pull some new fucked-up shit out of your back pocket . . .

"Saul, can we go somewhere warm and talk about this? You got me freezing my nuts off out here."

"What was her name again?"

He looked out over the water. "Melanie," he said. "And her mother's name is Annabel."

EMPTY COFFEE SHOP, blue-gray shingles, salt-rimed windows. Northern New England, deserted beach town, out of season. Mc-Clendon parked his Mercedes right in front of the place. I slid my battered Jeep just behind, shut it off, listened to it cough and sputter before it died. A cloud of faint gray smoke split apart and drifted away in the breeze.

Inside, a waitress brought coffee. She looked at the old man with a funny expression on her face, for a minute I thought she was gonna ask him if he didn't used to be on Happy Days or something. McClendon laid a twenty on her and told her that he just wanted to have a private conversation with an old friend. "I don't know why you're coming to me with this," I told him, after the kitchen door swung shut behind her. "I'm retired."

"No you're not," the old man said. "You're unemployed, and broke. There's a difference."

"How'd you find me? Who gave me up?"

"Don't be a sap," he said. "You can't hide from the world, not these days. I got friends in high places. Low places, too, for that matter. Not that I blame you for trying to stay off the radar. I was told they liked you a lot for that robbery at the Musée d'Orsay a year or so back. Didn't I teach you better than that? That painting you took was too high-profile. How'd you expect to make any money on that? Didn't they recover it about a week later? There was no way to sell . . ."

"I don't know what you're talking about." Actually, the painting was just a smokescreen. The real target was the Maximillian codex, which they didn't even realize was missing until two months later.

"I bet you don't."

There was no point in denying anything to a guy like Mc-Clendon, he was the kind of con artist that thought everyone else was just like him, only not as talented. And I had zero interest in what he thought of me. "Why are you bothering me with this? Why don't you go hire someone who does this for a living? You could probably afford Louie Freeh, for crissake."

"I did that already, and they come up empty. Not Louie Freeh, but someone just like him. Skinny, nasty, dried-out prick of an ex-cop. This ain't a job for a guy like that, anyway. This is a job for a guy from your side of the street."

"What are you talking about?"

"You. Listen, I know you got no reason to want to help me. I was too young when your mother and I were together, and I didn't know anything about being a father. Or a stepfather. And everything my old man did to me, which I hated him for, I did to you. And everything that's happened to you since . . ." He fluttered his hand in space, leaving his opinions of my history unspoken. "I'm not saying that it was all my fault, but I put your feet on the wrong road. I know that now. It's one of the great regrets of my life."

I didn't know what I was supposed to say to that, other than, you know, go fuck yourself, but that was the reaction he expected, he probably already had a play called for that, so I kept my mouth shut.

McClendon sat there looking tired and defeated. He was at a disadvantage and he knew it, because I had known him when. With the man I remembered, you might think you were getting to the real guy but all you really ever uncovered was another layer in his performance. If there was anything real to the McClendon I knew, he kept it buried so deep that no one ever got to see it. I would never say that I didn't learn anything from the guy, quite the contrary, but it wasn't anything you were gonna learn from the Sutras or the Bible or any university that I knew of. I'd never known whether to resent McClendon for it or be grateful. I didn't give him any indication I was buying his act. "This is quite a trans-formation," I said. "How'd you pull it off?"

"I'll tell you what happened," he said. "You can decide, after-ward, whether you want to believe it or not."

"Go ahead."

"About ten years ago," he said, "I finally hit the big one. The one we all dream about. And it was a total accident. Me and this guy I worked with were up in Canada, buying leases."

Alberta. It had been all over the news for the past couple years.

Oil. More than in Saudi Arabia. More than the whole Middle East, maybe.

"You're feeling me," he said. "You're with me, I can tell. Tar sands, everybody knew the oil was there. And everybody knew that you couldn't get to it. Couldn't dig it out. The paper we were buying was worthless, that's what we thought, hell, that's what ev-erybody thought. So we form a corporation, we buy every lease we can get. The scam was gonna be, 'Hey, this will never be worth a cent, not in your lifetime, but fifty, a hundred years from now when the rest of the world's oil is gone, they *will* figure out a way to get to the stuff. You buy in with us, you leave your shares to your kids in your will, someday they'll all be filthy rich.' Well, guess what? We were off by fifty years or so."

"You didn't even have to scam anyone."

"Right place, right time. The price of crude blew through the roof, and overnight, Alberta, Canada, is the new gold rush. Now all of a sudden the tar sand business is profitable, after all. It was like having the biggest pile of money you ever dreamed about fall out of the sky and hit you in the head."

"What did you do?"

"I didn't know what to do. Being a thief was all I ever knew, Saul, you know that. It's all I ever was. And all of a sudden, it's over. It was like I disappeared, Saul, when I looked in the mirror I didn't see nobody there looking back. I'd been chasing that score all of my life and now I didn't know what to do with myself. The game is over. I'm finished."

"Oh, wait, stop," I told him. "Let me guess. You got your pockets full of reasonably honest money, wait, don't tell me, you get on a plane to Vegas."

"A bus," McClendon said, wrinkling his face up in distaste. "I ain't too much for flying anymore."

"How long did it take you to lose it?"

"I didn't lose it all," he said, defensive. "I gave away a lot, too. I was very popular for a while."

"Yeah? How long?"

He sighed. "Eighteen months, give or take."

"You are unbelievable," I told him.

"Look," he said. "You got your problems, too. I know you keep falling into the same holes. Well, so do I. And to tell you the truth, I don't see where my blind spots are all that different from yours."

"Yeah? You have to be the only guy I ever met, give you a hundred grand today and you're broke by the weekend, and you got nothing to show for it." But I looked through the window at the reverend's Mercedes, parked by the curb. "So what changed?"

"You're gonna laugh at me," the old man said.

"Hey." McClendon had landed a punch there, he had me doubting my own skepticism. Was I really about to see a piece of the real McClendon, or was I just falling for the bastard's newest scam? "Wait. We telling the truth here? Do you even know what the truth is?"

The preacher leaned his elbows on the table and focused those blue eyes in on me. "Saul, as God is my witness. I had fifty cents in my pocket, a five-thousand-dollar bar tab, and the Trop was throwing me out. I'm walking down this street and I hear this guy." He closed his eyes and nodded, giving me permission to laugh at him. "Preaching."

"He must have been some goddamn spellbinder."

"Nah, he was awful. Still is, actually. Gets his hair cut like he's still in the Marine Corps, got no fashion sense at all, and his voice goes all high and squeaky when he gets excited. The guy is hopeless. Reverend Stillman."

"So? I don't get it."

He leaned back in his chair and looked around the coffee shop like he was expecting reinforcements to arrive; when they didn't he looked back at me and shook his head. "He was real, Saul. He believed in what he was doing. He *is* real. It was no act."

"Seriously, McClendon . . ."

"I know." He nodded again. "I know. But I tell you what, Saul, when he told me that I was a child of God, and that my father loved me, I bought it."

" 'Convince yourself that it's real, that's what really sells them.' "

"I remember telling you that. If I could go back and do different, I would, Saul, but that ain't the way it works. Anyway, I went to work for Stillman that afternoon. Swept the floors, wrote letters, kept his books. I'm still working for Stillman."

"Guess it didn't take him long to recognize your real talents."

"I am what I am, Saul. I've quit apologizing for it."

"And no more trips to Vegas."

He shook his head. "Can't afford Vegas no more."

I thought I saw a crack in the story. "Get real," I said. "You practically got your own cable network. You got to be making more now than you ever did."

McClendon shook his head again. "I told you, Saul, I work for the man. Stillman set up a foundation, and I get seventy-five grand a year. And my own bus. Well, actually, the foundation leases the bus, I think, but you get the idea."

"So what did you do? Go study old Billy Graham tapes?"

"You know what, I did look at some of those, sure, but Graham was a man of his times. Strictly fifties and sixties. Except for the hair, he had great hair. But if he was trying to break into the business now, he couldn't get arrested. 'Come down and kiss the altar' is all fine and good, but it don't work no more. These days you got to be more sophisticated than that."

"Who, then? Joel Osteen?"

"Osteen? You must be joking, it's like the man is channeling Jesus for Dummies. And that look he pastes all over his mug, come on, he looks just like a high school cheerleader on her first Ecstasy high. Osteen, gimme a freakin' break."

I was running out of candidates. "So who's left? That dipshit from California who keeps predicting that the world is gonna end any minute now?"

That got to McClendon, who shook his head and repressed a laugh. "Dipshit is right, how stupid can you get? Picking an actual date? Like, for instance, Thanksgiving Day? And then Friday morning you're standing there hanging on to your pecker and wondering why everyone is laughing at you. And even if God had Thanksgiving Day in mind, you know he'd have to reconsider, just to let you twist in the wind for a while. No, listen to me, Saul." He went all serious. "I ain't about any of that. You wanna know what I'm all about? It's very simple. That morning on that sidewalk in Nevada, I was a wicked person. Evil. You know that. And ever since then, because of the Reverend Stillman, you know something, I might still be a miserable son of a gun but I'm trying, Saul. I'm trying. I just hope that I'm trying hard enough."

"I don't get this. You're serious, aren't you?"

"Believe it," he said. "But anyway, Stillman's foundation gets the money, I don't. We're building a hospital in Haiti. I been to see it."

"Okay, so if you're an honest man now, how you gonna pay me? What's my incentive?"

He reached into a pocket, pulled out a bank card and flipped it across the table. "I still got a couple hundred thou in a bank in Barbados," he said. "I been wondering what I should do with it. The access code is 1066. I took the liberty of adding your name to the account."

"Battle of Hastings."

He nodded. "Keep it simple."

I didn't touch the card. "This was your seed money. This was your back door, you'd need this money to work up your next game. You always kept your seed money, it was like it was sacred. If you're giving it up now, you really are throwing in the towel."

McClendon looked down. "I could still go back. It's always easy to run downhill."

"The rev know about this?"

"Stillman? He knows."

"What'd he say?"

"He told me to leave the money where it is. Told me the foundation would pay."

"So?"

McClendon shook his head. "I'd rather do it this way."

"One last question. If the cops couldn't find this guy, what makes you think I can?"

He spreads his hands wide, palms up. "For one thing," he said, "I assume that this is my fault. Someone killed my daughter because of something I did. Or at least that's where the smart money ought to be. Chickens coming home to roost, and all that. So if I'm going to have someone rooting around in my past . . ."

"You trust me?"

McClendon looked sad, all of a sudden, less like the television preacher and more like the McClendon I remembered. "I know you, Saul. I know what you can do."

"Do you? I'm not that kid you remember. Been a lot of water over the dam since then."

"I know. I've . . . I been keeping track of you, Saul. Following your career."

"And how have you managed that?"

"I told you, I have friends in high places."

"You know what, I wish I had about one tenth your gift for bullshit."

"You wanna know what your real problem is? You don't, but I'm gonna tell you anyway. You're like a good car with a bad paint job. I told you, Saul, I know you. I know what's underneath the paint. Ninety-five percent of you is exactly the same as all the rest of us, and five percent is like nobody else on the planet. Now, I don't know what you think you gotta do penance for, but as far as I know nobody sentenced you to do time out here on the asshole side of Jabib. Yeah, okay, you pulled some messed-up shit before, but you're still young enough, Saul, you could still have a life. You ain't really that much worse than the rest of us. You just hit back harder than we do."

"You think that's it."

"I know it is. Listen to me. You got time. Shit, man, I was almost fifty when I found Stillman. Little bit of help, I changed everything. You can still be whatever you want. Although, no offense, that long hair and that beard ain't doing you no favors, you ask me. You're way too young for that John Brown shit you got growing on your face. And that nasty T-shirt . . . You look like you just stepped out of the pages of Hobo Monthly. Wasn't for me, that waitress wouldn'a let you through the door."

"I think I ate in here once . . ."

"Yeah, sure you did." He nudged the ATM card with a fingertip. "You see this piece a plastic? You're right, Saul, this was my back door. This was gonna be enough to pay for my next incarnation, if I ever needed one. Well, you know what, I'm going all in. I'm playing the cards I got. I'm staying with Stillman. I don't need a back door no more, but you do. This little card, right here? This is your next life. Find out who killed my little girl and it's all yours. And if you can't do it, then it can't be done. And if that's the way this plays out,

I can accept it. If I have to stand up and answer for my daughter's death, at least I can say, 'Lord, I hired the right son of a bitch to go looking, you know I did.' At least he's gotta give me credit for that."

"That's a real comfort, you know that?"

"You know what, it should be. Anyhow, she lived in New York City. My daughter. I know you spent some time there." McClendon, like most Americans, did not understand New York. He knew LaGuardia, he knew the theater district, maybe an overpriced restaurant or two. To him, New Yorkers were recognizably human but difficult to understand. They were suspicious, wary, hard to sneak up on, quick to strike back. Not exactly his kind of prey.

New York City saved me once.

McClendon sighed. "Listen to me, Saul. What do you want, more than anything else in the world? I'm gonna tell you, whether you want me to or not. Okay? You want to believe in us. All of us. You want to believe that the human race has a heart. And you'd really love it if someone came up to you and asked you to be on the team. If an ordinary guy said to you, 'Come with us, Saul, be one of us, just come and be a regular guy like us, love us and we'll love you back . . .' Well, I'm asking, Saul. Actually, I think I'm begging. Help me. I know that once you're in, you will never roll over on me. Not once you're on the team. And I promise that I will never lie to you again. Please, Saul, do this thing for me. You do this for me and I will be in your debt until the end of time."

TOLD YOU HE was good.

MCCLENDON HAD THE briefcase in the trunk of his car. There was a wet, greasy mist rolling in off the ocean, not quite what you'd call a good honest rain but enough to get you damp. The reverend's hair was suffering, losing its careful country and western twang and hanging limp down the sides of his face, he looked less like a preacher by the minute, more like an aging wino. He stood there behind his car, holding the briefcase awkwardly with both hands for a moment before handing it to me with the air of a man giving up his firstborn. "Please don't think bad of me," he said. "When you read what's in here . . . I was weak. And afraid. And selfish." Again I wondered if McClendon really felt any of that, or if it was just part of the show.

I took the briefcase, thinking, I'm really committed now.

Or should be.

"Call me, Saul," McClendon said. "As soon as you have any news. Or even if you don't. Okay?"

"Yeah, sure."

"I mean it," he said.

"You must be busy," I told him. "Writing sermons. Preaching, and all that."

"You could leave me a message," McClendon said, sounding wounded. "I'll call you back, I promise I will."

"I'm gonna have questions."

McClendon nodded sadly. "Yeah. I bet. You got e-mail? 'Cause I find it much easier to tell the truth in writing, if you know what I mean."

"No e-mail," I told him, smiling to myself, because I already knew how to get the truth out of McClendon.

THE WINNEBAGO DID not look like much from the outside. It was a vintage model, from back when they made them look like giant shoeboxes on wheels. From the outside it said, Stay away, whoever lives in here is not all there.

Which was okay by me. It kept my secrets. Not even the most determined of searchers could find everything I had stashed in here, not without losing a finger or two. Or maybe something more. Some of it was paranoia, I admit it. There may have been times in my life when I thought I was being followed by a couple of agents from the Invisible Bureau of Investigation, but by then I was over that, mostly.

Inside, it was more functional than it looked. I'd made a few improvements, and the thing suited me. When I drew the blinds I was generally left alone. It gave me a place to eat and sleep, and it fostered the illusion that I was safe when I was inside. I sat down and plopped the briefcase on the table in front of me and popped the latches open. Inside here, McClendon told me, I would find everything he had managed to learn about his daughter. It was sad to think that you could reduce a person's life down to a pile of stuff small enough to fit into your basic average-sized attaché. But that's what they do when anybody dies, it's what they'll do when I go, someone will dig through my camper and sort through the junk. What the hell do you suppose he was keeping this for? And into the Dumpster it will go. There are things in the Winnebago that cost me, and not just in dollars and cents, either, and it was depressing to think that one day it would all wind up in a landfill. Or somebody's yard sale. Or maybe, given the appearance of the Winnebago, maybe they'd decide that none of it was worth the trouble of sorting through it, maybe they'd tow it to one of those big salvage yards where they squash vehicles up into big metal cubes and ship them off to be melted down and reused.

I knew I was delaying. I really didn't want to open the briefcase, but after some more mental moaning and groaning, I did it.

The pile did not even fill the briefcase.

The coroner's report was on top, in a big brown manila envelope.

A body that has been in the water long enough will transform from something recognizably once human into a grotesquerie that will haunt your nightmares for the rest of your life. I didn't need anything new waking me up at night, so I left the coroner's report and the photographs that presumably accompanied it in the envelope undisturbed. I wondered if McClendon had looked at them. I marveled, and not for the first time, at the strength of the doctors, nurses, and orderlies who have to uncouple their humanity from their reason in order to discharge their duties.

Count me out.

As a matter of fact, the very idea of what might be inside that envelope was enough to knock me just a bit off-center, so I got up and made myself a pot of coffee. I was only feet away from that attaché but I turned my back to it and I focused as completely as I could on what I was doing. I filled the pot to the right level, which was not as easy as it sounded. Next I poured the water out of the pot and into the machine. I was immediately doubtful, given the disparity between the markings on the machine and the ones on the pot, that I had done any of this correctly, and I had to resist the impulse to upend the coffeemaker and start all over again.

Next the filter went into the basket, there was only one filter and one basket, thank the Lord for small favors. But after that I had to count out the correct amount of coffee grounds. It seemed all too easy to let my mind wander during that process. Was that four scoops, or five? How could you be sure? Memory is only a reconstruction, after all, a lie you tell yourself about how you wish things had gone. Pick up the filter carefully, pour the coffee back into the can. Start over again with a new filter . . .

This is not bad, really. There was a time when I was a lot worse.

By the time the machine began to gurgle, I was okay again, more or less. I had attained acceptance, for the moment, of the universe as it seemed to be, and of what had become of McClendon's daughter. The goonas were smiling on me again and I was ready to go back and look into the open briefcase again.

Goonas. It was a word I got from my mother, it was a term she used for the fates, the gods, the invisibles whose voices whispered in her ears. Some of the things you learn when you're eight, you can never get rid of; they stay with you whether they make any sense or not. So you do what works. You adapt. You get by.

I found that I could not, in good conscience, skip the coroner's report.

The pictures were even more horrible than I thought they would be. Someone had sliced her up pretty thoroughly. They hadn't touched her face, though, other than taking the bottom of her left ear.

There was another envelope, it had my name written on it in McClendon's handwriting. I decided to save that for later.

The police reports were next, and they said, essentially, that there was not a lot to say. The young lady in question, Melanie Wing, had been a nurse, about six months out of nursing school. She'd lived on Manhattan's Lower East Side, worked outreach out of Beth Israel. Plenty of acquaintances, a few close friends, no known enemies. One boyfriend. Did not report to work on such and such a day, missing persons report filed four days later. Pulled out of the water about a week after that.

Cause of death to be determined.

I worked my way through the pile and I tried to look at everything. I didn't take any notes; I'd do that later when I repeated the process. At the very bottom was a report from an outfit called

Whelen and Ives, with an invoice attached. It did not surprise me that I had not been the first to whom McClendon turned for help. I got up to turn off the coffee machine and I caught a glimpse of my reflection in the door glass.

Yikes.

How had I managed not to see what I had allowed myself to become? What it meant, I supposed, was that my brain had turned the page when I wasn't watching, that I was on to a new chapter whether I liked it or not. I silently promised both McClendon and myself this much: I would find out who this girl was.

From there, who knew.

Chapter Two

I AM NOT back in the game.

Yeah, there's a lie. The exhilaration I felt at the thought of what I would be doing in the coming days told me that I was bullshitting myself, a dumb and dangerous thing to do under any circumstances. But there is a sort of mad joy to it, a kind of freedom, a release from the prison of being yourself. Being back in the game meant that I could be someone else for a while, someone to whose character, accomplishments, abilities, and assets I held no legitimate title but which I would borrow and wear around like a better man's clothes. The dry cleaner had given them to me in error, and now I would try them on. Inhabit someone else's problems for a while.

"When you play this game you get in the ring with another guy," McClendon once told me. "He walks away afterward thinking he almost got it done, but you walk away *knowing* you did."

Oh, and the game is about the money, too, because that's how you keep score.

Now, of course, McClendon claimed to have reformed his

character and retired, now he worked the fields of the Lord. I was not entirely sure I believed that. It seemed to be a very real possibility that McClendon had simply gotten lost in his latest role. And me? I guess I thought that soloing in the Winnebago, sleeping in Wal-Mart parking lots, keeping my mouth shut as much as I possibly could might be able to show me some truth about myself, but as I stood there looking into the Winnebago's huge bathroom mirror, all I could see was a long-haired, bearded, smelly wild-man persona which felt as if it carried no more validity than any of the other roles I had inhabited in the past.

Damn.

And I really thought I'd been on to something. I thought I had taken a step, woken up a little bit. Was I that stupid, had I simply conned myself into believing that there might be a real point to what I'd been doing up on the coast? Call it the Zen of surfcasting. Right at that moment it felt artificial, an exercise in self-delusion, another hard lesson in the art of improv theater.

It was almost physically painful to think I could have been that far wrong.

I could almost hear the goonas laughing.

THE GAME CLAIMED its first victim, my Jeep.

I'd posted a handwritten notice on the Laundromat bulletin board, Jeep for sale. The next morning an old Yankee came to call, he honked his pickup's horn in lieu of knocking on the Winnebago's door, and he stood there waiting. I had seen him around before, and the guy had seen me, too; in the off-season the place reverted to its small-town origins. The guy wore a beard, too, but his was not like mine, his conformed to the traditions of his race and profession. He was a lobsterman, a local. A man with roots.

God, I envied him that.

"Sellin' ya truck," the guy said. It was more of a statement than a question.

"Yep." I can do Yankee pretty well.

He eyeballed the Jeep. It was parked behind the Winnebago but he made no move to inspect it any closer. The guy was probably more sure of the Jeep's provenance than I ever was, he probably went to school with the guy I bought it from. "Why so cheap?" the guy said.

"Two reasons," I told him. "One, I don't want to tow it."

The man's eyebrows went high on his forehead. "No? Headin' south? Had ya fill a peace and serenity?"

For whatever reason, I wanted to tell him the truth, if I could. "No. I was only getting started . . . but something came up."

"Ayuh," he said. "Know the feelin'. What's t'other reason?"

"Needs a valve job."

"That she does," he said. "But that's a nice straight six she's got in theyah. Good engine. Worth savin'. They don't make 'em like that no more. Treat her right and she'll run forever." We dickered over price for a while but the guy's heart was not in it, he knew he was getting a deal. I wound up taking a hundred less than I initially asked. The guy had lived up to the Yankee reputation for thrift and I had gotten most of my money back, but when the deal was done and the guy drove away with the keys in his pocket; I felt suddenly unsteady, as if I had come unmoored.

There was nothing keeping me there any longer.

I locked up the Winnebago and took one last walk up over the rocks, down to the water's edge. It was colder than it had been in a while and I had trouble reconnecting with whatever I had been doing before McClendon showed up. Maybe it was because, in my mind, I was already gone, I was already out there on the turnpike. Or maybe it was just this one unusually persistent horsefly who targeted me for his breakfast. He refused to be shooed away, in the end I had to kill him.

Stupid fly.

You have to know when you can push your luck, and when you need to cut your losses and run. When I got back the Jeep was gone, taken, presumably, by its new owner, and it was time for me to go.

DRIVING THE WINNEBAGO was a lot like driving a rubber-tired landslide, it was bumpy, rocky, noisy, and occasionally downright frightening. I'd done a lot of work on her but I hadn't been able to change the basic nature of the beast, and even though the engine, tranny, and most of the running gear were pretty decent, when a big tandem rig blew past me I began to understand how that bluefish felt when he got dragged up the beach. I was headed south, motoring down the northeast coast of Maine. My destination was the RV joint in Jersey where I'd bought the Winnebago, and my goal for the day was to get about halfway there before I holed up for the night. Maine has a long coastline, though, and pretty soon I was looking for any kind of excuse to pull over—a cup of coffee, a leak, a chance to stretch my legs, anything. It did not take long for me to get sick of driving.

Not a great attribute in your contemporary vagabond.

A truck stop beckoned, it had a big lot, so it was easy to park the beast. As long as you're not fussy, those places generally covered most of your basic needs, and for less than fifty bucks I was fed, watered, dewatered, and showered. I even sprung for a shave and a haircut. The Hispanic barber working in the phone booth–

sized shop stared at me, aghast. His own hair was about an eighth of an inch long and he sported a goatee, same length. "Look in the mirror," I told the guy. "That's what I want."

"You got money? I'll need to see, like, twenty bucks, pal."

I fished out a twenty. "Go for it," I said. The barber put me in the chair, stopped once more, clippers poised, looked at me in his mirror, making sure I was down for it, and I nodded. The barber dived in, and a couple of minutes later he had my hair all over his floor.

That was easy.

Gassing up the beast was a little tougher to take, two hundred fifty bucks vanished down a rat hole in about five minutes. When I finished with that I pulled the beast down into the far corner of the lot, as far as I could get from the roar of diesels.

I drew the blinds and opened up McClendon's attaché again. The envelope with my name on it, the one I'd skipped over earlier, was calling me. I took it out, held it up. My face, neck, and ears were not used to being so exposed, I felt like a tourist at a nude beach. I tore open the envelope.

It was not just Melanie Wing whose life was encapsulated in that attaché. McClendon had included a couple of handwritten pages about himself. The emphasis was more about his career path; it was his curriculum vitae, so to speak. He did not seem to be an introspective man, or perhaps he was not a writer. At the very least, he had chosen not to share many insights about himself, not on paper. What he had written was basically a greatest-hits list. It opened with a Ponzi scheme he'd taken part in back in the seventies, for which he'd been duly prosecuted, and he'd served four years in Indiana State. They seem to have schooled him well inside that hallowed institution, because thereafter McClendon had confined his ministrations to the commercial arena, and never again did he run afoul of the law. What followed read like an abridged version of Not Particularly Bright Slimeballs Running Mid-Size Corporations in the American Midwest, and How They Can be Screwed, although he'd sprinkled in a few from the East Coast, just for variety. In most cases, McClendon's victims thought they were getting an inside track with an unprincipled executive at a rival corporation, but some of them were angling for a beta version of an unpatented breakthrough, and in a case or two it seemed McClendon's targets paid him simply to go away. In short, Mc-Clendon had made a life and a career for himself proving that the maxims "You can't cheat an honest man," and "The hand is quicker than the eye" were just as valid in the corporate boardroom as they were on the street. He also provided a shorthand explanation of how his schemes worked, but really, they were all the same, they were all based on the same frailties of human nature. Technically, there are only four or five basic scams, though there might be a million variations on those few themes. All you actually needed was a greedy man's imagination and a magician's sleight of hand.

It was depressing, really.

Appended to the end of all this, though, was a short list of names. The offended parties, McClendon's list of suspects. He may very well have been correct in his assumption that his daughter was murdered by one of the people on his list, but I found myself disappointed by McClendon's dry recitation. I wondered what it must be like to be a priest. Personally, I don't care to hear that you committed this sin or that one, or that you'd repeated it so many times since your last update. I want to know what the object of your desires looked like, what she smelled like, what she said, what you whispered in her ear, what sort of fruit she used to entice you from the paths of virtue. And did you still think she was worth burning for? Afterward, you can go say as many Hail Marys as you cared to, but first, goddammit, I want the story.

I locked up the beast and went in search of a pay phone.

No pay phones. I was coerced by circumstances into buying a prepaid cell phone.

"Saul." McClendon sounded groggy on the other end of the line. Past his bedtime, apparently. "What the hell time is it? Where are you?"

"Truck stop," I said. "I'm heading south, but I got some questions."

"I bet you do. You still driving the Batshitmobile? You ain't thinking about taking that thing into New York City, are you?"

"No, I'm gonna park it. Did you know she was pregnant? Annabel, I mean."

"Yeah, I knew," McClendon said, his voice quiet. "I wanted her to get rid of it. A kid, did I need a kid? And the mortgage comes next, and the lawn and the station wagon, and the square life. I couldn't take it, so I ran. Listen, I told you I wasn't proud of what you were gonna find out . . ."

"I'm not asking just to beat you up," I said. "But I wanna see if she's got any family left. I'd like to know what I'm walking into."

"Yeah," he said. "I get you. Well, you ain't gonna find my name on the Wing family Christmas card list."

"Are they looking for you?"

"No," he said. "Not that I'm aware."

"Annabel still alive?"

"Yeah," McClendon said, quieter still. "Yeah, she is."

"Where's she live?"

"Flushing," he said. "Queens, New York. You want her phone

number?" He recited it to me. "The rest of the family is in Manhattan, why the hell anybody would wanna live in friggin' Manhattan I will never know, but that's where they are. Annabel wound up in Flushing all on her own. She always was a rebel and I don't think they ever forgave her for having my daughter. What's your angle here? You just gonna go walking in there, or what? What's your play?"

"I'm gonna be her half brother," I told him. "Father long gone, mother locked up, no other siblings. Then I hear about this girl and even though I never met her, I can't leave it alone, so I've decided to come see what I can find out."

"Not bad," McClendon said. "You know what, I like it, it even has the right smell. So you're gonna be my actual son for a while?"

I found myself suddenly annoyed. "That okay with you, Pops?"

"It could work," he said, oblivious. "Though I wouldn't go leaning on the McClendon family connection too hard. The less they associate you with me, the better off you'll be. We should probably be estranged, you and I. Like, you got my name out of state records—no wait, I got it. You found your mother's marriage certificate. Yeah, I like it. So from that you track me down, and I tell you to go take a flying leap."

"Let me think about it," I told him. "I'll get back to you with the particulars, just in case somebody walks it back in your direction. Next question. That PI firm you hired. Did you say they were ex-cops? I remember that right?"

"Yeah," he said. "You got something against ex-cops?"

"What if I do? But their report seemed, ah, perfunctory."

"They had connections inside the NYPD," he said. "They got

me copies of the police reports. The real ones, not that shit they gig up for public consumption."

"Yeah. I saw them."

"And they did some interviews. Neighbors, schoolmates, that kind of thing. Guy told me they'd keep on taking my money if that was what I wanted, but he didn't think they were getting anywhere. So I let it go. It kept me up at night, though. That's why I wound up coming to you."

"Did you ever meet your daughter?"

"Melanie," he said, exhaling. "Her name was Melanie. And, no, I didn't. I was halfway hoping she'd call me one day, but she never did. Maybe she would have. But what was I supposed to do? 'Hey baby, this is your father, I'm the guy who ran out on you before you were born, and now that you're all grown up and got a job, I wanna be Dad and carry your picture in my wallet . . .' I couldn't do it."

"So there was no contact?"

"Well, I don't know what you mean by contact. I called Annabel once in a while, I sent money whenever I was flush. In lieu of taxes, you might say. Paid for braces, Catholic school, college tuition, that kind of thing. I wasn't a complete asshole. Not quite, anyway. Listen, are you sure this is where you wanna start? My feeling was that someone I ripped off somewhere along the line killed her just to get back at me."

"Yeah? You get any calls to that effect? Anybody send you any gloating letters? Graphic pictures?"

"No. Nothing. I see what you're saying. Why snuff her if you're not gonna watch me squirm. I don't know if I'm with you on that, though. I'll tell you something, my experience, people mostly kill for the money. You got it, they want it, or else you're costing them and they're sick of paying. When in doubt, it's the money. You might come across a sicko once in a while, but that's the exception, and alla this 'crime of passion' shit, that's for the movies."

"Well, I gotta start somewhere, Mac, and I wanna find out who she was. I was thinking that I'd have liked to have met her. I mean, I didn't even find out she was alive until after she was dead, if that makes any sense."

"Wow, you're going all Method on me, here," McClendon said. "I can do Method." His voice was changing, he was waking up, recovering his performer's face. I figured I had probably gotten everything truthful I was going to get out of him on this phone call. "Listen, Saul, you are planning on getting a haircut, ain't you?" He was into it now, he was playing the concerned father. "I mean, these Chinese people tend to be conservative as hell. And I don't want no son of mine to go around looking like he sleeps on a god-damn park bench, you know what I'm saying?"

Yeah, the guy was fully awake now. "Don't worry about it, Mac."

"No, serious, Saul. I mean it."

"Mac, I was wondering. You ever wonder what your customers would think if they found out about your conviction?"

Mac chuckled. "Christians love people with convictions."

"Really? You're not worried?"

"Saul, you don't understand us at all."

"Enlighten me."

"Stillman put it in a press release, way back when I started. We know what we are, Saul. No point pretending otherwise."

"All right. Catch you later."

THE TWO MAIN reasons why I liked Porter's Perfect RV Warehouse were, first, it was located just off the Jersey Turnpike, and second, you could catch a bus to Manhattan from the center of the town just a mile or so distant. I piloted my ancient Winnebago carefully between the rows of shiny, modern, penile-enhancing lifestyle statements. Put a single scratch in any one of these things, I told myself, and the repair bill would likely exceed even the most optimistic estimate of the Batshitmobile's market value. I pulled up into the open space right outside the glass-fronted office building and shut down. I left my knapsack by the door and went in search of Frank, the unhinged little man who owned and ran the joint.

I didn't have to look far.

Frank stood inside the big window, phone clamped between his shoulder and his ear, arms out wide in disgust, the look on his face proclaiming that he'd just smelled something distinctly unpleasant. I repressed a smile and went around to the side door. "I gotta go," I heard Frank tell the phone, looking like he wanted to spit on the floor. "I'll get back to you." He snapped the phone shut and stuck it in a pocket. "I thought I seen the last of that damn thing," he moaned, staring up at the office ceiling. "God, why do you hate me? Couldn't you let that piece a shit catch on fire somewhere far away from here?"

I glanced over at Frank's mother, who was also his bookkeeper. She was seated at a desk against the far wall, and I had never seen more of her than the back of her head. "You weren't crying like a bitch when you sold it to me."

"Do you got any idea how much money I lost on that fucking thing? I only took it in trade as a favor to an old customer, you didn't pay me back half of what I had into it. If I'da known it was gonna come back to haunt me, I woulda drove it down to the Meadowlands and burned it up myself."

Frank's mother turned away from her computer, shifted in her chair to look at the two of us. "Relax," I said. "I'm not trying to trade it back in, quit whining for crissake. I just need to get some work done on it."

Frank's mother struggled to her feet, groping for her cane.

"Do you got any idea what my overhead is in this place?" Frank said. "Listen to me. You really oughta be doing business with someone who specializes in relics like that."

"You telling me you can't fix a lousy heater?"

Frank's mother wobbled across the floor in our direction.

"No!" Frank said. "I ain't telling you no such thing. What I'm saying is that I know a guy, and it'd be cheaper for you and less aggravation for me if you took it directly to him. He loves them old—"

Frank's mother elbowed him in the ribs. "Outa the way," she said.

"Ouch! Ma-aa . . ."

"Move it, I said." She shoved him aside and pulled a service ticket out of a drawer. "Hello, Mr. Fowler. If you could just fill out the top of this ticket, we can get you on your way."

"Of course. Thank you, Mrs. Porter. You remember me?"

"Ma-aah . . ."

"Shut up, Frankie. I never forget a customer, Mr. Fowler, especially one who pays cash. Was the heater your only problem? Would you like us to check the rest of it out for you?"

"Ah, yeah. Absolutely. Okay if I leave it here for a couple days?"

"No," Frank said, reaching for the service ticket, but the old lady snatched it out of his reach.

"Of course," she said. "Did you leave the keys in it?"

"Got 'em right here," I said, and I handed them over.

"You need a ride to the bus station? Frankie, give the man a ride."

Porter stared at her, mouth open, eyes wide. "Anything else?"

"Yeah!" she snapped. "Stop in Idaho and pick me up a bag a potatoes! What a stupid question. Gwan! Mr. Fowler is a busy man. He has things to do!"

Porter stared up at the ceiling, silently imploring his god, who was apparently occupied elsewhere.

"I NEVER SEEN her like that. Never. She just sits over there crunching numbers. She even look at you when you was here last time?" Porter had pulled his van around front to pick me up. I glanced through the big window, saw Frank's mother standing on the other side of the glass with an odd look on her face, a sort of lopsided sardonic quarter smile, like she knew something I didn't. Like if Mona Lisa had a sister who was a little older and a lot more street-smart. I nodded to her.

"Not that I recall," I said, climbing into the van.

"What the hell you suppose got into her? Maybe she had a little reefer with her lunch."

"Yeah," I said. "Maybe."

Interrugnum

He heard a voice, faint, somewhere above him. "Is he going to be all right?" It sounded like Aniri.

"Yeah, he's okay." It was the Babalao. "He's coming around now."

"Should we get him dressed?"

"You get your clothes on first, hon, 'cause I might be a priest but I ain't made outa stone, you know what I'm saying."

Corey stirred, raised a hand to his head. "What happened to me?"

"Power," the Babalao said. "Power happened to you."

"What was in that cigar?"

"Tobacco. That's what they make 'em out of, you know. Maybe I should change up to a better brand, but I like them plastic tips. More sanitary, I think."

"You didn't load it? Spike it with something?"

"Nah. Ask Aniri, she didn't even get woozy or nothing."

Corey's vision was returning. Aniri swam into view, she was pulling her shirt down over her head and shoulders. God, he thought, God, I love that woman . . .

"What was it for, then? The cigar." Corey was becoming uncomfortably aware that he was still naked, still sitting in the dirt of the courtyard behind the storefront on Eighth Street. The Babalao squatted next to him, supporting him with an arm around his shoulders.

"Eshu," the Babalao said. "The messenger spirit. He loves tobacco, and the cigar was really just a polite way of asking for his help. You think you can stand up, if I help you?"

"Yeah," Corey said. "If I take it nice and slow." He leaned forward, levered himself up onto one knee. "Why did I pass out?"

"Well, from the Western perspective," the Babalao said, "it's late, you're tired, you're under a lot of stress. And maybe your brain don't care for cheap cigar smoke."

Corey got the rest of the way to his feet, held on to the Babalao's shoulder with one hand, brushed the little pebbles off his butt with the other. "Yeah, okay. But what really happened?"

"Eshu came, and he brought someone with him. Oshun, who, I gotta say, would not have been my first choice, if it was up to me."

"Why not? Who is . . ."

"Oshun. The cardinal female, you might say. Divine, but unstable. And she's got some temper. I don't think she liked you."

"Great. Are you kidding me?"

"Don't take it personal. She threw out her first husband because he drank the wrong kind of beer. Listen, I gotta say, this might be unprofessional and shit, but you are in some kinda shape, my brother. You an athlete?"

"College boxing team," Corey said. "Oshun, you said. A goddess? Do you really buy that?"

The Babalao shrugged. " 'Goddess' is your word, not mine. Think of it this way: The fifth fundamental force can express itself in whatever form it chooses. Questions like why and how are not really rel-

evant to you and me, because we ain't got the software to understand the answers. Eshu, Oshun, and the rest are just part of a metaphor the ancients used to try to understand something they could feel but never see. Let's get you dressed, my brother, 'cause you got things to do before the sun rises. You still having trouble with this? Sometimes you just gotta roll with it. Know what I mean?"

"No."

"Tell you something a priest said, long time ago. 'The eye with which you see God is the same eye with which he sees you.' Aniri, give a brother some help, will ya? Make him put his pants on . . ."

Chapter Three

THE SUN ALWAYS seems brighter in Manhattan, voices are louder, the women are thinner, tougher, and have longer hair, even the taxis are painted a harsher shade of yellow. The midtown streets are a carnival ride, a freak show, a living episode of Survivor, a glittering, roiling stew of consumers and all the shit they chase. And everything that you own, owns you, believe it, my brother, but try selling that one around this town.

I missed the Batshitmobile . . .

I felt like a hermit crab without his borrowed shelter. The commuters flooding through the doors of the Port Authority bus terminal ignored me with practiced scorn. I was not one of them. I don't know if that mattered, because I think they would have still pretended not to see me even if I wore the right uniform, the right scowl, the right air of resigned fatalism. Suits, ties, umbrellas, briefcases, iPhones, newspapers, those were the marks of the real native here. I had only a knapsack, and I was appalled at how uncomfortable that made me. I had grown too used to my portable refuge, I felt incomplete without a place to hide. I'd shed most of what

I'd accumulated up north, all the stuff that had grown on me like barnacles on a ship. I was now without most of my hair, my Jeep, a home of sorts, not to mention the loss of that fleeting touch of serenity that had seemed just beyond my reach for all those months, and I'd given it all up for the promise of material profit. Seemed like a lousy bargain. We predators, we need our dark inner rooms, too. I was comforted somewhat, as I looked around, because I was pretty sure my fellow travelers had made similar bargains. They had exchanged the most precious commodity they had, their time, for stuff they probably didn't even care about all that much, like an Italian suit, a German car, or a South American girlfriend.

A wino sat in a corner and watched us flow past with thinly disguised amusement.

Yeah, who's the schmuck now?

I was pretty close to broke. The tin can burned through a lot of gas on her voyage south, and Porter had to get his, too. It occurred to me, and not for the first time, what a lousy businessman I was. Any prostitute will tell you how important it is to get the money first. I had Mac's ATM card in my pocket, and nothing but his word that it was worth anything at all.

Fortunately for me, the Barbadian bank where McClendon had hidden his seed money had a branch on Lexington Avenue, so I shouldered my bag and headed in that direction. It seemed half a lifetime ago that I lived in this city, and most of that time I lived in Brooklyn, which always felt warmer to me, friendlier. But it's the people you remember, not the geography. I'd been lucky in Brooklyn, back in the day. Met the right people. If I'd run into the wrong ones instead, things could have gone the other way just as easily.

I walked into the bank with some trepidation. Knowing Mac, I didn't expect things to be straightforward; with him there always seemed to be some English on the ball, but when I sat down with a bank officer, it turned out to be exactly that easy. The money was, indeed, on deposit and available to me. Yes, all of it. I considered putting it all into a new account, one that didn't have McClendon's name on it, but in the end, after making some financial arrangements with the bank, I left most of it where it was.

On my way out of the bank I thought I saw a reflection in the glass door; one of the tellers was looking at me with that same odd look on her face, that same crooked mix of leer and knowing smile that Frank Porter's mother had used, but when I looked around, she turned away.

Must have been my imagination. Get a grip, will you, I told myself. Nobody's paying any attention to you . . .

I WANDERED DOWNTOWN, stopped at a sidewalk café, and sat down. I took out the prepaid cell I'd picked up at the truck stop, punched in the number that McClendon had given me for his baby mama. A woman's voice answered. "Hello?"

She was an old-fashioned woman, apparently, one who didn't make you leave a message, didn't leave you hanging while she decided whether or not you were worth a return call. "I'm looking for Annabel Wing," I said.

She was silent for a moment. "And, now that you've found her?"

"Ms. Wing, my name is Saul Fowler. I know that name doesn't mean anything to you, but . . ." The lie stuck in my throat, but there was no help for it. "My father's name is McClendon."

Another moment's pause. "How is the good reverend doing these days?"

"I ah, I don't know. I really don't know him all that well. I never knew about you, for example, until a couple of days ago. I found out about your daughter at the same time. My half sister, Melanie."

Again she took her time responding. "What can I do for you, Mr. Fowler?"

"I don't mean to upset you, Ms. Wing, or complicate your life in any way. I'd just like to meet somewhere. Talk a little bit. That's all."

She exhaled into the phone, one drawn-out sigh. "I suppose. I can meet you tomorrow before I go to work. Can you be in Flushing, in the morning? Corner of Roosevelt and Union. Six a.m."

"Seriously? Six in the morning?"

"Take it or leave it, Mr. Fowler."

I heard the warning in her voice. "I'll be there."

MY NEXT STOP was an office building in the East Thirties. Both the neighborhood and the building were unremarkable, but you couldn't say that about the pneumatic young receptionist behind the front desk at Whelen and Ives, the PI firm McClendon had hired to look into Melanie's death. The woman was beautiful. Her only visible shortcoming was that her green eyes were set just a little bit too close together, which gave her a general air of befuddlement. That could have been a flaw or an asset, I suppose, depending on how you looked at it. I watched her from behind one of their dog-eared copies of Sports Illustrated. I decided, after a while, that an unkind person might conclude that she was as dumb as she looked.

They had a coffee machine in the waiting room, one of the modern ones where the coffee came in a little plastic cartridge. You loaded the cartridge of your choice in the machine, pressed the button, and the machine spit your coffee into a paper cup. The resulting product tasted all right, and since I needed the caffeine I was grateful for it, but the lack of ritual bothered me. I liked ritual, it could teach you the correct way to do a thing, how to do it for yourself instead of settling for how the designer of some machine decided it ought to be done. We are no longer either hunters or gatherers. We push buttons and accept what the machine gives us. Soon enough we won't even venture outside at all.

I laid my SI aside and walked across the ratty green carpeting to look out the window. Whelen and Ives was not what I expected. Dingy little office, beat-up couches, magazines from two years ago. They had, apparently, spent all their money on the coffee machine and the receptionist. It didn't speak of the kind of firm I thought McClendon would be drawn to; he was the kind of guy liked to have a show to go with his dinner.

"Mr. Felder?"

It was the receptionist, and she meant me.

She was a vision, standing there holding open the door to the inner offices. Maybe that's her purpose, I thought, maybe her real job is to divert some of the blood flow from your brain, get you off your game. "Right this way," she said, smiling mechanically, and she preceded me down an inner hallway. Maybe it's not her, I thought, maybe it's me, maybe I've deprived myself for so long that I don't react normally anymore. She stopped to knock on a door, then opened it and stood aside. I had to squeeze past her.

Get over it, I told myself. You're supposed to be a bereaved relative, and she seems totally uninterested in you.

"Hello, Mr. Fowler." Josh Whelen stood up behind his desk and held out a hand. He looked like a short, fat ex-cop who was trying hard to lose the short, fat, ex-cop look. He sported a stubbly beard on his round cheeks and his monogrammed white shirt pinched him at the neck so that the knot in his tie was mostly hidden by a layer of excess chin. To me, he looked like the kind of guy who'd let you out of a moving violation for fifty bucks, or maybe plant a bag of weed in your car if you pissed him off.

"Mr. Whelen," I said. "Thank you for taking the time to see me."

"No problem," he said. "You wanted to talk about Melanie Wing."

"If you don't mind. I saw the reports you gave to McClendon. I'm just curious to know if you might recall anything that didn't make it into print."

Whelen re-assed his chair with a grunt, motioning to his client chair. "You're putting me in a tough spot, Mr. Fowler. Technically, that's privileged information. Can I ask you what your interest in this case is? Did McClendon hire you to stir the ashes?"

"Melanie Wing was my sister."

"You speak pretty good English for a Chinese guy."

"Okay, half sister. McClendon was her father, and mine."

"Got it. McClendon was one of those, which ain't a surprise. My old man got around a little bit, too. I heard my uncles talking, after he died, found out I had relatives I'd never met, but I never pushed it. You know what I'm saying? What am I supposed to do, have 'em over the house? I don't even wanna talk to my real brothers all that much."

"I hear you. But suppose one of your brothers got hit." Whelen stuck out his lower lip and looked wounded. "Just saying. And suppose whoever did it took an ear, first, just for fun. And a couple of teeth. Wouldn't you be just a little bit curious?"

He rubbed the bristles on his chin. "Yeah. Yeah. You'd wanna see somebody bleed for it. That's only natural." He stared at me. "You weren't on the job, were you, Fowler? You were a cop somewhere once. Am I right?"

"No."

"Okay." He obviously didn't believe me. "Okay. Make me find out for myself. Irregardless, Mr. Fowler. Let's say you were the hitter. You, personally. You take reasonable precautions, right, you don't get no blood on your car, you don't leave no prints, you wear a hoodie so nobody can make a firm ID, okay, you're probably gonna skate. You know what I'm saying? You got a good chance of walking away clean. Exspecially if you make it through the first week. I mean, once in a blue moon something comes along that might trip you up, but that's not the general rule. So from where I sit, okay, going after whoever did this, it ain't a good use of your resources going after the guy. I mean, it's only human, and I do understand. But after all this time, nobody remembers much of anything, and if they do, they only remember what they think they saw, not what really happened. My advice to you, for what it's worth, let it go. Nothing good is gonna come from you poking around. Let's face it, Mr. Fowler, and if you're a cop you already know this, the guy is gonna get his. You know what I'm talking about. People are fucked up, pardon my English. They kill once, they get away with it, they like the rush, sooner or later they're gonna do it again. Second time, third time, fourth time, their luck runs out, someone drops a net over them. Either that or they pick on the wrong broad and she shanks 'em. That's just the way it works."

I'm not getting anything out of this guy, I thought, and I wondered why. There was an oil portrait on the wall behind Josh Whelen. "Karma," I said, and Whelen nodded.

"Everyone gets what they got coming," he said. "Sooner or later."

The portrait was of an older man, gray hair, gray suit, gray tie, thin patrician face, looked back out at me. "Your father?"

He shook his head. "Bought the painting at auction, thought it might make the firm look more, you know, refined and shit. Are you gonna let this go, Mr. Fowler?"

"I never met Melanie," I told him. "Can you tell me anything about her? What kind of person she was?"

He frowned, rubbed his chin again, and grimaced. "This is secondhand, okay? And nobody said so in plain English, but the impression I got from the people I talked to was that she was a good person, your sister, but she was a little bit like a girl from parochial school once she gets away to camp. You want it, she wants it. Not tryina be crude or nothing here, but you asked . . ."

"Yeah, I did. Nothing else you can tell me about her?"

He shrugged. "Grew up in Queens. Mother probably kept her inside too long. Girls that are too sheltered, you know what I'm saying, sometimes they never catch on. They never really get what the world is like. They never know who to trust."

Someone rapped on Whelen's door. "Come," he said. A woman entered carrying a stack of paperwork. She looked Italian or maybe Greek; she was older than the receptionist, a bit heavier, decidedly less perfect, much more interesting. She glanced at me as she placed the papers she carried down on Whelen's desk.

"Expenditures," she said. "Sorry to interrupt . . ."

"Ahh, Fowler, we done here? Okay if Maria shows you out? What I'll do, I'll pull my notes from your sister's case, and if anything jumps out at me, I'll call you. You got my word."

"Thank you for all your trouble."

"No trouble," he said, not looking at me. "No trouble."

Maria followed me down the hallway. Just outside the door to the waiting room she touched my shoulder and leaned in close. "Hotel Los Paraíso," she whispered. "Tenth Street."

"Thank you," I told her, and one corner of her mouth lifted in what might have been amusement, for a fraction of a second she looked like your best friend's older sister who knew more about it than you did, and then it was gone. Same look I'd gotten from Frank Porter's mother, and then that bank teller.

What the hell, I thought, but by then she'd steered me into the waiting room and closed the door behind me.

UNION STREET, NEAR Roosevelt and Main in Flushing, New York, at six in the morning. Very early for me but it was what she wanted, what she insisted upon, so there I was. The streets looked like two armies of garbage bags had fought a war there the night before, leaving the sidewalks and gutters strewn with the bodies and guts of their fallen. And the whole neighborhood smelled like death.

Or very old fish.

"You don't look at all like him," a woman's voice over my shoulder said.

I tried hard not to look like she'd just scared the shit out of me. "No. Ms. Wing?" She was about five-foot-six, and her long black hair was shot through with gray. I could not guess her age. She was a handsome woman, but thin and frail, like if you bumped into her she'd break apart.

She nodded in answer to my question. "That's me," she said. "Can I buy you a cup of coffee?"

The restaurants on the block displayed pictures of their offerings in their windows, none of which seemed appealing. I didn't know what bubble tea was, and I didn't wanna find out. I saw one sign in English, presumably the name of the establishment. FOUR CHOISE AND A SOUP. Thankfully, it appeared to be closed.

Annabel Wing watched my face, amused. "This way," she said. "There's a McDonald's up the block."

SHE DID NOT seem all that interested in her coffee. The place hummed with activity, even at that ungodly hour, people grabbing their breakfast before hurrying outside to line up for the bus. Ms. Wing appeared more interested in asking questions than answering them. "Where are you from?" she said.

"Have you ever noticed," I asked her, "with some people how you can never really get a straight answer to a question like that?"

She pursed her lips, waiting.

"The East Coast," I told her. "My mother moved around a lot. As far south as Baltimore, as far north as Bangor."

"Did you ever know him? Your father, McClendon."

The son of a bitch was not my father, I thought, he couldn't have been . . . I let it pass. I wondered how closely I needed to stick to my cover story. "After my mother got sent away, I found his name on her marriage certificate. No one is safe from Google, so I did find him, and he told me a few things. He talked mostly about Melanie. I can't seem to get past her death. I don't have any other siblings."

"Not that you know of," she said. It was a good point, and it torpedoed whatever I was going to say next.

"How long have you been out?" she said.

"Out of what?"

"Mr. Fowler. Your face and your hands are very tan, but your ears and your neck and your chin are white. Your shirt is new, I can still see the creases from the store. Your jeans are stiff, I doubt if you've washed them yet, and pardon me if I say that I can't imagine a man like yourself ironing his jeans. But your shoes look like you stole them from a homeless person. Who are you really, Mr. Fowler?"

"That's a good question." It came out before I could really think about it. "I think you missed your calling, Ms. Wing. And I wasn't in prison or anything like that. I was up north, on the coast. Near Canada."

"Doing what?"

"Getting away from it all," I told her. "I was trying to reboot."

She nodded, looked at me for a moment, pensive, and then she fluttered a raised hand. Two men seated at a nearby table stood up, glared at me, and left. Ms. Wing watched them go and then turned back to me. "If you are going to survive this quest of yours," she said, "you are going to have to learn to be careful."

I seemed to have passed some sort of test. "You're very perceptive, Ms. Wing."

"I have to be." She looked out the window. "He was beautiful, back when I knew him."

"McClendon?"

"Is that what you call him?"

"I've never been sure what to call him. He's been out of my life for a long time."

"I used to watch him on television sometimes," she said. "Not so much, lately. But he's still a fine-looking man."

"I suppose."

"He's a Christian now," she said.

"Do you believe that?" I asked her.

She shrugged. "I don't know what sort of life he's had since he left me, but the notion of forgiveness can be a powerful draw to some people. And he never really was a deep thinker, your father."

"You cared about him."

"Oh, I loved him," she said. "And he loved me, too, in his own way."

"Sounds like small consolation."

"No, he really did. But then again, he probably really did love nearly every other woman who smiled at him more than once. Your father is like a flat stone skipping over the surface of the ocean. It is only at the very end of his trajectory that he'll ever gain any real depth." She picked up her coffee cup, looked into it, put it back down almost exactly the way McClendon had done six hundred miles to the north. "You're not close with either of your parents, Mr. Fowler." It was not exactly a question.

"No."

"If that's true, it isn't going to be easy for you to understand Melanie," she said, "because to do that you have to understand her family. Not just me, and not just McClendon, either." She looked around the crowded restaurant, then back at me. "This is not a conversation that I'm willing to continue here. We have to go someplace private."

"DID YOU REALLY think that someone in that McDonald's might have been listening in?"

Annabel Wing did not answer the question. We stood on the top floor of a parking garage, in an empty corner far away from the stairs. Almost directly overhead, a Boeing 737 banked, throttled down and lined up for the approach into LaGuardia. Wing waited until the noise abated somewhat. "Fowler sounds like an English name to me," she said. "Is your family English?"

Her question surprised me. "Ahh, I'm not sure. I heard stories about my mother's grandfather coming to this country from

Belfast, in Ireland, but I never knew if that was true or not. My mother liked to reinvent her past as she went along."

"So Irish, maybe," Annabel said.

"Yeah, maybe. Who knows? He was supposed to be an Orangeman. My great-grandfather. Protestant, not Catholic. He may have thought of himself as an Englishman, I don't know. I don't even know if he was real. Why do you ask?"

Again she chose not to answer. She leaned her elbows on the parapet wall and stared off in the general direction of Citi Field and Arthur Ashe Stadium. "So you don't celebrate St. Paddy's Day, I suppose. What about McClendon? From his name I would assume that you are half Scottish."

"McClendon? Do you seriously think he came into the world with that name?"

She favored me with an appraising glance. "You do know him, then."

"I know what he is. But what I am, Ms. Wing, is your basic American mongrel. St. Paddy's Day never meant a thing to me." I waited to see where she would take it.

"An American mongrel," she repeated. "I wonder if you know how lucky you are. The kids are all worried, these days, about preserving their heritage. Personally, I always felt imprisoned by mine. A true conservative is merely someone who is haunted by the superstitions of his forefathers. Have you ever heard the expression 'Chinaman's chance'?"

"Rings a bell," I said.

"Long odds. As in, 'You don't stand a Chinaman's chance.' Sometime back in the 1860s, five brothers emigrated to San Francisco from a small village outside Canton. Four of them died building the transcontinental railroad. One survived."

"One in five," I said. "A Chinaman's chance."

She nodded. "It was very hazardous work. There were many fatalities." She sighed. "But, at the end of it all, it was possible to ride the train from New York to San Francisco. Or, the other direction, which is what my ancestor did. He knew quite a lot about demolitions by then. It was a skill that served him well in New York City, his new home. But anyway, all of his children, every member of his extended family was born in this country, and yet we are still not Americans. We are Chinese Americans."

"Why is that important now? You guys were probably already in Manhattan when my great-grandfather got off the boat. Whoever he was."

"Because I cannot escape my family's history the way you seem to have escaped yours, Mr. Fowler. I was born in St. Vincent's Hospital. I grew up on the Lower East Side. I'm as New York as a mugger with a brick in his pocket, but the choices made by the fifth brother, my earliest American ancestor, still hold me back today, all these years later."

"How is that?"

"Family lore has it that he was the founder of what is known in English today as the Mott Street Merchants Association."

"I think I begin to see," I said.

"Do you? The Mott Street Merchants Association is the American name for a very old Chinese institution. It is the tong that runs most of Chinatown. If you do business in that part of Manhattan, in one form or another you pay for the privilege. That money goes to the tong, which is still run by one of my distant cousins. Peter Kwok."

"Okay."

"Funny, how invisible we still are. Not so very long ago, Hoover and the rest of the FBI finally woke up and today the Italian Mafia is largely out of business. But they never bothered with the tongs. They still don't. We only hurt our own, that's what they think. Who gives a shit what they do to one another?"

"Is that why you moved out here to Flushing? No tong?"

"Please," she said. "Nature abhors a vacuum, Mr. Fowler. The tong that rules Chinese-American life in this part of Queens originated from the remnants of Chiang Kai-shek's army. They came here from Taiwan in the fifties. You see, when I got pregnant with Melanie, my family threw me out. I was offered refuge here, by Li Fat, who runs the tong in Flushing. Those were his men, back at McDonald's. They call themselves the Green Pang Tribe. Hip name for a very old institution. I think he just wanted to stick his thumb in Peter Kwok's eye. Kwok hasn't forgotten it."

"How long has it been since you've been to Manhattan?"

"I stay close to home," she said. "Where I'm safe. Peter Kwok can't touch me here. I tried to warn Melanie, I offered to send her anywhere, but she had to go to school in the one place where she couldn't survive. She thought I was foolish. Superstitious and ignorant.

"Now she's gone." She turned and looked at me, and all of a sudden she looked every bit as old as McClendon, every bit as ill-used by time. "I'll ask you again, Mr. Fowler. Who are you really? What are you after? Because I've been expecting someone like you ever since Melanie passed."

"Someone like me? In what way?"

"McClendon could never let this go. To him, Melanie was an asset, something of his that was taken from him. It's just like him to hire some mercenary, no offense, some guy not unlike yourself, and send him sniffing after whoever has done this to him.

Can a Christian do that, I wonder? Hire a killer to take his revenge for him?"

"What would you have me do, Ms. Wing? Let's say you had a sister . . ."

"I had a daughter."

"So you did. And someone cut her up." I watched her flinch. "They had their fun with her first, and then they dumped her in the river like a piece of garbage."

"You cannot change what is, Mr. Fowler. The person responsible will have to contend with his karma, as will you."

I sighed. "Buddhist," I said, and she nodded. I wondered if she believed in karma any more seriously than Josh Whelen did. "I never understood you guys. Don't you believe in history? From the Taoists in China six hundred years ago all the way up to Lon Nol in Cambodia, any time anyone wanted to wipe you out, you all stood there like a bunch of sheep and let them do it."

"We die in serenity," she said.

"That has never been one of my goals."

"Go home, Mr. Fowler. The path you are on leads only to more suffering."

"I can take it."

"It isn't you I'm worried about."

I shook my head. "Well. Thank you for seeing me, Ms. Wing." I turned to go.

"Are you in touch with Mac?" she said, looking away. "Do you talk to him?"

"I have his number. You want it?"

Once again she chose not to answer. "It wasn't his fault," she said, staring out over the roofs of Flushing. "Not entirely. We were so isolated, my family and I. And here I am, still in my own little neighborhood, all these years later." She looked back at me. "I never hated him. Resented him from time to time, sure, but never hate. My world is very small, by my choice. One neighborhood was never going to be enough for a man like McClendon, nor was one city. He wanted the world." She turned away again. "I'm glad I had him. For a while, anyway."

I HEARD SOMEONE say that we are, all of us, like men standing in a river, looking downstream: We can only see where we've been, not where we're going. I suppose that makes me blind by choice, because I have never liked looking back, it never seemed to me that I got much profit from it. If I could, I would just go forward from this point right here, clean.

Run away, run away . . .

But I could not come back to New York City without returning to Brooklyn at least once, back to one little corner of the borough, because if there is anything good about my life at all, it started down on Bedford Avenue. The big brick church was still there, of course, and they still had an NA meeting there in the basement, I could tell that from a half a block away. The most dependable sign of an NA or AA meeting is a bunch of guys hanging around by the back door of a church smoking cigarettes, and there they were. The neighborhood had changed somewhat in the years I'd been away, because there were a few white faces mixed in. When I first showed up on their doorstep, I was the only one. I was a lost dog then, half past dead, a homeless refugee, a white kid with a chip on my shoulder and a jones I couldn't handle.

Hard to say, sometimes, what changes and what doesn't.

The smokers nodded to me as I made my way to the door, and a couple of them stuck out a hand and gave me a name to go with it, Bobby and Michael and Kenny. With those guys the things that make them the same are bigger and more lethal than the trivialities that make them seem different. They are a brotherhood of pain, and of rebirth.

Inside, I stood in line for a cup of coffee. They had bagels, too, another sign the neighborhood had grown more prosperous. The coffee was dark and fragrant. Man, addicts know how to make coffee . . . I got my cup and scanned the room. The guy I was looking for wasn't there, and I stood in the back of the room thinking of all the reasons he might be gone, thinking, God, please let him be okay, don't let him be dead, bend the laws of time and physics for me just this one time, please, but I needn't have worried, he stepped through the door a couple of minutes later. He was of average height but he was not average. Sleepy eyes in a black, lined, street-hardened face, an unshakable calm, a gift for listening, and for asking you the right questions, after. He spotted me, made his way across the room. I held my hand out. "Hello, Tommy."

He ignored my hand and dragged me into a rib-crushing hug. "Hey William," he said to someone I hadn't met yet. "What do you get when you sober up a horse thief?"

"A sober horse thief," that someone said, and Tommy let me go.

"I have never stolen a horse," I said, but that was not true, strictly speaking, and Tommy spotted the lie on my face immediately.

"Yeah?" he said. "What?"

"It wasn't a real horse." It was a bronze, a signed Frederick Remington from the estate of a dead oil baron, and one of the bastard's ex-wives wanted the thing badly enough to pay me to go get it. Which I did. "It was just a statue."

"Hah!" Tommy held me out at arm's length. "But you get my

point. You look good, though. Got some color in your face now. How you doin'? And what brings you back to Brooklyn?"

"It's a long story," I told him.

"Stick around," he said. "We'll talk after." It was a ruse, it was just Tommy's way of getting me to sit for a meeting in case I hadn't been to one in a while. Tommy had a million of those. And it was okay, in fact it was better than okay. I've lost count of the number of times I've walked into a place like that church basement wondering what the point of it all was, sort of wishing it was all over, and walked out afterward playing with the idea that my life could maybe be okay if I could somehow manage to quit pissing all over it.

I don't like the word "spirituality" because it is too malleable, people squeeze it into whatever shape pleases them, and as a result it really has lost its meaning. One thing I am pretty sure of, though, when you can spot it from across the room, when it involves robes or jewelry or a beatific smile on a rich man's face, it's probably fake. I entertained unkind thoughts about Mac and his Bible as I watched Tommy after the meeting ended. Tommy was the sun of this particular solar system, it seemed like every stray cat in the room had to touch base with him at least once before they wandered back out into the merciless Brooklyn landscape. When I first met him, Tommy had only been a couple years removed from one of the more violent biker clubs in Brooklyn and I could sense the wildness in him then, maybe that was one of the things that had drawn me to him. He had changed, though, I could feel it, and it wasn't just a matter of losing some of the biker bling and covering up the tats with a long-sleeved shirt. It was easy for me to feel diminished, sitting there and waiting for Tommy, indicted because he had made that leap and I was still standing on the far bank, maybe not content, exactly, with what I was, but afraid to jump.

Tommy had been able to become something bigger than what he once was because he'd been willing to let go of some of the things that had kept him alive, once upon a time, but were holding him back in his new life. I've never had that kind of faith. Like a lot of addicts, recovering or otherwise, I had merely achieved a comfortable level of misery.

It seemed to take forever for that room to empty.

"Saul, my brother," Tommy said, after everyone else was finally gone. "How the hell are you?"

It wasn't a meaningless greeting, not like "What's up" or any of that. It was a real question. He wanted to know. "I'm okay," I told him. It wasn't the answer he was looking for but he accepted it.

"Listen, Saul, I'm sorry for that 'sober horse thief' crack. I shouldn't have said it."

Another sign of his progress. Admit it when you're wrong, that's one of the things they teach you in that kind of room. Make things right, don't let them fester. "You don't have to apologize for telling the truth."

"No? Maybe just for the way I said it, then. What brings you back to Brooklyn?"

I told him about Melanie Wing.

"I'm sorry to hear that," he said when I was finished. "I'm sorry for your loss. That kind of thing leaves a bruise that can take a long time to go away. But I didn't know you had a sister, you never told me."

"I didn't know. I still don't, actually. It would take more than a few DNA tests to untangle my family tree, and I'm not sure it would be worth the trouble. What it boils down to is this: Someone killed the girl, and her father, who may or may not be related to me, wants me to find out who did it, if I can."

"That the kind of thing you do, these days?"

I thought we'd come to that . . . "Not exactly. I've been sort of retired for the last couple years. The last job I had . . ." I caught the look in his eye. "All right, okay, the last horse I stole, if you want to think of it that way, involved a museum in France, and I did okay enough to take a step back for a while. So I don't know. I don't know what I do these days."

He nodded. "An uncomfortable place to be. Not a bad place, but uncomfortable. So with this sister of yours, do you have a plan? How are you going to pull this off?"

I shrugged. "So far all I'm doing is knocking on some doors, asking some questions. My operational theory is that whoever killed her will probably hear about it and start to get nervous. You know how it is, Tommy, when you stir things up, shit happens."

"Yeah," he said. "Even smart people will do some stupid things when they think they're under pressure. Anything I can do to help?"

"Thanks," I told him, "but I don't think so. Not unless you know something about the tongs."

He gave me a look. "Queens or Manhattan?"

"You're kidding me."

He sighed. "If you work in the pharmaceutical trades and you survive long enough to get up off the street, you learn the players after a while. Some of the biker clubs will transport product on occasion. So, yeah, I heard about the tongs, but it ain't like I met any of those guys."

"Oh. But it's true, then. I was told there are two tongs in New York."

"Two majors," he said. "Green Pang and Mott Street. Although, from what I hear, Mott Street ain't what it used to be. Plus, you got the dudes out in Jersey, and there might be some upstarts. From time to time some of the young turks will test the old men, just to see if they're still strong enough."

"What's wrong with the Mott Street crew?"

"Demographics, babe. The city is changing. You seen all them palefaces we had in here tonight, last time you was here you was the only white boy for miles. Those Mott Street mothers are getting squeezed because Chinatown ain't strictly Chinese like the way it used to be. Their business model don't work like it used to because the people they depended on are getting pushed out of Manhattan by the lawyers and stockbrokers. I mean, I don't wanna call you no names, Saul, but you know what these loser gang fuckwits are all about. If they can't make that easy money, they start to get restive. Start killing each other and whatnot, fighting over what's left."

"Interesting." But I didn't see how the problems of the Mott Street Merchants Association did anything for me, and I told him so.

"Ahh, you'll figure it out," he said, waving it all away. "So where does all this leave you? How you doin', really?"

I knew what he was asking me, or I thought I did. "I got a year and nine months clean," I told him.

"Not bad," he said. "Not bad. When you first showed up here, nobody thought you'd last a week."

"I didn't, either."

"Funny, how that works," he said. "You can never tell. Some people come around looking like they got it knocked, next thing you know you be going to the wake. Some sorry, hopeless excuse for a human being, got nothing left to live for comes through the door, a year later he's going to school and bitching about how much taxes he has to pay."

I probably should have felt insulted at that but I knew that

Tommy was yanking my chain. Laughing at me, and from him that was okay. "Was I really that bad?"

"Dude. Saul. Nobody comes through that door over there because he has it all together. This place right here? This is the knot in the end of the rope. You know how it is with us: First the men in blue come looking for you, then the men in white, and finally the men in black. You sound to me like you're still fighting all those same battles. Authority, the Almighty, the Meaning of It All . . ."

"What's your answer?"

"Mine?" The question seemed to surprise him. "You know what my answer is, man. Don't pick up, go to my meetings, quit behaving like an asshole."

"There has to be more to it than that."

"No, there doesn't," he said. "You always did overthink all this shit. You don't like authority? Guess what, nobody does. That the hill you wanna die on? Fuck, man, you don't have to fight every single battle that comes along, I tell you what, you sit still for five minutes, somebody crazier than you will come along and do it for you. Nobody says you gotta believe in the Great Cosmic Santa Claus here, you know what I'm saying. Stop wasting time on shit you ain't gonna figure out anyhow. Accept it: You ain't gonna think your way out of this. That ain't your job anyhow. Your job is to worry about how to deal with what's right in front of you."

"You make it sound easy, Tommy."

He reached out and put his hand on my shoulder. "Simple, never easy. Listen, if you're in town, I wanna see you. I wanna see you here."

And that, really, was what I came for. "Thanks, Tommy. I'll be back."

THE PHONE RANG seven or eight times before he picked it up, I thought he was gonna let it go to voice mail. "What the fuck?" he said, his voice fogged over with sleep. "Who's calling me in the middle of the freakin' night?"

"It's me, Mac."

"Son of a bitch, Saul . . . Don't you ever sleep?"

"Not that much. Listen, I met Annabel."

"Unngh." Sounded like I'd punched him in the gut. "How . . ." Deep sigh. "How'd she look?"

Like a tree in the desert, dying, starved for a lack of water . . . "She's beautiful, Mac. Little bit of gray in her hair."

Another deep sigh. "She ask about me?"

"Said you look fine on television."

He snorted. It was a sound freighted with self-derision.

"She seemed to think it was self-centered of you to assume someone killed Melanie because of something you've done. She figured you'd think it was all about you."

"That ain't it," he said. "That ain't it at all."

"What is it, then?"

"You oughta know this by now. Some guy chops up his wife and buries her in the backyard, why's he do it? Why'nt he just divorce her? Why don't he just throw her the fuck out? Why's he gotta kill her?"

"You tell me."

"Saul." Sounded like a teacher, exasperated by a particularly dim pupil. "He don't wanna pay child support. He don't wanna lose his house. And he wants the insurance. It's the fucking money, it's always about the money, and Mel didn't have none. Neither does Annabel, none to speak of."

"You think that's it?"

"You mark my words, you get to the bottom of this, it's gonna be about the green."

"Okay. Next question, this investigator you hired, you told me, if I remember right, that he was a tall and dried-out prick of an ex-cop. Guy I met was a short, fat prick of an ex-cop."

"You gotta understand, you can't do what those guys do for twenty years and come out normal."

"Whatever. But which was is, tall and dried-out or short and fat?"

"The fat guy runs the agency. What he does, he hooks up with one or two retired detectives from each precinct if he can, that way he's got guys who know the ground and know the players. They work for him when he's got something for them to do, the rest of the time they play golf. The tall, skinny guy, who I met maybe twice, he did the actual footwork on Melanie. The fat guy just delivered the bad news."

"The tall guy, you remember his name?"

He went silent for a moment. "No," he finally said. "I come up with it, I'll call you."

Chapter Four

MELANIE WING'S LAST address was a tenement building on Thirteenth Street, just off Second Avenue. She had rented a room from someone named Valerie Branch. Branch's phone number came up in a free online directory, so I called it and asked if I could come by. Branch, sounding somewhat guarded, delayed me until the evening, so I found a hotel room on the West Side, right near the Hudson River. I sat on one of the double beds and looked out the window. You couldn't see the river from my room, so basically I was staring at buildings and wondering if I'd made a mistake coming south.

It was after six when I found Valerie Branch's building. Like much of the neighborhood in which it was located, the fortunes of the tenement she lived in appeared to have waxed and waned over the generations. At present it seemed to be in a bit of a lull; the outer doors were beaten and battered, the inner door didn't lock, and the mailboxes in the hallway were heavily tagged with spray paint, which was the local gang's way of marking their territories. Better than peeing on the verges, I suppose, but not by a lot. The hallways smelled of cooking. I climbed the stairs to the third floor and knocked on her door.

A man answered. He was black, a few inches short of six feet, and built like a tree stump. "What can I do for you," he said.

"I called and spoke to Valerie Branch," I told him.

His expression did not change. "What can I do for you."

Not a happy guy. "My sister lived here once," I told him. "I wanted to see if Ms. Branch remembered her. If she could tell me anything about what she was like."

"Your sister." He stared at me, his eyes cold and unblinking.

"Okay, half sister."

"Toy?" It was a woman's voice, and it came from the dim interior of the apartment behind him. "It's okay, Toy. Let him in."

Toy? Dump Truck would have fit him better. He stood aside and let me pass.

You can tell a lot about a person by the feel of the place they call home. Ms. Branch was a cultured woman, organized, elegant, and cool. You got that just from her hallway; it smelled faintly like perfume, not sautéed onions like the rest of the building, and a jazz piano tinkled softly somewhere in the background. I liked her before I ever saw her, even if she seemed instinctively to distrust me. "In here, Mr. Fowler," she said, and I followed the sound of her voice down to the end of the hall and into a small sitting room.

She was in a wheelchair. I guessed her age to be something north of seventy. "Thank you for seeing me, Ms. Branch."

"I hope you don't mind," she said. "I wanted my son Toy to sit in."

"Sensible precaution," I told her. "Though unnecessary in my case. I am a pussycat."

"You don't look like a pussycat," she said. "In fact, you don't look anything at all like what I pictured."

And then she did it.

These women, they were beginning to give me a complex. Why did they look at me like that? It was as if I had a big pimple on the end of my nose, or a wart with hair growing out of it, or maybe I had forgotten to zip up my pants. With Branch, the look was there one moment and then the next second it wasn't; it felt as if someone else had come out of hiding to peer at me through her eyes, just for that heartbeat, smiled that odd quarter smile, and then vanished. The Ms. Branch who was left behind was a bit uncomfortable with me, even with her son standing by, but for that eyeblink of time, in the gaze of that other woman, I felt like the court fool, or maybe the last piece of cake. It was the same vibe I'd gotten from Frank Porter's mother, and with her, too, it had come and gone in a half second.

And then there was the bank teller, and the woman at Whelen and Ives . . .

I am not in the habit of imagining things. You come up the way I did, you learn early on that your powers of observation are your first line of defense.

But it made no sense. How could it? These women, I was sure, had never met one another, the odds against that were off the charts. File it, I told myself, and keep moving. When something happens that you cannot understand, chances are you do not yet have enough information. Eventually the answer will present itself.

"Melanie was a quiet girl," Ms. Branch said, once again somewhat distant. "You were hard-pressed to know for sure when she was home. She worked such odd hours, but she was always reading." She glanced over at Toy, who clearly took that as a shot. Maybe, in his mother's opinion, he watched too much television.

Your mother will never stop comparing you to your betters. "She was a worker. She was one of the invisible women who keep it all going while the men fight over the steering wheel so they can pretend to be in charge."

"Did she have a boyfriend?"

"There was a young man," she said. "I don't know how serious they were. I never met him. My agreement with her was clear: no men in my home."

"Did she tell you his name?"

"Marcus something. Jewish-sounding last name, Hammond or Hayman, something like that. Shouldn't you be writing this down?"

"No need, Ms. Branch. Did she have people that she hung out with? Regulars, close friends?"

Ms. Branch nodded. "A young woman. Klaudia Livatov. Klaudia with a K. Klaudia was even quieter than Melanie, if that was possible. Klaudia was Melanie's personal trainer, I think. When she met me she was so afraid that her entire body seemed to tremble. Klaudia was simply another invisible woman, and I think she was probably afraid every time she stepped out her front door. I think she was happiest when no one noticed her. She was quite pretty, but from the way she dressed I would say she'd have preferred to be plainer so that men would not look at her as much." She gave me a look. "I don't think a man can ever understand that kind of fear."

"We all got our demons, Ms. Branch."

She raised her chin higher and stared at me through her starboard eye. "Not the same thing," she said. "Not the same thing at all."

Yeah, maybe not. "Anything else you can tell me about Klaudia Livatov?"

"Very spiritual girl. She wore a cross around her neck, and she had a habit of holding on to it when you tried to talk to her. I could give you her address . . ."

She hesitated. She was afraid, on Klaudia's behalf. It was nice of her, really. "I'll be a gentleman, Ms. Branch. You have my word."

She seemed to consider it. "I'll have to look it up for you," she finally said. "I don't have your powers of recall." She wheeled herself over to a small table by the window and pulled a drawer open. "There was no one at her memorial service," she said, without looking at me. I felt indicted nonetheless. "No family, I mean. I know her father was gone, but I did expect to see her mother . . . It was only a few people she worked with, plus Klaudia and I, and some street girls." She glanced up, her eyes wet. "Prostitutes," she said. "They cried like babies."

"How do you suppose she got so friendly with prostitutes?"

"I didn't get the opportunity to ask her." She glared at me. "Her mother should have been there."

"I suppose," I told her. "Don't think ill of her. She was afraid, too. She's caught in a Hatfields and McCoys kind of thing."

"Crips and Bloods, you mean," Toy said.

"Something like that. She doesn't dare to trespass."

Ms. Branch found the slip of paper with Klaudia Livatov's information on it, and she read it off to me. "Thanks for all your trouble," I told her.

Toy showed me out. "Sorry for the distrust," he told me, out in the hallway. "Landlord's got rules against subletting, and he's been trying to get her out of here for twenty years."

IT IS GENERALLY only drug addicts, alkies, and teenagers who believe that they are immortal. Almost everyone else knows better, they have a visceral understanding that, although Life might be sacred and eternal, lives, specifically yours and mine, are fragile and very easily lost. I had scars to remind me of that, aches and pains that remind me of misjudgments past, and while they have not yet made me a coward, I do tend to be a bit more thoughtful than I once was, particularly when I am about to risk my ass in the pursuit of some new insanity. There were three of them, two on foot and one driving a gypsy cab. I picked them up shortly after leaving Ms. Branch's building on Thirteenth. My first thought was that I should walk over to Fourteenth and jump on the L train, ride it across town to Union Square and change there for an uptown train. The guy in the car would probably want to stay mobile, the other two ought to be easy enough to lose in the confusion underground, and I could walk away clean.

It was the logical move.

But every man, no matter how soft or genteel he may appear on the outside, carries deep within him the imprint of his reptilian ancestors, and when the beast awakens, logic is generally the first casualty.

The two on foot were still young, young enough to feel immortal.

I walked west on Thirteenth.

You can't kill the reptile, the reptile will not die because he is part of who you are, he is the reason we are still at one another's throats, and you can't really tame him, either; about the best you can hope for is that he stays asleep. I found what I was looking for a couple of blocks west, it was a building even more decrepit that the one Ms. Branch lived in. I stopped on the sidewalk right in front of it. I turned to look back where one of them was coming up the sidewalk behind me; I was probably a bit too theatrical but it was street theater, after all. The second one was on the far side of the street and the cab was laying back. I made eye contact with the one closest to me, he was Asian, with a wisp of beard on his chin. He stopped and pretended to retie his sneaker but it didn't have any laces, it had those Velcro things instead.

I could feel the reptile taking umbrage at that . . .

How stupid did this kid think I was?

I darted to my right, up the steps and into my chosen building. I heard a yell on the street outside as I pounded up the ancient wooden steps. Out on the street there is a certain amount of risk, no question, but in neighborhoods where the tenements are mostly the same height and stand cheek by jowl, it's up on the roof where the real shit goes down. I could hear them coming behind me before I was halfway up; I'd cut things a little close, plus they were each ten or twelve years younger than I and maybe fifty or sixty pounds lighter. I could hear two of them, I had to assume the third guy was still in the car, or else he was ditching it and would follow when he could. That gave me my strategy, such as it was. And my luck held, although it wasn't much of a stretch. If the street-level doors are broken and hanging open, you've gotta figure the roof door won't be much of an obstacle, either.

Or, if you prefer, the goonas were smiling on me . . .

Out on the roofs, it was perfect ambush country. The light was funny, most of the area was lit up by the ambient glow of early evening in the city, light from all the buildings, streetlights, cars, bridges, and all the rest, but there were pools of deep black everywhere due to the usual variety of roof structures like access doors, skylights, and HVAC ductwork. I picked out one of those blacked-out areas and stepped into it.

The first two came charging out of the roof door. The second one was Asian, too. Careless, I thought, both of them. It's the over-confidence that comes of being too used to prey animals that only flee. A tiger in the wild, for example, will run away from you but not for long, and never in a straight line. Instead, he will circle around behind you so that he can have a look at who you are. That gives him the option of killing and eating you, should he so desire.

But they were just kids, really. Sure, they would probably put the screws to me if I gave them the chance, but still . . . And if they were armed, they didn't show it. My best guess was that they weren't carrying, this being New York City and all. New York will not pass up the opportunity to put your ass away for a while if she catches you with a pistol. Most street gangs operate within well-defined boundaries, and within their respective territories each gang will secrete a pistol here and there, the hiding places being known to all the gang members. That way the weapons are available if they are deemed necessary, with much less risk of getting your soldiers jammed up by any of New York's Finest. I didn't think these two guys had had enough time for that.

They separated. One of them came around the corner of the air duct I was hiding behind and I clotheslined him. He went straight down, clutching his throat, and I kicked him hard in the ribs. Not hard enough to do any permanent damage, but hard enough to keep him discouraged for a while. The second one heard the noise and came running. Again I stepped out of the shadow; I hit the second one with a hard right to his temple. He was tougher than the first guy, he shook it off and went for a high leg kick but he was a little wobbly. I ducked the kick and hit him again, almost in the same exact spot. He staggered back, and I could see from the look on his face that he was reconsidering his career choices, but he had taken someone's money and now he had to earn it. He squared up and came at me again. Most of these guys think that you're going to back up or run, which is the instinctive and wrong reaction. Get up into their space, as counterintuitive as that seems, because then most of their practiced moves stop working. I threw an elbow at his chin, which he ducked. "Who sent you?" I figured Mac was wrong and Annabel was right, so it had to be either Peter Kwok or Li Fat. "What do you want from me?"

He didn't react at all, didn't even look at my face, but he kicked me in the outside of my thigh, which hurt a lot, so I head-butted him a little harder than I had intended to. He went down hard, his head caroming off the metal support for the ductwork I'd been hiding behind.

Done for the day.

You get so sick of this shit. If you're a plumber, I wonder if you get so tired of plumbing that eventually you reach the point where you never want to look at another broken toilet, ever again.

And it's the strangest sensation, even when there's a fire raging in one part of your brain, in another part of your head there's a voice telling you that you're an idiot and that you should have gone to dental school instead. Here were two more guys who were probably going to hate me for as long as they lived. That's the problem with this kind of thing—it never stops. Yeah, confound my enemies, God, but please don't let 'em find out it was me that dropped the dime or else we'll have to kill 'em all.

Call it the neutron solution . . .

I searched them both and I didn't learn much; they carried no ID, no weapons, not even a cent in their pockets. The first kid was still half conscious, he moaned when I touched him. "Who are you?" I asked him. "Who's paying you?" He didn't answer, not in English, anyhow. I still had no clue where he or his buddy came from. The only thing I picked up from these two was that they both had hard calluses on their hands, the kind you get from hours and hours of hard work, and not from hoisting bricks or turning wrenches, either. I finally decided that there was nothing more for me up there, and besides, there was still one more guy, the one who'd been driving the gypsy cab.

The two on the roof, you could think of them as freshly graduated engineers, they had all the qualifications on paper but they hadn't yet learned how things worked in the real world. I guess you've gotta learn somewhere. The thing is, man, it's hard to be something. It's hard to be anything. It's practice, and school, and late hours, and apprenticeship, and getting smacked around for doing it wrong, no matter what you're trying to be, you're gonna take some lumps along the way. So why would you pick street punk when you could learn how to do something normal for the same amount of work? Of course, the person I really needed to ask that question was myself.

The building roofs were divided by low parapet walls. I hopped the nearest one and tried the roof door for that building but it was locked, and so was the next, but the third door opened for me and I went down, trying to be as quiet as I could. There were a couple of kids playing in one of the hallways, they watched me with bright eyes as I went by. I silently wished them luck as I passed, because with that hallway for a front yard, they were probably gonna need it.

I slithered out the front door. Instructor I had once claimed that you could pull in your aura, sort of shrink your psychic emission to the point where no one would notice you. I never knew if it worked or not. I always figured it was me people noticed, not my aura, but you know, why not, what the hell?

Maybe it helped, who knows, or maybe my aura-shrinking

skills were weak. Further testing would be necessary. I got down to the sidewalk and maybe six steps closer to the guy before he noticed me.

Black guy. I gotta admit I was surprised, because the concept of integration still has a ways to go in the realm of street rats. The dude was out of his cab, standing in the middle of Thirteenth Street about halfway between his car and the open door to that first tenement when he saw me. He took two steps toward the car before he decided he wasn't gonna make it and took off running west on Thirteenth, toward Third Avenue.

I don't have the right build for running. Too much beef, for one thing, and my inseam might be a little short for a guy my height. I thought I had no shot to catch the guy, he put on a real burst, he went zero to max in a heartbeat, and to tell you the truth, I don't know why I bothered to chase him, if I'd had time to think about it I probably would have gone through his car instead. But I did it anyway, and I guess the patron saint of lost causes decided to cut me a break that night because when the guy got to Third and tried to cross in the middle of the traffic, he T-boned a yellow cab and went down in the middle of the street. In the midst of honking horns and drivers yelling in some pidgin combination of English and who knows what he bounced up and took off running again. I had gained on him some, though, I kept up my Gimli the dwarf imitation as the guy made the far side of Third. He wasn't looking so good anymore, though, I didn't know if it was the impact with the cab or too many cigarettes or what but his form was definitely suffering as he continued west on Thirteenth. His arms were windmilling all crazy as he turned to look back to see if I was still coming, he should have kept his eyes on where he was going because he tripped over something in the street, flew across the hood of a parked car and face-planted on the tailgate of the truck parked in front.

I stopped running at once.

I walked across Third Avenue trying to catch my breath and pull my aura back down again, but it's New York City, you know what I mean, so whatever you're doing, they seen worse, and they got business of their own anyway. Nobody paid much attention to the guy, or to me, either.

He lay senseless, facedown in the gutter between the car and the truck. I stood there looking down at him for a moment hoping he wasn't dead, waiting to see if anyone was going to come and see if he was all right, but everyone seemed to just flow on by.

I rolled the guy over. He was bleeding from a gash on his forehead and his right eye was closing up. He was going to have one mother of a headache. I wrestled him over onto the sidewalk and leaned him back against the front tire of the car he'd slid across. There was an empty pint bottle of Barton Reserve under the car, I fished it out and plopped it in his lap, just for effect. Somebody walks by, maybe they see the bottle, figure me for a soft-headed Samaritan instead of a creep.

"Hey, buddy." I put a finger under his chin and tipped his head back but he was still out cold. I let go of his chin, and his head rolled down onto his chest like all the bones in his neck had been removed. "Yo, buddy." I tried to find a pulse in one of his wrists but I couldn't feel anything, so I tried at his neck and there it was. He was alive, at least.

I sat back on my haunches and waited. It took him a couple more minutes to come around. "Fuck me," he mumbled, and his head stirred. He held one hand up to his face but he didn't touch it, it must have hurt him too much. "Oh my God . . ."

"You all right?" I asked him. "I was thinking maybe you broke your neck."

He looked up and focused on me with some difficulty. I think he recognized me after a moment; he had kind of a funny spasm and then he went all stiff. "Whaddaya want," he said, and then he looked around, like someone was supposed to show up with the answers. When they didn't, he looked back at me. "What . . . what'd ya do to the other two?"

"They wouldn't talk to me so I threw 'em off the roof," I lied. "Used to be, that always worked. Know what I'm saying? You talk to the first guy, right, and when he won't talk, you just chuck him over. That way, the second guy is cooperative as hell. Didn't work this time, though, the second guy just kept gabbling in Japanese, so I chucked him over, too."

"Chinese," the guy mumbled.

"Whatever," I said, warming to my role. "You come to this country, fucking speak English. So now what do we do with you?"

"Oh Jesus," he said, and he crossed himself convulsively, twice, wincing from the pain the movements caused him. "Jesus help me . . ."

"Jesus ain't here," I told him. "All's you got is me. So how come a brother like you is working with two Chinese guys?" I was still down on my haunches in front of him, maybe two feet away, and I was keeping my voice low. And that one quad where the guy had kicked me hurt like hell.

The guy began breathing faster and faster, his chest heaving like somebody running a race. "Oh God," he moaned. "OhGodohshitohJesusChrist . . ."

"Relax," I told him. "Just tell me what's going on. Was it Peter Kwok or Li Fat?"

"Ogun," he said, looking around wildly. "Ogun . . . he's gonna fuckin' kill me . . ." He squeezed his eyes shut and began to cry, and then all at once he screamed. "HELLLLP! Somebody HELLLLP!"

"What gun?" I asked him. "Nobody's got a gun. What are you talking about?"

"Ogun, you fuckin' moron! Ogun! HELLLLLLP MEEE!"

If it was an act, it was a good one. I became conscious of someone standing behind me on the sidewalk but I kept my eyes on my guy, who had quit screaming. "Ogun," he whimpered, "Ohshi-tohJesus . . ." His fingers closed reflexively on the empty whiskey bottle in his lap. He rolled over on his hands and knees and scrabbled away from me.

And I let him go.

It felt like dereliction of duty.

He jumped to his feet all spastic, looked like he'd gotten jabbed in the ass with a cattle prod, and he took off west again, ran unsteadily down Thirteenth Street, still had the bottle in one hand. I felt like I should have chased him, I should have done something but I didn't have the appetite for it so what I did was, I let him go. "Ya c'yan 'elp 'im," a voice behind me said. I stood up and turned to look; she was one of those religious women who wear their skirts down to their ankles. Island lady, by the accent.

"No?"

She shook her head. "Ya c'yan do nuttin' fer da man until he stop drinkin', stop smokin' nat chemical."

"Maybe not. Ogun, he kept saying Ogun. Is that a name? Does that mean anything to you?"

Her eyes narrowed. "I ain't hear 'im say nuttin'," she said. She knew who or what ogun was, I could feel it, but she wasn't going to talk. " 'Im gone now, anyhow."

Sergeant Schultz in a dress, just what I needed.

Anyway, picture a bead on a wire, one end of the wire is Mac and his money, at the other end is Annabel, the tongs, and their ancient hatreds. The bead just moved in Annabel's direction.

WHEN I GOT back to my hotel room I sat on the bed and listened to the movie the guy in the room next to me was watching. I couldn't hear the dialogue, assuming it had some; mostly what I heard was music, explosions, gunfire, and some occasional screaming. Ever notice how people who die in movies tend to just flop over dead? Screaming, in movies, is the exception. Too distracting, I suppose. It's usually the soundtrack that gets you. And why is it that there's music playing every time you're ready to press the go button on some irrevocable decision that your reptile mind has convinced the higher functioning parts of your brain to go along with?

Maybe it's just that there are some journeys that must be undertaken with the eyes of reason clamped resolutely shut. As the movie approached what I assumed would be the end of the final act, the pretend explosions crescendoed, echoing through the wall like the music of some manic bass player in the middle of a meth burn. No, wait, I was wrong. The next to the last scene. The final scene would be the wrap-up, the sunset, hearts and flowers, and the justifications for it all. Real life is ugly compared to the movie versions, sticky, messy, generally unfair, painful as hell on occasion. As science continues to push the limits of human lifespan, you have to wonder, really, how much of this shit do they think we can take?

I did not accept Mac's story of my conception, and I could not believe that Melanie Wing was really my sister, that she was any closer to me than anybody else on the planet, but I found I had adopted her somehow. My logical mind must have been otherwise occupied when my inner reptile decided, Yeah, she's mine. Otherwise, I think that first night in that hotel in Manhattan would have been my last. I even thought about it, sitting there on the bed listening to that guy's TV. It would have been easy enough, just take a little more of McClendon's money for my troubles and leave the rest where it was, call him up and tell him that Melanie was gone and nothing was going to bring her back, that it was most likely just some random creep who would eventually get his, somewhere along the line. Revenge being one of God's professions, why not leave it to him?

I couldn't do it. Just a bad day, I told myself. Don't give up this easy, give it another day. Go to see Klaudia Livatov, Melanie's scared and virginal little mouse of a BFF. Give McClendon a little bang for his buck, put on a show so he can salve his conscience.

And me, mine.

Growing up with a mother who saw and heard things that weren't there gave me pretty good powers of recall, because it became critical to me that I hang on tight to what my senses told me was real. I closed my eyes and mentally reviewed Mac's paperwork, and after a while I came up with the phone number for one Marcus Reiman, alleged erstwhile love interest of Melanie Wing. I called the number, got the recording, left my message.

Chapter Five

I SAT IN the hotel restaurant and stared at my greasy breakfast. I wasn't thinking of Melanie Wing or her father, the good Reverend McClendon. I was wondering how long I had to stick around before I could escape again, and I was wondering if I ought to cross the border and head up into Canada this time, really get lost, just keep heading north and east until I found a place with no other people at all, where I could stand on the shore until the racket in my head died away completely, no matter how long it took. I would have a few bucks this time around and brother, I knew how to be poor; if I lived on brown rice and fish I could stay up there a long-ass time, and when the noises stopped and the echoes died away maybe I could actually hear something, maybe then I'd know what to do with myself. Does every man dream this dream or is it just me, and why aren't there caravans of old Winnebagos driven by assholes such as myself, and why is it such a seductive thing, this idea that you ought to just hoist your sails and go? And when you got where you were going, would it be the same shit all over again, would I wake up restless and itchy, and . . .

Check Out Receipt

South County Regional Library
239-533-4400
leelibrary.net

Wednesday, September 5, 2018 9:56:47 AM
73752

Item: 33069075698536
Title: ILL Shadow of a thief : a thriller
Call no.: ILL
Material: ILL
Due: 09/19/2018

Total items: 1

Thank you for using the
South County Regional Library
Monday-Wednesday 9-8
Thursday 9-6
Friday-Saturday 9-5

My phone rang.

Scared the shit out of me.

I had to pull the thing out and figure out which button took the call. "Yeah?"

"Mr. Fowler?" Male voice, and not one I remembered hearing before. "Is this Saul Fowler?"

Bastard knew both of my names . . . "Who wants to know?"

"Mr. Fowler, my name is Marcus Reiman. I'm, ahh, I was friends with Melanie. Melanie Wing. You left me a message? We should meet up, Mr. Fowler, because if you, ahh, if there's a chance you can find out who, ahh, you know, whoever did it, I want to help. You know what I mean? Whoever did this . . . They shouldn't just walk away."

"No."

"If there's something I can do? There ought to be something. Can we get together and talk about this?"

"Yeah." Dreams of fishing for salmon up on the Labrador coast faded out and drifted away. "Yeah, absolutely. Where and when?"

"How about this morning?" he said. "I work at Beth Israel. If you got here in about an hour, that would work for me."

I MET HIM in the lobby. He was waiting just inside the emergency room entrance, just like he said he'd be. Pale green scrubs, short wiry hair, glasses, five-eight or so; he made me the moment I walked in. "Marcus?"

He walked up and shook my hand. He was beefier than he looked, had a strong grip. "Saul?"

"Yeah. Can I buy you a coffee?"

They had a Starbucks in the lobby. I found myself liking Reiman because he didn't order a mochachino grande or some shit, he asked for a coffee, large, and he didn't put any soy milk in it, either. We sat down at a table by a window. I couldn't be sure what McClendon had told him so I stuck to my standard story. "I never met her. After I found out about her I wanted to know who she was and what kind of person she'd been, but it seemed to me that she'd just vanished. Everyone I talked to had written her off. Even the PI firm that McClendon hired, Whelen and Ives, didn't seem all that interested in her, and they were getting paid."

"I didn't write her off, I assure you." The guy was intense. "Whelen and Ives, yeah, I remember the guy. Suspicious as hell, seemed disappointed he couldn't pin it on me. Wasn't a pleasant conversation."

"Tall skinny guy? Ex-cop?"

"Yeah." Reiman nodded. "What a dick. He didn't tell me he was retired, I only found that out when I talked to the real cops. They knew who he was, though. I was doing a Doctors Without Borders thing in Peru when it happened. And I still can't believe she's gone."

"You and her, you were happening, am I right?"

"No. I mean, truthfully, I was trying like hell. I was happening but she wasn't. How can I say this? I mean, you are her brother . . ."

"Spit it out."

"You know how you always want what you can't have? Melanie was the chick that no one could have. I mean, she'd go out with me, as long as I didn't call it a date. If she could say that we were just hanging, you know, she'd be all right with it. Just, you know . . ."

"Maybe she didn't like you like that."

"No, she did." His smile came and went like a strobe light. "I know she did. You ever date a nurse?"

I thought about it for a moment. The answer was yes, I had, and the lady in question wasn't hard to remember, but I wasn't all that sure I wanted to talk about her. Still, Reiman was being pretty open . . . "Yeah. I guess. I don't know if we were dating, exactly. It was in Bosnia."

"During the war?"

"Shortly thereafter."

"What was she like?"

Oh brother. "She knew what she wanted."

He pointed at me. "That's it! That's it. A lot of nurses are like that. They know what they want. Well, Mel was different. And it wasn't that she didn't know, it was . . . She didn't want . . . She didn't allow herself to want anything. She liked to keep everything contained. She kept her life small." His hands described a small square box on the coffee shop table. "Nothing bigger than this. Nothing that scared her. Nothing that didn't fit into her comfort zone."

"Must have been frustrating."

"You mean . . . Nah. It was fun. Mel was something else. And we were starting to get somewhere. I mean, I know I had a long way to go, but she was starting to trust me. She'd started to open up, just a little. Toward the end, I started getting a nicer vibe from her. I wanna say that we had a future, maybe."

The Melanie Reiman was telling me about didn't sound much like the woman who'd gotten out of her depth trolling Manhattan's night streets, like the one the ex-cop Josh Whelen described. "You sure? Maybe she hit from the other side of the plate."

Reiman shook his head. "Listen, I'm not so egotistical as to think that any woman who doesn't want me must be a lesbian, but you know, no. She was coming out of her shell, but on her own time. You had to give her the space, and the time. And someone didn't give her the time."

"No."

"Do you think there's any chance it was an accident?"

"Did you see the postmortem photographs?"

All of a sudden Marcus Reiman looked old and tired. "No. And don't tell me."

"I wasn't going to. But it was no accident."

"Jesus Christ." He turned away.

I decided to shift gears. "Did she have any particularly close friends? Someone she may have confided in? Other than yourself."

"I'm not sure. The people she worked with, I suppose, to a certain extent, but even with them . . . Mel was easy to be friendly with, but hard to be friends with. She was so guarded it's hard for me to believe she'd be too intimate with very many people, that's not who she was. There was this one chick, though. Not a nurse. What the hell was her name? Strange bird. She lives downtown, just off Houston Street. I met her a couple of times. She was a lot like Melanie, only more so. She was so self-contained, so hermetic, she was so shut off from you that you never got even a clue about who she was. I always pictured her showering with her eyes closed so she wouldn't catch a glimpse of herself naked. I think she's Polish. Of Slavic extraction, anyhow. Loves her some baby Jesus. She's like, a dog walker, poet, personal trainer, editorial assistant, blogger kind of a chick. You know what I mean? Like, vegan, PETA, fur is murder, gluten-free, nonviolent, sew a quilt for peace, like that's going to make any goddamn difference."

"Melanie was like that?"

"Yeah. Yeah, she was, but with Mel, behind the mask there was this other person, I'd get a quick look at her every now and then.

But with Klaudia, that's it, that's her name, Klaudia. With her, I never got the impression that there was anyone inside there. Livatov, Klaudia Livatov. I don't have her phone number but I know where she lives. Second Street, right off Houston. With Mel, I sort of knew I'd get to meet the real person someday but whoever Klaudia is, I never saw her. I don't know if anyone ever did."

"So Melanie worked here at Beth Israel?"

"Yeah. But she had some other things going on."

"Like what?"

"One of her jobs, okay, she was working for the city. They had an outreach program, I don't think it's still running because the budget got cut, but they were trying to help the street girls. Health care, which is a nice thing to have even if you're not a hooker, disease prevention, reproductive counseling, all of that. And that was Mel, if she thought you needed help she would really put herself out there."

"Socialism! I can see why they cut the program. So the prostitutes that showed up at her funeral, I guess that's how she met them."

"Well, yeah, she got to know some of the girls. You know, who they were, where they were from. What they did. She once told me that she never wanted to do any of the things the girls did to their johns, which don't leave a lot of unplowed ground, you know what I'm saying. She claimed that a lot of the girls had been forced into it. Which is true enough, I suppose. And the whole thing with oral sex, you know, how unhealthy it was for the girls, and so on, and so on. She would always be over the moon when she convinced one of them to get out of the life, you know, and go home or whatever. For a while, she had started to hate us."

"Us."

"Yeah. You, me, everyone with a pair."

"What did you do about that?"

"What could I do? My strategy was time, which was how I knew I had it bad. I was thinking I would wait her out. Like I told you, she was coming around. Listen, do you mind if I ask you something?"

"Go ahead."

He considered his question for a moment. "When you were seeing that nurse in Bosnia, you were, what, like an MP or something? Do you know how to do this? Were you some kind of an investigator?"

"No. You're a doctor, am I right?"

"Yeah," he said, somewhat cautiously.

"What kind of doctor?"

"A gas passer. Anesthesiologist."

"So you're a specialist. Not a surgeon."

"No."

"But you could do it, if you had to. Set a broken leg, maybe. Something like that."

"I been around. Where you going with this?"

"I'm a specialist. I'm not an investigator, and I'm not a shooter, but I been around. My theory is, whoever did this, they were probably breathing a little easier up until a couple days ago. I wonder what they're gonna do when they start hearing footsteps behind them. You know what I mean? Just when they thought they'd gotten away with it. If they're human at all, they gotta wonder, once in a while, when the shoe is gonna drop. Maybe they'll react, maybe we'll see something. Maybe their karma catches up with them."

"Yeah, karma. Maybe." Reiman looked out the window for a

while. "You know something, it would be nice if that were true. Like the guy in Crime and Punishment, right? In the end it was his own belief system that got him. Always thought that ending was a fucking copout. I have a neurologist buddy who says that religion and superstition are essentially the same thing, they're both a product of the mapping function of the human mind. Trying to make sense out of things. Impose some kind of order on a random universe."

"I was thinking more along the lines of, nobody wants to go to jail, everybody wants to get away with whatever shit they're doing. I wanna make the guy nervous, I wanna bait him into doing something rash. Smoke him out."

"Okay. Yeah. I hear you. Serious question," he said. "How can I help?"

"I don't know yet," I told him. "But I have your phone number. I'll let you know."

I WONDERED WHAT to do about Klaudia Livatov. Two people had brought up her name, Branch and Reiman, and from what they both said, it seemed to me that Livatov was the kind of person who would take one look at a guy like me and run away, either run or shut down like a snail, pull up into her shell and slam the door shut behind her. I know myself well enough to know that I'm not very good with that kind of fear, but I could picture Reiman sitting down with her, holding her hand, telling her that he knew how much pain she was in but that she needed to be brave for Melanie's sake, she would have done it for us . . . Yeah, Reiman would do a much better job of that than I ever would, I should leave her to him, plus, since she already knew the guy, she might be more comfortable with him. But I decided to go by and ring her bell first.

Houston Street is like the Colorado River, it chokes before it ever reaches the sea, strangled by the needs of men. It starts out strong on Manhattan's East Side, it flows west toward the Hudson, but it dies in the middle of a desert of concrete and steel, leaves you standing there wondering what the hell happened.

The building where Livatov lived was steps off the eastern end of Houston; it was a tenement not too unlike all the other tenements, three broken slate steps took you up to the ancient, paint-crusted outer doors. In the entryway there were rows of aluminum mailboxes; each had an ivory-colored button on it whereby you could harass the occupant of the mailbox's corresponding apartment. I leaned on the one marked Livatov and waited.

Nothing.

Maybe she's not home, I thought. Maybe she's hiding . . .

Out in the street, I heard someone yelling.

I pictured her up there, a bookish sort of woman wearing clogs, glasses, and a too-large-for-her denim dress, afraid to answer the bell. I leaned on the bell again, but that time I heard her.

"Hey asshole! HEY! Who's ringing the goddamn bell?!"

Maybe I had the wrong Livatov.

I went back out on the sidewalk and looked up, saw blond hair obscuring the face that leaned out of a window and looked down at me from several floors up. "Klaudia Livatov?" I said.

"Yeah? What?"

"We need to talk," I said.

"About what?"

"Melanie Wing."

The blond hair disappeared, but a moment later a key floated down through the air, a piece of bright green yarn fluttering behind it like the tail on a kite.

This was not the Klaudia Livatov that Reiman and Branch told me about. Must be a cousin, or maybe a roommate.

I caught the key and went up.

She wasn't waiting behind a chained door, like I'd expected, her door was wide open and she stood halfway out into the hall staring at me. I had the sudden feeling that someone had left the tiger's cage open. I was immediately hyperaware of everything about her. I could hear the sound of her breathing, I could see her taut musculature, and there was no fear in her face as she shook her blond hair back over her shoulder. This was not the Klaudia Livatov they'd been telling me about. This was no mouse . . .

I dropped the key in her hand.

"Who are you," she said.

My cover had started to sound stale, at least to me, but I repeated it all over again. A half sister, my only sibling, dead before I'd ever known she existed . . . I could not tell from her face whether she bought it or not. "Come inside," she said. My pulse seemed, all of a sudden, quicker than it ought to be, and I felt too warm, like I should lose the sweater, except I wasn't wearing one. And whatever it was that I had glimpsed looking at me, however briefly, out of Frank Porter's mother's eyes, and later, through the eyes of those other women, Livatov had it in its raw, undiluted state; something or someone inside of her stared out, straight down into me, I could feel it. "You coming in or what?"

It was a small apartment, even by New York standards. A couch that looked like it doubled as a bed, a canvas rug on the floor, movie posters on the walls, a small glass-topped table with two chairs, a phone booth–sized kitchen, and in the corner by the window, a rickety little wooden table, the top of it maybe a foot square, adorned by a lace doily. On top of the doily rested a statue of some sainted woman, I assumed it was the Virgin Mary. The statue was about eighteen inches tall, she had a semicircle of burnt tea candles at her feet, and an unopened half pint of rum. Myers's Dark. Who drinks half pints, I wondered. A half pint ain't nothing but a tease. The table and everything on it looked like a relic left over from a previous administration, it didn't fit the Klaudia Livatov that I was seeing. Maybe if she'd been fifty years older . . .

"Have a seat," she said.

I chose one of the chairs next to her table, felt it creak and strain as it took my weight. "You're not what I expected," I told her.

She sat down across from me. "I know, I know." She tossed her hair back again. She could not sit still, she did not so much sit in the chair, she occupied it, she pushed its limits, the thing could not have been engineered to cope with so much . . . what? Energy? Emotion? I wasn't sure. She had a vaguely Eastern European face; I looked at it in profile as she turned and looked over her shoulder at her tiny kitchen. "But after Melanie died, I got pissed off and now I can't seem to shake it."

"Why?"

She whirled back to glare at me, her left forefinger pointing at my face. "Because she was a fucking person! She was a human being! She wasn't just some cat you could strangle and throw in the river just because you didn't want her anymore! She had never even . . ." She paused a second, lowered her arm, then went on in a calmer tone. ". . . done anything yet. Listen, I'm sorry. I shouldn't be yelling at you. Jesus. I was going to offer you something to drink."

"I'm good," I told her.

"I'm not." It took her two steps to reach the kitchen. She reached into a cupboard, pulled out a half-empty bottle of Johnnie

Red and two chipped white coffee cups. She turned and caught me admiring her ass but she didn't react to it. She hefted the bottle. "You sure?"

"Yeah, no, I would rather have water." She poured whiskey into one, water in another, then brought them back and reoccupied her chair. "Thanks," I told her. "You don't look old enough to drink."

"Chronologically I'm twenty-six," she said. "But lately I been feeling like I'm about ten thousand and twenty-six."

I could believe it. In fact I could hardly credit the stories I'd heard of that other, earlier Klaudia. In contemporary America it seemed that the ingredient list for the ideal woman generally included silicone, anorexia, and a Barbie doll face, no matter how you got it. Klaudia was oh for three and didn't seem to give a shit. "Tell me how you came to this, Saul. Or how Melanie's story came to you."

A bit more of the truth, then. "One of my mother's exes looked me up." I told her about McClendon, about the beach where he found me, and about what the man told me he wanted, and about his list of targets. Klaudia was nodding before I was halfway through. McClendon's assumption that one of his victims had been the murderer seemed to rub her the wrong way.

"Men," she said, after I was done. She got up out of her chair and stalked away to stand by the window. "The guy's daughter is murdered and he automatically assumes it's all about him, not her. It wasn't her life, it didn't happen because of what she was, it was only because of something he'd done. Someone he'd screwed, and they killed her to get back at him."

"In your story," I asked her, "aren't you the hero?"

"Point taken," she said. "Regardless. Some son of a bitch killed Melanie. And that's awful enough, all by itself, but when I think about what he might have done to her first, when I think about what her final hours might have been like, it makes me want to scream. And if it wasn't even about her, if it was all just because of some dickhead she never even met . . ."

Stop staring at her ass, I told myself, and I hitched my chair around so I could see the religious statue she kept in the corner. "How do you know it was a man?"

"Isn't it always?" she said. "The real question is, can you find out who it was? And what are you gonna do about him if you do?"

I realized that she wasn't looking out the window at all, she was looking at my reflection in the glass. Our eyes met, and I felt her gauging my interest, but rather than act insulted, she looked like she'd merely coded the information and filed it away for reference. "There's a chance," I told her. "It really depends on how our guy plays his hand. If he's smart enough to lay low and do nothing, he'll be hard to catch. But whoever he is, he already heard my name, and he already put some of his people on my tail. So he already made one mistake. I'm thinking he'll make another one sooner or later. That'll be my best shot."

She turned around, leaned her butt on the window sill, and crossed her arms on her chest. She nodded at the statue. "Admiring the goddess?"

"Goddess? I had assumed that she was the Virgin Mary."

"Did I say goddess? Sorry. No, that's Our Lady of Charity. I don't know if history is clear on her sexual experience, or lack thereof. She bothering you? You could turn her around if you want. Or I could put her away in a closet."

"Somehow I don't think that would be a good idea. Back to McClendon's list of offended parties, okay? Let me tell you how good

McClendon was. I would bet that all or most of those guys still like McClendon, and even though they lost money on him, they probably all think they came up just short on one of the greatest business opportunities they ever had. And if he called them up tomorrow with some wild-ass scheme, I'm guessing most of them would at least think about going in on it."

She threw herself back down in the chair. I was already learning something about Klaudia, that she had too much energy, she was like a pot on the stove, too full of boiling water. "A real professional," she said, leaning forward, planting her elbows on the table and staring at me. "How are you with computers, Saul?"

"I'm okay . . ."

"Well, I'm better than okay. I cut my teeth on databases and I am fucking phenomenal. I tell you what, you give me McClendon's list. I will find everything there is to find on these guys, and if I need to talk to them I'll be a reporter working on a story about McClendon. I'll call you in a day or so and by then I'll know whether or not any of these assholes hate McClendon enough to do him dirty." She threw herself back up out of the chair, took the two strides to reach her kitchen, pulled a tea candle and a book of matches out of a drawer. She lit the candle, turned and plopped it down in front of the statue. "Save me Lord, but not tonight."

"Wait. That wasn't her, that was some other guy . . ."

"Augustine," she said. "But it was hardly an original thought, even back then. And I have this feeling that Our Lady of Charity was probably more human than she gets credit for. If murdering an innocent like Melanie and throwing her in the river doesn't piss her off, then nothing will." I saw it again, that sidelong glance, that quarter smile, that maddening air of superiority. "Doesn't hurt to have the Lady on your side, Saul."

"I'll take all the help I can get. Do you have something to write with?"

She walked off, bent down to fish through a drawer. I couldn't take my eyes off her. "Okay," she said, coming back. "Give 'em to me."

I started out. "Boyd, William C. CEO of Midwest Power and Light." I went all the way through the list, giving her everything McClendon had given me.

"Got 'em," she said, after I finished. "Where did you learn how to do that? Remember all that data?"

" 'Twas in another lifetime,' " I told her, quoting Dylan. " 'One of toil and blood . . .' "

"I go crazy when men sing to me," she said. "Give me a day or two. You got a phone number?"

As I gave it to her I got the feeling I was wasting my time. The bead on the wire shivered a little farther away from Mac and the money, a little closer to Annabel and the tongs.

LATE THAT NIGHT I placed another call to McClendon. He tried to answer the phone but he dropped it with a clunk. I heard him say "Oh shit," and he came on the line. "Goddammit . . . Do you know what . . . What time is it?"

"Hi, Mac, it's me. I got a question."

"You got a pair of balls, that's what you got. No, honey, not you. Go back to sleep. It ain't nothing."

"Why, Reverend. I am shocked."

"Saul, if I could reach through this phone . . . Why you gotta call in the middle of the night?"

Because the only times you tell the truth are when you're

drunk or half asleep. "Whelen and Ives. Where did you come up with those guys?"

"Unnnnh . . . Jesus Christ, I can't even think. It was the guy. The cop. Shit, what was his name . . ."

"One of the detectives working the case?"

"No, no, the guy in the precinct house. Desk sergeant. I was mouthing off, because they weren't giving me much. The guy at the desk says, call this guy, he used to be the man in this precinct and he knows all the players. Had one of their cards in his wallet."

"So you called them, they didn't call you."

"Yeah. I mean, the desk sergeant was an old-timer, you gotta know how these things work. The retired dick is probably his buddy, okay, so the guy at the desk gets a bogie for every customer he refers. But the PI, Whelen, he seemed to know what he was doing. And the other one, the tall skinny guy, he was sharp as shit. Maybe not a guy you'd wanna have a beer with, but sharp. Good guy to know, long as he's on your side."

"Okay, so the way it works, the guy at the desk gets paid, the investigator gets paid, you get jerked off, everybody's happy."

"You suck, you know that? No, not you, baby, go back to sleep. Did you get anywhere with my list? Those names I gave you. My unhappy customer list."

"Your victims, you mean."

"Yeah, them."

"I'm getting there. Do you remember the tall guy's name? The guy who actually did the footwork for Whelen on your case."

"No. I don't think so. I only met the guy a couple times, I mostly dealt with Whelen."

"Well, what do you remember about him? You must have some impression of the guy."

"Old, as in seen-too-much-bad-shit old. You got to hang on to some of your illusions, you know what I'm saying? His name will come back to me. I'll call you when I think of it."

"Okay."

"Tell me something, Saul. What was she like? Melanie. I mean . . . you know."

"She had some friends. Some people loved her. She worked at her job, and she did some volunteer work. Angel of mercy. Had a nice Jewish boyfriend. I'm thinking she was probably okay."

"Do you think it was me?" His voice was quiet. "Do you think it was one of those guys, from the names I gave you."

"That might be the most plausible explanation, Mac, and it still might turn out to be the right one, but I don't see anything that points that way. Think about it. I'm in town a couple days, okay, I talk to a few people. One, Whelen the cop. Ex-cop. Two, Annabel. Three, Melanie's landlady, and what happens? Three goons try to jump me. How the hell were they on to me so quick? How did they know who I was? Whelen could probably have found out if he really wanted, but he didn't seem very interested, and I haven't seen him since. And if your theory about the money is right, I haven't seen much of that, either. Other than yours."

"You got jumped? By who? You okay?"

"Yeah, I'm fine. Two Chinese guys, had a black guy backing them up."

"Wow, that's interesting. Integration. Be careful, Saul."

Chapter Six

On Tenth Street, steps away from Avenue C, a short awning hung over the sidewalk, sheltering the doorway to the Hotel Los Paraíso; it was the joint Whelen's office manager had told me about. The building that housed the hotel differed only a little from her neighbors, principally by being a taller pile of shit than they were. The front door was held open by a cinder block, and through the doorway I saw only steps going up, nothing more. I walked on past, headed up to the bodega on the far side of the avenue and bought myself a cup of coffee. It was Puerto Rican coffee, strong and somewhat harsh, cut with a dollop of condensed milk. I went back outside, leaned on the insulated box where they stored their ice, and watched.

There were kids out in front of Los Paraíso, sitting on the hood of a parked car. They were too young to be jaded, too old to be innocent, and they watched each car that came down Tenth.

Marketing at its most basic level, and no need for a sign.

A woman came out of the hotel doorway, she was tall, thin, with long black hair. The kids left off what they were doing to watch her, but none of them moved or said anything. She was NYC postmod-

ern cool and she carried a large handbag, the strap over one shoulder. She strolled up to the corner right across from where I waited.
She did not favor me with a glance. She held one hand out, fingers
spread gracefully, and cabs dueled like hungry fish, each wanting
to be the one. I finished my coffee after she left, watched as several
more people exited the hotel doorway. None of them seemed re-
markable, but maybe they only suffered by comparison.

A young black kid bounced down the steps of the building
across Tenth from the hotel. He was younger than the gang kids.
Too young for sales, maybe, but still too old for innocence, although
I had to wonder if that concept had much relevance in a place like
Alphabet City. The gang kids hooted and yelled at the younger kid
and one of them threw an empty plastic juice container at him, but
he ignored them, walked up to the avenue and headed north.

I tossed my coffee cup in the trash can that was chained to the
light pole on the corner and followed the kid. I waited for a block
before I called to him.

"Hey, kid."

He turned, walking backward, wary. "What?"

I had a twenty in my hand and I let him see it. I stopped and
so did he, he sauntered back and we slapped hands, and then the
kid stuck the bill in his pants pocket. "Walk," I told him. We continued north, up toward the red bricks of Sty-town, up on the far
side of Fourteenth. "That building you came out of," I said. "You
live there?"

"Uh-huh." He wasn't sure about me, he kept his distance. "You
a cop?"

"No. Inside front door locked?"

"Nah-ah, busted. You could go right up."

"I bet you know everybody that lives in there."

"Yeah."

"Okay. On the front side, looking down at the street. Who's the craziest person living there who's got a window looking down at Tenth?"

"Luisa," he said, without hesitation. "She be up on five. You gonna go mess wit' her?"

"Never. I just wanna see the street, that's all." I palmed another twenty and passed it over as before. "You never saw me."

"Got it." He pocketed the second bill, turned and walked away without looking back.

I went back and loitered for a while.

It was not yet spring, not quite yet, but the ladies were tired of winter and some of them had apparently decided to jump the season and get started on their warm-weather wardrobes. You had to wonder how they kept from freezing, dressed in such thin and insubstantial clothing, but some flowers, like daffodils, insist on going first, poking up through the snow before the sun is really ready for them. I thought of Klaudia for a moment, then forced that thought away so I could concentrate on what I was doing. I crossed the avenue and walked up Tenth. I ignored the kids sitting on the car, but they watched me as I climbed the steps to the building across the street from the hotel and went inside.

Tile floors at least a century old. Thick marble stair steps, equally ancient, worn concave by generations of feet. Railings made of cast iron, bolted together clamshell style. The layers of paint on the walls were peeled and chipped in changing and unrelated depths, leaving the stairwell and hallways dappled by time and color. Each landing informed on the people who lived behind the closed and locked doors there, smells of garlic, onion and cilantro, dogs barking, music, television, people arguing.

Life.

On the fifth floor, two doors led to apartments that fronted on Tenth. I folded a fifty up in my fist and knocked on one of them. A middle-aged woman with a tired face answered. "Luisa?"

"No," she said, and bobbed her head at the neighboring door. "Sorry."

She had her door closed before I got the word out. I heard the security chain slide into place. I had to smile. We place our trust in such frail things . . . That which we believe shields us from the dark is mostly hot air and wishful thinking. Now, a door with an old-fashioned Fox lock where the iron bar clicks into a slot in the floor, that can be a bitch to get past. I moved along to the next door and raised my fist to knock but Luisa was faster than I was. She opened the door before I could touch it. "Sí, señor?"

The fifty stuck its head up between two of my fingers, and she stared at it, wide-eyed. "Luisa, I have a problem. I think you can help me."

"Men always have prollem." She opened the door wider, waiting for me to hand her the money.

Luisa was a vision . . .

She was dressed in what appeared to be layers of nightclothes, cotton, polyester, silk and lace, with worn furry slippers on her feet. She had white Spanish skin, eyelids painted in graduated shades of color, black eyeliner and red lipstick applied by an unsteady hand, hair jet black, unconvincingly black because Luisa appeared to be immensely old. I held out the bill. "Do you think you can help me?"

A tiny exhalation through the nose, the smallest expression

of amusement, and that irritating, knowing quarter smile, there for the briefest interval of time and then it was gone, along with my fifty. "Help is my especiality," she said, and she motioned me inside.

The hallway smelled of old perfume, old age and old dog, of incense and weed and tobacco, strong coffee and dust. Once she closed the door behind us it was too dim to make out much detail, which I took to be a good thing. A small dog stuck his head out of a doorway, saw me and retreated silently. A larger dog in the form of a stooped, gray-whiskered man wearing a pink flowered corduroy bathrobe stepped into the far end of the hallway, blinking, and he did not retreat. Large patches of the corduroy on his robe were worn away, leaving behind only the base material. "Raul, my cousin," Luisa said, and she followed that up with a barrage of machine-gun Spanish. Raul retreated then, too, and Luisa ushered me the rest of the way down the hallway to the front room.

"Can we sit by the windows?" I asked her.

"Yes, sí," she said. "Can I get you son-thing? Coffee? Water? Son-thing estronger?"

"No, Luisa, thank you. Sit down, please. Talk to me."

She put me in a kitchen chair by one window, seated herself by another a few feet away. "What you wan' to talk about? Politic? Giuliani getting berry berry old. His brother, too. Then you gonna see son-thing, maybe." She shot me with a forefinger. "Money to make, down in Cuba. Firs the blood, then the money."

"I'm more interested in the politics of that hotel across the street."

"Los Paraíso," she said, grinning and looking at me through heavy-lidded eyes.

"What can you tell me about it?"

"Whorehouse on the top two floor," she said, and her smile faded. "Thass what you want to hear about." Distaste puckered her lined face. "Such an ugly word. Whore. That word use by a rich man, come to get a little son-thing on Saturday, go to church and repent with the wife on Sunday. To me you don' look like this man."

"Maybe not. If you don't like the word, tell me a better one."

She sighed. "Mujer. Mujer de la vida."

I had her repeat it several times, trying to wrap my thick Anglo tongue around the musical Spanish phrase. "So what does it mean?"

"The life," she said. "You know, the life, a lady of the life." Her hand fluttered in the air, dancing in the dusty sunlight.

"A party girl," I said.

"Exactamente," she said. "Party girl. Is it such a terrible sin, to be party girl? A little dancing, a little drinking, a little fun . . . I don' thin' so God gonna burn you too much for this. A little bit, maybe, on the bottoms of the feet. Nothing more."

I agreed with her. "There are worse things."

"I was a dancer once, long time ago." She shifted in her chair, her shoulders swaying to the beat of some long-forgotten music, audible now only to her. "I dance in the revue three time, at the Apollo," she said. "And at all the clubs in Spanish Harlem. Back then, all the rich man come uptown, dance a little bit, listen to music, laugh and sing." She raised her chin, waiting for me to disapprove. "Better then," she said, "back when things were worse. Because the black, the white, the espanish, we all know each other then. Not like now. Now I live downtown, you don't see me. You live uptown, I don't see you. You live uptown, señor?"

"No," I told her. "I live far away. Far up north, where there are no people, only the ocean."

She eyed me speculatively. "Give me your hand," she said, and she leaned forward and reached for me. She turned my hand over, explored the skin on my knuckles with her fingertips. "I don' thin' so you get these hands from working on your car," she said.

"No."

She hitched her chair closer, turned my hand palm side up, and again she explored the topography of my hand with her fingertips. I found myself wondering how much she could actually see. "Your lifeline is broken," she said. "Two pieces, one here, one there. Cut in half." She squinted at me. "You feel okay?"

"Yeah, I'm fine."

"Good, good. You see?" She traced the line in my palm with a finger. "One life here, and stop. Young, maybe thirty, finito. T'hirty-five, no more. Dead. Now here, your second life. Different line." She tilted her head back and stared at me. "You gonna die soon, but don' worry. You get one more chance, different track. Sometime the old has to die before the new can live."

"Well, that's comforting." Movement on the street caught my eye. Another tall woman walked out of Los Paraíso, dressed in the same way as the first. All the boys stopped to watch her, their silence a mark of their respect. She didn't have to hail a cab, there was a limo waiting, a real one, whose driver got out and opened the door for her. "Mujer," I said.

"De la vida," Luisa said, glancing out the window. "But no club. No music. No dancing. Just a car, and a hotel room. So sad."

"And the pimps. You forgot about them."

"I forget nothing," she said.

"Is 'pimp' the right word?"

She nodded. "In Spanish, chulo. Bad man."

I pointed at Los Paraíso. "In that building over there, how many chulo? How many bad guys?"

She sighed. "In the upstair, three. Two Chinese, one Haitian, the Worm. He is the worst. And El Tuerto, he come for the money, he make four. Downstair, you know, on the other floors, they come and go. One woman moves in, one chulo follows her to take the money. Then they don' pay the rent and they go. But they are not like the one you saw. They are tire, like old horses, and ogly, but with no time for resting."

"Is that a real hotel? Could someone walk in there and get a room?"

"I thin' maybe so. At the top of the stair you find a little room, like a cage. A man sits inside. A Jew." Her fingers traced invisible curls next to her ears.

"Orthodox," I said.

"Hasid," she said. "I thin' maybe his father own the building."

"Got it." I stirred, started to think about leaving. "When does he come out of the cage?"

"To get the mail," she said. "The mailman, she don' going up inside there, so the boy comes down."

"What time does that happen?"

"One-thirty, two o'clock. And at night, somebody comes to take his place. An older man, and the boy goes home."

"Have the cops ever busted the place?"

"No. Never."

"Can you tell me anything about El Tuerto? Is he the money man?"

She shrugged, palms out and up. "Anglo," she said. "El Jefe, the big boss. Mean. His greed make him look hongry. Think about money alla time. The rest of them are just soldiers."

I stood to go, and she rose with me, and that's when I saw the altar on a corner of her kitchen countertop. Two cold candle stubs and a mostly empty half pint of Old Duke red sat around the plastic statue of a robed woman. Like Klaudia's, only not as tall. "Is that . . ." I tried to remember what she'd called hers. "Our Lady of something . . ."

"Charity." She crossed herself, an unconscious gesture. "How do you know her?"

"I don't, really. Tell me about her."

"For Catholics, Our Lady of Charity. For the old religion, from the Yoruba, in Africa, she is Oshun. The first woman, become spirit."

"Oh. Like Eve, from the Bible."

"No, baby, no, not like Eve. Oshun is power, she is the power of the woman, and if you make offense to her she will cut out your heart and eat it."

I was willing to bet that an honest man had invented this particular saint. "Thank you, Luisa, you've been a great help." Then I remembered something. "Ogun." It was the name my assailant had been shouting. "Does that name mean anything to you?"

"Male spirit," she said. "Strong, but not too smart. Like most men." She stood with her chin high, waiting for me to judge her. Pride, and fear, and a little suspicion. "I think so you need more help than I can give. Let me see your hand, one more time."

I reached out to her and she felt my palm with her fingertips, as before. "You better be careful," she said. "I feel trouble, in this hand."

NYC WAS ALWAYS funny that way, the place felt like it had more Russians than Russia, more Jews than Israel, more Turks than Turkey, more Cubans than Cuba. And when they came to New

York they brought more with them than their language and native cuisine. I wondered how much time I really needed to spend learning about African deities, but when the same goddess, or whatever she was, shows up twice in as many days, there had to be a link. Anyway, the bead on the wire shivered again but it didn't move, because you had El Tuerto the money guy on Mac's side and you had two more Chinese bad guys on the side of Annabel and the tongs.

THERE WAS NOT a single person named Tuerto in the Manhattan phone book, with or without the El. Bronx, either.

Nickname, maybe.

I remembered that Mac spoke Spanish, so I called him. "Tuerto?" he said. "I don't think that's a word. You sure she didn't say suerto? Means luck."

"No. Tuerto, with a T."

"Don't mean nothing to me," he said. "But Spanish is like that, it's regional. Might be a local thing. I learned mine on the West Coast, and I don't think I ever heard the word before. How you doing, anyway? Or shouldn't I ask."

"You ever swindle any Chinese guys?"

"I don't remember any."

"I'm starting to think Annabel was right and you were wrong."

"Never happen," he said, sounding completely sure of himself. "Keep your eyes on the money, Saul. It's always the money, believe me."

I STARED AT my reflection in the window of The Gap store. Melanie Wing, my sister. Maybe. A nurse. It takes a special kind of person to be a nurse, misadventures and consequences will acquaint you with nurses, and the hands of a good nurse can have enormous impact on how well you heal and how quickly you walk away. Or even if . . . Wouldn't that make you a couple of points with the goonas? Probably a better person than me. Made more of a contribution, no question.

Probably hadn't stolen many horses.

So, okay, maybe she wasn't a saint, not according to one J. Whelen, ex-cop and current private eye, and I had little cause to doubt him. This was his city, his neighborhood, in fact, and I would have to live in it a long, long time before I could read the signs better than he could. And was it so bad anyhow? She'd been a woman, after all, among other things a sexual being. If God had given her a Ferrari, who was I to tell her she couldn't drive it?

Please. And if there was a real deity, wouldn't he, she, or they be disappointed in you if you'd never once in your life gone out and swung from the trees a little bit? Otherwise, why make trees?

Then it hit me.

Whelen had given me an out.

It was perfect.

What father really wants to hear about his daughter's sex life? That meant that long and detailed explanations would not be necessary. 'Mac, this isn't going to be easy for you to hear . . . A pretty girl all on her own in a big city, hey, these things happen.' And if that didn't do the trick I could beat him down with some words out of that book he loved to carry around. 'Vengeance is mine, saith the Lord. I will repay.' The guy would get his eventually, and probably in exactly the way Whelen said he would, either he'd slip up and wind up in prison or he'd mess with the wrong lady and catch a knife in the ribs. A girl from a less sheltered background, maybe, one who would think to have a shiv secreted somewhere about her person. Survival of the meanest . . . That was the way these things were supposed to work. Isn't nature, after all, God's primary testament?

Mac would buy it, I wouldn't even have to sell it to him, he'd do it to himself.

And then I could go back.

Really? To what?

Who was I kidding?

Shit.

I could hear the goonas laughing at me.

Interregnum

COREY JACKSON SILENTLY *thanked Providence that he happened to have put on loafers that morning because he did not think he could have faced the prospect of bending over to tie his shoes. Aniri would have done it for him, he had no doubt of that, but he was not at all comfortable with that prospect. He was the one that was supposed to be the strong one . . .*

Yeah, he decided, looks like that one's bullshit.

"My brother, you think you're gonna hurl?" the Babalao said.

"No." Corey prided himself on his level of physical toughness. I will be damned, he thought, if a single two-dollar cigar is gonna make me puke.

If that's all it was.

"Do we go now?" It was Aniri's voice, thin and frightened. "What do we do?"

"Don't worry, sister," the Babalao said. "I got you. First we gotta go back into the shop. Take his elbow." Corey sensed the man up close. He blinked his eyes, trying to bring the world back into focus.

"My brother," the Babalao said. "We're goin' in now. Watch the steps. Do you see them steps?"

"Yeah," Corey said. "Remind me to pick up a box of those cigars, will you?"

"Coreee . . ." Aniri sounded like she was freaked.

The Babalao chuckled. "I know, I know. Twenty bucks for five. But if I used better ones, they'd probably hit you even harder. Here we go. Up the stairs."

Back inside the shop, Corey leaned against the counter to steady himself. The Babalao's assistant absented herself while he puttered around. Corey's vision slowly began returning to normal; he watched the Babalao dig through a cardboard box and come up with a bottle of Bacardi 151. "Here we go," the guy said. He handed the bottle to Aniri, who began dusting it off. "That's not for you, that's for Oshun," the Babalao said. "It isn't a payment, though, and I don't want you to think of it that way. This is important. It's not a bribe. It's a token of your regard." He peered into Aniri's eyes. "Do you understand what I'm saying? You know her, you know she likes, so you brought. Just like any other old friend. Okay?"

"Yes," Aniri said. "But . . ."

"No buts. This is what seals the deal. So what we're gonna do, okay, and I'm gonna go with you just to make sure, we're gonna walk this down to the park. Once we get there, we're gonna open the bottle and toss it into the river."

"Isn't this expensive?" Aniri said.

"Certain times," the Babalao said, "and this is one of them, honey, it don't pay to go cheap."

"Okay," Aniri said. "And then what happens?"

The Babalao paused, his mouth wide with amusement. "Well," he finally said. "That is the question, isn't it?"

BY THE TIME they got to the end of the first block, Corey was feeling normal enough for his sense of skepticism to return in force. Primitive spirits, he thought. Ghosts, kitchen gods, demons, ghouls, and the night sweats . . . The Western perspective was, no doubt, still the best and most logical explanation. Praying for some kind of help from a spirit, fundamental universal force or not, was a mind fuck at best, a way to shelve your despair for another day, to rally your fading strength and get yourself out there one more time. And at worst it was a cruel trick, a false hope. Better to face reality. If Corey was going to free Aniri from Los Paraíso, he was going to have to break some eggs. Sure, cheap cigars and good rum might be more palatable than sacrificed chickens, but neither approach made much sense to him.

I should never have let her talk me into this, he thought. But she'd have done it on her own anyhow. The question that troubled him now was, was his presence making her safer or more vulnerable? He'd already been warned away from her twice, first by one of the Chinese pimps and the second time by their Haitian enforcer. The big man had made it clear that there would be no third warning, that if they caught him near her again he'd wind up with a stay in the hospital, or worse. That was the reason he and she usually arranged to meet way uptown, as far from Los Paraíso as they could. To be together this close to the lion's den was madness.

Cigars. And you didn't even get to taste the rum. Really? Corey wanted to spit the vile tobacco taste out of his mouth, but he didn't have any saliva. Aniri and the Babalao preceded him down the sidewalk. The Babalao touched her softly on the shoulder to indicate where he wanted her to go, and she glanced back at Corey from time to time, beseeching him with her eyes to please just keep it shut and go along. When this doesn't work, he thought, she's gonna be *heartbroken. He'd been thinking about driving home to South Carolina for a pistol. But, after the inevitable happened, after someone got shot with it, how did you live with a thing like that? And if things went far enough wrong, he might just wind up destroying what slim hopes they had left.*

They crossed Avenue D and walked into the dim courtyards between the buildings of the Jacob Riis projects. Corey felt eyes on him. Paranoia, he thought, listening to the cars roaring past on the FDR Drive. The Babalao steered Aniri north between the buildings, heading for the pedestrian bridge that spanned the roadway and led to the narrow strip of green that lay between the highway and the East River. Corey's sense of misgiving grew as they crossed, and it continued to get worse as they neared the water. We get through this, he thought, and we are never coming back here, no matter what.

Lights burned like stars on the far shore, glittering off the uneasy surface of the river. There was a fence right at the seawall that held the river in place, and it had a large man leaning on it. Corey looked back, his stomach sinking when he saw two more guys cross the pedestrian bridge behind them. One of them loitered there, cutting off their escape, the other sauntered closer.

He was one of the Chinese pimps from Los Paraíso.

Corey called softly to Aniri. "Babe?"

The tall guy detached himself from the fence and walked over. The Haitian.

He stopped about ten feet away, looking at Corey, shaking his head in mock sorrow. "This is on you," he said. "Because you were warned." A gray-haired guy loomed out of the darkness. Senior management, Corey thought, coming to safeguard his investment. The Haitian nodded to the guy. "You see this man? He is going to punish Aniri. And you are going to watch." Corey glanced at the guy, saw him flash a sick smile. "And then I am going to hurt you."

The Babalao was the first to move. He stepped up and took the bottle from Aniri's shaking hands. He unscrewed the top, which crackled as it tore loose from its retaining ring. He dropped the cap on the ground and looked at the Haitian. "You should reconsider," he said.

The Haitian hesitated, looked at the Babalao, then shook his head. "You can't help them."

"That remains to be seen," the Babalao said. "But allow me to take care of this one little detail first." He twisted back and sideways from the waist, wound up and slung the bottle hard, throwing it so that it spun as it arced, silvery rum spraying in wide circles. Corey watched it soar out over the water, which was a mistake, because when he looked back the Haitian was up close, gritting his teeth as he punched Corey in the face.

Corey tasted blood, felt the dirt of the park against his face. He heard Aniri crying, heard the splash as the bottle hit the water, and then he heard a man screaming. He wondered if it was the Babalao.

Guy sounded like he'd been skewered . . .

Chapter Seven

I STOPPED AT the same bodega, got another cup of that Bustelo coffee. I didn't think I would survive a steady diet of the stuff, but once in a while, man, when you wanted all your brain cells standing up and paying attention . . .

The mail carrier made her way up Avenue B, and I went to work on my face. Eyes too wide open, brows up too high on your forehead meant that you were a little too desperate for them to like you. Too many lines on your face, too much tension meant that you were too angry, that you might be working yourself up to something. Nothing at all, that's what I wanted, no wide eyes, no tension, no nothing. A little resigned fatigue, maybe, but just a little. That would broadcast the message that I didn't give a fuck one way or the other, and in this momentary role as an inspector for the NYC Department of Buildings, not giving a fuck was exactly right. Got my face, got my pen, got my clipboard with violation forms printed out courtesy of my hotel's Internet connection, got my attitude, I was ready.

I crossed the avenue just as the mail carrier turned onto Tenth.

When she got to the open doorway to Los Paraíso, she stopped and shouted up the stairs. I thought I probably had her figured, from just that much. West Indian adult female, skirt down to her mid-calf, I figured that made her likely to be a good Christian woman, the USPS might have their regulations but she was not about to put a foot inside a joint like Los Paraíso.

Good to know some people still had standards.

As I came up the sidewalk a tall, skinny duck-footed Jewish kid came out for the mail. Probably not yet twenty, the sort of orange hair that would turn brown in time, glasses, wrinkled white shirt, black pants, yarmulke, Hasid curls, premonition of a beard, big black shoes. "Excuse me," I said. The kid jerked to a stop, the parcel of mail in his hand. "You work here?"

He nodded. His face looked squeezed, his eyes squinted in an attempt to focus, his features all out of proportion due to the distortion from his glasses. "Yyyee, um, yeee, um, yeah."

I took out my pen, held it poised over my violation form. "What's your name?"

We had attracted the attention of the gang kids and they all stood expectantly, waiting. "Ahh, Schhh, um, schhh, um . . ."

"Shmuley!" About half of the kids yelled his name, almost in unison.

I shook my head and looked down at my form. Minor show of sympathy. "Are they right?"

"Um, um, um, yeah."

"Last name?"

The gang waited in expectant silence.

"Gel, um, gel, um . . ."

"Gelman!" Their harmony was better this time. "Shmuley Gelman!" They dissolved in laughter.

I glanced over at the kids. They were not afraid of me, but they seemed to sense that their fun was over for the moment. They stood around us in a ragged half circle. Behind them, a car honked. One of the taller kids turned around and held his hands out, palms up as he shrugged, miming a salesman with nothing to sell. "Mr. Gelman, can we do this inside? Do you have an office?"

He stared at me for a moment, his pained, constipated expression firmly in place. Willing me away, perhaps, but I didn't go so he nodded, turned, and clomped up the stairs. I followed a few steps behind, feeling as though each step transported me back to a New York City that I hadn't seen in a long time. There were no smells of cooking in this building, this place was the flip side, this was the last stop before that long slide down into darkness. At the first landing, I watched while Gelman unlocked the door to his iron and glass cubicle.

The lock was a joke.

There were two chairs inside, one was an upright wooden office chair behind a desk next to the window to the lobby, and the other was an overstuffed, moth-eaten affair over in a corner, suitable for sleeping. I would have worried about its cockroach population but I didn't think there was anything in the building for them to eat. I plopped down in the soft chair, which was more comfortable than it looked, and I threw my clipboard on the floor. "Gelman, I need you to listen to me. Okay? I don't work for the city."

He froze.

"Gelman, turn your chair around so that I can see you. Attaboy. Relax, kid, I'm just here to talk, you got nothing to worry about on my account. I'm not going to hurt you. I work for a branch of the government that you've never heard about."

"Ah-duh-ah, do you have any ID?" he asked, his eyes squeezed almost shut. He looked like his stomach was killing him.

"I got all the IDs you want," I told him, "but they're all phony. What's the point?"

"Wha, ahh, what do I call you."

"Saul."

Something came and went across Gelman's tortured face. Was that a smile? "The faithless king," he said.

"Yeah, that's me," I told him. "God's not so favorite son. Gelman, I think you got the worst job in New York City. What did you do to deserve this?"

"Emmmah, my uncle owns the hotel."

"Wow, I finally get to meet a guy who really does have a rich uncle."

Gelman squeezed his eyes shut and shook his head. "Nnnn-not really. Hee only owns the hotel, not the building. It's the lease that's worth something, nuh-ah not the hotel, because when someone decides to build condos here, they gotta b-b-buy him out. Hotel barely pays the bills."

"Interesting. What about the street-level space? He got that, too?"

Gelman shook his head.

"You know who does?"

He shrugged. Stutterer's shorthand.

"Still, why'd he stick you here? Are you being punished?"

He gestured at a dog-eared copy of something called Elementary Mathematics from an Advanced Standpoint. There were a couple others, with equally fascinating titles. I mean, I can make change for a buck, but you know . . . "Ennn-ahh, not very spiritual," Gelman said.

"Seriously. You understand that shit?"

"Um, yeah. Buuuut I don't understand the Torah. So here I am."

"How the hell did you get interested in mathematics?"

"I can't remember being, ah, nnot interested in it."

"Does your uncle know that someone's running a whorehouse in his hotel?"

Gelman shrugged.

"He doesn't care?"

"He heee's in Israel."

"I see. So he's in the Promised Land looking for God while the rest of us chase pussy in Los Paraíso."

Gelman nodded, grinning, then caught himself at it and looked around nervously to see if anyone was watching.

"Is it true what I hear, that some of you guys smear Vaseline on your glasses so that you can't see the girls?"

"Y-yes. Bee-cause what you can't see won't tempt you." Gelman took off his glasses and held them out for me to look at. Although his expression didn't change, he didn't look quite so tortured without them. "But I don't nnnneed to bother."

Coke bottles. "You know something, Gelman, the next time I start thinking my life sucks I'm gonna come here and hang out with you for a while. Okay?"

He snorted and put his glasses back on. "Okay."

"Do you read the papers? Did you hear about all the trouble the Secret Service got into down in Colombia a while ago?"

He nodded. "Reading the Nnnew York Times is aaah-nother sign of being Esau and not Jacob."

"I know all about being Esau. And Jacob was a fucking weasel. Anyway, the thing in Colombia happened because one of them didn't want to pay the girl. Well, between you and me, someone in D.C. decided that we need to take a more proactive approach.

And apparently some of the ladies upstairs have become very popular in some political circles uptown, up by the UN. Uncle Sam is very concerned about that. There is some thought that the whole thing leaves some of the people on our side vulnerable. You with me so far?"

He nodded again.

"How many girls do they run out of that space?"

Gelman reddened and his vocal cords slammed shut.

"Schmoo. God made 'em look like they do for a reason. You're a young guy, you're supposed to notice. Looking ain't a sin and I won't tell your uncle. How many?"

He looked down at his shoes. "Ahh, sssss, ah, um, seven regulars, and a few part-timers."

"There, that was easy. And how many guys?"

"Thhhh, ahh, thhhhh, umm, thhhh . . ." He gave up, held out three fingers.

"Three guys. Same ones all the time?"

"Yeah. Two um, Japanese. One black."

"You sure? You think they could be Chinese?"

"I, ahh, wow. Could be. And wuh, ahh, one white guy, comes on Mondays. Usually."

"The money man," I said. "El Tuerto. You know anything about him? He ever talk to you?"

Gelman shook his head. "Nnnever. He never even looks at me. Enn-ah, nobody ever talks to him."

"What's he look like?"

Gelman shrugged. "Older. Skinny. Face like a fuh-ah, fist."

"Okay. On the back of the building, do you have fire escapes?"

Gelman nodded.

"Okay. I want a room. At the back of the building, okay, and one floor under theirs. Put mine next to a fire escape. I'll pay you cash for two weeks, plus an extra hundred to stay quiet about it. Does that work?"

IT WAS NOT easy to see unless you were looking for it but the place might have been something, once upon a time, she might have been a bit of a mujer de la vida herself, but now she was just another old blowser, way past her expiration date. The stairs to the upper floor ran around a central atrium, and dim light filtered down from a filthy skylight far above. The staircases were slowly losing their battle with gravity, the steps leaned toward the inside, and each of them groaned when I put my weight on it. The key in my hand did not have one of those plastic drop-in-any-mailbox tags on it, either; that system relied a little too heavily on the goodwill of the user. At the Hotel Los Paraíso you paid a twenty-five-dollar deposit on your key. No honor system here, strictly capitalism. No tickee, no washee, sucka.

Three more flights up, that made it the fifth floor, and that's where I encountered my first sign of life. It was a kid; he stood frozen stiff right in front of one of the room doors. Looked to be about five or six. Dark hair cut by someone in the bowl style, obsidian eyes, white shirt and tie, pants carefully creased, old-fashioned tie shoes all shiny, tiny sport coat. But for his environment and uncertain ethnicity he looked for all the world like some little red state preschool shitbird all dressed up for church. He had a large paper name tag on a string hanging around his neck, it was the kind used by the New York City school system so as not to lose too many kids. Emblematic of how bad this kid had it, the name tag wasn't even his, the original name printed on the tag had been crossed out and his name was scrawled underneath. It was hard to read the writing, particularly in that dim light, but the first name might have been Hector, and the second one might have been Sammikrishnasomefuckingthingoranother. When the kid saw me he trembled from the top of his head all the way to his shoes, but he stood his ground.

Six years old, max.

The goonas have some sense of humor.

The room behind Hector's door was apparently in use, because the sounds made by the current occupants came through clear enough. Squeak, unnh, squeak, unnh, and then, rapidly, squeak-squeaksqueak Aaaaaaagh. Not a great performance, really, but sometimes the actors are too used up to do much more than read the lines.

I looked at the number on my key; my room was next door. Perfect. "Hello, Hector. You don't need to be scared of me, okay?"

The kid didn't answer but he quit shaking. Maybe he nodded, or maybe I just imagined it, who knows. I stood there looking at the kid, fishing for something else to say. Ask him if he's hungry, I thought.

Yeah? Why? You gonna feed him, I asked myself. You gonna fix that stupid haircut that somebody gave him? Buy him a coat if he's cold? What? Ask him if he's okay? He's not okay, he's fucked, he's fucked worse than his five-year-old brain can comprehend, and there isn't shit you're gonna do about it. I took another step, meaning to walk on by, and just then the door behind Hector opened and a guy came out. No distinguishing features, just a neighborhood guy getting his nut, not seeing anything he didn't wanna see, stepping past the kid like he wasn't there.

Saw me, though.

A woman appeared in the doorway behind Hector, the resemblance told you she had to be the kid's mother, and she, too, was way past her prime. I got one good look at her before she flopped down behind the kid and wrapped herself around him, her hands shaking, but not just with fear. Hers was the more frantic, fluttering palsy of the confirmed cokehead. She squeaked, dragged the kid backward into the room, and kicked the door shut.

The kid's eyes never left my face.

The guy looked at me, then looked past me to see if there was anyone else with me. Nobody. He saw that I was alone; to him that meant I wasn't a cop. He put a hand in a back pocket, stuck his chin out. "You got a prollem?"

"Yeah, I got a problem." Nobody with any brains carries a pistol in their back pocket, it's too easy to shoot yourself in the ass that way. Probably a knife. Maybe seeing Hector had gotten to me. I leaned in and whispered to the guy. "Pull it. Let's go, *cabróne*, pull it."

The guy froze, the wheels turning slowly in his head, and then he edged away slowly, his back to the wall, both hands in view. I watched him go down the stairs.

MY NEW ROOM had a distinct smell, but I could not quite identify what it was. It was probably a combination of things; call it overtones of human sweat, hints of dead mouse behind a wall, strong undercurrent of a not very clean bathroom, stale and dusty finish due to the window being closed for a long time. I stepped into the room anyway, closed the door behind me. One window. One metal bed frame, twin size, topped by one mattress that I would not allow any part of my body to touch. One metal desk, two drawers, graced by one metal lamp. One metal straight-backed chair. A closet-sized bathroom. One metal steam radiator under the window, with no steam in it.

My lost paradise.

The light in the ceiling didn't work but the lamp on the desk did. I closed the door to the bathroom, undid the latches holding the window closed and forced it open. I hoisted myself over the radiator and out onto the fire escape. The metal steps leading to the upper floors were missing, I guessed that whoever ran the enterprise up there was more concerned with uninvited guests than with burning up in a fire. No matter, the lack of steps was not a barrier and I climbed up the rusting framework as quietly as I could.

Which was pretty damn quiet.

Incursion was one of my specialties.

They'd painted the inside of their windows black.

Again, it was not a barrier, one of the windows was missing a little triangle-shaped section of glass in an upper corner. Someone had taped a piece of paper over the break but another someone, presumably someone who'd preceded me to that exact spot, had poked a needle-sized hole in it. I stood up slowly and looked in, waited for my eye to adjust.

I was looking into a room pretty much identical to mine, only this one had a woman in it. She lay sprawled unmoving on the bed, long hair hanging down over the side. There was a large bag on the desk; it looked like the sort of thing a lot of women carry with them everywhere. There was something beside it on the desk, roughly the size and shape of a prescription bottle. Not for nothing, but when you have to knock yourself out at night, you are in trouble. Her door was open. Someone in the hallway outside her room stopped and stood in the doorway.

The guy was massive. Overbuilt, head too small for his body, arms forced out from his sides a bit due to the size of his guns. I couldn't see the guy's face but I assumed that he was the one my friend Luisa from across the street had called the Worm. He had to be the enforcer. I waited, completely still, watching him and wondering if he could sense my presence, somehow. After a moment or two, he moved on.

Barriers to a successful incursion come in various forms. In a newer building, your obstacles are generally electronic. You have to worry about security systems, which usually include perimeter alarms, guards, closed circuit TV, and so on. The answers to these problems are not always high-tech, despite what you might expect. Say for example that you are targeting a building which has a perimeter alarm that you must get past. You must assume that there will be sensors at all of the points of entry. So, about a week before your projected date of entry, you visit the building during the day, preferably late in the afternoon, and you disable one of the sensors. If you choose wisely and work carefully, this can be done with something as innocuous as a tiny piece of cardboard with some foil on one side and stick-um on the other. What typically happens next is that the alarm refuses to set that evening, and at least one of the security guards will make some overtime because management will have to pay someone to babysit overnight. As soon as the building opens the next morning, you visit and you remove your cardboard strip. When the service tech arrives, everything works normally. He pronounces the system healed and moves on. A day or so later you repeat the whole performance. Keep it up and soon enough the management will be sick of paying overtime and everyone will be cursing the alarm system.

You get the idea.

In an older building, or an ancient one like the Hotel Los Paraíso, the obstacles tend to be physical in nature, like a window that hasn't been opened since Moses' boat ride through the bullrushes. The wooden windows at Los Paraíso were of the standard casement variety, and not the kind assembled in a factory somewhere, either. When the place was built, they had a craftsman on site who basically put the windows together from scratch using strips of wood and panes of glass. In theory, the window slides up and down in a wooden track, or at least it would if it hadn't been painted about a hundred times. The sliding part of the window is held in place by a wooden slat, one on each side, nailed in place. Remove one of these slats and the window will swing open just like a door, and you're in. Of course, the wooden strip has been nailed in place for a century or two and will not come off without a lot of loud shrieking, which, for my purposes, would be counterproductive. There is, however, a particular brand of penetrating oil, and if applied liberally and allowed to soak in for a few days . . .

I climbed the rest of the way up, checking the windows as I went. The rest of them were all painted black, too, and were intact, besides. Up on the roof there was a small hatch instead of a door. Probably had a ladder inside to let you climb out, but it's too easy to wire up an alarm on a hatchway, and too easy to rig a booby trap inside it, too. No way I was going through there until I'd had a look at the inside of it. No, my entry point was going to be the drugged woman's window. I went back down the fire escape and climbed back into my room, mentally going over the supplies I was going to need. This being New York City, they'd all be easy enough to find, and thanks to McClendon, price was not an issue.

My room smelled a bit better than it had, and I toyed with the idea of leaving the window open, but that was not a great idea. I was not the only B&E artist in the city. I latched the window closed again, went over to the inside of my door and listened.

I opened the door a crack and looked out.

No kid.

He was inside, I guessed, sheltered for the moment in the questionable graces of his mother's well-traveled bosom. Drop it, I told myself. There's nothing you can do. My own mother hadn't exactly been Florence Nightingale, and I'd made it okay, hadn't I? Nature sows her seeds with mindless enthusiasm, and if a thousand fall for every one that makes it, or ten thousand, or ten million, what of it? As long as one or two survive, life can go on. A salmon gives her life to lay fifteen thousand eggs in a cold mountain stream, and of that number maybe one or two will live long enough to return the favor. A bull shark's pup, alive in its mother's womb, will kill and eat as many of its siblings as it can, and will so enter the world having already murdered and cannibalized to improve its own chances. You're looking for sympathy, it's in the dictionary, as the saying goes, in between shit and syphilis.

But how could you not root for the kid?

Yeah, okay, so his mother made her living on her knees. Yeah, if another customer came along she'd stick him back outside in the hallway, and yeah, she'd feed her jones, of course she would, she had no other choice. Still, she'd managed to iron the kid's pants and shirt, she'd given him that haircut even if she'd butchered it, she had, for crissake, shined his fucking shoes. She had gotten him all dorked up and ready for school just like all the other mothers had done to their sons.

And every afternoon when he got home from school he'd do

what he had to do, he'd stand out there in that hallway with more backbone than any five-year-old ought to have, or need.

God.

It made me want to pray even as it trod on whatever shoots of faith might still be alive inside me. Dear God . . . What the fuck are you doing?

I heard the stairs creak as someone climbed up. I pulled my door shut again. I heard a heavy thump as someone knocked on her door, heard murmured voices.

Bet your house that the kid is back in the hallway again.

There it is, man.

Deal with it.

I listened carefully to see if I could hear the goonas laughing, but there was nothing.

It was another twenty minutes before I could leave. I wanted to head for my other hotel room, the relatively clean one over on the West Side, but I still had a couple of things to do, first.

I NEEDED TO get somebody who worked out of the top floors of Los Paraíso to talk to me. Obviously it wasn't going to be one of the pimps. Yeah, we'd probably reach that point eventually, but I wasn't ready for them yet. My best bet was one of the ladies, if I could isolate her somewhere away from the hotel, I could wave some money at her, and since she was probably a capitalist at heart, I felt pretty sure she or one of her compatriots would talk to me. Once I got back down on the street, I waited over by the bodega to see if any good candidates came out, and it didn't take long.

They made an odd couple. The woman was a tall, healthy blond in high heels, the guy was a relatively short Asian dude in a gray hoodie and shades. Guy kept the hood pulled up over his head, he looked a bit like a turtle that had not yet decided whether or not it was safe to come out; but the woman walked as if she were on display, modeling for an invisible audience. My cabdriver and I watched from down the block. They reached the corner and the blond hailed a cab. When a yellow taxi pulled over to pick them up they did a bit of a role reversal, the guy hung back, took another drag on his cigarette before throwing it in the gutter, acting exactly like a guy who was worried about being seen by someone he knew. His companion walked over and opened the cab door for him, he scuttled inside, then she walked around to get in behind the driver, tossing her hair back and swinging her butt, oozing confidence and availability as she went. If my driver thought their behavior strange, he didn't say so, he just pulled out into traffic as the taxi accelerated away from the curb.

It was a short trip, they stopped in front of a big hotel in the East Forties. The guy got out, leaving the blond in the back of the cab. I got out of the Town Car and followed. The guy went in past the hotel front desk, turned left and went into the hotel bar. I don't much like bars but I went in anyhow, stopped just inside the door while my eyes adjusted to the gloom. My mark chose a table in a far corner, where he was almost invisible. I took a seat at the end of the bar, right next to the servers' station where the waiters from the adjoining restaurant did their business. I was half hidden behind the draft beer taps and stacks of glasses, but I could still see. I had a mike clipped to my shirt pocket, thing looked just like a pen. I clicked the top of it to turn it on, thumbed the earpiece into place and fiddled with the mike until I had it focused on my mark's table.

It didn't take long.

Guy and a kid. Guy looked fat and successful, wore a pale gray silk suit, kid was mid to late teens, dressed like a kid, jeans and T-shirt, baseball cap pulled down low. There was something about his face, I didn't catch it right away, but I got a better look when the two of them sat down across from the guy in the hoodie. Kid's face looked like melted plastic and his nose was mostly gone. I got one look and then he was slouched low, looking down at the floor, hiding as best he could.

"Mr. Salazar?" the suit said. His voice was a bit muffled but I heard him clear enough.

The hoodie heaved a giant sigh. "You didn't tell me about the face."

"Does it matter?" the guy asked, his tone harsh. "You need more money? Because . . ."

"C'mon, Dad, let's go," the kid said, his voice barely audible, and he started to rise.

"Mikey, you sit your ass down in that fucking chair and you don't move until I tell you to." The kid collapsed back down, sat with his chin down on his chest and his shoulders hunched. I felt my plan slipping away, and I swear this time I could hear the goonas laughing at me.

Yeah, funny.

"My girl's gonna hafta say," the hoodie guy said.

"Look," the suit said. "We're both businessmen here . . ."

"I can't make her do something she don't wanna do."

"Dad, let's just go." The kid was, again, almost inaudible.

"SHUT UP, Michael."

"Let me call her." The hoodie guy got on his phone, murmured something I didn't catch. A hefty waitress walked up and stood at the service bar, her bulk between me and the table in the corner. I leaned back, peered around behind her and watched as the hoodie guy put the phone back into his pocket and they all waited in uneasy silence. The waitress got what she came for and departed. A moment or so later the blond walked in behind me and swayed across the floor, over to their table. "Charlene," the guy said after she sat down. He gestured at the kid. "This is Michael."

"Hello," she said, and she must have seen his face then. "Oh my gawd."

"Your call, hon."

The kid was crying, I think. The suit spoke up, his voice husky. "Listen, I can make this worth your while . . ."

"You hush." Charlene stood up out of her chair, walked around behind the kid, knelt and put her arms around him.

"It's okay," the kid said. "You don't hafta . . ."

"Poor Michael," she said. "You must be so lonely."

He started crying in earnest then and we all waited for him to get a handle on it. I should have gone, it was obvious that my brilliant plan wasn't going to fly because there was a line there I couldn't cross. I found I couldn't move, though, I had to see what she would do, but the booze behind the bar was starting to look good, so I knew I had to get out soon.

The blond still had her arms wrapped around the kid. "All right, Michael," she finally said, and she held her hand out, palm up toward the hoodie guy, and she waggled her fingers. Gimme . . .

The kid started to say something and she hushed him.

"No, now, no talking. You do what I say and everything will be fine. Come with me, now." The hoodie guy laid something in her palm, probably a key card, and she and the kid got to their feet. She almost enveloped him, and when they walked past me and headed for the elevators, I was the one hiding his face.

YOU ARE NOT safe.

Not from me.

If I want your social security number, I can get it. If I want access to your credit cards or your bank accounts, I can get that, too. I can beat your alarm system, and if you lock your baubles up in a safe I can open it, or failing that I can steal the whole goddamn thing, and there really isn't much of anything you can do about it. Neither the gentry nor the serfs have really caught on yet but the feudal system is finally dead, your castle and your moat cannot protect you no matter how many locks you put on the door or how many passwords you put on the account. This is the new reality and the shape of human life is slowly changing to accommodate it. Privacy is finished, and personal property is on life support. Get used to it.

Two o'clock in the morning, the hour when lost dogs and lonely old men die, when honest people are asleep and both the cops and the bad guys have forted up somewhere, their real business done, and they're either passed out or in the station house filling out the paperwork. I made my way up the battered and rusting trellis that was all that remained of the fire escape at the Hotel Los Paraíso. It took me a good half hour to get my targeted window open, but it was not a barrier, not really, all that was required was patience.

Once inside, I stopped and waited. The whole place was asleep, if felt as though the hotel had a heartbeat of her own and it had slowed down to almost nothing. A woman lay on her stomach on the bed in the room I was in, long blondish hair obscuring her face, which was turned to the wall. Her breath rattled in her throat. I could hear a mouse scratching inside a wall somewhere, mouse made more noise than I did. He'd left behind a few turds about the size of caraway seeds, and I left behind a few camera lenses about the size of the buttons that hold a preppie's collar attached to his shirt. An exceptional housekeeper would have had no problem finding either, really, but exceptional housekeepers are even less common than exceptional thieves, and I had no fear of encountering either one inside the Hotel Los Paraíso. I did find one thing of more than passing interest, up on the top floor, most of the room doors were missing. One of them seemed to pass for an office, and they had a safe bolted to the floor. I didn't bother to open it because they had a shopping bag sitting on top of the safe and it was about one quarter full of bills, banded into little stacks. Leave the shit alone, I told myself. You did what you came to do, get out now . . .

Hey, man, I'm a thief. I mean, I knew I was in there for information, not for money, but it's like this: You invite a plumber over your house, he's gonna find something wrong with your plumbing. You go see a proctologist, what do you think he's gonna wanna look at? I took four of the stacks. Thought about taking the whole bag but I didn't do it. It made me think, though. No more room in the safe? I guessed that they hadn't wanted to move the cash, probably not since I started hanging around. Seemed a good bet that El Tuerto, whoever he was, didn't want to show his face, but he couldn't wait forever. Cash in a paper bag is the sort of thing that will give almost any coward the heart of a hero, at least for a half hour or so, and who wanted to deal with that?

I went back out into the hallway. I decided to check out of few more of the rooms on the top floor before I left, and the first one I passed by was occupied by one of the Chinese pimps. He was asleep in a chair, cowboy-booted feet stuck straight out in front of him. I stared at him a little too long, I guess, and he stirred, and it was then that I heard it.

Sounded like someone had left a television running, tuned to some foreign language station, it was just a low mumble, barely audible. I backed away from the door, headed further up the hallway as I heard the guy coming the rest of the way awake. You see what you get, I told myself, if you had kept your mind on your business and left the money alone . . . We were on the top floor, just below the roof, and I was rapidly running out of hallway. It was a little easier to see there, too, ambient light pollution filtered through the dirty glass of the skylight over my head, not a good thing at all. One of the rooms I passed had a woman in it, she was down on her knees, holding a rosary, clicking the beads; she was the source of the low mumble I'd heard. I didn't know the words, not in her language and not in mine, either, but I got the drift. Mother Mary, I'm really in some deep shit this time, could you cut a girl some slack . . . Just past her room, on the opposite side near the very end of the hall there was a tiny alcove that held another window, but this one had been painted black like the others, and that's where I took shelter. The Chinese pimp clomped down the hall, not bothering to try and be quiet. I think the only reason he didn't spot me was because he had his mind on the girl.

"Stupid bitch!" he yelled. "What did I tell you about this shit? You fucking wake me up with this bullshit . . ." She rolled into a ball on the floor, and he kicked her in the small of the back. She cried out in pain, and the noise seemed to energize him. "Shut up! Shut the fuck up!" He kept on kicking her, she kept on crying out, not six feet from where I stood.

I could have killed him. Should have, maybe. He got tired of it, finally, pulled a pistol out of his jacket pocket. He went down on one knee, grabbed a handful of her hair and pulled hard, stuck the barrel of the pistol in her ear like he wanted to shove it right into her skull. "Do you want to die right now?" he hissed.

All I could do was watch.

She just cried.

"I might even be doing you a favor," he whispered. "There are worse ways to go, you know."

She inhaled sharply, went silent.

"That's better. This is the last time I'm telling you."

I heard the wooden floorboards creaking as something heavy made its way in our direction. It was the Haitian. He halted just behind the pimp, his back to me, so close I could have reached out and touched him. He just stood there silent, waiting. The pimp stood back up, ignored the Haitian and stomped back to his room. The Haitian watched him go, then he went into the woman's room, knelt down, held out a hand. "Take this," he told her. "It will help you sleep. Take it. Now swallow it. Let me see you do it."

Apparently she complied, because he stood back up, stood there looking down at her a moment, then he, too, made his way back down the hall.

She pushed herself into a seated position, reached up, fished the pill out of her mouth and tucked it into a pocket before lying back down and curling herself into a fetal position on the floor. I'm guessing she was saving them up, waiting until she had enough to take her out.

I waited another forty minutes before I moved. She wasn't sleeping, I know she wasn't, but she didn't make a sound when I left. It felt like I should have done something, but I didn't know what that something might have been.

Chapter Eight

MY PHONE RANG twice that morning. It didn't wig me out like it had at first; I was getting used to it. For a couple of years I had been so disconnected from everything that I had forgotten what it was to have people wanting to talk to me. Initially I thought that losing the phones, the Internet, my fixed addresses and my profession would free me, and it did feel like that for a little while, but looking back, I thought, that day, that maybe my whole take on that experience had been based on flawed assumptions. For one thing, the fault with me had never been in the technology. And my problems had not been with the other people, either; that may have been the answer I wanted but it was the wrong one. Okay, maybe my sabbatical from the world had been therapeutic for a while, but I think I got it that morning. Maybe it was Michael, the suit's kid, or maybe it was Hector, the kid in the hallway, who knows, but I got it. A single molecule, in and of itself, is nothing, does nothing, has no effect on anything. I cannot exist all on my own, I have to be a part of something.

People were calling me now.

I was alive again.

Go figure.

The first caller was Annabel Wing. "Mr. Fowler," she said.

"Yes, ma'am."

"I . . . I have a confession to make." She spoke as though each word pained her, like she didn't want to talk to me at all, but forced herself anyway. "I haven't been . . . entirely truthful . . . with you."

"Why Ms. Wing. I'm shocked." I expected to get some kind of reaction out of that, maybe a little chuckle, but I got nothing, she went on as if I hadn't spoken at all.

"Could you stop out . . . and see me . . . this morning."

"Of course. Where should I meet you?"

"My home." Her voice broke and she coughed, a shallow little rasp with no air behind it. Then she gave me her address, and she asked me how soon I could be there.

I looked at the hotel's alarm clock beside the bed, guessing at the severity of the morning rush hour traffic and my ability to get my ass in gear. "Give me about an hour and a half, Ms. Wing," I told her. "Look for me around eight o'clock."

"I'll see you then," she said, and the line went abruptly dead.

Odd. But then I didn't know her very well, and she did strike me as an odd bird. What kind of mother blows off the memorial service for her only daughter? Even if there'd been some risk involved, you'd think she'd have gone.

The second call came when I was walking through the hotel lobby. It was Klaudia Livatov. "How about you stop by and see me this morning," she said. "I've got a couple things I'd like to show you."

I looked at the clock in the lobby, and then I looked outside at the cabs waiting by the curb. I figured I could make it if I grabbed a taxi instead of riding the train. With a little luck I could see Klaudia, check out what she wanted me to look at, and maybe even make arrangements to go back and see her later. You know, to discuss.

Yeah. Cab fare didn't count for a lot, not when you were thinking about someone like Klaudia . . . I figured, worst case scenario, I might be a little bit late to see Annabel. I figured she could live with that. "On my way," I told Klaudia.

I FIND IT difficult to reconstruct with any clarity what happened when I got to Klaudia's place. There are some things I think I know for sure: I know for a fact that she made a pot of coffee when I got there, that she had an old laptop up and running on her little glass table, and that she'd printed out some stuff for me to read. I know we spent some time talking about her research, although I think she did most of the talking. I know I found it hard to concentrate, I know she was wearing a pair of black running shorts and a polyester T-shirt, and I know that at some point, as I sat there vainly trying to focus on the computer screen, she sat down next to me and put her hand on my thigh.

Everything else is subject to interpretation.

The problem is that I cannot be sure that I am not amplifying my memory of those events in light of what happened later, that I do not color in those images now as I look for meanings that may not have been present at the time. Or is it simply that all prophecies are initially misunderstood? That all messages from all gods are only unraveled long after the fact, when you look back and ask yourself, how come I couldn't see that? I have the impression that I unwrapped Klaudia Livatov like a little kid who had just gotten the most incredible Christmas present of his life, and that she was much more like the kid who tears the box in half to get at what's inside. I have no memory of any conversations we may have had, I don't recall any talking, really, although there must have been some . . . I don't think either of us thought to close the blinds. I think I remember the feel of that rough canvas rug against my back. I think I may have lost track of myself, that for a while I was no longer clear about exactly where Saul stopped and Klaudia began. For what seemed an eternity I hardly felt anything at all, my brain seemed too stunned to comprehend much of the input, but then right near the end I think I felt everything for both of us, through her nerve endings and mine, I tasted her thirst and mine, I was burned by her fire and mine. I/we/she had come through a long, dry, and difficult passage, but now that baked and arid country was behind us and by God we were finally and gloriously drenched.

She got up, afterward, padded across the room to her kitchen. At the sight of her walking away and then coming back with those two white coffee mugs I was reborn. I remember her laughing. I remember the coffee was cold by the time we got to it.

We talked, afterward, some small part of my brain made conversation, whether intelligent or not I cannot say, and again it was about the work she'd done on McClendon's list of names. Anything else we may have said has escaped me now. I think I would have sworn, at the time, that Klaudia Livatov knew far more than I did about who we were, she and I, but I may have been profoundly wrong about that. In the gray landscape of memory where information slowly morphs into conjecture and wishful thinking, it's very hard to know any one thing for certain.

I will say this: Ignore the data at your peril.

I say that I remember, and I think I really do, but I can't swear to it. I came out of a fog walking aimlessly on Houston Street, unsure if I was headed west or east, feeling like a man who wakes up out of a dream fighting to hang on to the images even as they fade like smoke in the breeze. I thought I had to check myself, see if my shoes were on the right feet, or if I had my shirt on inside out. I stopped on the corner of Houston and the Bowery and waited for the world to come back into focus. When the cobwebs were mostly clear, I flagged down a passing taxi to take me out to Flushing.

I WAS ALMOST three and a half hours late getting to Annabel Wing.

What was I supposed to do? It was Klaudia, man, it was freakin' Klaudia . . . I felt like I was miles away from understanding her, and I couldn't get her out of my head. Maybe it was her kinetic physicality, that sense of restless power and energy that seemed to boil just beneath her surface, maybe it was the way my interactions with her seemed to run counter to everything everyone had told me about her. Maybe it was just, you know . . .

The way I was choosing to see the thing with Klaudia was that she had decided to trust me. That was not something that happened a lot in my life. I was too used to being the strange new kid with the weird clothes, I had always been the kid who didn't fit, and all of a sudden the coolest girl in the neighborhood was hanging with me. She'd let me past her defenses, she'd reached out, and with the touch of a hand she'd incinerated everything I'd been using to keep everyone away from me.

The cab fare was twenty-four bucks, I only had twenties and the driver's English had deserted him, conveniently, but hey, the goonas had finally smiled on me that morning and I was feeling too great to stiff the guy, so he drove off with a sixteen-dollar tip.

I stopped and bought a bottle of wine as a sort of peace offering to Annabel, wondering as I did so if she even drank, if she'd maybe take the bottle and clock me with it.

Annabel Wing lived on a sort of quiet side street. Quiet for Flushing, anyhow. It was a one-way street of adjoining two-story brick buildings that looked like they'd all been built sometime back in the seventies or eighties; they had commercial spaces in the street-level units, God-only-knew-what going on in the basement units, and apartments up top, each with its own balcony. Guy on the sidewalk out front was handing out flyers and mumbling "Ten dollar," and a couple of the girls were hanging, giving you the eye, trying to tempt you down the stairs. I barely noticed them. The doors to the upper-level units were the sort of barred metal security doors that you see everywhere in the city, although they're not great for security if you leave them unlocked the way Annabel had.

The light in her stairwell was out.

I should have taken another half hour or so, late or not, I should have waited for my vagrant mind to reassemble itself . . .

Something brushed at my face, it felt like a hair or a strand of spider's silk, and when I went to wipe it away it was gone. I stopped in the doorway and waited, but nothing happened, so I went up the stairs. The door at the top of the stairs was open, too, and I finally woke up. Without moving my feet at all I checked all around the door for a trip wire or some sort of trigger, and when I found none I pushed the door the rest of the way open with my elbow.

"Ms. Wing?"

Nothing.

I put the wine down on the hallway floor behind me and took two careful steps into her apartment, which allowed me to look left into her dining room. There was a kitchen beyond that but it was open enough for me to see that she was not in it. I took three more steps.

"Ms. Wing? Annabel?"

Straight ahead was her sitting room, to the right, her bedroom. I could see the bottom third of her bed. Someone lay facedown on the mattress, I could see their shins and feet.

I would like to have remembered Annabel Wing the way she looked the morning I met her, tall and exotic and nice. I should not have looked into that room.

Death does not reside easily in the mind, there isn't a good space for its odd shape and sharp corners, it always seems to push back at you somehow. How could she be dead, hadn't I talked to her just that morning, and yet she was, with so much of her blood on the walls and floor there could not be enough left inside her to support life. Her face was darker than the rest of her, she was discolored from the middle of her neck on up because someone had taken a wire coat hanger, wrapped it around her neck and tightened it up until it was imbedded in her flesh. They'd twisted the wires together behind her neck the way an electrician does, wound the strands tightly around one another and cut off the excess, all I could see was maybe an inch and a half of it sticking out behind her. No human being that I'd known, including me, would have been able to loosen that noose without a pair of pliers, so even if I hadn't been hours late, I'd have been too late.

Her left earlobe was missing.

I heard footsteps pounding up the stairs behind me. There wasn't any point in trying to run, whoever had set me up must have been a pro. "In here," I said. "I'm unarmed."

Two cops, one young guy in blues and an older guy in a brown suit. "Freeze!" the younger one said, holding his pistol out in a somewhat unsteady combat stance. The older guy slid past him in the narrow hallway, he was the one I worried about, he pointed his pistol at my chest, almost casually.

"Don't move, asshole," he said. "Move and you're dead."

I SPENT A couple of hours handcuffed in the back of a squad car, exercising my right to remain silent. The cop in the brown suit came to talk to me once, but it was a short conversation, something about my best chance at cooperation and fair treatment and my desire to see a lawyer. I wouldn't talk. It wasn't that I didn't want to make a statement, but cops are pros and you have to know when you're outclassed. After that we rode down to the precinct house and I spent a couple more hours shackled to a metal pole that was bolted to the wall behind the perp bench. When I finally got to make my call, I called Mac. More accurately, I called his voice mail . . .

A cop I once knew told me that there used to be an unwritten rule in the NYPD: You never took a suspect into the station house if he was still upright and walking under his own power. So there are worse places to get arrested but I don't think the margins are huge. It's a little like getting your arm caught in some giant, slowly revolving machine, the thing is going to pull you in and you're going to die slowly and horribly and there isn't a damn thing you can do about it.

That's what it felt like, anyway.

I HADN'T NOTICED much about the cop in the brown suit back at Annabel's, I mean, I remembered he was black and had some gray in his hair but after two days in lockup I could not have picked him out of a lineup. I was pretty sure this was the guy, though, he was seated on one side of a table when they brought me in and shackled me to the chair across from him. I didn't know about his chair, but mine was bolted to the floor. When the security detail went through the steel door and it clicked shut behind them, he looked over at me. "Mr. Fowler," he said. "We meet again."

"Mr. Fowler?" I said. "Last time I was just an asshole."

"Forgive me. That was before I found out you weren't just any old every-day asshole. My name is Sal Edwards."

"Nice to meet you, Sal. I'd offer to shake hands, but . . ."

"No thank you."

"How'd you arrange all this, Sal?" I nodded at the empty room. "I didn't know you guys still pulled shit like this. No lawyers? No DA? Nobody does anything without a lawyer these days."

"We're old school here," he said. "Call it interdepartmental cooperation. Besides, this isn't really happening. I'm not actually here. But in principle, communication is good, don't you think?"

"Okay. I'm listening."

"I worked counter-intel before I came home to the cops," he said. "Funny, isn't it, but in every steaming shithole on this planet, there always seems to be someone like you around. There's always some guy who can get shit done even when there's no legal way to do it. I always wondered what they did with you fucks once Uncle Sam didn't need your talents anymore."

Technically that was a statement and not a question, not that I could have answered it anyhow.

"Why are you in my city, Mr. Fowler?"

"I just have this thing about New York, man."

"Why did you let us take you, back at the apartment?"

"You were properly ordained agents of the law . . ."

"Yeah, stop," he said, cutting me off. "Who are you working for?"

"Melanie Wing," I told him.

"You're probably gonna burn for Annabel Wing's murder," he said.

"I didn't do it."

"Are you saying you don't believe I can stick you with it?" I didn't have an answer for that. "Who are you working for?"

"Melanie Wing."

He acted like I hadn't answered him. "Your name pulled up a red flag. I'd never seen one like it before. 'Inform immediately.' I got to make the call myself. You wanna know what was the first thing they asked me? They wanted to know if I thought you'd gone active. I told them we had you for criminal trespass. You know when someone's laughing at you on the other end of the phone, right, you can't hear them but you know they're doing it?" He leaned in, motioned me closer, and I responded. It's the natural reaction. "Who are you, anyway, and what the fuck are you doing in my town?" he whispered, presumably to defeat the mikes. "How much trouble are we in?"

I leaned back. "You ever work a case out in Podunk, Sal?"

His eyes narrowed, but he shook his head. "Brooklyn born and raised."

"Thought so." I had his complete attention. "I'm gonna tell you something you'd know if you'd worked much outside of the five boroughs. When it comes to white trash families, it ain't all in the computers. Now I don't give a shit if you believe this or not, but this is the truth. My truth, anyway. I suppose a DNA test could prove me wrong, but unless and until, I'm going with it. Melanie Wing was my half sister. Melanie, Annabel's daughter. Six or seven months ago someone killed Melanie and dumped her into the East River. And once I started sniffing around, they killed her mother and set me up to take the fall for it. I really wanna find out who did it." I surprised myself, laying it out there, for one, believing it, for another.

Edwards exhaled, like he'd been holding his breath, and then he leaned back and stood up out of the chair. My read on him was that he was relieved. Funny, how the things you fear the most so often turn out to be something other than what you expected. He walked over and knocked on the inside of the steel door. He didn't turn around. "The forensics are gonna place you at the scene. Where we found her."

"How'd you pull that one off?"

"Wasn't me," he said. Someone unlocked the door and pulled it open for him. "Either you ain't as good as I was told, or somebody tied you up in a nice neat package. I'd say you got a real problem. I know you don't wanna talk, I know that's the way you guys play the game, but if it was me, I think I'd consider my circumstances before I made up my mind to clam up. This situation, right here, this could be your whole ball game."

He walked out.

Chapter Nine

I THOUGHT IT was gonna be Mac, a day later when they came to tell me I'd made bail I just assumed he'd finally gotten it done, so when I saw the guy through the reinforced windowpane in the metal door it felt like I'd gotten shot, that jolt of unexpected recognition blows through you and then all your nerve endings wake up and go Oh shit . . .

His name was Dick Plover and he was a nightmare of a client.

He was fifty or so, fat, florid, with a fringe of gray hair. He wore a blue suit, flag pin on the lapel, white shirt, red tie, I'd never seen him in anything else, I could not picture him as a child or a high school student; there was no way any kid I'd ever known could have turned into something like Dick Plover. I mean, he was human, he had to be, sired by a man just like the rest of us, born of a woman, but God, I couldn't picture it. His was a face from another lifetime, one I had sincerely hoped I'd never see again. They say that America needs men like Plover and I suppose it might be true, but we're still pretty good at building things, we're still pretty good at feeding people. I always wondered what the world would look like if we spent a little more time and money doing that and a little less blowing shit up.

Then again, since I am not a builder, I suppose I have no right to speak.

Plover was not a builder, either.

This is as close as I ever got to understanding the guy, and as close as I want to get: He was an Unformed Man. You see guys like him on occasion, running a corporation, a school or a church. They can sound like us when they want to, they can laugh and cry and pat you on the back, but they are nothing like you and me. They believe in the primacy of the mind, they have never had to run or hit, never held the rifle or the knife themselves, only by proxy. They never had an older brother to slap the shit out of them for straying too far from normal, have never felt physical pain themselves and are therefore all too ready to cause it in others. I have no doubt that Plover went to church on Sundays. I am equally sure that the people sitting next to him would move to another pew if they had any idea what he was.

I watched him watching me as they processed me out. He walked me out, after, he had a car and driver waiting in the tow-away zone outside. The people going by, cops and lawyers and families of the unfortunate, they all eyed us speculatively as the driver, who aside from the black suit looked like USMC standard issue, got out and opened the back door. Plover motioned me in first. I looked back at the building, then up at the sky, and then I sighed and got in.

The car was a cocoon, a bubble, nothing of the outside world intruded. "You should have called me, Saul," Plover said, oozing phony compassion.

Yeah, sure. I owed him now, and owing a guy like him could

be bad for your health. "What happened, Dick? We get into another war?"

"The enemies of freedom never sleep." I never knew if he was serious when he said shit like that. "I think I may be of some use to you when it comes to resolving the manner of Ms. Wing's death. But I'd like to know that I can count on you." Tit for tat, that's what he was telling me.

"I didn't kill her, Dick."

His smile was eloquence itself, he was letting me know that he didn't really care whether I'd done it or not. "They have your prints at the scene."

"Impossible. I never touched anything."

"A water glass in the kitchen sink. You took your pleasure with the woman, then you killed her. And, despicable bastard that you are, you stopped in the kitchen for a drink of water on the way out."

Son of a bitch. "Someone set me up."

He nodded. "And a fine job they've done of it, too."

We rode in silence for the space of a block or two. "Why do you need me, Dick?" I finally asked him. "I'm not a shooter."

"We have plenty of those." He turned and looked at me, for all the world looking just like your favorite uncle giving you a red bicycle on your birthday. "Saul, you are a man of talent and resourcefulness. We consider you an asset, I want you to know that. Despite what you might think, we do care about you."

"Bullshit. You already have something, don't you."

The look on Plover's face was not exactly a smile. "Your cynicism disturbs me, Saul. We were so happy to see you get out of Zurich. Europe was a bad situation, all the way around. Maine, on the other hand, seems to have agreed with you. You look great." His eyes narrowed. "You had us all very worried, there, for a while."

"Yeah, sure." He knew, that's what he was telling me. He knew I'd been using. Wouldn't have surprised me if he had my old dealer's phone number. And it was more than a little unsettling to find out he'd been keeping tabs on me. "Must be a comforting thought, if you need me to become permanently silent, you just stick a lethal dose in my arm and a syringe in my hand."

"May that unfortunate circumstance never become necessary," he said. "I told you, Saul, we consider you an asset. We want to see you prosper."

There was probably no real way to tell what Plover wanted, other than me, willing to work for him again. "All right," I said, knowing I'd regret it, agreeing to it anyway. One last time, I told myself. One last time and I'm free. "I owe you one."

He nodded. I could almost see the checkmark next to my name in his little book. "Good," he said. "Now, if you don't mind, you and I are going to go sit down with a gentleman who represents the interests of the NYPD, and we're going to see if we can clear this whole mess up."

WE MET AROUND a conference table at the Midtown Sheraton. The guy was technically a lieutenant. Calabrese was his name, and he stood like a boxer, looked like he was waiting for a good time to hit you. Plover introduced us. "The lieutenant works for the chief of detectives," he said. Calabrese didn't offer to shake hands, and I didn't push it. "Lieutenant," Plover said. "If you would."

Calabrese glared at Plover but I guess Plover outranked him; either that or he had something on the guy, or the guy's boss. Calabrese shifted his attention to me, sucked in a big breath of air, let it out slowly, as if he were praying for patience. "We believe we're dealing with a serial murderer," he said. "We know of five women that he's killed in the last two years. There may be others that we haven't found yet. So far we've managed to keep this out of the media, and we'd like to keep it that way."

"I've already vouched for Mr. Fowler's discretion," Plover said, a tone of warning in his voice.

Calabrese grimaced.

"Five women," I said. "Does that include Melanie Wing and her mother?"

"No. It would appear that those two murders are the work of a copycat."

"I thought you said nobody knew about this guy yet?"

"I didn't say that. I said that the media didn't know. There are at least four precincts where rumors have started."

"Oh. Okay. That means he's one of yours. The copycat. Otherwise, how would he know what to copy?"

Calabrese just stared at me.

"To speed things along, here," Plover said, "we have established to Lieutenant Calabrese's satisfaction that you were in Switzerland at the times of the first two murders, and that you were in Maine for the next three, as well as at the estimated time of your half sister's untimely demise."

Calabrese didn't look satisfied to me. "And you're sure of all that," he said, glaring at Plover. "You are confident that—"

"We know where Mr. Fowler was," Plover said calmly, and Calabrese shut up at once. "And we know what he was doing."

I felt a sudden chill. Of these two characters, I was much more afraid of Plover, and the idea that he'd had me watched, though useful as an alibi, was not comforting. Focus, I told myself. Keep your mind on business. "So you have two problems," I said to Calabrese. "You have a serial killer working in your city, and you have someone inside your department who murdered two women and tried to pin it on him. Are you sure it's a copycat?"

"The serial murderer has a couple of signature moves," Calabrese said. He looked like he wanted to bite someone. "Not all of the details have gotten out. For example, he has sex with his victims, postmortem. That was not the case with either Annabel or Melanie Wing. And there are several other markers that are absent. Minor, taken individually, but together they are significant enough to indicate a copycat."

"A cop."

"We are exploring that possibility," Calabrese said, seething.

Plover did not seem interested in the problems of the NYPD. "In any event," he said, "we have our Mr. Fowler in Zurich or in Maine for six out of seven of your cases, and it would seem that he simply stumbled onto the scene of the latest murder." He glanced at me again. "The lieutenant has established that at the approximate time of death, you were in the company of a certain young lady at her apartment in Manhattan." He looked back at Calabrese. "I assume you will relay the necessary information to your investigation team . . ."

"I'm telling them nothing," Calabrese growled.

"And that would be because . . ." The warning in Plover's voice was clear.

"Sal Edwards is not an idiot," Calabrese said. "He's got the time of death and he's got Miss Livatov's statement. That's all he needs to know."

Plover walked me out through the lobby. "I don't think he liked you," he said.

"I don't think he likes anybody."

"He's had some setbacks," Plover said. "Have a little compassion. He thought he had you for two out of seven, and now he doesn't. And one of the things he didn't tell you, his killer has hep C. So whoever the guy is, he's really already dead. Hardly worth looking for him. I wonder if he knows it . . ."

"I suppose I'll be hearing from you."

"Well, you know how it goes," he said. "They say it's easier to get forgiveness than permission, but the next time it seems like the oversight committee will give us neither, we may give you a call."

I KNEW IT was her, even from a block and a half away. My eyesight was okay, not outstanding, but there was no mistaking Klaudia Livatov's athletic grace or her blond hair dancing in the breeze that blew northward between the buildings up Avenue C. Sitting on her stoop, I don't think I stood out the way she did but she did not act surprised when she saw me. "Hey, hotshot," she said. "No flowers? No candy?"

She was right, I should have brought something. Man, I had a lot to learn. "Sorry."

She snorted at that.

"Actually," I told her, "I am sorry I didn't call you. I was unavoidably detained."

"I heard about all about it," she said. "Come on up."

SHE HAD HER back to me as she hung up her coat. "About last time," she said.

"Yeah . . ."

She turned around and stared at me. "I don't know what that was."

A thousand smart-ass answers occurred to me, all of them wrong, so I kept my mouth shut, but apparently my poker face still needed work. "Okay, okay, you idiot," she said. "I know what it was. But what I mean is, I don't know what came over me." I opened my mouth to reply but she pointed at me so I shut it again. "Let me just, you know, let me just say this."

God I wanted her right at that moment. I had never known another woman as intensely and fiercely alive as she was. "Okay."

"Normally," she said, and then she shook her head. "Start over. Before you. Yeah, that's better. Before you, okay, I have never been . . ." She looked around, searching for the right words. "That motivated. Physically. I don't know why. It's just that guys . . . All the men I've ever known were just guys. Just guys. Beer-swilling, TV-watching, sex-starved slobs. I don't know what it is about you."

I didn't know, either.

"It was like a kind of seizure. I felt like I had a thunderstorm go through my head. Too dark to see, you know, and too loud to think, rain drumming on the roof, and lightning . . . All I knew was . . . I don't know how to explain it. I just felt all of a sudden like I'd been waiting for you for one hell of a long time, and once we started, I could not let you loose until . . ." And then it seemed to be my turn to talk. "Am I making any goddamn sense to you at all?"

"Yeah. Yeah. No." Very smooth, Casanova. "The thing is, nothing like that ever happened to me before. Nothing like you. I mean, with me, it's always been sort of mercenary. Only, that's not really the right word. Impersonal, I guess that's what I'm trying to say. Howling at the moon, okay, and I'm not complaining, but then afterward, nothing. No connection. I always figured that was going to be it for me. That was as much as I was ever gonna get." There it was, the thing that I'd always been afraid to say, now it was out there and I couldn't get it back.

She walked past me like a boxer going to the center of the ring just before a fight. She stopped at her little statue, paused to light one of the candle stubs with a kitchen match. "I can still feel it," she said, without looking at me. "I got it locked down right now, but if I give in to it . . ." She turned and stared at me. "I don't know if I like giving some guy that much power over me."

"I'm not some guy."

"No?" She flipped the match into her kitchen sink, walked over to me, stood too close, inside that zone, but I didn't back away.

"No. I am a grown-ass man, not a guy. There is a difference."

"I've heard that." She reached out, put a hand on my chest. "You're gonna have to give me a little time with this."

"I can do that."

"Good," she said. "We got other things to talk about anyway."

Yeah, but . . .

"Two cops came to see me," she said. "Day before yesterday. They got my number out of your cell. They didn't wanna tell me but I got it out of them eventually. They said they were holding you but they wouldn't say why."

"Melanie Wing's mother was murdered," I told her. "They think I did it."

"Holy shit," she said, her face turning paler than normal. "Are you serious? What happened?"

"She called me that morning. Maybe a half hour before you did. She told me she'd lied to me when I talked to her the first time, about Melanie. I was on my way to see her when you called me. My original intention was to take the subway out to Flushing, where she lives. Lived. So after I talked to you I grabbed a cab instead, I figured that would save me enough time so I could stop here, talk to you, and still be more or less on time to see her."

"Didn't work out that way," Klaudia said.

"No. I should have pressed her, when I had her on the phone, but I didn't think it was a big deal. I mean, I was already headed out there . . ." I broke off, staring at Klaudia, remembering what had held me up. "What did the cops ask you?"

"How I knew you. Did I know anything about your past. What time did you get here. What did we talk about. What time did you leave. Did I know where you came from. And on and on, in circles, same questions over and over, just phrased a little different each time. I told them they could get the times you came and went from the cab companies. Told them I wasn't interested in where you came from. Which was a lie, by the way. And I told them I called you over here so I could fuck your brains out." She colored, just a bit. "What happened to Melanie's mom, exactly?"

"My gut feeling is that whoever killed Melanie killed Annabel, too. Word must have gotten around that I was in town and asking questions. And if they find out about you and me, whoever they are, that would make you the next logical step. I think we need to talk about getting you some—"

"I can take care of myself," she said.

"Listen, Klaudia, I know you're a tough lady, but . . ."

"Saul!"

I shut up.

"I'm on it."

"Seriously, if anything ever happened to you, I would . . ."

"If someone comes after me, I'll try to remember to leave a piece big enough for you to identify them. Okay?"

"Whoever he is, this guy doesn't play."

"Neither do I. I made some more progress on your list."

"I'm not feeling good about this."

She gave me a look that said the subject was closed. "I made some more progress on your list."

"All right." She took me through it, and it didn't really feel much like progress. Eight more names disqualified because they still liked Mac too much to do him dirty. "Well, thank you for doing the work. Are you up for a little more?"

"Sure," she said. "What do you have?"

I told her about the building on Tenth Street that housed the Los Paraíso Hotel, gave her the shorthand version of why I was interested in it. "What I really want to know," I told her, "is who owns the actual building, and who holds the leases. Who are the interested parties."

"I'm on it," she said.

MAC, I FOUND out, had been in town for two of the three days I spent in the arms of the Corrections Department. He'd been staying at a small boutique hotel over on the East Side, just north of the UN. I was hungry, for a couple days I'd been thinking about a steak at The Palm, but Mac didn't want to go out so I met him at the bar in his hotel. Not my kind of joint, but it was a nice enough place in a traditional sort of way, dim lighting, lots of dark wood, a piano but no piano player. Mac was sitting alone at a table in a dark corner, which surprised me quite a bit.

Mac was born talking.

He raised his head when he saw me, struggled to his feet and waved me over. He looked good enough from across the room, his shaggy mane of white and his country and western suit making him look like a red state politician in town to raise hell and get laid, but when I got closer I saw that he hadn't shaved in a while and his face was gray. "Mac," I said. "Are you okay?"

He sat back down, pointed at a chair for me. "Tell me something, Saul. Did you ever think you'd live this long?"

A fine young waitress wandered over just then, and her musky scent and flawless smile lit up our dark corner, just for a second. I asked her for a coffee and she went off to get it. I watched her walking away, confident that Mac was doing the same, but when I looked back at him he was staring down into the depths of his glass. He looked up at me, waiting for his answer. "It would be easy for me to tell you that I shouldn't still be here," I told him. "But the fact is, I'm always pretty sure I'm gonna make it. If this place catches on fire, you and everybody else might get burned up, but not me. I'll get out."

He sighed. "Not as much fun as you might think," he said, "outliving all your friends."

He did look old. Facial stubble is a fine thing on a young man, and it can look good on a middle-aged guy too, but past a certain age, it just makes you look like a wino. "I'm really sorry about Annabel, Mac."

He nodded. "So am I. She didn't deserve to go like that. She was not a bad person." He picked up his glass, swirled its contents, then took a drink. "I wish I'd been a better man. Wish I'd have taken better care."

"I know what you mean."

"Do you? You have any kids?"

"I've had plenty of times when I wanted to be someone else. Some guy drives a Toyota to work every morning, watches football with his buddies on Sunday. You know what I mean? Anybody but me. But it's all bullshit, Mac. If I can't learn how to be who I am, what makes me think I could cut it in some other guy's shoes?"

He nodded. "Escapism."

She came back with my coffee, and she still had that smile. It didn't seem to be working on Mac. "How'd you get loose?" Mac said. "I was tryina get you out, but all I got was doors slammed in my face. It ain't normal, when your money don't talk at all. It ain't American. What the hell? How'd you get them to let you go?"

"I made a deal with the devil." I told him a little bit about Dick Plover.

"Ah, shit. I'm sorry I ever got you involved in this thing, Saul. Really, I mean it. Who the hell is this guy, and what are you gonna have to do for him, you don't mind me asking. The devil."

"Something he can't get caught doing. It'll be an incursion of some kind, probably. Go in, get something or somebody he wants, get back out without leaving any evidence. I think Plover works for the Department of Defense. He's the kind of guy that management will tolerate because they know he 'gets things done.' "

"A patriot," he sneered.

"I'm sure he thinks he is."

"Those guys are the worst," he said. "Their minds don't work like yours and mine. God help you if you get mixed up with them."

"God might. Or he might not."

"Yeah, sometimes not," he said. "Sometimes he'll leave you to it. Or maybe it just feels like he ain't hearing you. Does this mean you're in the clear on Annabel's murder?"

"Well, I have an alibi, but the NYPD still considers me a person of interest. They still wanna think I killed Annabel, no matter who's leaning on them to let me go. I got set up, Mac. Somebody boxed me in pretty good."

"Someone musta heard you were asking questions, and they got nervous. Any idea who it was?"

"There are a few possibilities. I had someone working on your list of names. Nothing face to face, just computer searches and some phone contact. We had a good cover story. 'Hey, I'm a reporter and I'm researching an article I wanna do on this guy Mac, what can you tell me about him,' and so on. We got a couple possibles but nothing that jumps out at you. Seven out of ten, if you knocked on their door right now and told them you had a great opportunity for them, they'd be so in they'd get the money up tonight, so we crossed them out. Couple of them thought hanging with you was the most fun they ever had. Two others didn't wanna talk about you, so I'd guess they deserve a little more exploration. Maybe. One's past caring, since he got run over by his ex-wife's Mercedes, with her driving it. I mean, there were no red flags, Mac. But I got a call from Annabel a couple days later, she asked me to stop out and see her. Time I got there, she was gone."

"If you were a rich guy," Mac said, staring at his glass, "and you were enough of a prick, you'd probably know somebody who could make this all happen. Kill Annabel, set you up to take the fall for it. Problem solved."

"Yeah, maybe. But it ain't as easy as it looks in the movies. Easier to have someone put a couple rounds in the back of my skull."

He swirled the contents of his glass again. "I think it's time we walk away from this, Saul."

"Are you serious?"

"Two people I cared about, in my own limited and dysfunctional way, and now they're both gone. And you, look at you, look at the trouble you're in. The thought of you all jammed up sitting in a cell because of something you didn't do . . . I don't think I could handle it. Vengeance belongs to the Lord, Saul. Maybe we oughta leave him to it."

"Yeah, I thought of that." I watched him for a moment. "Do you remember the pictures you gave me? The postmortem stuff on Melanie?"

Mac squeezed his eyes shut. "Yes."

"All those cuts on the body."

"Stop, Saul."

"She'd been in the water too long. Nobody could say definitively if they happened before she died or after she went into the water."

"Please."

"I can tell you now." I waited for a reaction. If he really didn't want to know, I wasn't going to inflict it on him.

"Go on, then," he finally said.

"They were knife wounds," I told him. "He bled her out first, then he dumped her. She was alive when he cut her up."

"How do you know that?"

"Because he killed Annabel the same way." I had a terrible thought. He'd been with her when she called me . . . "When she called me that morning, she was weak. She had a hard time talking. She had to stop for breath in the middle of every sentence. He was with her, Mac. She was already dying. She was bleeding to death, right then. The son of a bitch was right there." I wondered what he'd promised Annabel, to secure her cooperation. Probably told her he'd stop something he'd been doing . . .

"You're sure of this?"

I was getting pissed off at myself, thinking about it. "I should have known, Mac, just from the sound of her voice. I should have called the cops right then. If I had, this thing would already be all over."

"Strangulation, they told me. Annabel, she died from . . ." He couldn't continue.

"Yeah. Technically, that may have been cause of death, but I was there, Mac, I saw her. There wasn't a lot of blood left in her."

"Same . . . Same as Melanie."

"Yeah. Same guy. Same person. And I'll tell you one more thing."

Mac closed his eyes, rubbed the bridge of his nose with a thumb and forefinger. "Go ahead."

"He took a piece of her with him. I keep saying 'he,' but I'm not assuming that, not yet. But Melanie had one earlobe missing. Earring still in the other ear. Same with Annabel."

Mac opened his eyes and looked at me and I saw the anger flowing into him, pulling him back from whatever brink he'd been standing on. Saving him. "Son of a bitch. Then it was the same person."

"That's what I've been telling you. And we can't walk away. And not because of ego, either. Not because I don't like getting beat." Not really . . . "We can't let this douchebag walk free."

Mac stared at me for a moment, then nodded. "I agree."

"Good. Next item, you need bodyguards. Right now. Today."

"The Reverend Stillman told me that yesterday. He wants to send me a couple of his guys."

"Well, he's right, but I think we should hire local."

"Just because they're born again don't mean they forgot how to shoot. Stillman's guys will be bad enough to get the job done." He grimaced, looked like I'd told him he had to drink a quart of cod liver oil.

"What?"

He sighed again. "You wouldn't believe the kind of buzzkill these guys are. I'd rather tour with Attila the Nun."

"Sorry, Mac. You're gonna have to put up with it for a while. Take one for the team. Maybe they'll be a good influence on you."

He gave me a withering look. "Yeah? Want me to ask for a couple extra? They could follow you around, too. See how you like it."

"Can't do it," I told him.

"Why not?"

"We don't wanna scare off our guy."

"So where are we with this?"

"Well, there's your theory, some guy that you stung, mad because you took his money. That one ain't looking too good." Mac grimaced and shook his head, he was that sure. From his way of thinking, it had to be about the dough. "And there's Annabel's thing about the tong trying to settle an old score. I'm not in love with that one, either."

"What else you got?"

I told him about the building on Tenth, of Melanie's work with the street girls. "Maybe the pimps just got sick of her hanging around, asking questions. I'm still trying to get someone inside there to talk to me."

"Good luck with that one," he said. "Better make sure they don't get sick of you hanging around, asking questions."

Maybe they already had . . . It occurred to me that they could have been behind Annabel's murder, and the attempt to set me up for it. But it didn't seem like the kind of thing a pimp would know how to do.

"Anything else?" he asked.

"Well, the fourth scenario is the worst, at least for us. It could have been a random thing. Just some stray cat, and we'll never catch him."

"It can't be that," Mac said. "Can't be. What's your gut tell you?"

"It was a cop."

"What?" he said, shocked. "What? I mean I know you don't like policemen, but . . ."

"In the past two years, five women, apart from Melanie and Annabel, have been murdered, all with the same MO. Very similar to the way Mel and her mother were murdered, but there were enough small differences to make the cops think they have a copycat." I told him about the postmortem sex, and the hep C.

"Okay," he said, "but that doesn't mean a cop killed . . ."

"Yes it does," I told him. "Nobody knows about the first five murders yet, except for cops."

"The guy with hep C," Mac said.

"That's right. So nobody would know to stage copycat murder scenes except a cop."

"This just keeps getting worse," Mac said. "I was so sure. 'For the love of money is the root of all evil.' I woulda bet my house on it, if I had one. Do you have any idea what to do next?"

"Yeah."

"You know who the bad cop is?"

"No. But I think I know what trees to shake."

Chapter Ten

I SAW A bunch of people dressed in black; they were walking up Avenue C when I came back to the Hotel Los Paraíso. The gang kids seemed to be a couple members short, and they backed off, wary of the clump of newcomers.

Groups make me nervous. Sometimes they can, like this one did, reignite a lot of my old resentments about always being the new kid. The outsider. It is because groups are hermetic, they are self-referential. The insiders cannot be strange or out of balance, no matter how they look or how out of sync they are with the rest of the world because their metric is the group, the only opinions that matter come from those others they surround themselves with, the ones who look like they do and talk like them. There may not have been any Hasidim in the trailer parks of my youth but I saw plenty of the same dynamic, always from the outside: If you dress like us, if you spend all your free time in our company, you have our assurance that God has your name inscribed in stone somewhere, right next to ours. But if you don't, we don't want to know you, we don't even want to see you. The funny thing is, that's not what hooks you, because in the human animal, immediate gratification always trumps long-term good. What draws you in, even when you know better, is acceptance. Be with us, stand with us and we'll like you, we might even love you.

It was how Mac had hooked me.

Appalling, now that I thought about it, how easily he'd reeled me in.

THE HASIDIM POSSE stopped on the sidewalk right out in front of the Hotel Los Paraíso, and tension radiated off them like heat from an August sidewalk. They were coming for Shmuley, the orange-haired Orthodox kid who worked behind the desk, don't ask me how but I knew it. Kid wasn't even old enough to drink yet, his group was all he'd ever known. It came back to me in a rush: He was risking expulsion and alienation from his family and his religion by committing the mortal sin of trying to learn something real about how the universe worked. I could not wrap my skull around the extent of that kind of intellect, that kind of curiosity, and that kind of courage. Bad enough, when you're a kid, if no one is much interested in helping you learn, but when the people who are supposed to be on your side take an active interest in keeping you down in the dark with them, that was just too wrong, that was the kind of thing that brought my resentments roaring back to pulsating, venom-dripping life.

They stopped outside the entrance to the hotel, rehearsing, I suppose, five men and one woman, dressed in the manner of one of the more radical Jewish orthodoxies. Intentionally rude, I elbowed my way through. "Excuse me. You mind? Get out of the fucking way, for crissake . . ." I went up the stairs two at a time, hoping I'd delayed them enough. "Gelman!" I hissed, when I got up to his cubicle, trying to rouse him without alerting them. "They're coming for you! Gimme your math books! Gimme all your shit. Hurry!" His eyes went wide and he froze for a second, and then he sprang into palsied life, piling books and papers up with shaking hands and shoving them at me.

God, I could hardly carry it all. How could one twenty-year-old kid be reading this much shit at once? Really? I could almost hear the goonas howling with amusement as I clomped up the stairs to my floor carrying all that stuff.

Hector was there, rigid and attentive. "Hello, kid."

His black eyes were wide. "Books," he said.

"Yeah, you want one?"

He shook his head once. Probably figured he had enough trouble already. "You're pretty smart for a guy your size," I told him. I had to put the pile down on the floor so I could unlock my door. I dumped them on the desk once I got inside, right next to the laptop, which was, miraculously, still there. I kicked the door shut, sat down in front of the laptop, and started to run through the program that would connect my laptop to the cameras upstairs. While it spooled up I went into the bathroom to take a leak and I noticed that the water glass that had been sitting on the sink was missing.

Son of a bitch. That's how he'd done it, that was how he put me at Annabel's murder scene. Snuck into my room and stole a glass. I sat with that for a little while, then I got to work.

Gelman knocked on my door about an hour later.

"Come in," I told him. "Want your stuff back?"

"Maybe I should leave it with you." His stutter was gone. From that moment on, Shmuley Gelman and I were brothers. "For safe-keeping."

"Come on in."

He did, and he sat down on that disgusting mattress. But then, you know, he was just a kid, kids are immortal and they don't think germs are real, and besides, he had other things on his mind. He didn't give the laptop a second glance.

"You figure they'll be back?" I asked him.

"Maybe." The kid looked miserable. "Probably. Yes." He gestured at the pile of books. "Those would have been a felony, but they already got me on a misdemeanor."

"What do you mean?"

He got up, yanked a book out of the stack. It was trade paper, the title was gobbledygook, and when Shmuley opened it, what I saw on the pages was worse, some insane and indecipherable stew of numbers, letters and symbols that would never make any sense to me. He'd scribbled a lot more of the same right on the pages, in pencil. "I had questions," he said, "particularly when it comes to the relationship between . . ."

"Yo, Gelman."

He looked up. "What?"

"I ain't gonna understand your questions."

"Oh." He closed the book, alone again with no one to talk to, at least on that level. "Anyway. The author is at NYU. Right across town. The man who wrote this." He tossed the book back on the pile, sat down on the bed, and put his face in his hands. After a moment he looked up at me. "I wrote him a letter. Stupid, right? But why can't I ask?"

"I don't think I can help you with this."

He stood up long enough to grab his book again, the one he apparently did not completely understand. "I've been thinking about this for a long time," he said. He opened the book to a random page and held it out so I could see it. "You are the only person I've ever talked to about it. This is not what they think! Do you want to know what this really is? Past all the formulas, past all the equations, it means one simple thing. I'll tell you what it means, okay? I can tell you everything you really need to know about this in one sentence."

"Okay. I'm listening."

"When God makes the world, okay, this is the language he speaks."

Yeah. All right. Goonas, if you're listening, this kid is trying really hard, and I got nothing. You got to give me a clue . . . I inhaled, hoping some more oxygen would spark my brain into thinking something smart. "So what happened to your letter?"

"I am an idiot," he said. "I meant to put the hotel as the return address, but I didn't do it."

"Oh shit. So the guy answers you but someone at your house gets his letter."

Gelman looked disgusted. "Correct. My mother. And she didn't even let me read his answer."

"I know this is big for you, but it sounds to me like you might have to give up on arithmetic for a while."

"Arithmetic, he calls it." He stared at me for a good thirty seconds. "No," he finally said, shaking his head. "I won't do it."

I thought back to the stuff I couldn't quit doing when I was his age. "I suppose it's out of the question, sitting down with them and explaining."

"Really," he said after a minute. "You don't get it. They're going to hold a funeral. They'll put a headstone in the cemetery with my name on it. I'll be dead to them."

"That's pretty cold." Not even the goonas could think this one was funny.

"It's coming," he said. "It's only a matter of time."

"So when it comes, what do you do?"

He looked at me. "I'm not the first person this happens to, you know. I know a guy."

"A former, ahh, you mean, someone who got away? Before you?" Call me Mr. Smoove.

He nodded. "Yes. But it won't happen today. Thanks for your help." He finally noticed the laptop. A file was running, a feed from one of my cameras upstairs. The Worm occupied most of the screen, but there was a young girl there, too, down on her knees. "What?" Gelman said, pointing. "What in the world? Is that, um, upstairs?" He looked at me, wheels turning. He pointed at the screen. "That's why you're here."

"Yeah."

"But . . . You put cameras? You went up there? How?"

"Even bad guys gotta sleep sometime. These are wireless, and motion activated. Batteries are good for about a month before I have to go back and change 'em."

"Can I ask?" Gelman said. "What did they do, to bring you here? Those guys upstairs."

"They may have killed someone. Or at least they may have been there reason someone got killed. I'm not sure yet."

Gelman shuddered. He looked at the image on the screen, then looked away. "Maybe it's better I shouldn't see," he said. He stood up.

"You want your books back?"

He thought about that for a moment or two. "Yes," he finally said, and it felt to me like he was deciding about a lot more than just books. "I do. Thank you."

EVERYBODY KNEW THE Worm.

Tall guy, maybe six-seven or-eight, Haitian, pale brown, pocked face, skin stretched hard over a bony skull, ridges sheltering small brown eyes. Plus, the dude was ripped. He was even more impressive in person than he was on camera, and he walked through the hotel with the kind of Superman strut that told you he was pretty sure bullets would bounce off. He was coming down the stairs when I exited my room.

In certain situations, testosterone will mess with your head. If I stood aside to let him pass, would it be because the halls were narrow and I believed that basic consideration for the other guy was the last thing holding civilization together? I'd do it for anyone else, right? Or was it because I knew my punk ass was outclassed? I was delivered from too much angst by Hector, who stood in his usual spot outside his mother's door.

The Worm stopped in front of the kid and held out a massive fist that was almost the size of Hector's head. The kid was not afraid, and he bumped fists with the Haitian. Watching the two of them, it was hard to believe that they came from the same species. "Koman ou ye," the Worm said.

Hector answered, "Mujen la."

The Worm stood back up, rose up to his full height and looked down on me. "Hey, Pink," he said, meaning me. "Why you here, man?"

It ain't like I've never been called names before, and I was almost grown up enough for the opinion of a guy like the Worm not to mean a hell of a lot. Really, what irked was his unspoken certainty that he was better than me. "Hey, Taupe," I said. "I sleep here. You got a problem with that?"

He was thinking about what to do with that when I noticed

Hector, who all of a sudden looked terrified. The kid had flattened himself right up against his mother's door. It wasn't right and I knew it. Hector already had enough shit to deal with. I ignored the Worm and squatted down in front of the kid. "I'm sorry, Hector," I said, and I meant it. "Everything's okay. Nothing bad's gonna happen. We're all friends now, okay?"

He nodded once but he didn't move.

I stood back up and looked at the Worm. "Not here, okay?"

He looked over my head, off into the distance. "Don' get many Pinks here," he said. "Let's keep this simple. I tell you what I tell 'em all. Dis place is mine, you understand? Don' mess with my ladies. Don' bother my people. Don' try an run no girls outa dis buildin'. Dis buildin' is mine."

"Got it," I told him.

He stared at me. "Member what I tell you, vale." It sounded like he'd called me a "valet," but the pronunciation was a little off. He reached down then and rubbed the top of Hector's head, barely ruffling the kid's hair. "Adieu, mon ami," he said. The kid watched him in wonder.

The Worm glanced back at me. "Later," he said.

It was a tactical victory, but I didn't know it at the time, I was too busy wondering what kind of a guy pimps out a bunch of girls and yet takes the time to teach some little kid how to say hi in Creole.

BIG SURPRISE, THE lock on the door to the building across the street from the Hotel Los Paraíso was still broken, so I yielded to impulse and decided to go on up and knock on Luisa's door. I heard her voice somewhere inside. "Ola . . ." A moment later I sensed movement at the spy hole, and then I heard her locks opening. She was, as before, layered in lace and nightgowns, slathered in perfume. "Señor," she said. "You come back."

"Yes, ma'am. So sorry to bother you. I wonder if I could talk to you a little bit more."

She didn't smile but I got the impression she was not unhappy for the company. "Please," she said, and she stood back, holding her door open. "Come inside. But I have to tell you, Ramon is berry mad with you."

"Ramon? What'd I ever do to Ramon?"

"I don't let him open the bottle I bought with the money you give me," she said, as she slid by me in the dim hallway. "Because for Ramon, open is empty."

I followed her to her front room and we sat in the same two chairs by the window. "Well, that's what bottles are for. They're for drinking."

"No, no," she said, wagging a finger. "Not for him to give me one lilla sip and then drink the rest and go sleeping the whole night and the next day. Too bad for him. Did you come for me to look at your palm again?"

"No thanks. I'm more interested in Ogun. What can you tell me about him?"

She rocked her head back, looked at me through half-lidded eyes, her chin held high. I thought I was beginning to understand Luisa, a little bit. This was her posture for threatened pride. She wasn't sure if I was mocking her or not. "Male spirit," she said, after a minute.

"Good male spirit? Bad male spirit?"

"Male," she said, shrugging. "Sometime you find a woman who can be good without the bad, but never the man. Even when the man is good, is only because he tries so hard, but still he carries the bad with him." She stared at me. "You know what I mean."

I feigned outrage. "I think that was a shot."

"Señor, please," she said, and some of the tension went out of her. "You only try for being good because you think that is what your lady wants, but this is ignorance."

"Okay, so Ogun is a male spirit. He wants to be good but he can't always pull it off."

"Exactamente."

"So a guy on the street tells me that Ogun is going to kill him," I said. "What's he talking about? Is he really afraid of a spirit?"

She glanced past me, at her little statue in the corner. "Oshun," I said. "I remember her. She's the female spirit. Maybe not completely sane."

"The first woman," she said reproachfully. "I don't think so you want to mess with her." She had her chin held high again.

Counselor, you're badgering the witness . . . "Luisa, please understand. I'm not trying to poke holes in any of this. My problem is . . ." I paused for a beat or two to let her hear that, to let her see that I knew it was my problem.

Which it was.

"I am not a believer. But I need to understand, when this guy on the street, just the other day, says to me that Ogun is going to kill him, what's he thinking?"

She was still feeling insulted. "You are like the blind man in the train station," she said.

"How's that?"

"You think maybe something big is up next to you but you can't see nothing, and everything that you're thinking is wrong."

"First of all . . . Okay, never mind. Back to Ogun. The male spirit."

"Okay," she said.

"Ogun wants to be good, but because he's a guy, he messes up now and then. Who comes up with this stuff?"

That got a smile. "Ogun is very old. From Africa first, then Cuba, now here. You ever hear somebody say, I don't gonna do this an' that until the spirit moves me?"

"I suppose."

"So your friend from the street, he doesn't think so Ogun comes down from the sky to step on him."

"No? So what's he afraid of?"

"When a spirit looks at you," she said, "how does he see?"

"Luisa, you're asking the wrong guy. I could never . . ."

"From up there?" She pointed up at her ceiling. "He watches us from the sky? Like ants? No. I don't think so you are that stupid. The spirit sees you from in here." She pointed at her eye. "Or maybe he goes inside you so he can see what you see. Feel what you feel. Do you know what is a shadow?"

She'd lost me.

"A spirit comes to you sometimes. Happen to everybody once in a while, but nobody knows what is it. Work this way: Say Ogun hate that guy you see on the street. Okay? When you see that guy next time, maybe Ogun comes to you and fill you with his power. Ogun become your shadow. So what happens?"

"Yeah." I couldn't deny having felt the phenomenon, of being momentarily stronger than I had a right to be, or less sensitive to pain. And angrier, no doubt, but I wasn't going to attribute that to Ogun, just to adrenaline and my own loss of control. But being shadowed by Ogun was a way to understand it. "I get it. You're saying that God goes inside you . . ."

"You felt the shadows, then. Most men have. And all women."

"You mean Ogun could shadow a woman?"

She shook her head. "Boys with the boys, girls with the girls."

"So my man on the street, he thinks he did something to piss off Ogun and he was afraid Ogun would come to me and make me kill him."

"No," she said. "Your man on the street is too stupid to understand what I tell you. He is only escare of a man who pretends to have the shadow of Ogun."

"How do you know?"

She closed her eyes. "I know," she said, and she bobbed her head in the direction of the Hotel Los Paraíso.

And then I did get it. "You're talking about that big Haitian guy. The one they call the Worm."

She nodded once.

"Why do you think he's just pretending?"

"God is never the chulo," she said, and she had her chin up again, but not like before. Her face was twisted into an expression of disgust. "Never."

"Chulo?"

"Pimp." She filled the word with disgust.

"What if it isn't God? What if it's Ogun?"

She shook her head. "All spirits belong to God."

"Luisa, your universe is a complicated place."

She gave me a look. "Not so much, I don't think so."

"But you're sure the Haitian is pretending."

"Just a man who use the dark to escare the children, and the weak," she said. "This is an old story."

THE COPS HAD been to my hotel to talk to the night manager. The nice one, over on the West Side, not Los Paraíso. The guy didn't say he'd seen the cops but he didn't need to, I don't know what they told him but he was shaken. He apologized all over the place because he'd packed up my shit and rented my room. "They told me they had you in custody," he said, quivering. "They said it wasn't likely that I'd ever see you again. They said to hold your belongings until they came back with a warrant. But look at it this way, we saved you three nights' worth of charges."

"Yeah, great," I said, counting the days. "Don't you mean four nights?"

"Well, technically, since checkout time is eleven . . . You're right, let's make it four days." He took back the bill and revised it, seemed happier after I paid him. He even rented me another room.

Next to the elevators.

They were hydraulic, and they groaned and sighed as people went out for the night or came home to bed. I can't say it bothered me; elevators or not, my new room still beat the hell out of the last place, because if there were any rats in this one they stayed politely out of sight. I expected I'd feel better after some room service and a nice long shower, and I did, but only marginally. I didn't feel like watching television, and my window did not provide much in the way of distractions. There are some nights when you can't think, at least not productively. The committee convened, those inner voices from my past came out and they sat in judgment, comparing my present difficulties to my historical flaws.

I did not care to wait for a verdict; in that court I have no shot.

It occurred to me that, for once in my life, I did not have to be alone.

I got dressed again, went outside and took a cab downtown. She did not answer her phone in the usual manner, she just picked it up and waited. I knew she was there, I could feel her. For maybe ten seconds we breathed at one another over the phone like a couple of pervs. "Where are you," she finally said.

"Houston Street."

"I knew you'd come."

I walked back out of there a couple of hours later feeling so wrung out that I could barely navigate. The world was not as pointless as I'd thought, or so it seemed, and I knew, at least for that one night, what life was for, for that one night I believed utterly, because while I was clearly the product of a long evolutionary process of trial and error, Klaudia, just as clearly, had come directly from the hand of an artist; there was no other explanation that made any fucking sense. My life would never reach any higher, that's what I thought that night as I stumbled down Houston Street looking for a cab, I worshipped at the temple of Klaudia, and no church bell ever rang louder.

Chapter Eleven

I WANTED TO talk to Marc Reiman again. He was the guy who'd fallen hard for Melanie. He was also the guy who had told me what a shy and retiring budding spinster Klaudia was. He'd known Mel in life and I hadn't, and he'd known Klaudia, too. He seemed like a rational guy.

The discrepancy bothered me. Could he have been wrong about them both?

He worked out at a gym right next to the Fifty-Ninth Street Bridge, which was a block south of his apartment. When I talked to him on the phone, he agreed to meet me at a greasy spoon downstairs from the gym. "I guess you're an East Side guy," I told him.

"Funny, isn't it," he said, "how New Yorkers will go uptown or downtown a lot easier than they'll go east to west, or vice versa. Must be those long avenue blocks, they must make you feel like you're walking farther. Hey, wait a minute . . ." He shook his head. "Never mind. Doesn't work."

"What doesn't work?"

"I was gonna say that whoever killed Mel must be an East Side guy, otherwise he'da put her in the Hudson, but I was only assuming he'd dumped her in the East River. But where they found her, it could have been either one."

"True. It's a thought, though, because she was an East Side girl. Lived over here, worked over here, too. Assuming this wasn't a totally random thing . . . But that doesn't really work, either. You remember that guy from Long Island who was driving in, picking up prostitutes in the East Village and offing them? So our guy could be from anywhere."

"Couple of years ago," Reiman said. "Yeah. Guy probably knew the neighborhood, though, probably knew where he could find a parking spot for his truck. Is this what you wanted to talk to me about?"

"Not exactly. I'm getting some very mixed messages about what Melanie was like. And the same thing keeps happening with Klaudia Livatov, too, for that matter."

"Really? Like what?"

"Well, with Klaudia, for example, you gave me the impression that she was a timid little mouse."

"Yeah," Reiman said. "Timid is exactly the right word. Quiet, scared . . . that's her."

"Okay. And it ain't just you. Melanie's landlady described Klaudia in almost the same exact terms. But when I met Klaudia, I didn't get that from her at all. With me, she's been . . ." Yeah? What? "Aggressive," I told him. "Confrontational. Anything but timid."

"Wow," Reiman said, eyeing me. A waiter stopped by and interrupted his speculations. He repressed a smile and ordered his breakfast, and then I did the same. Most of the women I'd known tended to make you want to scratch your head, but Klaudia made you want to smile.

Which, apparently, I'd been doing. Something new, for me.

"Wow," he said again. "I know that look. You and Klaudia? Really? I'd have never guessed that, not in a million years. What do you mean, aggressive? I mean, apart from the ways that aren't any of my business."

"She told me that she'd gotten pissed off. She said when nothing much happened after Melanie died, when no one seemed to care all that much, from then on she's been angry all the time. She said she felt like she'd been invaded by this other personality, one she doesn't recognize."

Reiman shook his head. "Personality is formed very early in life, and it's generally not a very malleable thing. The only way what you're talking about makes any sense is if this new Klaudia is who she really was all along. I mean, from what I know of her I can't see it, but it's possible."

"When I asked her how old she was, she said she was twenty-six, but that she felt like she was ten thousand and twenty-six."

He'd stopped smiling. "Odd," he said. "You might want to tread carefully with her, Saul. I mean, it's not hard to subscribe to the theory that all women are crazy, at least to some degree, but Klaudia might be . . . Okay, what I'm trying to say is that if she really did suffer some kind of psychological dislocation after Mel died, there might be some serious issues there." He scratched his chin. "You know what, I just assumed that Mel's killer was a guy. I'd hate to think it even possible that someone like Klaudia . . ." He looked at me. "Might be useful to know a bit more. Where she came from, what kinds of things she's been through." He shook his head. "I hate this. I hate thinking that someone I know might have killed Mel."

"I don't care for it much, either." It had not occurred to me until that moment that Klaudia was as much a logical suspect as anyone else. "But here's the really odd thing. I've been getting the same kind of conflicting stories about Melanie, too. And again, it's her landlady and you telling me one thing, and outside parties telling me something else."

"Really? I'm not wrong about Mel, I know I'm not. Who is this third party, and what are they saying?"

"The good Reverend McClendon hired a private dick to look into Melanie's death, not too long after she was found. The guy didn't come up with a lot, but his impression of Melanie was very different than yours."

"Yeah," Reiman said. "I remember the guy. What did he say?"

"Said Melanie had been a good woman, but a bad girl. Said he thought she'd been repressed by her mother. That when she got out on her own, she went a little wild. Indulged in some risky behavior, and ultimately she paid the price."

Reiman was shaking his head. "Bullshit," he said. "No fucking way. Besides, Mel wasn't repressed. She was just a late bloomer. No way."

"You remember anything else about the guy? The ex-cop investigator that talked to you."

He thought for a moment. "It isn't fair for me to talk about him, I only met him that one time, but . . ."

"Do it anyway," I told him.

He shook his head. "Cops always think the worst about you," he said. "It's just how they are. Nobody likes that."

I GOT A call from Klaudia. "I checked into that flophouse you told me about," she said. "Down on Tenth. The building is owned by a holding company that turns out to be the Diocese of New York. Huge company, got stuff everywhere, they seem to like to buy and hold for the long term. I called them up and talked to one of their property managers. I would bet they don't have much to do with anything that goes on there. I mean, yeah, they own it, but it's like one tiny piece of a big picture. Lady I talked to said they had a number on the books for it, meaning, someone comes along and offers them more than they have it valued for, they'd sell. The lease on the upper floors is held by Gelman and Gold, LLC. They're pretty small, they got some warehouses in Queens, the building on Tenth is the only residential property they have. Lease for the bottom floor is held by Shield Investments, which is an incorporated proprietorship owned by a guy named Francis O'Neill. I assume it's a guy, although I suppose Francis could be a woman."

"Or a mule," I said. "Gelman and Gold, that's gotta be Shmuley's uncle, who's in Israel. You suppose the Diocese of New York knows that someone's running a cathouse out of one of their buildings?"

"You know, the same thing occurred to me, so I when I talked to their property manager, I asked. She got a little huffy. Said they probably had thieves and adulterers in every property they owned."

"Some people got no sense of humor. You talk to anyone at Shield?"

"No," she said. "Number I got for them connects you with an answering machine, says please don't leave a message, text your issues to a second number. I texted my number to them but nobody called me back, not yet." She gave me the phone numbers, and I texted Shield Investments, told them I wanted to discuss the property on Tenth.

JENNY SOO WAS a freelancer who wrote mostly for Chinese-language newspapers, but she'd gotten a story about Mao's legacy in the Daily News, which was how I found her e-mail address. She agreed to see me and I met her in Flushing, in that same McDonald's where I'd had coffee with Annabel Wing just days before. Jenny was on the short side, and chubby, with a round face, bright eyes, and a quick smile. It was midmorning in Queens, and the usual mad currents of humanity swirled all around us: halal street vendors, an old man in a blue turban selling papers, a fat white guy in an MTA inspector's uniform, an old black lady carrying a Macy's shopping bag that was almost as big as she was, Falun Gong protestors setting up a gruesome display about the black market in human organs, all right there on the sidewalk outside the windows. Every minute or so it seemed that the whole cast of characters changed, but there was something timeless about the way it all flowed by while we sat there inside Mickey D's. "Thanks for seeing me," I said.

"How can I help you?" She had the bubbly sort of personality you don't often see in a reporter, and I guessed if she stayed in the business she'd lose it before long.

"What can you tell me about the Green Pang Tribe? I understand that's the tong that sort of runs this part of Queens."

The lights in her eyes dimmed with caution, or maybe it was fear. "Are you in trouble, here?" she said.

"Not yet," I told her. "But I expect I will be soon." I told her about Melanie, and about Annabel Wing's murder. She was shaking her head before I finished.

"This doesn't sound like them," she said. "Not to me. Green Pang is super-organized. They are all about discipline. Nothing gets done without permission, and a high-profile killing of a civilian is completely opposed to everything they believe in. If Annabel Wing, or her daughter, had done anything to merit this kind of response from the Green Pang, she would have simply disappeared. Completely. Or she'd have suffered an apparent heart attack. You have to understand, Mr. Fowler, these guys are not cowboys. They've been doing business for centuries. Maybe not in Queens, I'll give you that, but they come from a very old tradition. The Green Pang is about money, first and foremost, and they handle their business quietly. And they are extremely good at what they do. I'm surprised, frankly, that you've heard about them at all."

"Okay. What about the Mott Street Merchants Association?"

She eyeballed me for a moment before she answered. She may have been a reporter, but she was obviously uncomfortable with my chosen subject matter. "The same answers would apply, for the most part. Although there are some subtle differences."

"Like what?"

She looked away and swallowed, then came back to me. "Green Pang is run by a guy named Li Fat. Rumor has it that there are a bunch of warrants out on him, but I don't know that for a fact. He hasn't been seen in public for years now, but I don't know if anyone is trying all that hard to find him."

"What about Mott Street?"

"Chinatown," she said, looking at me sideways. "Downtown

Manhattan. Run by Peter Kwok. Kwok took over when his father died. At the time, no one thought Peter would last a month."

"Too soft?"

"Not at all," she said, and she glanced around. "Peter has a reputation . . . They say he is unstable, and short-tempered. A Chinese man without patience will be thought of as a baby. Immature, weak. So everyone thought that the old men would take him out, but that never happened. Not yet." She stared down at the table between us. "Annoying Peter Kwok is not something anyone is liable to do more than once."

"Okay. Say someone in either organization had a kink of some sort. A problem dealing with women, for example . . ."

"Violent, you mean. Toward women in general?"

I nodded.

"Long term," she said, "I'd say that man's prospects for survival would be very poor. Maybe if he kept it quiet, and buried . . ." She thought about it some, then shook her head. "These are very traditional men, Mr. Fowler. Very conservative. They frown on individuality. I can't see them tolerating much of that sort of deviant behavior in the ranks. And if a body turned up? Publicly? Forget it."

"Okay. Last question. Any outsiders in the ranks?"

She just shook her head.

"You couldn't picture any of these guys working side by side with someone from, say, Mexico?" Or Haiti . . .

"Never. Do business, sure. But work together? On the same team? Not on your life."

Disappointing, to say the least. "But they would have no problem working with a crooked cop."

"Of course not," she said, grinning. "Where you been?"

I grinned back, thinking of the tree I was about to shake.

THE BUILDING WAS not far from the Whitestone Expressway, it was mixed in with the junkyards, chop shops, and taxi garages of Willets Point. It was a bus garage, a big empty barn of a building with a fenced-in parking lot out behind. I watched it for hours, sitting in a few different vantage points. No one seemed to pay me the slightest attention. I was, it seemed, the only unemployed person hanging around, everyone else was busy, nobody looked like they had any time to contemplate me or what I was doing. Late in the afternoon, when the buses started coming back to the garage, I decided I'd waited long enough.

The first driver I approached was around forty, looked more or less like a guy who sat on his ass for a living. "Excuse me, sir," I said, walking up to the guy as he headed up the sidewalk, away from the garage. "I wonder if I could talk to you for a minute."

"What?" the guy said, guarded. "I ain't buying nothing."

"I'm not selling anything. Do you work for the bus company?"

"No," he said, "I just went in there to use the men's room. Take a hike, buddy." The guy turned his back on me, walked up the hill, got into a car and drove away.

I tried again a few minutes later, I walked up to a thin, gray-haired white guy but he just ignored my questions and walked away. A third guy did exactly the same thing. Funny, I thought, when none of the guys working at a place want to bash the management. It ain't natural.

An ancient, bald-headed Chinese guy came out of the building carrying a push broom. It was an open question whether he was holding up the broom or vice versa. I watched him sweep the sidewalk and driveway in front of the building. I kept trying, approaching the bus drivers as they headed out for home, and I got nowhere. I finally got a response of more than two sentences; it came from a stocky middle-aged black guy who looked like he could be bad news if you pushed him too far.

"You a reporter?" the guy demanded. "You tryina dig up some dirt? You barkin' up the wrong tree. You don't like gooks, that what ya problem is? Lemme tell ya somethin', asshole, them are good people up in there. Lemme see you try ta get a decent job when ya got a coupla felonies on ya sheet. Don't matter none, you got ya GED and ya CDL, ya kissed ya parole officer's twat fa two fuckin' years and ya go ta church every muthafuckin' Sunday, okay, let's see you find a gig where ya make more than minimum. Okay? So fuck you. Them are good people in there, they know how ta treat a man like a man. So tell ya story walkin'."

I liked him. Good to see a guy with some backbone, a guy who knew the meaning of loyalty. Still, I found the whole thing perplexing, on two levels. First, it was odd that not one of the guys I tried to talk to would bitch about his job, and second, I had really expected a couple of hard cases to come strolling out of the garage and tell me to bounce before I got hurt. I walked up closer to the place, considered going inside, but what that would accomplish I didn't know, apart from scaring the dispatcher and whoever else was in there. The old guy with the broom looked like he was about finished, so I decided to give him a shot. "Hello, Gramps," I said. "You speak English?"

"Hello yourself," the guy said, straightening up a little. "Yeah, my English is okay, seeing how I was born in King's County Hospital."

"Sorry. Seemed like a valid question."

"Nuttin' to it," the guy said. His accent was homegrown New York. "You lookin' for a job? You gotta go inside and fill out a application."

"No, I don't want a job. Besides, driving a bus in New York City traffic sounds like my idea of hell."

The old man nodded. "Kinda like bein' the fattest guy on the dance floor."

"What I'm looking for is some information about the bus company."

The old man shrugged. "What's to know? Sign up forty, fifty a ya closest friends, youse can all ride down to Atlantic City together. Okay? Now you know everything."

"I heard this place was owned and run by one of the tongs."

The old man shook his head. "Tongs? Are you for fuckin' real? All my life I lived in this city and I still can't get past the Chans."

"What Chans?"

"Charlie and Jackie. Buddy, this is only a bus company. You already talked to about half the drivers, I seen ya. Inside there you got three mechanics and a oiler, all of 'em too fat and outa shape to hit you with a karate chop. Pork chop, be more likely. You got two office ladies, one of 'em is pretty mean, I'll give ya that, but I still don't think you got nothin' to worry about. I think you could take her. And you got the dispatcher, worst he could do is maybe run over ya foot with his wheelchair, and you got the manager, who's dumber than a box a rocks. And you got me. That's the whole story."

"Now I am disappointed."

"Why?" the old guy said. "You was expectin' a fight? You lookin' to take a beatin'? That's ya thing, it's okay by me, but ya wastin' ya time around here. I hoid they got a place over in the Village, fa fifty bucks a naked girl will tie ya up and slap the shit outa ya. Sounds like a gas ta me but I don't think my ticker would hold up."

"Some other time, maybe. You ever hear of a girl named Melanie Wing?"

"Melanie Wing?" He scratched his head. "Melanie Wing. I don't think so. Knew Dickie Wing, him and his brother Raymond used ta bootleg cigarettes up from Virginia someplace, but I think they're both inside."

"You sound like you got a million stories."

"Million and a half," he said.

"I should come over here and buy you lunch sometime. You can tell me all about the old days."

He shrugged. "I ain't hard ta find," he said. "Just look for this broom, you'll prolly find me on one end of it."

IT FELT LIKE a wasted day.

I went down to Avenue C and looked at the Los Paraíso but I couldn't think of a reason to go inside. I stopped in the bodega across the street, got a cup of that Puerto Rican coffee. Once is an experiment, twice is an affectation, but three times implies a commitment. One more and I would have to find out how to make the stuff myself, carry the pot and the makings with me. Maybe, though, it would turn out to be one of those things tied to a certain place and time. Maybe, once I got away from Avenue C, it would lose its power and I wouldn't want it anymore.

"Vale," a voice said, pronouncing the word oddly, almost as though I had done a poor job laying out someone's suits. "We t'ought you gone, man."

It was the Worm, and the guy had cat feet, I had not heard him coming. To find him behind me, unexpected and very close, was perturbing, but I tried to sound normal when I answered him. "Still around," I said. "Why do you care about what I do?"

He came around my left side, stood there staring out across the avenue in the direction of the hotel. "What gods did we piss off," he said, "to draw a snake like you into our little garden?"

"From what I hear, you're something of a god yourself."

He laughed softly. "Believers think," he said, "that when it rain, got to be someone to make it rain. Funny, no? Between god and da weatherman, listen to da weatherman."

"So it's wrong, then. They tell me you are shadowed by Ogun."

"Believe what you want, I don't care," he said. "But you should know that Chang and Eng want you dead."

"Chang and Eng? You mean, your partners. That what you call them? So how come you haven't killed me yet?"

He stood silent for a moment, staring at the cars passing by. "Hector maybe miss you," he said, finally.

"Hector. The five-year-old that stands in the hall outside his mother's door."

He shook his head. "Listen to me, vale. I take dere money." I could feel his eyes boring into the side of my head. "You ever done that? Sell your soul to another man?"

Dick Plover's fat and rosy face popped into my mind. "Yeah."

"Den you know," the Worm said. "Dere are times, you wanna live, you do your job. Do you know what I'm saying?"

"You're telling me you and me ain't going to the ball game together any time soon?"

"I mean, if you got any sense, do what you got to do, and get lost."

"I'll try to remember that."

"I had a sister once myself," he said. A moment passed, and his words hung between us. The cabs on Avenue C steamed past, dueling in a ritual form of automotive combat. So he knew about Melanie. I wondered how. "It wasn't me. And the two Chinamen would not lower themselves."

"Is that so."

"We never touch her," he said. "I knew her, I admit it. But she was pure, vale, not like us, not like you and me. She could look at a man and make him sorry for not washing his hands and brushing his teeth like he should. She walk down da street over dere and all of us, man and boy, we look down when she pass, promise ourselves to be better from now on. Took a special kind of evil to touch that."

I had stopped breathing.

"Yeah?" I finally said. "You know anybody that evil?"

"Who could tell? A man like that, he hide his blackness behind a white veil. Was a priest in Cap Haitien, where I was born. Best priest in Haiti. Fed the poor. Cure the sick. Walk on water, maybe. But if you was a small child, you don't wan to be the girl who bring him his shirt, pick up the dirty ones." He grabbed a handful of his crotch. "He was so big, down there, that sometimes the girls died. No one ever find out what he done with the bodies."

"What happened to him?"

The Worm sighed. "One night, my father and my uncles, they come to his house and they bring him out. They pull two car tire down over his head." He stood stiffly, his arms clasped at his sides, unconsciously pantomiming his memories. "You know. Gasoline inside the tires. He scream, vale, after they light him up, but not like a man. And in the hills outside of town, the loups-garous hiding there hear him screaming while he burned, and they howl back, all that night. He was one of theirs."

"Loups-garous?"

"Werewolves."

"You believe in that?"

He shrugged. "There was a special kind of evil in the hills around Cap Haitien. Simple people had to give it a name." He glanced over at me. "But they make him pay, for what he did to my sister. And the rest of them."

I remembered something I'd been wondering about. "What does 'vale' mean?"

He blinked, surprised, perhaps, that I hadn't bothered to look it up. "Thief," he said. "They say this is what you are. No?"

"Not exactly," I said. "I'm really just a contractor."

He chuckled softly. "Too bad," he said. "Don't forget what I tell you." He walked away, then, crossed Avenue C without waiting for the light, and the cabs parted like water in a stream to let him pass.

I was tempted to believe him. Sure, he was in a bad business, and there was little doubt in my mind that he colored outside the lines, but still, I got the impression that he had his code, that there were lines he wouldn't cross. A lot of guys in his line of work will do anything, say anything to get what they want, but most politicians are like that and no one is surprised by it. What bothered me most about the conversation was not the implied threat to my person, but his impression of Melanie. She was an unfallen angel, according to the Worm, although I had to admit that his judgment might be skewed, somewhat, by his line of work. Maybe to a guy like him, a girl who didn't sleep with farm animals qualified as pure, or relatively so. But all my instincts had been pointing me at the Hotel Los Paraíso, and I had to wonder if all my instincts, and all my theories, too, had been wrong.

And then I thought of what he'd called me. "Vale," thief. Called me that the first time he saw me. I wondered who told him that.

Chapter Twelve

THERE WAS A flea market in Greenwich Village, and idle curiosity drew me in. There were people selling bongs, terrariums, tie-dyed shirts, old manual typewriters, cheesy jewelry, collectibles . . . I suppose you could consider anything collectible, the question is, why? Anyway, I bought a camera, an SLR from the predigital age. The thing came with a long lens and an auto-winder. It was in great shape apart from some scratches on the lens, and totally useless. The camera reefed and snapped but I didn't know where you'd ever find film for it, or where you'd send the film to be developed into pictures. The vendor told me all about how rare and valuable it would be someday and why it was therefore worth the perfectly reasonable price he was asking. I told him how its only foreseeable useful employment would be as an oddly shaped doorstop to hold my screen door open so my cat could get out when he wanted to go take a shit. He offered to throw in the batteries and a shoulder strap, and I wound up giving him twenty-five bucks for it.

Such a deal.

That's how I came to have an antique camera slung around

my neck as I sat in a gypsy cab on Avenue C. I'd found a driver who was okay with an hourly rate, I think the guy was Bengali but it was hard to say for sure because he had a speech impediment to go along with his accent and incomplete grasp of the American language. He was a talkative guy, though, and my lack of comprehension did not seem to discourage him at all. He got all excited when the first girl came out of the Hotel Los Paraíso and got into a waiting limo. She was tall, thin, carried herself with a regal air. She was accompanied by one of the men who worked with the Worm and since I still suffered traces of the emotional hangover from the last time, we stayed put. Guy on a motorcycle pulled out and followed the limo. Nice bike, I think it was a Triumph T-Bird, but the guy looked too big for it. I wondered who the hell he was. Looked like he was from Kansas. I wondered what tornado had dropped a shitkicker like him in Manhattan's Alphabet City.

The next girl came out alone, and there was no limo waiting, just a yellow cab that stopped at her hail, so we followed her.

No cowboy, and no motorcycle.

I thought of them as girls, even though they were probably not all that much younger than I was. Ten or twelve years, maybe. The terms "hooker," "prostitute," and "sex worker" might have applied, but they felt a bit harsh to me, even unspoken. "Young adult who has made some seriously poor choices," although accurate, was too unwieldy. I had certainly made more than my own share of stupid choices, and since my continued survival sometimes felt attributable more to dumb-ass luck than to good judgment, who was I to look down my nose?

"Girl" would have to do.

All the girls from Los Paraíso were tall, it seemed.

The one we were following had brown hair framing her somewhat angular face, and although not conventionally beautiful, she was striking enough in her own way. Her cab delivered her to a giant hotel in midtown, and I followed her inside. I was just in time to see her shake hands with some guy in the hotel lobby. Neither of them seemed awkward or nervous in any way, they could have both been Bible salesmen for all anyone could tell. The guy was obviously prosperous, you could tell from the Cartier tank watch and the wardrobe, but he was overweight, thin on top, and sported an old-fashioned skinny mustache, the kind most men would only grow if they lost a bet. He seemed totally at ease, right up until the moment he noticed me pointing my empty camera at him, reefing and snapping, reefing and snapping. Funny how fast some fat guys can move when they want to, he ran like a man afflicted with a sudden and violent urge to void his bowels.

The girl turned and glared at me. "You asshole!"

Some guy wearing a hotel jacket was at my elbow a second or two later and he came on very strong. "I'm gonna have to confiscate that," he said. "No pictures on hotel property." He tried to move me but I wasn't moving. I handed him my camera.

"You really want this? Be a collectible someday. For twenty-five bucks it's all yours."

He stopped trying to push me and he took the camera, saw what it was, and scowled. "What the hell?"

I handed him a fifty. Hey, it was Manhattan. "No trouble here."

He backed away a step, glanced over at the girl, then handed the camera back to me, looked like a guy holding a dead rat by the tail. I took it and he sidled away, muttering. I walked over to the girl. "Did I cost you some money here? Because I'm good for it."

She waited just a heartbeat too long. "Sixteen hundred bucks."

"Sixteen? Really? I'm gonna guess the tab was eight hundred, and that you'd see four, max. Am I close?"

"What do you want," she said, eyeing the exit.

"I'll go five hundred, cash, for a half hour's private conversation."

"Yeah?" She hefted her bag, probably wondering if she could take me out with whatever she had in there.

"It won't come to that," I told her. "Just talking."

Her eyes narrowed and she hefted the bag again. "All right," she said.

The money first, naturally. We sat down at a table in a quiet corner of the hotel lobby and I passed over five crisp new hundreds. She stuck them in her bag and looked pointedly at where her watch would have been if she'd worn one. "Meter's running," she said.

"What do I call you?"

Her look was halfway between a sneer and a grimace. "Heather," she said.

"Did you know Melanie Wing?" I asked her.

"Yeah."

"What kind of person was she?"

She shrugged. "Do-gooder. Do this, don't do that, blah blah blah blah."

"Sounds like you didn't like her much."

She shrugged again. "She was all right. I didn't have no problems with her."

"How about your bosses? The Haitian and the two Chinese guys. They have any problems with her?"

"At first, yeah, they were like, what's your deal, what are you doing here, and all like that. After that, no. She didn't have no attitudes or nothing, you get what I'm saying. Just did her little nursey thing. Talked a couple of the girls into going home, or wherever."

"That didn't piss off the management?"

She shrugged. "Ain't that big a deal."

"If she had any problems with anyone on the street . . ."

"The Worm would have kicked their ass," she said flatly.

"Really."

"Yeah."

"She sleep with him?"

She shook her head. "Nah."

"How about the Chinese guys? She go with either of them?"

"Far as I know, she didn't crack that thing open for nobody."

Not what I expected, but that's why you ask the questions. "Do you live at Los Paraíso?"

"No."

"No? So where do you live? Can I ask?"

"You just did," she said. "I live in Delaware."

"No kidding. So, what, you drive in . . ."

She looked at me and sneered again, as if she found my interest in her life, as opposed to her ass, inexplicable, if not distasteful. "I usually work one week, take two off. So, yeah, I'll sleep at Los P six, seven nights, and then I go home."

"Your bosses okay with that?"

"Why would they give a shit?"

"So, you weren't forced into this, then."

She glared at me. "Whaddaya want? You want a sob story? You wanna hear how my old man molested me? How neglected I was and shit? What?"

"I'm not looking for stories. I just assumed, forgive me, that there's usually a certain amount of coercion in these situations."

She shrugged again. "Well, you would be wrong about that," she said. "But it ain't a union gig. Everybody has to make their own deal."

"So if the Worm and his bosses aren't holding you hostage, what's their function?"

"Make sure I don't get hurt. Make sure I get my money. Keep the cops happy."

Again, not exactly what I was expecting. "So they take care of you. They're not 'holding' your money for you, they're not pretending to be a bank."

"I get mine," she said. "Don't you worry. Heather's coming up on retirement pretty soon, baby."

"How much does it take to retire?"

"Two mil," she said, without hesitation.

"Wow. Okay. So everybody makes his own deal, nobody's there against their will . . ."

"That ain't what I said."

"Okay, maybe I heard you wrong. Talk to me."

"I'm an American," she said. "I do what I want. Some of the other girls, like the Ukrainians or whatever, they got expenses they gotta work off."

"What do you mean?"

She looked like she was starting to burn. "Okay. Say you live in Crotchnia or some shit, you got too many kids, you can't feed 'em all. One a your daughters, okay, let's say she's eleven or twelve, she's old enough so you know she's gonna be tall and not hard to look at, so you take her to town and you sell her. Now you got money to put gas in your tractor or some fucking shit. You starting to get it?" She was getting hotter. "And the buyer, okay, maybe he uses her, maybe he puts her to work or maybe he sells her up the line. Some of them wind up here."

"Nice. So some of the girls you work with . . ."

"I don't work with nobody."

"Some of the other girls at Los Paraíso, then."

She stared at me, almost as if she were daring me to have a human reaction. "Yeah."

"They're stuck," I said.

"No more than you."

"You think? Some of the girls don't have any choices, that's what you just told me."

"No," she said, some of the steam going out of her voice. "I guess they don't." A look crossed her face, it was almost like a spasm. I didn't say anything, I waited to see where she'd take it. "There's a girl from Seconal . . ."

"Seconal?"

"That's somewhere in Africa."

Oh . . . "Oh."

"Her uncle sold her to an Italian syndicate. They took her to Milan, worked her there for a few years, and then they sold her here. She speaks Italian, English and French, she's smart as shit. She's fucking high-end, man, the gooks paid a fortune for her. They'll never let her go. They might kill her, but they won't ever let her walk."

"Why would they want to kill her?"

"She's breaking the rules."

"So?"

"Client is just a client. Understand? He's not your friend, he's not your benefactor, he's not your business partner and he sure as shit ain't your fiancé."

"She fell in love."

"She fell all right."

"What's her name?"

"Aniri."

"Must be tough to be her. Okay, almost done. The Worm and the other two, any of them have problems with women? Some kind of kink?"

"What would you call a kink," she said, but then she went on. "Nah. You know what, when you work in a candy store, after a while you get sick of it, you know what I'm saying. And I like what I do, don't get me wrong, but I got no desire for any of those guys, so we're all like, you know, don't put yourself out none on my account."

"So you don't know anyone who would've wanted to hurt Melanie Wing."

"No," she said, looking down at her lap.

"Any cops associated with the enterprise?"

She glared at me. "You already got your money's worth."

Aha. "Do I take that for a yes?"

"Take it for whatever the fuck you want. That's none of my business, I do my job, management does theirs. I don't know nothing I don't need to know."

All in all, aside from making the fat guy run away, I had to admit that I was disappointed in the whole transaction. "Thank you, Heather. Take care of yourself."

"Believe it," she said, and I noticed that she had one hand inside her bag and that the thing was pointed in my general direction. "You mess with me and I will fill you fulla holes, right here and right now."

Yeah, sure. Easy enough to demonstrate the problems with that assumption, but I saw no profit in arguing the point. If a piece in her handbag made her feel safer . . . "Good luck on your retirement."

She stared at me for another second. She had this look on her face, it was almost as if she wanted to sneer at me again, but she couldn't, because she didn't know what I was. Maybe her opinions about men had gotten too set, too often reinforced by every new guy she did business with, and I didn't fit her preconceptions. I suppose I found that comforting.

She stood up and stalked out.

IT FELT LIKE I was running out of options, so I decided to give the Green Pang Tribe another go. Found out they upped their game.

I was camped out just uphill from the bus garage, and four guys, none of them what you would call young, made their way in my direction. They didn't seem overtly hostile, even though one of them had a pistol. He carried it discreetly in his jacket pocket but he made sure I saw it before he tucked it back out of sight. "Mr. Fowler," he said. He stayed back out of range, which meant I would't be able to attack his weapon unless he got close, and he seemed too smart for that. The other three kept their distance, as well.

"Don't tell me," I said. "You'd like me to go away."

"My employer would like the opportunity to have a private word with you," he said.

"The bus company wants to talk to me?"

He permitted himself a small smile. "I am not a bus driver, Mr. Fowler."

"Well, then we got a problem. See, out here on Willets Point Road, I ain't afraid of your gun. In under cover, though, there's too much chance of something bad happening. You know what I mean?"

He gestured with his non-gun hand. "I didn't come to fight."

"Really."

"Mr. Fowler. I was told you wanted to talk." He nodded down the hill, in the general direction of the bus garage. "Your opportunity awaits." He grinned. "You wanna do this, you're gonna have to have some balls."

Prick. "Fine. All right." I glanced at his compatriots. "Nobody behind me."

He looked at the other three and nodded, and they walked down the hill in front of us, then he and I followed. It was like a dance, almost, he and I each aware of every step the other took, each nuance of movement carrying its own message. I'm not sure what my body English was telling him but it was clear to me that his intention was to get me inside that garage without getting either of us jammed up. We did okay until we got right up to the building, but once I got close to the cavernous maw of roll-up doors fronting the comparatively gloomy interior, I became less comfortable with the whole idea. I still didn't think he'd use the pistol, not out in the sunlight, but inside the garage it'd be another equation altogether. The other three were still keeping away from the two of us, if I wanted to try for the gun I might have had three or four seconds to disable him before any of them could interfere.

The old man with the push broom limped out and stood blinking in the sun. My friend with the pistol nodded to him, then turned his back and walked off to lean on a parked car. I looked over at the old guy, he was wearing a janitor's green uniform, with cotton work gloves and running shoes that looked a couple sizes too big for him. "You gotta be kidding me."

The old man shrugged. "Best place to hide something," he said, "is out in plain sight."

"You're Li Fat?"

"I decline to answer that question, your honor, on account of it ain't nobody's fucking business. What can I do for you, Mr. Fowler?"

I racked my brain, trying to remember if I'd told him my name when I met him last time. "You have good sources."

"Information is the lifeblood of all business," he said. "Yeah, I know who you are. I just can't figure out what the fuck you want."

I sighed. It bothered me, every time I had to go into this. "I had a half sister, I guess you might have known her after all. Melanie Wing."

"Yeah, Melanie. We knew her." He kicked at a pebble on the ground. "She was your sister? Can we go inside and sit down? My back is killing me."

I hesitated.

"Come on, Fowler, what the fuck. It's us that ought to be worried about you. We got a lotta flammable shit up in here. I was told you blew up a fuel dump outside of Sarajevo. That true?"

Sometimes the reason for an incursion isn't to take something away, but to leave something behind . . . "I respectfully decline to answer your question, counselor," I told him. "That was an accident. Lead the way."

THE GARAGE WAS relatively empty, almost all the buses being out on their appointed rounds. They had a ready room for the drivers, it had a couple of folding tables, a scattering of mismatched chairs, some vending machines, and a small kitchenette. A Hispanic kid was inside pretending to clean up. "Jimmy," Li Fat said. "Give us a few minutes here, willya?" He fished in his pants pocket, came out with a five. "Go have a cup of coffee someplace."

The kid accepted the five. "Yes, boss."

"Coffee," Li Fat said, pointing at the kid. "No beer. No ser vesa, pendejo."

"I promise, boss," the kid said, and he departed in haste.

"Fuckin' kids," Li Fat said. He gripped the edge of one of the tables and lowered himself into a chair. "Park it," he said.

I sat down across from him. Li Fat peered at me. "The guy who got Annabel in trouble," he said. "He the connection here? He your father?"

I sighed. "That's my current misunderstanding."

Li shrugged. "These things happen. He do any better by you than he did for Melanie?"

"No."

"I watched her grow up, you know."

"Melanie?"

He glared at me. "Who the fuck we talking about? Anyway, she was our unofficial mascot for a while. Everybody loved her. The office people, all the drivers, you name it. Some a them desperadoes we had driving back then, they woulda walked on hot coals for that little girl. I still can't believe anyone woulda wanted to hurt her."

"Annabel gave me the impression that she believed that one

of you did it. Either one of your guys or someone from the Mott Street group."

Fat grimaced in discomfort and hitched himself up straighter in his chair. "If I thought one of mine killed her," he said, "I'd have his fuckin' cock nailed to the wall, I fuckin' promise you that." He sounded like he meant it. "Listen, when Annabel first come out here she asked us to watch her back, and we did it. Tell you the truth, nobody showed much interest."

"What about the other side? What about Peter Kwok? Annabel thought he might have wanted to get back at her, and poke his thumb in your eye at the same time."

"Why would he bother? Because she was with us? I ain't buyin' it, Fowler. Vendetta is a Latin thing, it don't translate into Chinese all that well. I ain't in the Peter Kwok fan club, okay, but I can tell you one thing about him, and you can bet your fuckin' house on it: Kwok is a capitalist. What he's interested in is making money. You think he's gonna put his whole business and all his money at risk to hit some chickadee because she crossed the river to go to school in his backyard? I don't see it. Not even if you paid him. Too much risk, not enough payoff. Suppose you went to Kwok right now, today, told him you wanted to pay him to take out some guy for you. How much money do you think it would take? Half a million? Those guys clear that in a month. Why would he put his cash flow at risk for some stupid low-rent shit like that?"

"Annabel seemed very sure."

"That ain't about us," he said. "That's about her."

"I don't understand."

He shifted uncomfortably in his chair again. "Old-fashioned girl," he said. "She dishonored her family, so she thought. Once, by givin' it up to a white guy. A second time, by gettin' knocked up and having the kid, and a third time by movin' over here. I mean, she didn't work for us or nothin', but in her mind she was a turncoat. She never got over being ashamed. But that was her thing, man, not ours. This is America, for crissake, who really gives a fuck about alla that old country shit? Not me, and not Peter Kwok, neither. Listen, her parents weren't exactly right off the boat. Even if they were pissed, okay, alls she hadda do was take that baby over the house one time and let them see her. Her old lady woulda took one look at Mel, I'm tellin' you right now, pissed or not, it woulda been over, right there. And I told Annabel what I'm tellin' you, right when she got home from the hospital, and I wasn't the only one." He shook his head. "People are fucked up, man. She could never see any other way except what she knew. What she thought she knew. She was raised traditional, and she thought she was tainted. And she never had another guy, not since Mel's father. As hot as she was? How fucked up is that? But she was a true believer. Do you know what that means?"

"Yeah. Means logic doesn't apply. Don't confuse me with facts."

"That was Annabel, she knew what she knew and she didn't wanna hear nothin' different. Even if it didn't make no fuckin' sense to anyone else."

"What can you tell me about Melanie?"

He looked away from me while he thought about it. "Earth shoes," he finally said. "Vanilla chai with soy milk. Feed the fuckin' pigeons. Walk to cure this, run to cure that. NPR. Eat the rich. Save the children, and the whales." He stared at me then, his eyes two black holes in an empty face. "I ain't talkin' politics here. She didn't mean nothin' bad by it, that's just who she was. I grew up on the street, Fowler. You see me right here? This is me, this is what I grew into. I don't know where you grew up, but I see you sittin' right here too, muthafucka, so you ain't all that different from me. Okay? But Melanie grew up right on that street out there. And she managed to turn into a good person." He stared at me a moment. "You on Facebook?"

"No."

"Me neither. 'Ooh, be my friend, like me, like me . . .' Mel was never all that hung up on whether or not you liked her, but she really wanted to like you. There's a big fuckin' difference there."

"I get it. She have any bad habits that you knew about?"

"Yeah, givin' her money to bums." He sighed and shook his head. "I'm not sayin' she was perfect. I kept waitin' for her to break out, you know what I'm sayin'. Follow the Dead for a year, sleep with the horn section or some damn thing. I kept thinkin' she'd come around, that eventually she'd wind up doing what me or you woulda done. But that's not who she was."

"You must have a theory."

"Okay, you wanna know what I think, I think it was probably one a those random things. I think she was walkin' home some night, some sick fuck seen her and he had to have her. And they'll never make him for it."

"Yeah," I said. "I heard that theory. A cop told me the guy will keep it up until his number comes up."

Li Fat spread his hands out, palms up, eloquently expressing his agreement. "Which don't make either one of us happy."

"Do you think it would be a waste of time for me to try to talk to Peter Kwok?"

He laughed at me. "You sure you wanna stick your neck out that far? Kwok's a fuckin' head case." He scratched his chin. "Thing about the guy is this," he said. "The man's got his hands full right about now. Having a hard time keepin' his kids in line. You don't want him comin' down on you just to show them all what a hardass he can be when he wants to. I tell you what, I'll make a call for you. Tell my man Brian to give you his number, I'll have him back you up." He grinned. It was a predator's smile. "Just to keep everybody honest."

"Brian the one with the piece?"

Li Fat nodded. "Good luck," he said. "Whoever the guy is, I hope you get him. Give me a couple days to set it up with Kwok."

Chapter Thirteen

GELMAN WAS IN his cubicle. I got the impression he was pissed off but I went on by, climbed those creaking stairs up to my floor. As usual, Hector was doing his lonely sentry duty outside his mother's door. I tried to smile at him on the way past but it was asking a lot and I don't think I pulled it off. Eyes on your own paper, I told myself. Quit worrying about the kid, you can't help him.

Inside my room, I sat down, powered up the laptop, and scanned through the new video feeds. The only thing of interest that I found was some footage of the Worm and his two Chinese pals having an argument. The sound was too degraded for me to tell what they were fighting about but it seemed clear that none of them could agree with either of the other two. And right in the middle of it all, one of the Chinese dudes made a phone call, and whoever answered, they all argued with him, too. It was the first time I was seeing the Chinese guys without the shades and hoodies, and maybe it was me getting old, I didn't know, but they both seemed way too young to be doing this. There was some footage of Heather, too, the girl I'd met in the hotel in midtown. It appeared that she might be the one I'd seen on my first night at Los Paraíso, the one I saw passed out in bed from my perch on the fire escape. It wasn't easy to tell for sure but it looked like she swallowed a couple of capsules and went off to lie down. Maybe she was less at ease with her career choices than she wanted me to believe. And maybe I should have used better equipment, too, so I could hear and see clearly what was going on instead of merely guessing at it, but then again the whole enterprise was starting to look like a waste of my time and Mac's money, anyhow. It took me a couple of hours to finish going through the new files, and when I was done, I dumped them all.

I thought back to that first assault, back when the two kids had followed me up onto the rooftops. I'd figured that it meant something at the time, but now I was beginning to think it was nothing more than a lame attempt by the Worm and his buddies to run me off. I made them uncomfortable and they wanted me to go away, but I get that a lot. It didn't mean they had anything to do with Melanie's death. Besides, the goons they'd sent after me weren't exactly varsity.

The setup at Annabel's building, though, that felt like it came from an entirely different kind of douchebag. As I sat there thinking about it, I remembered feeling something brush against my face as I entered the hallway behind her security door. Probably a trip wire of some kind, but it had been so fine and I had been so distracted that I hadn't thought to stop and look for it. And they got my prints on a water glass in her kitchen sink. A water glass had gone missing out of my bathroom. Planted evidence, a bad cop's best friend . . .

I felt confident that both Li Fat and the Green Pang Tribe had the money and the smarts to put something like that together, and I was equally sure that both of them had cops on their pay-roll, but Li Fat hadn't really shown a lot of interest in what I was doing. I had a sinking feeling that Peter Kwok would be essentially the same, focused on his own business interests and not all that concerned with another casualty of the street. You know, Too bad about the girl, really. We done here? I tried to push that thought out of my head. Don't prejudge the guy, I told myself. Wait until you see him face to face, if that actually happens.

When it was finally time to go I walked across the room and stood still for a moment facing the inside of the door, wishing I could see through it so I would know if that goddamn kid was still out there in the hallway. Why are you so afraid of the kid, I asked myself.

You know why, an inner voice said.

I can't help him, I thought.

The voice did not reply and I stood there motionless, accused by the silence.

Really, I thought. Whatever he needs, I don't have it.

This is stupid, I thought, and after another minute I opened the door, rattled the outside doorknob to make sure it was locked, and stepped out into the hall.

No Hector.

I felt a wave of relief wash over me, followed swiftly by a subtle whiff of dismay. Am I so hollow, I wondered, that I can't even bear to look at the kid? But the truth was, Hector needed an answer and I didn't have one for him. I looked up at the dirty skylight far above my head. What do you want from me, I asked it. What am I supposed to do? And all of those voices, goonas, gods, the editorial committee, angels, spirits or demons, they were all silent. The earth spun on her axis, the solar system whirred like the guts of an ancient pocket watch, and the Milky Way, unseen by me, was just a small eddy in an unfathomably enormous stream. I tried to put Hector out of my head and I went down the creaking stairs.

SHMULEY GELMAN HAD gotten a haircut.

I'd missed it on the way up. He'd shaved, too, somewhat inexpertly; his face looked like it lost a fight with his razor. He was wearing a purple shirt, which clashed magnificently with his reddish hair, even in the dim light of the lobby of the Hotel Los Paraíso. I walked over and let myself into his cubicle. "Holy shit, Gelman. What happened?"

He turned to look at me, and he did not seem at all surprised that I'd gotten through his locked door. "You noticed," he said, scowling. "So far, you're only the second one."

"You expected the world to be different." I sat down in his soft chair. "You turn your life upside down, but when you step outside your front door, everything is just like it was. You thought the world would be shocked but then it goes about its business without giving you a second glance. Who else noticed?"

"Aniri," he said, looking at the floor. "One of the girls from upstairs. She didn't say anything, but I saw her looking at me, and she smiled. I think she knew."

"So what happened?"

He seemed to think about it for a moment, and then he hitched his chair around so that he was facing me instead of his window. He leaned over, put his elbows on his knees, and went back to staring at the floor. "He sent me another letter," he said.

"The arithmetic guy? The guy from NYU, that wrote the book?"

"Yes." Gelman nodded miserably. "But I got the letter this time. Before she did."

"She?"

"My mother." He infused the word with bitterness. "But she caught me reading it."

"Oh-oh."

He looked up at me, his face a study in pain. "I thought she would understand," he said. "Isn't she supposed to be on my side? She's my mother . . ."

"Because she's your mother, you think she's gonna look out for you?" I wasn't able to keep my face entirely neutral, but then again, Gelman had broadsided me. I realized, sitting there in his cubicle, that I hadn't ever talked about it, either. "Whatever gave you that idea?"

Gelman stared at me with an odd expression on his face. "Really? Was your mother as nuts as mine?" he said. "Tell me about her."

Man, I wasn't prepared for that. And the truth was, I had done my best to forget about her.

"I'm sorry," Gelman said. "I shouldn't have asked."

"No, it's all right." I stretched out in his chair, stuck my feet way out in front, leaned my head back. "She was very pretty when I was young. I remember brown curls in her hair, and white skin. She was very thin, back then. Still had all her own teeth."

"What happened?"

I swallowed. "She was a paranoid schizophrenic. She heard voices in the dark. And whenever the voices convinced her that someone was after her, you know, she'd pull me out of school and we'd wind up on another bus, on our way to some new town, someplace where nobody knew who she was, and she could start over again." I glanced over at him. I had Gelman's complete attention. "I mean, she probably did the best she could, but . . . So anyway, I was always the weird new kid in school. And I think the biggest thing I ever learned in school was how to take a punch."

"Came up short in arithmetic, though," Gelman said, and he managed a weak smile.

"Well, yeah, that and a few other things, too. I guess. But she taught me. Read to me when she could. Although you had to be careful what kind of book it was. I mean, if it was sci-fi or fantasy or whatever, I'd lose her, she'd wig right out. But she tried to teach me what she knew."

Gelman nodded at his cubicle door. "She teach you how to open locks?"

"No. I picked that up that later on. But you know what, Shmuley, she did what she could. She gave me what she had to give. You know what I mean? If you really need a buck from your mother but all she's got is a quarter, the quarter is all you get. You ain't gonna do no better. Your mother is probably about the same. Maybe she gave you her quarter, and that's all there is."

"Yes, but . . ." He shook his head, decided not to say what he'd been thinking. "You're no dummy. How'd you get your education?"

"She gave me away once, and I got most of it then, I think. And I read a lot."

"Whoa. Wait. She gave you away? You mean she left you with relatives or whatever?"

"No. It was more like what happens when your dog has puppies. 'Hey, mister, you want a puppy? Your kids will love him.' Like that. So I got through a couple years of high school, for what it was worth. But mostly I got my education the way you got yours." I pointed at his pile of math tomes. "On my own. But during my stretch in high school, I felt like I was getting close, you know what I mean? I felt like I had almost figured out what I was supposed to be doing, but then she came back and got me and we were off and running again."

"What kind of stuff did you read?" he said.

"Not a lot of math," I told him. "I seemed to gravitate to what-the-fuck books."

"What? You read what kind of books?"

I nodded. "What-the-fuck books. Isn't that the real question? Like, what's the real point? Yeah, so I worked my way through guys like Alan Watts, Suzuki, Thomas Merton, Stephen Hawking, Sun Tzu, Karen Armstrong, Harris, Peck, and on and on, anyone who was trying to answer the question. Does it matter what you do? Are we missing something? Is it all gonna make sense, one of these days?"

"You're asking the wrong question," Gelman said, and he stared at me. "The right one is, are we simply biochemical phenomena, or are we something more? Everything else is inferred."

"I think that's just the smart person way of saying it."

"Those books you read," he said. "Did any of them teach you anything?"

"Malcolm X."

"Really? What'd he say?"

"To be honest with you, I can't remember what he said, I only remember what I heard."

"Which was . . ."

"There's nobody looking out for you. Nobody's gonna take care of you. If you sit around and wait for a handout, or even a hand up, you're gonna be sitting there a long fucking time. If you want something, if there's something out there that you wanna do with yourself, better get up off your ass and get after it. And, like I said, I don't know if that's what he said, but that's what I heard."

Gelman thought about that for a while. He looked up, eventually. "What happened to your mother?"

"Crack. She got to where she'd take anything that would make the voices go away for a while, but when she wasn't high her paranoia got a lot worse. I mean, a lot worse. She tried to kill me once, and she came a little too close so I took off. And not too long after I was gone, she did kill someone. Some john picked her up, I guess she'd been too long between rocks and she thought he was trying to take over her mind, so she cut him. She's locked away now, she's in a prison hospital up outside of Boston."

"Do you ever go to see her? Does she know who you are?"

"Oh, she knows who I am all right. She thinks her whole life is all my fault. Wasn't for me, she'da got everything she ever wanted. What did your professor say, the math guy that wrote to you?"

"Why didn't I answer his first letter," Gelman said. "Can I come to see him. Actually, I have an appointment to go by his office on Saturday."

"Wow. Really? Saturday? Are you serious?" That was a hell of a step for a so-recently Orthodox kid.

"Yes," he said, staring at me with his jaw clenched. "And I'm going. I don't want to blow this on account of some bullshit superstition." It was the first time I ever heard him swear. "Of course, that's assuming I have the courage to actually go, when Saturday comes. You think God will hate me for this?"

He was overreacting, and I got why, I understood. If he lived long enough, he might have the chance to revisit the whole mess, but for the time being he was going to be pissed off. "Can't imagine why she would," I told him. "But you still have a job?"

"So far," he said. "I don't see anybody lining up outside to take it."

"You got a place to sleep?"

He nodded at the chair I was sitting in.

"You got another key to my room upstairs? Use it if you need to, I ain't sleeping here."

"Thank you," he said. "How long are you staying?"

"I'm not sure. But listen, if you need company on Saturday, I'll walk across town with you. I'm not gonna say I know how you feel, but I do know what alone feels like."

The tension bled out of him and he sort of deflated in his chair. For a second I thought he was going to cry, but he just wiped his nose on the sleeve of his purple shirt. "Thank you," he said. "And for the use of your room, too. Those guys upstairs, did they do what you thought they did?"

"We'll find out shortly."

I WATCH FOR cops, pretty much all the time.

Maybe it's a function of my profession, I don't know, but I'd always assumed that any interaction between the police and myself carried too much potential for ill and too little for good, so I've always kept an eye out. I'd done it for so long that I suppose I'd stopped being conscious of it long ago, but I am rarely surprised by policemen, whether it be driving, walking around the city, or in the pursuit of my chosen profession. I walked through the front door of my hotel over on the West Side and I saw them before they saw me. I was back out through the hotel's front door before they could react. One of them was Sal Edwards, the guy who came to talk to me in lockup.

I melted back into the New York City night.

I suppose a normal citizen would have been willing to talk. Although I don't know this for a fact, I assume that a regular guy, comfortable in the knowledge that he hadn't done much of anything wrong, would figure that he was safe enough. He might even think that the cops were on his side, and would treat him fairly.

I harbored no such delusions.

They'd already put me inside for something I hadn't done, and they'd probably do it again if they could. It's like a parent who beats his kid even when he's not sure of the kid's guilt, operating on the assumption that the kid must have done something, somewhere along the line, and so deserved to get his ass kicked either way. That had always been my mother's working hypothesis.

No wonder I had problems with authority.

I sought refuge in the back corner of a coffee shop a block or so away. Something I'd heard years ago in a 12-step meeting somewhere came into my mind, you could call it an aphorism, although I'd always preferred to think of that stuff as new age bumper sticker psychobabble bullshit. 'Nothing will change until it becomes what it is.' I probably sneered at it at the time, but I finally understood, maybe, some of what the guy was saying. So long as I kept on pretending that I was okay, that I was coping with my situation, I would not be able to do much of anything to change it in any meaningful way. It came to me then that I needed to do what every successful enterprise must do from time to time. I needed to take inventory.

To begin with, I was still pretty shaky about who had murdered Melanie Wing. I had to admit that I'd zoned in on the Hotel Los Paraíso, specifically the Worm and his two Chinese pals. I mean, they looked so guilty . . . And yeah, they'd probably been behind that first halfhearted attempt to scare me away, but from their point of view that could be seen as nothing more than normal prudence. How they'd gotten on to me so quickly, though, that was still puzzling. It was like they knew I was coming before I even showed up.

Next, the ex-cop PI Josh Whelen and his tall, skinny, ex-detective pal hadn't come up with much, either. Two guys who were, unlike myself, professional investigators, looked into Melanie's murder and came up empty. On top of that, Whelen had what I had to admit was the likeliest take on what had happened to her, which was the Random Fruitcake Theory. Some guy with a twist had done her in, and he'd gotten away with it, and short of God coming down and pointing a finger at the bastard, that was that. And, okay, maybe the guy would get his somewhere along the line, because everybody pays in the end, but we weren't gonna make him for killing Melanie.

Third, someone with strong connections to the NYPD, someone who knew what he was doing had, very carefully and very professionally, set me up to take the fall for Annabel's death, and if it hadn't been for the auspices of Dick Plover, who probably had more blood on his hands than the rest of us put together, I'd still be behind bars while I tried to explain myself. Bad enough I wound up owing a guy like Plover, but to make it worse I wasn't sure I was in the clear on the murder charge.

So now the cops were looking for me again. Could that have been simple paranoia talking, could the cops have had a perfectly rational reason to be in the lobby of my hotel, one that did not necessarily involve further pain on my part?

Yeah, no. Not this time.

If Edwards had just wanted to talk to me, he had my phone

number. In fact, he'd had physical possession of my phone for the whole time I'd been in custody, so yeah, he had my number, but he also had names and contact information for everyone I'd talked to, and that included Annabel, Mac, Klaudia and Reiman. I fished the phone out of my pocket and looked at it. I thought about losing it, but I had gotten used to it. Would the cops bother tracking my cell? I turned it off. From now on, I told myself, you wanna make a call, you can turn it back on, and then shut it back off when you're done.

It bothered me that the Worm had known that I was a thief, right from the beginning. Why had it taken me so long to pick up on that? "Vale," I could still hear that word rolling off the Worm's Creole tongue. It's not like I advertise or anything. He'd been on to me so quickly . . .

And finally, the criminal enterprise known by some as the Green Pang Tribe had known Melanie Wing while she was alive but didn't seem to demonstrate a lot of interest in catching her killer. Li Fat had wished me good luck, and had volunteered to introduce me to Peter Kwok, but not a lot more.

I still hadn't talked to Kwok, though.

Also, I'd studiously ignored the guys on Mac's list, the ones that Klaudia thought merited further attention. I'd been too focused on Los Paraíso. At that rate, it was looking like my chances for making the Flatfoot All-Star Team were pretty dim.

THERE WAS A resale shop on Avenue B with a sign in the window that promised you they specialized in "gently used clothing," which was a lie. I spent about thirty bucks in the joint, came out the proud owner of an old trench coat, which from the look of it was also pre-urinated-on, also a wrinkled fedora with a nice wide brim, a pair of shades, and a ratty, snarled grayish wig, which was more comfortable than it looked once you got the hair out behind you in a ponytail, secured by a bunch of rubber bands supplied at no extra cost by the proprietor of said establishment. The worst thing about my new get-up was the smell of mothballs, which I think came from the coat, but I figured that wouldn't last forever. I didn't need the shopping bag the lady gave me because I wore all the stuff out of the store, but I kept it anyhow. When I hit the sidewalk I affected a homeless guy's pace and I stopped at the first few trash cans I came to for some newspapers to fill out my shopping bag. Hey, who says I don't have my shit together? Got it right here in this bag. Wanna see? Funny, though, I would have been appalled to go digging through the garbage on any other occasion, but hidden as I was inside my hat and trench coat it didn't seem like a big deal, and no one paid me the slightest attention. Good practice, I told myself. If things turn bad enough, I could just, you know, go with it . . .

I STOPPED IN a dollar store and picked up that most basic of B&E tools, a screwdriver. Mine would suffice to get me past the front door of the building where Klaudia lived, mostly because that lock had been jimmied about a thousand times before I ever got to it. And the locks on her apartment door were hardware store specials, they were the sort of locks that only kept honest people honest. I stowed the screwdriver in an inner pocket of my trench coat.

People avoided me as I walked south. They wouldn't look me in the eye, they gave me a little more room on the sidewalk because now I was a bum, a homeless crank, a threat. They pretended I was invisible, that I wasn't there at all, I could feel them doing it. I thought about talking loudly to my imaginary stockbroker on my pretend Bluetooth but I wound up shuffling along more or less in silence, perversely uncomfortable. It's one thing to fly under the radar but it's another thing to be in a city like New York and be deemed untouchable by nearly everyone. It was a crawling, itching sort of unease. It's a bit like the feeling you get when you think you might throw up at any moment. I knew that a hit or a toke or a snort would make it all go away, that I wouldn't care, after that, what anyone thought, which made that stuff pretty effective medicine. The side effects suck ass, though, like dying and everything.

I got through it. I felt it, but I thought about my friend Tommy from Bedford Avenue in Brooklyn, I thought about how lousy it would feel to have to admit to him that I was starting all over again, again, so I swallowed the urges and kept moving. It's a stupid thing, really, I imagine a normal person might write it off as a sort of emotional hangover that would disappear in an hour or two, or a day at worst. And a trigger is nothing more than a simple mechanical device, harmless in and of itself.

It's the bang afterward that kills you.

I popped the front door to Klaudia's building; it would have taken longer to open it with a key. Once inside I climbed up to her floor, but when I got to her door I hesitated. For the record, it's never a good idea to pause for soul searching right out in front of the place you're planning to break into. You should already have your doubts safely anesthetized by then, no good can come from hanging around outside someone's front door with your shims in one hand and your conscience in the other. It was a first for me, though, and it caught me by surprise. I was about to invade another person's private space, which was something I'd done more times than I could count, but this would be the first time it was someone I cared about. A lot. But you can't call her, I told myself, because that might mean inviting the cops to the party, but you can't wait for her in the hall, but you can't not see her, either, not when you're this close . . .

I went in.

I folded my hat and gray wig up inside my trench coat and stuck the whole mess inside my shopping bag, and then I turned her lights on. I moved one of her chairs to where she'd see it as soon as she opened the door, and then I sat in it and waited. There have been many times in my life when I wished I could silence those inner voices, but never more than right then. Several times I thought of leaving. Write her a note and walk away, I told myself, but that felt like the coward's way out. It mattered, what this girl thought of me. She mattered, and that was another new experience. I began to wish fervently that I had never set foot on this road, that I was still up on the Maine coast standing knee-deep in the Atlantic, still cut off, still alone, still lost. I could hear the goonas laughing at me again because they'd given me pretty much exactly what I wanted and now I couldn't deal with it. They'd given me a connection, and all I could think about was running away. You hear all this shit about love and you wonder if any of it is real . . . I found out that day that love does not cure you of the disease of you, that it is made of both ecstasy and pain, and that the pain will be at least the equal of anything else you have ever felt.

Her door eased open, some blond hair and one blue eye peered inside, then she flipped the door open wide and walked through. She had her keys clenched in a fist, and the metal bits poked out between her fingers.

Yeah, city girl.

"I don't know whether to be pissed off," she said, "or happy to see you."

For the second time in a single afternoon I thought about a joint and about the release it would give me, and then I thought about everything it would cost me in the days that followed, because there's no such thing as one, not with me. And the shit's gonna come to mind, there's nothing you can do about that. The question is, do you play with the thought? Do you starve the idea or do you feed it? That's the part that's on you.

She walked around behind me. "How do you know I'm not one of those crazy women? How do you know I don't keep an ice pick in my pants?"

I didn't see one, last time I was in there . . . I wanted to say it, but I didn't dare. "Go on," I told her. "Do what you gotta do. I made my decision."

She came around front again, restless, feral as ever. She kicked her door shut, turned and glanced down into my shopping bag. "The cops came to see me again," she said. "Looking for you. Detective Edwards and some other guy. Is that why you didn't call?"

"Yeah."

"Then it's true, what he said about you."

"What did he . . ."

"He said you are a thief. And a drug addict."

"I never touch anything stronger than aspirin."

"That's not what I asked you."

Honesty does not come easy, not at first. But if I really wanted to get anywhere with this girl . . . "Well, okay yeah, I guess, technically, I'm an addict."

"How long you been clean," she said.

"Two years." Hey, I rounded up. Sue me.

"You got a sponsor?"

Oh-oh. The girl had done her homework. "Yeah. Guy name of Tommy."

"Will he talk to me?"

"Probably."

She walked over to her table, dragged the other chair across the floor to face mine and threw herself into it. And even then she couldn't keep completely still, her foot was going the whole time. "So what do we do now?" She leaned the chair back on its rear legs like it was a recliner.

"I'm not running away, I'm staying with this. I'm in too far, and now I really wanna know what happened to Melanie. The cops are not gonna scare me off. And neither are you."

She chewed on that for a moment. "What about the rest of it? Are you really a thief?"

I sighed. "I suppose that would be one way to put it. I like to tell people that I'm a contractor. I'm sort of like the guy who repos your car if you quit making the payments."

"Does that mean it isn't stealing? Edwards said if my mother was stuck in a South American prison, that you'd be the guy to go and get her out."

"That might be stretching it."

Her foot quit tapping. "I figured you weren't a choirboy, but Jesus. Are they right about you, Saul? What are you?"

"You ever hear of Bill Parcells?"

"Yeah. Football coach."

"He used to say that you are what your record says you are." I shook my head. "I keep hoping that there's more to it. I keep hoping that I'll do better. Or that I'll find the operating manual, the one everybody else got when they were born." I stared into her face but I couldn't read a thing in it. "I can't answer this for you, because I don't have the answer. You're gonna have to make the call. I'm throwing myself on the mercy of the court. You tell me to walk, I'll walk, and I won't bother you again."

"Laying it all on me, huh?" She dropped the chair back down, leaned forward, rested her elbows on her knees. "I used to be so contained," she said. "My whole life woulda fit in five or six of those little plastic boxes from the dollar store, all neat and clean. I coulda carried 'em all in that shopping bag." She nudged it with her foot. "This new getup of yours means you're going native, doesn't it."

"I need to stay out of sight for a while. And I don't want anyone trying to get to me through you."

"God, why does everything have to be such a mess? Ever since I laid eyes on you I feel like my head is on backward."

"I'm sorry if I complicated things for you. It wasn't what I intended." I started to get up.

She sat back up and her foot started tapping again, like a relief valve blowing off excess pressure. "I didn't hear anybody tell you that you could go yet," she said. "Sit."

Chapter Fourteen

WHEN I CAME up out of the subway in Brooklyn I powered up my phone and saw that I had a voice mail. My first thought was that it was from Klaudia but it turned out to be from Francis O'Neill, of Shield Investments. Took me a minute, then I remembered that he was the guy who held the lease on the bottom floor of the building the Hotel Los Paraíso was in. I was walking up Bedford Avenue in Brooklyn in the direction of the NA meeting wearing my new raincoat, wig, and hat, must have looked funny as shit, some homeless wino walking up the block talking on his phone. I called the number O'Neill left me, and he picked up. "Francis O'Neill," he said. "How can I help you?"

"Mr. O'Neill," I said. "My name is Saul Fowler, and I'm trying to find out what happened to a woman who disappeared from the Hotel Los Paraíso about six months ago."

"Don't know that I'd be much use to you," he said. "I hardly go near the place."

"I won't take much of your time, Mr. O'Neill . . ."

"I understand," he said. "You want to cross all the Ts, I know. You busy tomorrow?"

"Where and when?"

"I'm supposed to look at a building first thing in the morning. In Corona." He gave me the address. "I don't think I'll be there long. Why don't you meet me there."

I shut the phone off, stuck it in my pocket.

I got to the church, and as I went through the parking lot I got basically the same reception I'd gotten the last time, handshakes and first-name introductions. Inside, a young kid stood by the door greeting people on the way in. He held my hand a heartbeat or so longer than he needed to. "You're welcome to come in and listen," he said. "Have a cup of coffee, eat some cookies. And you can share, if it comes around to you." He dropped my hand. "But don't disrupt the meeting. Okay? Disrupt the meeting and we gotta put you out."

I was finding it hard to stay in character, I wanted to tell him that putting me out might be tougher than he thought, but I stared at the floor instead and mumbled my okays. Once I got past him I looked around for Tommy, but like the last time, he showed up a few minutes after I did. I saw his eyes go around the room; they stopped when he got to me. He made his way back over to the door and put a hand on the kid's shoulder. "William," he said. "What'd I tell you about letting all these goddamn winos up in here?"

William bristled. "He's got a right," he said, and he stuck his chin out. " 'Cause if he can't come in here, why we here? Huh? What are we doing?"

Tommy grinned and leaned in to whisper something in William's ear, I'm pretty sure I saw the phrase "sober horse thief" but I didn't actually hear it. William's eyes went wide once as he looked over at me, and then he shook his head and glanced up at the ceiling. Tommy laughed, slapped him on the back, and then he came over and sat next to me.

"Seems like a nice kid," I told him.

"He gets it," Tommy said. "You shoulda seen him six months ago. I think he's got a shot." He glanced up at my hat. "What's with the big disguise, chief?"

"Cops."

"Ah," he said. "You done anything to merit their attentions?"

"Not yet. But they probably think I have."

A girl in her twenties stood up at the front of the room and cleared her throat. The room went silent and she began the usual litany. "My name is Melanie and I am cross-addicted." The editorial voice started up in the back of my head. Did she mean she was addicted to crosses? But the voice was so faint that I could barely hear it. I think it was because Melanie had my sister's name. She asked someone to read a passage out of a book, my editorial voice had always gone up a notch when they did that but this time I couldn't really hear it, I just sat there and stared at Melanie. She wore a bit of a fro-hawk and she had tattoos on the side of her neck, but she also had a Madonna's face and I sat there thinking, You go, Melanie, I hope to fucking Christ you make it. Tommy took a cookie out of my hand and ate it, I saw a raised eyebrow or two when he did that because, you know, who knew where them hands had been? I ate the rest of them as I drank my coffee. Good stuff, too, I never knew if it was because of those big urns they made it in or maybe they just took extra care putting it together. When the reading was finished Melanie introduced the speaker, some woman whose career as a pharmacist had crashed and burned, and for predictable reasons. She was funny as hell and easy to listen to. The discussion afterward never got around to me, which was just as well. It occurred to me then that when it came to getting fucked up, everybody in that room was already pretty well up to speed and probably didn't need to hear my take on it. It's what you do without the shit that's the real trick.

"I like this look on you," Tommy said, after. We were the last two out of the meeting except for William, the kid who'd met me at the door. He was washing out the coffeepots with an addict's single-minded intensity. "I mean, you don't have the smell exactly right, but you could pass for a homeless guy in my neighborhood."

"How about I piss my pants once or twice? Will that help?"

"Probably," Tommy said. "But don't start up on that just yet. The men in blue, are they really looking to pick you up?"

"Yeah. Two of them showed up at my hotel."

"You sure they were looking for you? They got cops everywhere, you know."

"Yeah, but I recognized one of them. He was the guy that came to see me while I was locked up. And they stopped to talk to this lady friend I been seeing."

"Jesus Christ, Saul, you're barely in town five minutes, already you been locked up, shacked up, and now the cops are looking for you. A second time? You even pause for breath?"

"I guess there's a few things I could catch you up on."

"Yeah? You think? We oughta go get a cup of coffee someplace. Yo, William, you finished with that damn thing yet?"

The kid looked up, scowling. "This pot is all black inside."

"Perfectionism is a flaw, William, not an asset. You gotta reckanize the value of adequacy. Rinse that mother out so's we can get the hell out of here."

"Yes, boss."

I told Tommy about the Hotel Los Paraíso while we watched William finish up. Tommy seemed intrigued. "Let's go have a look at it," he said.

"Yeah? You wanna see it? Now?"

"Why not. William, you ain't gonna get that damn thing no cleaner. What you doing tonight?"

"I don't know," William said. He rinsed the urn out one last time, then gave up on it. "Tell me, Tommy, what am I doing tonight?" He stuck the coffee urn in a closet and wiped his hands on a paper towel.

Tommy dug in his pocket, fished out his car keys and tossed them to the kid. "You're driving me and Saul here into Manhattan. We wanna go look at a building down in Alphabet City."

WILLIAM DROVE CAREFULLY and well, with little of the aggression common among city drivers, and me. He kept glancing at me in his rearview mirror. "Saul," he finally said. "You look like you got a story."

Tommy smiled and looked out the window. William glared at him. "Tell me why," he said, "the craziest motherfuckers in the room always know you, Tommy. Tell me why."

"What's that make you?" Tommy asked him.

William didn't reply, he looked at me in his rearview mirror again.

Why not, I thought. "I met Tommy . . ." I had to stop and think about the math, which, as my friend Gelman has observed, isn't my strong point. "A lot of years ago. When I walked in off Bedford Avenue, I didn't know anything about you guys, I didn't know what you did and I didn't think anything would work on me, but it was a shot in the dark. I'd been on the street a couple years, at that point."

"You was on the street? For real? In Brooklyn?"

"Here and there. I'd been in Brooklyn a while. I'd been living with my mother before that, but she was locked up by that time."

"Why they lock her up?"

"She went crazy."

"They put you away for that?"

"I don't mean crazy in the usual sense. Criminally insane."

"Oh shit," William said. "Sorry, man."

"Nothing to it," I told him. "But you know how it is, William, you're just a kid, you're on your own, you got no one to point you the right way. Picked up a few substances, you know how that goes, found out too late I couldn't put 'em down. Started wondering what would be a good way to kill yourself. I mean, I figured the shit was gonna take me out eventually, but it seemed like it was taking way too long. What I came up with, right, was I was gonna take a nice warm bath, shoot up after I got into the water, then try to cut my wrists just as the rush hit."

"You're still here," William said.

"Yeah. Couldn't find a bathtub."

Tommy was laughing softly and William glared at him again. "Motherfucker, you got no fuckin' heart, you know that?"

But by that time I was laughing, too.

"So how was you makin' it? You get into sales and distribution?"

"No. I was a thief."

Tommy snorted.

"Was. Past tense. Now I'm a contractor. But I started out stealing cars, there was a joint down on Flushing Avenue, they would tell you what they needed. Guy liked Hondas and Toyotas. Then the dude got busted, none of the other chop shops would trust me so I had to start doing break-ins and whatever. I liked warehouses the best, if I was careful I could hit them a few times before they woke up."

"Then you found us down on Bedford. Did you stick?"

"I did okay for a while."

"What happened? Was it a skirt? Skirt take you out?"

"You got to leave the ladies alone a while, William. Didn't Tommy tell you that?"

Tommy threw the kid a look. "Yeah," William said. "I do recall, you know, hearing a word or two about the subject, 'bout once every five minutes . . ." He looked back at me. "So you gonna stick this time?"

"I'm here now. What about you?"

"No, man, I'm stickin'. I know what I want."

"You like Brooklyn that much?"

"It ain't Brooklyn," he said. "My pops took off when I was six. My moms left me with her aunt. She was around for a while after that, but I ain't seen her now in years. My mom's aunt, she was okay. They made a place for me. But, you know, what you said, you got nobody to do for you, you start to run with the wrong people and shit, and they use you. You know, they get caught with the product, they goin' away, but you just a kid, what they gonna do? Put you in juvie? So what? But then the day comes, man, you know how it is. You gotta go one way or the other. That's when I found Tommy and them . . . And once you know, it's just different. You know there's a way. You know you don't have to do none of that shit no more. Tommy went and fucked up all my excuses. And when you go into that meeting and everybody is glad to see you, and shit, and you miss a couple nights they come looking, you know what I'm saying . . . It's different. Bedford is where I need to be at. You know what I mean."

"Yeah. I do."

"So, you been in Brooklyn this whole time?"

"No, William. I been all over. I only got back to Brooklyn a few weeks back."

"Where was you at before this?"

"Maine."

"Maine?" He said it like I'd said Mars. "What's up there?"

"Ocean," I told him. "Rocks. Fish."

"Yeah? You hit meetings while you was up there?"

"No."

"They didn't have no meetings there?"

"I'm guessing they probably had enough meetings, but I didn't want to hear it. Not right then."

"You was still tryina figure it out," William said, nodding. "Done that. Mix up a little bit a this and a little bit a that, some of this in the morning and some of that at night, I get it right this time, man, you'll see, no, serious, I be all right this time around, don't look at that, that ain't nothing but a little blood, you know what I'm saying, that'll heal right up . . ." Tommy and William were both laughing, but it was all right, because the kid was right. The oldest lie in the world, and the most lethal, is the one you tell yourself. I'm okay, I can do this myself. This time will be different. I got this.

William turned on to Tenth Street and parked next to a hydrant halfway up the block. Tenth was quieter, that time of night, than I had thought it would be. "That's it, up there," I said. "Where the awning is. Los Paraíso."

"Bet you didn't think you'd be looking at paradise right here in Manhattan, did you William?" Tommy said.

"Nah," the kid said. "Way I figure, Garden of Eden was probably down where they got Rio now. I seen pictures, they got Jesus up on the hill, blue ocean, blue sky, green jungle. Good place for snakes. Didn't even look real. Looked like a painting."

"Tenth could be in a painting," I said. "Van Gogh, maybe."

"This block ain't so bad. Why did they brick up them hotel windows? One on each side of the door right there. Did a shit job of it, too."

"I don't know," I said. "Your eyes must be better than mine."

"Bricks be all crooked," he said.

"Well, anyway, those street-level spaces are not part of the hotel. Hotel starts on the second floor. You don't think this block stinks? Got your gang kids up on the corner . . ."

"No," William said. "This place is happening. Gentrifyin'. All the gays, the waiters and the musicians and all them have packed up and went out to Greenpoint, they can't afford to live here no more. You could buy one of these buildings right here, you could double your money in about five years. Double your money, man. If them bricked-up storefronts ain't part of the hotel, what are they?"

"I don't know. Probably empty."

"Empty?" William sounded skeptical.

"You would live on this block?"

He looked around. "Little close to the projects. Not horrible, though."

"What about the kids up on the corner selling dope?"

"I see 'em," William said. "But they ain't selling nothing."

"What do you mean?"

"Look at 'em up there. They just hanging. Ain't got they minds on business." He was right, the few kids that were left didn't seem to be paying much attention to the potential customers coming up the block. "Boss man come by and catch 'em, he tear they little candy asses up."

"Maybe he's scouting for a better corner to do business on," I said. "If the neighborhood is coming up like you say, maybe he won't last here much longer."

"Tell you the truth," William said, "he shoulda been gone already. And them guys runnin' ladies outa that hotel, they ain't gonna make it neither. New people ain't about puttin' up with that shit, not around they kids. You said these guys ain't been busted yet?"

"That's what I was told."

"Funny. I'ma go talk to them kids one minute. Be right back." He reached for the door.

"No, I'll go." Tommy and I said it, almost at the same time.

William turned and looked from my face to Tommy's and back. "You guys are old, man. Them kids ain't gonna tell you shit. Sit tight."

Tommy sighed and sat back. We watched William go. "Nice kid. You got him living in your house, am I right?"

"How'd you guess?" Tommy said.

"You set this up?"

"No," Tommy said. "But I was watching him wrestle with that coffeepot while you were telling me about this joint. Seemed to me that William would probably see things that you and I might miss. Us being old, like he said, and whatnot."

"Speak for yourself. For real, that's why you had him drive?"

Tommy was watching William. "Do you remember what it felt like, when you first came in? Remember the first time you found out you could do something useful? Wash a pot, say. Put some chairs away. Sweep up the butts out by the back door."

"Yeah."

"Wasn't that a revelation? In that one moment you go from a lying, thieving, conniving punk-ass junkie to a contributing member of something. Why are you still here, Saul? Why are you still alive? You ever think about that?"

"Yeah."

"What possible reason could there be for you and me to be here? When I was in the life, I should have died a hundred times over. William up there, he gets to know you a little bit better, maybe he'll tell you about the bucket of shit he was in when he walked through the door a while back. He could have gone away for a long time, but he didn't. Got lucky, did some of the right things. And if your mother was just a little bit quicker, she could have stuck you good and proper. And I'm guessing that wasn't the only time you went dancing with Mr. D."

"No, maybe not."

"I'm gonna make you a promise, Saul. If you really make it, okay, if you get your shit together this time, you're gonna be sitting in a room some night, and some guy is gonna come walking through the door who needs to hear it from you. Not from me, not William, not anybody else, either. You. And if you ain't there, he turns around and walks right back out." He stared at me. "I don't care if you believe this or not, but there's a reason you're still here."

"Maybe you're right."

William was squatted down on his haunches, making him shorter than most of the kids who were gathered around him. "The kid was right. They wouldn't have talked to either of us."

"No," Tommy said. "Probably not. So maybe you'll see some good from tonight. But William will, too."

"Doing something for me, you mean. Something he ain't getting paid for."

"Saul, you know what they call us in the emergency room? Users." He laughed. "How's that make you feel? Where I work, they don't even know. They got no idea what I was. All they know about me is that I'm good to have around when you're in a tight spot. Guy who did my performance review last summer told me so. Said, 'I can't promote you and I can't get you no more money, Tom, but you're a good man and we're lucky to have you.' I woulda took the money, don't get me wrong, but I don't mind, Saul. I don't mind being a good man to have around."

"Beats being a user."

"That it does. Here come William, let's see what he got."

William slid back into the driver's seat. "Fernando," he said. "Fernando was with the 10–60s, some bunch a losers who mostly run downtown from here. Fernando used to come once a day, more or less, drop off the product, pick up the money, keep everyone in line. The kids ain't seen Fernando in a couple weeks. Day or so after he went missing, some friend of Fernando name of Domonic showed up, said he'd be running things a while, but he got himself put in the hospital and he ain't been back. Kids don't know what to do, they still scared of Fernando, they know if he shows back up again, they better have his money, so they sittin' on it."

I didn't see what all that had to do with me. "Interesting. Was it a big Haitian who bounced Domonic around?"

"No. Kids say it was cops. I mean, you always hear that, but it don't happen that often. Cops don't generally put you in the hospital and then walk away, not no more, anyhow. They go to that much trouble, they gonna lock your ass up, that's the business they're in. But the kids are convinced it was two white cops worked over Domonic. Busted him up, told him not to come back."

There it was again. "So you don't think it was cops?"

William looked up and down the street while he thought about it. "I woulda said no," he said. "But in this neighborhood, okay, them kids ain't been rousted outa here, and them ladies doin' business up in that hotel ain't been busted, and two and two don't add up to five. You know what I mean? And cops go with hookers like salt go with pepper. Just sayin."

"What'd you tell the kids?"

"What could I tell 'em, man?" he said, in a sadder, quieter voice. "Go home? Go back to school? Them kids are throwaways, man. They got nothing to go back to. There's nothing I can tell them."

"The more I see of Manhattan," Tommy said, "the more I like Brooklyn. Let's get the hell out of here. Saul promised us a cup of coffee."

Chapter Fifteen

I SPENT THE night in a noisy little hotel in Sheepshead Bay that Tommy knew about. I was not, initially, a big hit with the night manager, given my general appearance and lack of luggage, but there's nothing like a couple of crisp Ben Franklins to inspire confidence and win new friends. After those two bills changed hands, all I got from the guy was one raised eyebrow. "It's a long story," I told him.

"I have no doubt." His tone said that he'd heard them all.

But, of course, I couldn't sleep.

A late-night NA meeting will do that to you sometimes. It can wind your mental mainspring tight and set you digging in your attic whether you like it or not. I sorted through the junkpile for a while, but there was really no profit in it, not that night. I was not what I could have been, I got that. Some other time, I told myself. Some other time I'll figure it out, see if there isn't some path by which I might become a good man to have around when you're in a tight spot. In the meantime it seemed an unrealistic goal, so to break the spell I forced myself to think about William, and his reaction to the Hotel Los Paraíso. It seemed obvious that William had come to the that meeting right off the street, because he knew more about the retail drug trade that any casual observer would. But credit where credit is due, I found out over late-night coffee that the kid was back in school. And in the years I'd been gone, Tommy, the ex-biker, had gotten his EMT ticket and now worked for a private ambulance company.

I'd never had much luck with school. And how do you do that anyway, how do you decide, okay, I've had enough of being a thief, now I want to go about the process of becoming . . .

What, exactly?

Shit, thieving was all I was ever good at.

And someone had my prints on a water glass. Ironic, I guess, someone had broken into my room, for a change, and stolen something of mine, with my prints on it, then planted it at a crime scene. Funny, even, I suppose.

What were the chances that someone had been a cop? Someone with hep C had killed five women in NYC in the past two years. And someone else, a cop or someone with good cop connections, had heard about it, killed Melanie Wing first and then Annabel, copied the MO.

Another thing that bothered me was William's confidence that the drug kids would not be tolerated on Avenue C and Tenth, not if it was a neighborhood on the rise like he said. "No street girls, neither," he'd said. "You didn't notice? No street corner ladies." Yeah, but there were plenty inside the hotel, I told him. Even some independents. "Different business," William said. "But it is funny that they're still there."

You think the cops made the street girls move, I'd asked him.

William hadn't thought so. "The serious money is up inside

that hotel. They got a real nice spot. You think them guys wanna drag ass all the way out to Long Island City someplace? No way. They wanna stay right where they at. Last thing they wanna see is the neighbors saying, 'Look at these damn kids selling that shit up on that corner, we got to clean this block up.' Nah-ah. Something big and bad out there in the dark, comes out once in a while to keep all the little fish scared off."

I owed William.

"MAC, YOU SLEEPING?"

"You fucker . . . I'm too old for this shit, Saul, I need to get my sleep."

"You remember the place I told you about, down on Tenth?"

Mac sighed. "Yeah. Hookers."

"Mujer *de* la vida."

"Okay," he said groggily. "Call girls, not hookers, so what?"

"You told me to follow the money, you remember that?"

"Yeah," he said, coming awake. We were in his backyard now, talking about something he knew. "So how many girls they running?"

Nine, Gelman told me, plus a few part-timers. Did he say nine? "Call it ten or twelve. We talking a lot of money here, am I right?"

"You kidding? Do the math, Saul."

"Arithmetic ain't my forte."

"Okay, figure ten, to make it easy. Ten ladies times a net of what? A grand a day, per? Something like that. Figure you got a thirty percent overhead . . ." I could almost hear the gears spinning in his head. "Annual net of something over two million, would be my seat-of-the-pants estimate. But I'm probably close."

"So if you got four principals, they're clearing a half a million each?"

"Something like that. Probably ain't an even split, but they're doing more than okay. And a few cops pulling some heavy green to let the door stay open."

"Worth killing to protect."

"Saul, are you kidding? I know guys who'd skin you alive for a tenth of that, and so do you."

THE CAB LEFT me on a sidewalk in Corona, Queens, early in the morning, and then hastily departed. It didn't look like the kind of neighborhood where you'd want to raise your kids, but there seemed to be plenty of people who were trying to do just that. I had an appointment to meet up with one Francis O'Neill, and the building he was looking at was a joyless gray brick lump that would not have looked out of place in Magnetogorsk. It was located on a joyless gray semi-industrial street in a neighborhood populated with similar buildings. The gang tags on the front of the place were the only touch of color, but you could hardly call them cheerful. I leaned on a light pole out front and waited. After some time, three white guys came out of the building; two of them were slight, Eastern European–looking guys dressed in suits and the third guy was a tall, long-nosed dude with a short gray beard and a gray ponytail. I figured O'Neill for the nose, and I was right. He paused to shake hands with the two suits. "I'll get back to you if I decide to do something here," he said. "I'll have to give it some consideration."

"Don't considerate too much," one of the suits told him. "This won't stay on the market long."

"No? You mean you're gonna be dropping your asking price? Because at two and a half, I'm not sure you're going to find a buyer at all." They went back and forth in that vein a few more minutes, and then one of the suits went back inside the building and the other one started walking away. The tall guy walked up to me and stuck out his hand. "Mr. Fowler?" he said.

"Mr. O'Neill. Thanks for seeing me. Two and a half for that place? Million? Seriously?"

"I know, I know," he said, glancing back over his shoulder. O'Neill, it turned out, was the sort of garrulous soul who starts a conversation with himself every morning and keeps it going all day long. Those of us who wander in and out at random are expected to know our lines. "But that's just their opening number, they know they'll never get it." He dropped his voice down. "Actually it's not a bad price, to tell you the truth. The whole damn place is section eight housing." He must have noticed my blank expression. "Government subsidized. What that means, my friend, is the state pays the rent, and the state is never late, the state never sneaks out in the middle of the night, the state never holds out on you behind a leaky toilet or mold or a broken window or some damn thing, figure, twelve hundred bucks, average, for every apartment in the place, direct deposited in your account every month. What's not to like? And I'll tell you another thing. The gays have started moving into this neighborhood." He tapped his temple with a forefinger. "You can't go far wrong, following the gays. You know why? Everyone else follows them. The creatives, your artist types, then the young professionals, then the rich people. You buy this place for, okay, two and a half is a big nut, say you get them to go two and a quarter. Commercial, that means you gotta come up with five hundred thou. Okay? So you buy it, you suck up that section eight money for a couple of years, then you sell to some schmuck who watches too much HGTV, okay, let him sweat the new roof and replacement windows and the new boiler and all that shit. Probably get three for it. Maybe a little more. Listen to me, I'm talking myself into this and probably boring the shit out of you at the same time. You had breakfast, Mr. Fowler? Because I'm starving."

We started down the sidewalk. After a moment, his phone chirped at him. He looked at it, then glanced at me. "Excuse me," he said. "Gotta make a call." He punched some numbers. "Come on," he said. "Pick up, dammit, pick up . . ." He stared up at the sky, a look of supplication on his face. "Babe?" he said to the phone, looking relieved. "Babe. It's time to get up. You gotta get out of bed."

Pause.

"Why?" He looked my way and shook his head. "Because you gotta. It ain't no good to stay up in that bed alla time. Go on out to the kitchen now, okay? Open the fridge. You see them pills? Top shelf. Says 'brain' on the bottle. Yeah. Brain. B, R, A, okay, okay, I'm just tryina help. I know you can read. Take two of them pills. I'll wait while you do it. Shit." He looked at me again. "Fuck, man, she put the phone down." He made as if he wanted to throw his own phone, but went back to talking into it instead. "Babe . . . BABE! Okay, okay, sorry. You took the pills? You took 'em? Good. Now don't go back to bed, okay? Look at some television for a while. I'll be home soon. Yeah. Love." He made kissy noises, then ended the call and stuck the phone back in his pocket. "Doctors," he said to me. "Don't you wish they would just admit it when they don't know what the hell to do? The money I pissed away on rehabs and drugs and every other damn thing, and what did they do for her? Nothing. I should strangle every one of 'em. I finally found a homeopathic guy, treats you with natural shit, he's the only one managed to help her at all."

Alzheimer's was my guess, and the guy didn't want to admit to it. What do you say to someone is a fix like that? To watch someone you love die from a slow corrosion of the soul, that had to do something to you. "Sorry."

"Not your fault," he said. "Not mine, neither, for that matter. Where were we? Coffee, that's where we were. Come on, I know a place."

It was a Lebanese joint. One of the interesting things about NYC is that, from every ethnic group on the planet and probably a couple from outer space, a few native sons move to the city, and in any random neighborhood you can find a hole-in-the-wall where some guy cooks with reverence and care, the way his mother did.

O'Neill ordered half the menu.

"You weren't kidding, you must really be starving."

"Takes a lot of calories to keep this much self-esteem operating," he said with a grin. "So tell me about your problem."

Melanie.

I was weary of telling her story, but I gave him the shorthand version, I left out her mother, the tongs, and my family history. Just a nurse who went missing, used to frequent the Hotel Los Paraíso.

"Did you know I used to be a cop?" he said, when I finished. "Don't hold it against me. I spent more than a few years in that precinct. That's how I got interested in that place on Tenth. I bought in out of sentiment, and sentiment will screw you every time. You spend too much time there, after a while you don't see the hookers no more, you don't notice the burned-out car halfway down the block. I figured someone would buy the place and put in a bunch of million-dollar condos, first they gotta buy out my lease, and they will, but it's taking a hell of a lot longer than I thought. I'll never get my money back out." He eyed me. "So now you wanna know what to do. I guess going home ain't that high up on your list."

"Wasn't what I had in mind."

"In my day," he said, "you hadda know the streets. You hadda know the players. What I woulda done, I woulda started working all the contacts I had, figuring someone knew something. Some you hadda bribe, some you hadda threaten, some you hadda bounce them around a little bit. You know how that goes. I mean, I know it ain't right, not now and not then, but back in the day, certain guys in the precinct, they knew someone was holding out on them, they put the guy in a box and started squeezing. You get what you want, you let the guy go. Not the right thing, like I said, but that's the way the game was played. Don't happen that way no more, not much, anyway. I know that probably don't help you too much."

"Not sure that approach would work for me."

"No," he said. "You gotta know the players. And I been gone outa there awhile now. 'Course, I still got some friends in the precinct. How they would catch your guy these days, you gotta have a crime scene, you gotta have the body. You get the forensics guys to do what they do, maybe you get the guy that way. Or maybe he's in a bar, right, and he runs his mouth and somebody gives him up. But I mean, there's usually a life span to that kind of skell, your guy ain't gonna die in a rest home. You know what I mean. He'll get his, somewhere along the line. Which don't make you feel much better, I know. I tell you what, let me think about this for a while, okay? Like I said, I still know a few characters down there. Let me ask around, maybe someone seen something, maybe we get lucky. But to tell you the truth, Mr. Fowler, I wouldn't hold my breath. Sometimes there's nothing you can do."

THEY GOT NEW cabs for the outer boroughs now, a sickly green instead of bright yellow, but at least you have a prayer if you need a ride out of Queens. I got lucky, flagged down a greenie and he rode me into Manhattan, let me out right across the avenue from Los Paraíso. I thought about the shopping bag sitting up there on the top floor, the one on top of the safe. Probably more than half full by now . . . Gelman told me that he had not seen El Tuerto, the money man, come to make his regular pickup, not since the first time I showed my face in the joint; the pimps were sitting on an uncomfortable bunch of cash and they didn't want to move it, not while I was around. I even gave some thought to going back in and taking the rest of it; man, how funny would that be, but their money was not my objective.

It was a thought, though.

I wondered, again, who El Tuerto was. Wondered how he got the nickname.

A woman walked out of Los Paraíso, and she annihilated all thoughts of money from my mind. She was tall and very dark, she had hazel eyes, long lashes, and short hair, I remembered her face, how could you not, she'd been accompanied by one of the Chinese pimps the last time I'd seen her, and the two of them had been followed by a cowboy on a Triumph. Big tall white kid. This time she was alone. I thought I knew who she was: Aniri, the African, from Seconal. I'd heard her story from Heather, the girl from Delaware. The goonas had been particularly unkind to the girl. Sold as a child to an Italian syndicate by her own uncle, moved on from

Milan to Alphabet City. I have always had a tough time understanding why some people become the object of so much cruelty. I'd had my share and more of second chances and I had spurned them all one after another, always confident that I'd get another shot . . . But maybe it's a statistical thing, maybe out of seven billion people there's a certain number who are going to roll snake eyes every time they touch the dice, no matter what.

I wondered what was keeping her erect, but then you never know, strength comes in funny shapes sometimes.

A cab pulled over but she waved him away, she stood there as cool and serene as Buddha until a limo pulled up, and then she walked over and got in the back.

I had to follow.

Yeah, another hotel in midtown.

I followed her inside. She went straight past the front desk and punched the button for an elevator. I actually got in with her, punched the button for the floor below the one she'd chosen. I didn't know what else to do, I hadn't thought this through and I didn't have any kind of a plan. She did not favor me with a glance but her image watched me calmly from the elevator car's mirrored surface. When we got to my floor and the doors closed behind me I began breathing again, and then I raced for the stairwell and ran up one flight. I got to her landing in time to see her disappear around a bend at the end of the hall. I was wondering what to do next when I heard the elevator doors rumble open again.

A short Hispanic woman dressed in a housekeeper's uniform pushed a cart out into the hallway. She was followed by three red-faced college-age kids, a little on the beefy side. They looked like they didn't know whether to stare at her ass or hide their faces so they tried to do a little of both. The maid ignored them; she pushed her cart up to a door close to my end of the hall, knocked twice, then opened the door and vanished inside. The three kids looked at each other, two of them balled their fists up, the third one held up a hand to stop the other two. "No visible marks," he said, his voice somewhat muffled through the hallway door. "She gets marked up, we don't get paid. Got it?" The other two nodded and then the three of them walked in the other direction, the one Aniri had taken.

Not good.

They ain't come here to party, I told myself. Heather told me that the pimps were mad at Aniri because she'd fallen in love, or in something, and this looked like a setup. I shoved the stairwell door open and ran after them, they were almost to the end of the hallway and they ran when they saw me coming; by the time I got to the far corner one of them had a door open and I got there just as he went through and tried to shut it behind him. I banged my shoulder into the closing door, heard the kid go sprawling to the floor inside.

How stupid will you look, I asked myself, if she isn't in there?

But she was, she was backed up against the far wall, standing stiff, eyes wide.

I could feel myself ogreing up, inflating, Ogun was definitely pissed at these three clowns, he filled me with his power; they might have been young and strong but they were out of their weight class. The first one was clambering back to his feet, as he turned to face me I caught him with a short left just above the ear and he went straight back down again. The first guy through the door had Aniri by the upper arms and he was grinning like he'd just pulled the ace to match his flush, she still had that blank look on her face but she reached one hand slowly down into her bag.

The other kid looked undecided. I didn't give him time to think, I vaulted the bed but he bear-hugged me so I couldn't hit him. "I'll kill this bitch!" the other one yelled, but then he made this weird noise, kind of a gargling shout; the one holding me turned to look at his buddy and his eyes went wide just as I head-butted him, he let go of me and reeled backward, blood blooming out of his nose. Aniri stepped past me then, her hand held straight out in front of her, she was holding a small spray can, she pushed the nozzle down and the stuff came out in a stream and the kid began clawing at his face. The one who'd been holding Aniri was in a fetal position on the floor; all of his attention was focused on the act of breathing.

"Pepper spray," she said, strangely calm. She stowed the can back in her bag.

"I think your employers might be unhappy with you," I told her, panting slightly.

"You might be right," she said. Her hands were shaking, and she swayed on the spot.

"We should leave. Are you gonna be okay? Can you walk?"

"Yes," she said, almost inaudibly, and she moved, pausing next to each of the fallen men, and by the time we got to the door she had three wallets, two watches, about a half an inch of loose bills, and a whole bunch of keys. "This way," she said, wobbling in the direction of the elevator.

"You sure you don't want their shoes?"

"Come," she said, her pronunciation betraying her origins for the first time.

Outside on the street she stopped for a moment, stood blinking in the sun. "Do you know which way to the park?" she said.

"Uptown," I told her, trying to focus. The last of my adrenaline was still ebbing. "That way. Do you think we should sit down somewhere . . ."

"I would like to stay outdoors," she said, and she turned and headed uptown.

I followed her. "What happens next? If you go back to Los Paraíso . . ."

"I'll be all right," she said, her voice belying the confidence of her words. "No use to anyone if I can't work." She glanced at my face. "I know you," she said. "I've seen you drinking coffee in front of that bodega on C."

"I had a sister . . ."

"I was at Melanie's memorial service," she said. "The Worm and the other two have been talking of nothing but her, and you, for days now." And then she did it, she hit me with that knowing little quarter smile, for an eye blink there was something or someone very familiar in her eyes, something I should have expected. Someone I knew.

Someone who knew me.

"Don't worry about me," she said again. "I'll be all right. Do you know about the four . . ." She stopped, looked away for a moment. "Five. Do you know about the five fundamental forces?"

I shook my head. "My education is incomplete."

"The first four are gravity and whatever."

It sounded like something she'd memorized out of a book but didn't understand, and it felt like I was supposed to ask the obvious question. "Okay, what's the fifth?"

"Right about now," she said, "I think you are."

Sirens sounded a couple of blocks behind us. I turned to look as cops in blue disgorged from cruisers pulled haphazardly in front of the hotel we'd just left. I stopped to watch them make their unhurried way into the building. "Maybe you should reconsider," I said. "Maybe we should get in off the street for a minute . . ." I turned back, but she was gone.

SOME GUY I didn't recognize occupied Shmuley's chair inside the cubicle, and it dawned on me then that it was Saturday and Gelman didn't work Saturdays. I was wearing the raincoat, the guy in the booth growled something at me but I just showed him my key and kept going.

No Hector, the kid was not in his usual spot in the hallway. Inside, maybe, sleeping, or maybe he was at preschool. I wondered if they did preschool on Saturdays. I wondered if he was okay, did his mother feed him breakfast, was that the only pair of pants the kid owned, was he better off with his prostitute of a mother, who seemed to be really trying, or would he do better in some foster home where nobody really gave a shit? I went through the same inner debate every time I went past his spot, whether he was in it or not. It never changed much and I never got close to any kind of answer, except the usual one: God, isn't there something you could do for this kid? What the fuck?

It was in that frame of mind that I opened my door to see Shmuley Gelman sitting on the bed looking at me. "I thought you'd forgotten," he said.

" 'Course not," I lied. "Gelman, if you ain't gonna wear a tie, you don't need to do up all them buttons. Undo that top one, at least, you look like you're trying to strangle yourself."

"Well, he's a professor," Gelman said. "What do professors wear? Do you think I need a tie? Mine are all back at my mother's house and I don't wanna go back there. How much does a tie cost? Is there somewhere on the way where I could stop and get one?"

I breathed a sigh of relief as I remembered promising to accompany the kid across town. "Gelman, relax, you don't need a tie. The guy don't care what you look like." The kid was in a state, he looked like he was gonna vibrate right out of his shoes. I started to wonder how I wound up with this job, it seemed to me that the kid deserved better than me, but it looked like I was all he had. Besides, Tommy and William had taken time out for me just the night before and they weren't gonna see a thing for it. What the hell, Saul, it's not going to fucking hurt you to do something for someone besides yourself for a change. "Is it time? Are you ready to go?"

He rubbed his forehead and started to hyperventilate. "No," he finally said. "But I think I need to go now anyhow. Where did you find that raincoat? It looks like you slept in it. Do you have to wear that?"

"I think I do, but when we get close to where we're going I'll take it off and carry it. No one will notice. Does that work?"

"Yes," he said, and he stood up somewhat unsteadily. "I hope I can walk." He looked at me. "Saul, if you weren't here, I don't think I could do this."

"Shmoo, this ain't Lucifer we're going to see. Guy's a freakin' math teacher."

That broke the spell, and he laughed, but then he quickly got serious again. "Just so you should know," he said. "When I wrote him the letter, I used my middle name. Samuel."

"Sam Gelman." He stared at me, a bleak look on his face. "Yeah, I can see it. It fits you."

"I think that's what pissed my mother off the most." He looked like a man walking to his own execution. "I'm ready."

GELMAN'S ABILITY TO speak completely deserted him when he met his professor. The guy reminded me of pictures I'd seen of Ulysses S. Grant taken during the war. He was kind of a stocky guy, had a very short salt-and-pepper beard, and you could see the mileage on his face right through it. I put my arm around Gelman and got him calmed down a little bit, once the two of them got started up on whatever the hell it was the guy really taught, Gelman forgot about his nerves, and when a couple of post-grads showed up and joined the party he hardly missed a beat. They all could have been speaking Latin for all I knew. After a while I excused myself to go take a leak and I don't think any of them even heard me.

I decided to hang around. It wasn't that Gelman couldn't find his way back. I didn't know why, really, but I sat on a bench outside of the room they were in, rolled my coat up, stuck it in the bag and shoved it all underneath. But just say he was your kid. Say he'd just started to find himself, what he was, what he was going to be. How could you cut him loose, even if you didn't approve of mathematicians? Or whatever? "If you don't give up this normal shit you're studying, kid, we're going to throw you out and you can't ever come back."

And I thought I was a rat.

I sat there on the bench kicking it around while I watched the girls go by. Some of them looked to me like they had to be around fourteen, but you had to be older than that to go to college, didn't you? Made me feel like Aqualung, especially when they smiled and said hi on their way past. It was probably about an hour later when Gelman's professor came out and flopped down on the bench beside me. "Where on earth did you find this kid?" he said.

"Just ran into him, I guess."

"He thinks the sun shines out of your nether orifice," he said.

"I spread cheer wherever I go. You don't sound all that happy to have met him."

He shook his head. "Is he really . . . He's completely self-educated? Let me tell you something. I spent the last eighteen months concocting a model for string theory that doesn't require the existence of eleven dimensions . . ." He glanced at me, decided I didn't need to hear the fine details. "What it is, Gelman just blew up my whole program. Just like that. There's little pieces of equation all over the floor in there. I mean, I'm still right, I know I am, but I have to rethink . . ." He looked at me again. "He doesn't even have a cell phone. When I asked him where he lives he got so nervous he could barely breathe." He shook his head again. "Not for nothing, okay, and please don't take this the wrong way, but you two don't look like you'd ever inhabit the same room, at any time, for any reason."

"Works that way sometimes, but I don't know shit about string theory." The professor tilted his head back and regarded me through slitted eyes. Reminded me of Luisa. "Funny, though, how the universe uses you. One molecule bumps into another one, changes its trajectory. And from then on, everything is different. That ever happen to you?"

"Yes," he said. "It has."

"And then you find out you got a new obligation you weren't looking for."

"That's the way society is supposed to function," he said. "Ideally."

"Maybe. Gelman's story ain't mine to tell. Safe to let you know, he's got nothing."

The guy leaned his elbows on his knees and stared into space.

Took him a minute to get there. He glanced over at me a couple of times while he added it up. "Hasidic," he finally said.

"Until just a few days ago. His mother found the first letter that you wrote him back, and the shit hit the fan."

"Dios mío." He stared into space awhile longer. "He have a place to stay?"

"For the moment."

"This kid's extraordinary." It was almost like he was talking to himself. He sighed, and then he shook his head. "All right," he said, sounding like a guy who'd just agreed to adopt a cat that he knew his wife would hate. "I'm in. We should work something out, you and I. He's going to need a lot of support. If you're game. You and I, maybe if we work together we can keep him going. I mean, I can't just let him walk out of here, what a mind that kid's got. Are you really up for this? You got a cell number?"

I GOT A call from a number I didn't recognize. I stared at the screen for a few seconds and toyed with the idea of ignoring it, but I hate voice mail, and I hate suspense. There must be something imbedded in the human psyche that makes you need to answer when you're summoned by a mechanical clatter, or even the electronic approximation of one.

It was Brian, Li Fat's lieutenant. "You still interested in talking to Kwok? If you are, you gotta do it right now."

I went inside the classroom and made my apologies to Gelman, but they were hardly necessary, he was locked in. His professor waved me away, absolving me, at least in my mind, from seeing to it that Gelman made it back to Los Paraíso.

Brian picked me up about a half hour later. He was in a new Lincoln, the one with the grill that looks like Geraldo Rivera's mustache. And he had a driver, too, an older guy who looked like he wanted to kick my ass. Which I thought was funny, because it's usually the young guys who want to make their bones, not the old ones.

Dude glared at me.

"Even if you're the toughest meatball on the block," I told him, "you're still just a meatball."

He took a step in my direction.

Brian cleared his throat, and his driver froze.

"Mr. Fowler?" Brian said. "Please don't stick your fingers through the bars. They might get bitten off. If you don't mind? I just need to pat you down. Since we're vouching for you and all." He stepped around behind me while I assumed the position, right there on the Manhattan sidewalk. He searched me quickly and thoroughly while the older guy and I glared at each other.

"Your associate doesn't seem to like me."

"His is not to question why."

"A gangster who quotes Tennyson! I must have been misinformed about you guys."

"I like Tennyson," he said. "Running dog imperialist, to be sure, but a great poet." He pointed at the car. "If you would."

"Who picked this thing out?"

"We own the dealership," he said mournfully.

"Into the valley of death, rode the six hundred."

"I only see one of you."

"Maybe he was talking about my IQ."

"Six hundred?" he said. "Probably a lot closer to sixty. I feel compelled to tell you that Peter Kwok is not known for his sense of humor. And, on a related subject, if things get ugly here, which is a distinct possibility, we, ahh, we are not here to back you up. Just to be clear."

"How'm I doing so far?"

"Well, you're not dead yet," he said. "So you got that going for you."

"Wow. From Alfred, Lord Tennyson to Carl Spackler, all in the same conversation. Astonishing intellectual breadth in such a young man."

"Get in the fucking car, will you?"

DOWNTOWN MANHATTAN, SOMEWHERE under the western end of the Manhattan Bridge, in a confusing warren of tangled streets, we stopped in front of a new six-story steel and glass office building with an attached parking garage. It was on a short block of ancient redbrick buildings. We parked on the third floor of the empty parking garage. Strange for anything in Manhattan to be empty. "Park facing out," Brian told his driver. "And keep the engine running."

"Kwok that bad?" I asked him.

"One never knows," he said, giving me the eye. "Just remember what I told you."

We walked through a connecting doorway into the empty office building. Almost empty. We were in a large, gray carpeted room that looked like it was fated for cubicles. A short fat guy in a suit was at the far end of the room. He was putting golf balls at a glass that lay on its side on the carpet. A half-dozen men stood around behind him, looking stiff and uncomfortable. And behind them, the inner office walls were in place. As I got closer I saw the signs of what might be called a history of physical confrontation in the faces of the six men, a cauliflower ear here, a broken nose there, a scarred lip on another. One of them hung back behind the others, but I caught a glimpse of his face.

I'd seen him before, wearing a hoodie, down on Tenth Street. Aha, said I. To myself.

Brian leaned in close and whispered in my ear. "Try to follow my cue," he said. "And let me speak first."

I nodded.

I assumed the fat guy was Peter Kwok. His hair was mostly white on top, and he had it cut in a fifties USMC flattop. He paid us no attention at all, he seemed completely focused on his putting practice. I didn't know much about golf but the guy seemed pretty good to me, consistently on or close to his target from about fifteen feet away. We stopped at a distance that I guessed Brian considered either prudent or polite. Kwok still had five or six balls to go, lined up at his chosen distance, and he stood over each one in succession, lining up his shot and connecting with the same careful, measured stroke. After the last one caromed off the lip of the glass and came to rest a short distance away, he stood erect, leaned on his putter like it was a cane, and looked at Brian.

Brian cleared his throat. "Li instructed me to thank you for your forbearance in this matter."

Kwok nodded at him and then looked at me. "As a personal favor to Li Fat," he said, "I'll listen to your story. Make it short."

"My name is Saul Fowler," I told him. "I had a half sister named Melanie Wing. I have pictures."

He stared at me for a few seconds. "Okay."

I walked closer and handed him the printouts. "This is Melanie in life. This is what was left of her when they pulled her out of the river. And this last one is her mother, Annabel Wing. Annabel was murdered a few days ago at her home in Flushing. I don't have a picture of her body but the MO was the same."

Kwok looked at the picture of Annabel for maybe twenty seconds. "He's Flushing," he said, gesturing at Brian with the printouts.

"She was your second cousin."

"So?"

"She was terrified of you."

Kwok snorted. "She was afraid of ghosts. She . . ." He left off as a car pulled up outside, next to Brian's Lincoln. Kwok handed the printouts back to me. "Give me a moment, please."

I retreated, went back to stand next to Brian. Maybe it was my imagination, but Brian looked a little tenser than he had. Kwok retrieved his golf balls, lined them up about the same distance from his target as before and started again. Three men came through the door in single file. The center one had wet his pants. They, too, stopped and waited while Kwok practiced. When he was lined up over the last ball, Kwok spoke without looking up. "I thought we had an arrangement," he said.

"Mr. Kwok," the guy with the wet pants said. "Please. My daughter . . ."

Kwok waved a hand and a light went on in one of the inner offices. A girl stood just inside a window and looked out at us. It was hard for me to judge her age, but I guessed she was somewhere in her mid-teens. A large man stood behind her with his hands on her shoulders.

"Oh, Jennifer," he said, and tears started to run down his face. "Oh my God, Mr. Kwok, please . . ."

"You decided to go into business for yourself. Against our agreement. In Jersey. I don't do business in Jersey. Now I have to go out to Union City and apologize for your indiscretions. None of the people out there are going to believe that I had no hand in this. Do you have any idea how much trouble you have caused me?"

"Mr. Kwok, please, it had nothing to do with you . . ."

"I FUCKING OWN YOU NOW!" Kwok screamed, his face suddenly the color of raw beef. He abandoned the last golf ball and strode up to the man in the wet pants. "YOU DON'T EVEN TAKE A SHIT WITHOUT ASKING MY PERMISSION! DO YOU FUCKING HEAR ME?"

The guy didn't answer but he folded up his hands as though he were praying.

Kwok swung his putter, catching the guy in both hands as the guy tried to shield his face.

The girl screamed.

Kwok got in three more good licks with the putter as his target melted to the floor but he went long on the fourth and the club head snapped off. Kwok grunted with the effort of each swing, and again when he flung the shaft of the golf club across the room, and then he started kicking the man, who had rolled into a ball and clasped his arms around his head.

That's what you're supposed to do if you get attacked by a bear.

Kwok was fat, though, and out of shape, plus he was wearing the wrong kind of shoes for the job. Italian loafers don't provide much protection for your toes. He stopped after about a minute and a half, walked a short distance away, stopped to look at the girl, who was still screaming. He made a chopping gesture at the office window and the large man dragged the girl away, and after a moment her screams became fainter and fainter until I could no longer hear them. Kwok turned and went back and knelt down next to his target. "These men are going to take you away," he said. "And they are going to ask you a lot of questions. If you love your daughter, do not lie. Do you hear me? If you love your daughter, do not lie." He struggled back to his feet. "And after I hear what you told them, I will decide on your punishment." He waved at the two men.

We all stood silent as the two men dragged the guy back out to their car.

Kwok ran his hands through his hair.

Then he turned back to me. "They were early," he said calmly, his voice betraying only a very slight embarrassment. "My bad." He stood there looking at me.

"Annabel Wing," I told him.

"It wasn't us," he said.

"Is that all you got? Somebody murders your cousin and that's your reaction? I know people who would consider someone murdering their cousin a bit of an insult."

"I didn't really know her. I hadn't seen her in years. I know there was a thing about her getting knocked up, but that was a family matter, and it was a long time ago. None of my business." He stared at me for a few seconds and I started to wonder if he had another golf club stashed somewhere close by. "Let me explain something to you. New York is a dangerous place. You can make money here, but if you fuck around you pay the price." He gestured at a small pool of blood on the gray carpet. "That's the chance you take. Now, I don't know what Melanie was into, or Annabel, either. And frankly I don't care. Now, if you don't mind, I have a business to run." He turned away.

"C'mon, Pete, we both know you're smarter than that."

He turned back, his face growing red again.

"I start asking questions about Melanie Wing, and very shortly thereafter two Chinese dudes working with a black guy try very hard to discourage me. And when that doesn't work, someone puts a hit on Melanie's mother and sets me up to take the fall. Something stinks, and I got this feeling that you know what it is."

He pointed a fat finger at me. "Number one. I am not an equal opportunity employer. Got it? If a black was mixed up in whatever is going on, it has nothing to do with me, I don't use blacks. Number two. I. Don't. Care. Stay away from me, Fowler, and stay out of my business. I won't say it again." He turned and walked away, deeper into the depths of the office building, leaving his golf balls, and the small puddle of blood, behind. His men followed a short distance behind. The guy I'd seen before, wearing a hoodie, seemed particularly nervous.

"You're as crazy as he is," Brian said, after they were gone. "Let's get the hell out of here."

I didn't move. "How far uptown does he go?"

"Nothing north of Houston, I would think."

"You know the guy better than me. Between you and me, Bri, what's your read on what just happened?"

"Between you and me?" Brian looked around. "He's afraid of something," he said, dropping his voice. "I don't know if that routine with the golf club was supposed to impress you, me, or those guys he's got working for him. Come on, Fowler, let's go. Train's leaving."

Chapter Sixteen

I LOST MY raincoat and stuff, I must have left it all wadded up and shoved underneath the bench at NYU. Funny, how naked I felt without my disguise, funny how people looked right past me while I was wearing it. I could stand the coat collar up, tuck my face, shamble along and become almost invisible. But funniest of all were the feelings that crowded in on me when I did it. Sure, it was safer for me to be invisible, but at those times I was oppressed by a bone-deep loneliness. It was a horrible sensation, that even strangers going past in the street, people I'd never met and probably never would, they, too, ignored me, turned their faces away and pretended I wasn't there. I'd had to keep reminding myself that I had good and valid reasons for wanting to be overlooked, and that would suffice, barely, to keep the coat in place, but as I walked back to Avenue C and Tenth Street, in spite of the increased risk to my person, I had to admit that I was glad to be rid of the damn thing.

Much harder for me to look past a homeless person after that.

Yeah, man, I see you.

And I know you're fucked up. Maybe just a little bit more than the rest of us, but we're probably more like you than either of us think.

I saw the tall kid with the motorcycle again. It took me a moment or two to remember where I'd seen him before, but he was Aniri's boyfriend, I'd seen him following the limo that bore her off to her next appointment. And those of us for whom lurking is a profession are always amused by the efforts of those who suck at it. The kid was loitering in front of the bodega where I liked to get my coffee; he was drinking bottled water and pretending to read the newspaper. He was too big to blend in, for one thing, and for another, he was a white boy to a degree rarely attained by native or even transplanted New Yorkers. He had a cowlick, for God's sake, he wore the bottom two inches of his jeans turned up, and he wore a blue denim jacket that almost, but not quite, matched his jeans. Made you wonder where he'd left his horse. I looked around for the motorcycle, spotted it parked a block south on C.

I walked up behind him. I didn't have to go all Snidely Whiplash on the guy, either, his entire being seemed focused on the front door to the Los Paraíso. I got up close, and in what I thought was a passable imitation of the Worm, I said, "We thought you gone, man."

His startle response was almost all physical. He hardly made a sound but his water bottle went straight up in the air and his paper devolved into a bunch of litter blowing down the street. He whirled around, his hands turning to fists and taking up residence on either side of his chin.

Not bad, really.

"Not funny," he said, breathing hard. "Are you with them?"

"What would you do if I was, you fucking idiot? These are not Boy Scouts you're messing with."

He dropped his hands. "I know. I just wanted to see her."

"Walk with me," I told him.

"WE CAN'T GO to the police," the kid said. We were a couple of blocks south on C, still out on the sidewalk because he didn't want to go in anywhere. He didn't want to be with me, either, he was so antsy he could hardly stand still. He couldn't wait to get back to his corner.

"Why not?"

"She's undocumented, man. If the police did raid that place, they'd arrest Aniri along with everyone else, and they'd put her in jail, they'd try her and put her away. And when her time was done they'd deport her."

"So run away. Get on a bus and take her back to Alabama with you."

"It's South Carolina," he said sourly. "And they know who I am. They know where my folks live. They'll never let us go, for two reasons." He ticked them off on his fingers. "One, there's too much money involved, and two, it would set a bad precedent. They got some girls from the Ukraine. What about them? Don't you think they'd like to take a walk, too?"

"Okay," I said. "So your answer is that you're gonna stand there on that corner all lovelorn and shit? And you couldn't stick out any more if you wore a cowboy hat and a pair of shitkickers, for crissake. And just in case they don't notice you, honky, you got your goddamn motorcycle parked right there on the avenue. Why don't you just wear a sign?"

"Doesn't a person have a right to fall in love?" he said, indignant. "Isn't this still America? Don't I have a right to stand where I want?"

"Yeah, okay, sure. Your South Carolina is showing. You're in Alphabet City, dumbass. They'll kill her. Or worse, they'll sell her. You ever consider that possibility?" From the look on his face it was clear that he hadn't. "Six months on the street in Juarez, or some other garden spot, her own mother wouldn't recognize her."

"Aniri has a plan," he said stubbornly. "She said she had something figured out, but she wouldn't tell me what it was. And I trust her."

"Great. Does that make her the one with the brains? She the member of this collective that's in charge of thinking? I hope so, buddy, because I don't see much sign of it coming out of you."

He ground his teeth. "You work with them, don't you. They sent you out here to scare me off. I'll kill 'em all, you tell them that for me. They hurt Aniri and I swear to God I will blow away every swinging dick in that place, I don't care. The Worm, those two Chinese assholes, the white guy who comes for the money, and you, too."

Paranoia. It was good to see, actually, because maybe it meant he wasn't as stupid as he looked. "I do not work for anyone at Los Paraíso."

"Who, then?" he demanded.

"Melanie Wing," I said. "Someone at Los Paraíso killed her, and they dumped her body in the river."

Corey went a little pale. "Don't know her," he said, after a minute. "You sure of this?"

I had to admit it. "No."

"Well then, you got a problem, don't you." He turned and headed back to his corner.

"Hey, kid." He stopped and looked at me. "At least move the bike. I mean, show a little effort, for crissake."

He turned and stalked away. Guess my bedside manner needed work.

SOMETIMES YOU GET a feeling that you're riding too high, that the situation you're in is inherently unstable and that far below you something has begun to crack, which ought to tell you to start looking for a soft place to fall. Either that, or find an exit door. Avenue C and Tenth had started to look like that, every time I showed up. Funny, how something can go along for years, everybody thinks it's permanent, and then suddenly you realize that there ain't enough air in the balloon anymore, and down she comes. I watched Aniri's boyfriend as he stomped back up the avenue. Kid surprised me, though, got on his bike and rode away.

A black gypsy cab pulled up to the curb and two guys got out. One of them was Sal Edwards, the cop who had arrested me at Annabel's, and the other one was a fat white guy who looked and dressed like a used furniture salesman.

"Mr. Fowler," Edwards said. "So nice to see you. Could we have a word?"

"Do I have a choice?"

"Yeah," the fat guy said. "I could sit on you right here while Sal goes to get a warrant, but you don't want that, do you?"

"I get the picture."

We sat down at a table in a dark bar over on First Avenue. I didn't know if it was a cop bar or a wino bar, it was early enough for the place to be empty, and what distinctions there are between the two are probably too subtle for me. Sal and his portly friend drank something imported and I settled for coffee, which was pretty horrible.

Sal had notes and he took me back over everything that had happened on the day Annabel got killed. We went over it several times, from her call to my cell, through my stopover at Klaudia's apartment, right up to the moment he arrested me. Sal had done some homework, he had the exact time of the phone call from the cell company, statements from the cabdrivers who'd taken me to and from Klaudia's, and he even had the transaction time from the liquor store where I'd bought Annabel's peace offering. He grilled me over and over about everything I remembered from that morning, what I had for breakfast, the appearance of the cab-drivers, and the time I spent with Klaudia. I drew the line there, though. If Klaudia wanted to tell him how we passed the time it was her business, but he wasn't going to hear about it from me.

"Well," he finally said, flipping his notebook shut. "I could get past all of it, even the cabdriver who remembers you because of the sixteen-dollar tip, but I can't get past Livatov. Time of death, you were with her inside her apartment, so she says, and I can't shake her. Wasn't for the fact she bushwhacked you that morning, you'd be on your way upstate. I guess that means you owe the lady something."

"You sound disappointed."

"I am," he said. "My job is to put miscreants such as yourself away."

"So much for truth, justice, and the American way."

"Listen," he said. "Truth is for philosophers. It's like my old man used to say, maybe you didn't do what I'm gonna beat you for, but you done something I didn't catch you at, you deserve it and you know it. You're dirty, Fowler, the hair on the back of my neck tells me so."

"Isn't your hair ever wrong?"

"Rarely," he said. He drained what was left of his beer and pushed his chair back. "I gotta piss."

The fat cop watched Edwards walk away, and then he looked at my coffee cup. "You got a problem with the booze?"

"Not as long as I don't touch it," I told him.

He nodded. "Scanlon," he said. "Vice. I asked Edwards if I could tag along. I had a talk with Frank O'Neill. He told me why you're here."

"O'Neill. Retired cop, does real estate now. He a friend of yours?"

"Moneybags? No, but I used to work with him. That place on Tenth, where your sister used to work. What do you have on it?"

I looked at Scanlon and the hairs on the back of my neck started tingling. Call it instinct, call it prejudice, whatever, but something told me Scanlon wasn't one hundred percent. And one of my wandering brain cells must have bumped up against another one. I was, all of a sudden, pissed at myself for being so slow. "Vice, you said."

"Yeah."

"I know where there's a shopping bag full of nice dirty money, the kind that's got no memory and no conscience." Maybe it had taken me too long to figure it out, but I had it now, and the next steps seemed obvious. "The shopping bag is sitting on top of an old safe that's full of the same stuff." I had Scanlon's complete attention. "And there's probably a lot more where that came from. You ever hear of a guy they call El Tuerto?"

"The twisted man," Scanlon said. "Could be anybody."

"The twisted man ain't just anybody. It's one specific guy."

"I assume the money you were just talking about belongs to him."

"He might think it does, but I'm thinking it probably needs a new daddy. I got a few things I gotta take care of. This could turn out to be a very sweet deal. Can you give me another day or two? And are you willing to do what needs to be done?"

"Here's my number," he said. "I'm your man."

I BOUGHT AN old Toyota Corolla. Thing had a million miles on the clock and there was a hole in the dashboard where the radio used to be but it looked okay if you didn't get too close. It ran okay, too, although it shivered like a dog too long in cold water if you went much over seventy, it smoked a bit when you first cranked it up, plus the tires weren't great, but I figured no bad guy in New York City would ever get caught dead driving it, which meant, nobody I had to deal with would look at it twice. The price was right, not that it mattered, and I planned to dump it long before the temporary tags ran out. The first time I drove it I was pretty worried because Peter Kwok's driver went a little faster than the Corolla really wanted to follow, but after a while I quit worrying. Freakin' Corolla would probably keep going long after I was dead, as long as someone thought to put a little oil in it once in a while.

Kwok lived in Westchester, about an hour north of the city. Surprised me, really, I had him figured for a Trump Tower kind of douchebag. His house was beautiful, though, an old stone farmhouse out in the woods, historic as hell, George Washington would have had no problem crashing there if he'd ever been in the neighborhood. It had a three-car garage styled to match the house, with three cars in it, one of them a Morgan three-wheeler that gave me a serious case of lust. After I followed Kwok there the first night I went back twice to scope the place. The first time there was a car in the driveway, sign on the car door said HANDIMAIDS, and I had to wait for them to leave, which cut my margin a little close. The second time the place was all mine, I had plenty of time to handle the alarms, set up my entry point, and do all my other due diligence. The toughest part of the whole exercise was finding a place to stash the Corolla while I was inside. I wound up parking in the grass behind the garage. You couldn't see it from the house unless you were looking for it. Kwok had the kind of perimeter lighting that goes on by itself when you got too close, but that stuff isn't much use after you've taken the bulbs out and chucked them in the woods. I spent the better part of the afternoon going through the place. Old habits, maybe, or idle curiosity. The guy had an amazing porn collection, and he had a lot of weapons. Guns, knives, and two baseball bats. I policed up all the ordinance and stashed most of it where Kwok wouldn't find it in a hurry, but I left the porn where it was.

I hung around until I saw lights in the driveway around nine that night. I watched from an upstairs window as Kwok and a woman got out of the back of the car. The driver stayed put until I heard the front door open, then he reversed back down the driveway and took off. After some murmured conversation, Kwok came upstairs and took a shower while the woman waited for him in the entryway downstairs.

He was naked when he came out of the master bath. The GI Joe haircut was the only macho thing he still had going, the dude was fat, his arms were flabby, and he was basically hairless. I was sitting on his bed; me and the goonas were all laughing our asses off, I don't think he noticed me until the flash from my cell phone camera lit him up, and even then I'm not sure the light was good enough for him to tell who I was. "Goddammit!" He wasn't too loud at first but he built up volume as he went, inhaling more air than he needed, puffing himself up like a blowfish. "Do you know who I am? Do you have any idea the kind of shit you just bought? What the fuck are you . . ."

I racked the slide on the Colt 9mm I'd found in his desk drawer. "Wow," I told him. "You got the tiniest schwantz I ever seen. Now I know why you're so pissed off all the time."

"What the fuck are you doing in my house?" he screamed at me, his big belly shaking. "I'll show you what I got, you fucking—"

I fired a round into the floor between his feet. He jumped and fell over backward. I got off the bed and walked over, pointing his gun at him. "Now that's what you call a dinkie."

"Shut up!" he screamed. "Shut the fuck up!"

I squatted down so that I was at eye level with him. I pointed the gun at his face. His meager chest heaved and his belly shook as he fought for breath, and for self-control. "Do it," he finally said. "See if I give a fuck. Get it over with."

"It's a thought," I told him. "But I didn't really come here for that."

"How much is he paying you?"

"Who?"

"Li fucking Fat!" He practically spat the name at me. "You won't live to spend the money, you realize that, don't you? You fell for his crazy grandfather act, and you probably won't figure him out until he chops you into little pieces and feeds you to the sharks somewhere off Montauk, you fucking piece of shit . . ."

"I don't work for Li Fat."

He leaned back on his elbows, his legs splayed wide, fat guy style. His belly sort of flattened out and his little wee-wee pointed at the ceiling. "Who, then?"

"I am here on behalf of Melanie Wing."

The air went out of him and he shook his head. "You fucking dope," he said. "The fuck you want from me? I already told you, I got no time for that shit."

"I'll tell you what, Kwok. Gimme something. You give me something, I'll give you something."

"What you got for me?" he sneered.

"You first," I told him.

He gritted his teeth, then spoke slowly, like he was talking to an idiot. "On my mother's grave," he said. "Her name never one time left my lips. I don't think I ever seen the girl. I don't care about Melanie Wing, alive or dead, and I never did."

He stared at me while I thought it over. "Why the picture," he finally said.

"The picture is so I don't have to kill you," I told him. "See, all those people jumping off your bandwagon, I think they're making a mistake. I think you're a survivor. Okay, you had a run of bad luck, but I don't see you going down this easy. But if the picture comes out . . . Everybody laughing at you? Calling you Shorty behind your back? Nobody could survive that, not in your business. You can survive everything but disrespect."

Kwok's expression was a mixture of contempt and fear. Mostly contempt. "You said you had something for me."

"You didn't give me all that much, apart from your solemn oath." I paused long enough for him to figure out how much I thought of that. "But I'll give you some of what I got. That sound fair? Two of your meatballs are jumping the fence."

His face flushed a deep red. "That fucking Li Fat . . ."

I shook my head. "Li Fat is not your problem. Two of your guys are freelancing. They moved uptown." Melanie had been murdered a little over six months prior, and the operation at the Hotel Los Paraíso had been in full swing by then. "I'm guessing they been running their sideline for at least a year, maybe longer. My connection says their operation is probably clearing two million a year, and I'll bet you this pistol right here that you ain't seen dollar one out of it."

His face got even darker.

"No bet? I'll give you one more thing. I saw one of them, last time I saw you. In that empty office building. I don't know the dude's name, but you're a smart guy, you'll figure it out. Gotta be a lot of money sitting in someone's sock drawer, that's for sure. I don't understand how come the cops haven't shut them down yet, but then, you know more about that kind of shit than I do."

He stared at me for a moment. "Are we finished?"

"Yeah, more or less." I stood back up. "Okay, get up. You and Little Willy get back in the bathroom."

He gritted his teeth as he struggled to his feet, but his eyes went wide when I picked the baseball bat up off the bed. "Don't worry, this isn't for you. In the bathroom. Go."

He eyed the bat as he backed away from me, kept going until he was at the far side of the bathroom. I swung the bat hard, broke the knob off the inside of the door. He finally thought to cover his wee-wee, which he did with both hands. He looked like a chubby little kid, angry and ashamed, embarrassed, short-changed by life. The goonas had to be pissing in their pants.

If they wore any.

"Your secret is safe with me," I told him. "And I'll stay off your block, if you stay off mine. Mess with me and your picture goes viral."

I closed his bathroom door, made sure it latched. As I walked out into the hallway I could hear him screaming and throwing shit. His date for the evening was still waiting in the entry, her face white. "Take me with you," she whispered. "Please? For the love of God, don't leave me here . . ."

I dropped her at the bus station in Yonkers.

I HAD A voice mail from Francis O'Neill. I listened to his message, he said he'd been thinking about my problem and he had some ideas; maybe he and I ought to meet and have another conversation. O'Neill knew the neighborhood, and he was no desk jockey, my impression of him was that he'd been a street guy. He had even intimated, in our last conversation, that his investigation skills were centered on the more, shall we say, physical aspects of interrogation.

I punched up his number.

He answered, which surprised me, given the lateness of the hour, and he dropped me into the middle of the conversation he'd been having with himself, no surprise there. "I hadda put her in a home, Saul."

What do you say to a guy who just had to have his wife committed? I assumed it was his wife. "Damn. I'm sorry to hear it."

He was silent for a second, then I heard him sigh. "I really wanted to get with you, Saul, what you were telling me before, it bothered me. But I can't even think of . . . I can't remember what I was thinking. I can't remember what I was going to do with you."

"I understand," I told him, even though I didn't, there was no way I could. "Don't worry about me, I'll be fine."

"Twelve grand a month," he said. "Can you believe that? Twelve grand a month and they can't even . . . She kept getting lost. She'd go out for a walk and she'd forget the way home. They tied her to the bed, Saul. I pitched a fit. I mean, I pitched a real fit." I pictured it, all six-foot-six of him, pissed off. "They tied her to the fucking bed, and when I went off on them they called the cops. Okay, I got loud, and whatnot. But can you blame me?"

"No. But you being an ex-cop, that must have helped."

"Damn right it did," he said. "We take care of our own, you can believe that. Twelve Gs a month and they tie her to the fucking bed. Son of a bitch. So I wanted to take care of you, Saul, if I could, but I can't. I can't do it. I can't even think straight."

"Forget it. She's lucky to have you."

He snorted. "Yeah. Right. I tell you what, for a long goddamn time it didn't look that way. So, anyhow, I'm jammed up right now, Saul, but I won't forget you. I'm gonna call, as soon as I can get my head straight. I'll get to you yet."

"Thanks," I told him.

Chapter Seventeen

So that's how it all came together, it's like when you're trying to remember someone's name and you can't, you go through the whole alphabet and you still can't come up with it, then later on when you're thinking of something else, it comes to you. It was like that. And Mac had been half right, it was about the money after all.

I had a brief last-minute case of cold feet, you know, what if I'm wrong, but I screwed up my resolve, sent my questions out there into the universe, and then I texted Scanlon, the vice cop, and I gave him the particulars. He texted me back a half hour later. He and his boys were coming. I had known it would happen, just not so quickly, but Scanlon was not a guy to leave money lying on the table. He'd taken an educated guess on the identity of his target and he already had his search warrants. Smarter than me, I suppose, but I had my guess, too, finally, just not so educated. I had enough time to go wrap up my stuff at Los Paraíso and get out. Klaudia had never seen the place, so she tagged along.

I read somewhere that in some primitive tribal societies, when you see children misbehaving, you are considered rude if you do not discipline them as you would your own. In other words, you see something obviously wrong, it's on you to do something. Not the cops, not some other faceless government entity, not your mother.

You.

Okay, more specifically, me, since I was there. And maybe outrage would have been the correct response all along, and maybe I would have felt something more than pity had not my humanity been eroded by the insanity of my own path. Hector, the five-year-old kid, watched me climb the stairs and walk down the hallway. "Where's my mom," he said.

Five fucking years old. Maybe six.

You had to know this day was coming. Selfish, I know, but I had figured to be long gone before it arrived, that way I could feel bad for Hector in the abstract, him and all the other kids just like him, not Hector in the flesh, not right then and there. I wanted to blame the goonas for it, or the system, or his mother, or whoever, and walk away.

"Where's my mom?" He stood there in his clean white shirt and his black pants so carefully ironed and creased, his shiny black shoes and his bowl haircut. Sounded more worried than before. I reached over his head and knocked on the door.

No response.

Bitch probably OD'd, I thought, she's probably right there dead on the floor inside. You want the kid to see that? Shit, man, I didn't even want to see that. "She's probably downstairs, Hector. She probably had to go down to the corner for something."

Go ahead, lie. Get away while you can. You got business, man . . . Klaudia was with me, she was right downstairs hanging with Gelman while I wrapped things up, and I wanted to get back to her. "I gotta get something inside my room over here." I pointed at my door. "Then I'll go downstairs and check for her. You stay right there, okay?"

He just looked at me.

I went into my room and shut the door behind me. I closed the laptop down and unplugged it, and then I paused to wonder what the hell I even wanted it for. There was a suspended ceiling in that disgusting bathroom, the kind with four-foot by two-foot foam panels hanging in a white metal grid. I stood up on the toilet, pushed one of the panels up, shoved the laptop and its power cord up inside.

The hell with it.

The kid was still in his spot. "I'm gonna go look right now. Okay?"

He just watched me.

Funny, how easy it is to believe in God when you really need a favor. You wanna see an atheist turn agnostic? Just add hot water.

One floor down I saw Heather, the girl I talked to in the hotel in midtown, and I yielded to a sudden urge. You can't help the kid, I told myself. Do something for someone else.

Anyone.

"Heather, don't go up. The cops are coming."

"What?"

"There's gonna be a raid. Tonight. Right now. I got the high sign from a guy I know in vice about a half hour ago."

She seized my elbow. "Walk me out," she said. "Get me the fuck out of here . . ."

I gave Klaudia the high sign on the way past, sort of a give-me-five-minutes kind of wave. She and Gelman watched us go by, she said something to him and he turned red and laughed. How cool was this lady, I knew women who would have wigged right the fuck out . . .

Outside on the sidewalk Heather turned her head against my shoulder and we headed north on Avenue C. She didn't make a sound until we were a couple of blocks away. "Are you some kind of cop," she whispered harshly.

I didn't see the need for whispering. "Are you really so far short of your retirement number? Are you close enough to your two mil?"

"This wasn't supposed to happen," she said, still whispering. "The Worm told me they were dialed in. He said they were connected, he said the guys in the precinct got theirs."

"Maybe some of them did," I told her. "I found one who didn't."

Avenue C stops at Fourteenth, and when we got to the corner we saw several black Chevy Suburbans with darkened windows whoosh by us. Heather watched them pass, then shivered and turned us in the opposite direction. "I'm close enough," she said. "I'm retired, as of right now. Can we get off the street somewhere?"

"If you want," I told her. "I figured you'd want to be on your way back to Delaware."

"I do," she said. "But I owe you for this, and I don't like owing anyone." I wondered what she had in mind, opened my mouth to tell her thanks just the same, that I wasn't in the market, but she was already pulling me into some restaurant we happened to be passing. It was a glorified Jewish deli, common in New York, rare elsewhere, and a pretty good reason to visit. She asked for a table in the back.

Her hands shook as she fumbled with an electronic cigarette. She got it in her mouth and sucked. "Was Melanie really your sister," she said.

"I don't know. It doesn't really matter anymore."

"I've known guys like you before," she said, nodding. "Not happy unless you got something to hunt. Something with claws."

"I'm not sure that I—"

"Don't talk," she said, pointing her finger at me. "Listen."

I shut up.

"Your timing sucks," she said. "The Worm and the two Chinamen are not in the building." She toked on her plastic cigarette again. "They're down in the park, down by the projects. By Tenth and the river. They're gonna put a beating on Aniri and her boyfriend."

I started to say something but she pointed her finger at me again. "You ever wonder what happened to the asshole who was runnin' those kids that used to sell dope right there on the corner outside the hotel?" She didn't wait for an answer. "He's dead. You wanna know why? He was drawing too much attention. They warned him off but he wouldn't go. They want Tenth Street nice and quiet, so that nobody looks too hard at Los Paraíso. You ever wonder what used to be on the first floor? In that street-level space under the hotel?" This time she did wait for an answer.

"I heard it was a pork store or something like that. Some kind of butcher shop."

"It's still a butcher shop." She stood up.

"Ah, Heather . . ."

"The name ain't Heather. And I don't live in Delaware." Her face twisted up into something between a smile and a grimace. "That's where he killed her. You know who he is, by now. You must."

"Yeah. El Tuerto. The twisted man. I know who he is, what I don't know is why."

"She made the same mistake the guy running them kids made. El Tuerto warned her away but she wouldn't go. Stubborn, just like you. You get in front of the money train, you get run over. And that really does make us even." She sucked on the plastic cigarette. "Happy hunting." She stood up, took two steps, then looked back at me one last time. "Don't leave him alive," she said, and then she did it, with her it was almost a sneer, but it was her just the same, that other woman looking out through Heather's eyes, and then Heather turned and she was gone.

HEATHER, OR WHOEVER she was, headed west on Fourteenth, clicking down the street in her high-heel boots like she had someplace important to go. She didn't look back and I never saw her again.

I went back to Los Paraíso. The cops weren't there yet, I wondered if maybe they wouldn't come after all. Maybe those Suburbans we'd seen on Fourteenth belonged to some politician, some sheik, some captain of industry on his way to see his girlfriend. I ran up the stairs. Klaudia was still sitting with Gelman inside his little glass booth. She started to rise but I motioned her to stay put. "How do I get into the space downstairs?" I said to Gelman. "Where's the door?"

He pointed to the rear of the building. "Down the back stair," he said. "Go out into the alley, I think there's a door . . ."

YOU CAN TELL a lot about a guy from the kind of work he turns out. I had to believe that the same guy who'd bricked up the front windows had set the gray metal door into the back wall of the alley. He'd gotten the courses so crooked out front that my friend

William had noticed it from a half a block away. Same douche-bag had hung the door, had to be, thing looked relatively new but it was on crooked and the hinges were installed backward, the dope left the pins exposed. All I needed was a hammer and a drift punch, I could have taken the door right off, locked or not, but I didn't have a hammer, I didn't have a punch, and I didn't have time. Did have my shims, though.

The cylinder was protected by an escutcheon plate, also installed crooked, but it protected the lock well enough. There was a hole in it where you stuck your key, and that's where the shims went, too. The cylinder was a contractor's special and it only took a minute to line the pins up. I got them all popped, turned the cylinder a quarter turn before it stuck.

Fucking shoemaker.

I had to lean my shoulder into the door and bounce my weight against it while I torqued the shims until the lock finally opened with a loud snap; to me it sounded like a gunshot in the quiet of the alley. I could have opened it without a sound if the lock had been installed right, but there was nothing for it. I jerked the door open.

The lights were on. I was in what looked like it had been the back room of an old deli. There was a walk-in cooler to my left. An ancient belt-driven refrigeration unit sat on a metal rack, chugging away. Through the small glass square on the door to the walk-in I saw the torso of a naked man, he seemed to be hanging from his feet. I guess now we knew what happened to the guy who'd been running the drug kids on the corner.

I didn't take the time to look.

I tiptoed past the walk-in box even though I knew any hope for surprise was lost. I had to be careful where I put my feet. The floor was made of old fashioned quarry tiles. They looked pretty new but they were unevenly applied.

Same craftsman.

In the main room, old store fixtures were shoved back against the walls. There was an open drain in the center of the floor, and about a hundred cockroaches scuttled for it when they felt me coming. I don't know why they bothered to come out, they could have fed on the blood easily enough down in the relative safety of the drainpipe.

Curiosity, maybe.

It was Hector's mother.

She was naked, stretched full-length on the floor, facedown. Plastic tie wraps bound her wrists and her ankles together, and she had about a dozen steak knives imbedded in her body, from two different sets. One set had what looked like bone handles and the second had the more common ebony wood.

I think she was still breathing.

To my right, a couple lengths of chain, about three feet each, were anchored to the wall. Each chain ended in a set of handcuffs. To my left, a noose of what looked like satin rope hung from a sprinkler pipe, and directly under the noose was a footstool, about a foot high, covered with a beige silk brocade.

Hector's mother coughed.

I swear I never heard that back door open, never felt the presence, not a hint of warning from the reptile brain, but the voice hit me, it went through my stomach like a raw electrical current.

"Where's my mom?"

God, you gotta be kidding me. The kid followed me down here? Couldn't you have done something?

Hector's mother made her last sound, it was a kind of rasping exhalation.

I don't know exactly what happened next. I am only a man, prisoner to my senses, tied hand and foot to what I see and hear, and I can never know for sure when my mind is lying to me. Maybe I had been touched by Ogun once before, in the hallway of a midtown hotel where three assholes targeted Aniri, I wondered about that, after, but right then all I know is that it felt like the air I breathed was on fire, that when I inhaled, the air burned my mucus membranes away, it incinerated whatever was inside my skull, it torched everything I thought and felt, there was barely room for consciousness, everything else was obliterated by fire, now I knew why they called it blind rage.

"Where's my MOM?"

The fire raged in my guts, I could barely keep from screaming.

"Where's my MOMMM . . ."

And then Klaudia was there, she must have followed Hector down the back stairs, she was on her knees wrapping herself around the kid, he fought her but I doubt she even felt it, she pulled him to her, crushed his head to her chest and shielded his eyes.

I looked at Klaudia.

It wasn't her.

I mean, it was, but it wasn't. It was gone, that . . . what? That other person who'd been inside her, the one that had hooked me, was gone. The real Klaudia, the little mouse that Reiman and Ms. Branch had described to me, that small and frightened human being was all that was left. I couldn't speak and she wouldn't look up. She was shaking, and it knew it wasn't the butcher shop she was afraid of, and it wasn't the dead woman on the floor.

It was me.

I couldn't comfort her, I couldn't touch her, I couldn't stand still, the flames wouldn't let me. I wanted to take them both into my arms but I could not, O'Neill, the man who'd killed Melanie, and probably Annabel, too, was somewhere in the park between Tenth Street and the river, and I was on fire, burning.

The twisted man.

I vaulted over the two of them and ran.

Finito

COREY JACKSON LEVERED himself up to one knee. *No referee in this fight,* he thought. *The Worm could kick you in the face right now if he wanted to . . . But the Worm was distracted.* Several of the harsh sodium vapor lights that illuminated the park blinked and went out, leaving them in relative darkness. The Babalao touched Aniri's elbow, guiding her to stand back behind him. The older guy, the one Corey assumed was the money man for Los Paraíso, stood with his head cocked, listening to the sound of a man screaming off in the distance. He had gray hair, gray eyes, and a hard face. He also had a snub-nose pistol in his right hand and he held it pointed at the ground. The gun looked like a .32 to Corey. He had grown up around guns and he knew the limitations of the small caliber piece but he also knew that in the right hands the thing could shoot you just as dead as any of its bigger brethren. One of the Chinese pimps stood off to the side, shifting his weight uneasily from foot to foot. "Go on," the gray man said, and he gestured back in the direction from which they'd come with his gun hand. "Go find out what the hell his problem is."

The pimp took off, running back toward Avenue D.

You can't do a damn thing about the gun, Corey told himself. And maybe you can't do much about the Worm, either, but maybe you could spoil his fun. Make him earn it. He stood the rest of the way up, spat a mouthful of blood onto the Worm's shirt. "That all you got?"

The Worm exploded into motion but Corey Jackson had thirty-six amateur bouts, and God had blessed him with a lot of quick. He saw the punch coming from a mile off, watched the Worm turn his upper body, dip his shoulder, saw the right elbow lift, watched the fist go back before it started to rise and come arcing in his direction, classic haymaker, and he leaned back just far enough. The Worm's knuckles whiffed past his chin but the follow-through left the man exposed. Corey backhanded him across his face with his right hand. "Come on, motherfucker," he said, surprised at the softness of his voice. "Show me something."

The Worm gritted his teeth and glanced over at the gray man, the unvoiced question clear in his eyes, but the guy was unmoved; he just stood there with his piece pointed at the dirt. "You heard the man," the guy said. The man's face looked like it was incapable of anything as human as a smile, but Corey saw something there that told him how much the gray man wanted it. You saw them at matches sometimes, and they always had that same look, it was the vulture's leer, the face of a man getting off by watching you bleed. Funny, how seldom you really hated your opponent, how often you hated the ghouls who came just to watch. For the gray man the pain would be an aperitif, something to whet the palate.

"That your buddy?" Corey muttered, knowing the Worm could hear, wondering if the gray man could as well. "Loves you, don't he." The Worm looked at him, hesitated a second, then ducked his head and shuffled forward. Corey danced to his left. The Worm, more cautious now, began throwing quick hard punches, using mostly his left hand. He was stronger than Corey, bigger, and he looked just about as quick, but he'd never seen the inside of a ring. Every time he threw a punch, he loaded up first, telegraphing his intention, and Corey was able to evade the worst of the blow. He took some shots on his arms and shoulders, slapped the rest away.

Yeah, he thought, but even on points I don't know if I can beat this guy, and points wouldn't help anyhow. Corey knew that his biggest flaw as a fighter had always been his lack of a nose for the kill. You better man up, he thought. This time you got some skin in the game.

The Worm started getting angry, his punches were getting sloppier, less crisp. He's thinking, Corey told himself. Getting ready to change tactics. He could try to grapple, and if he gets his hands on me I'm probably finished. Either that or he'll try to go for Aniri . . .

Like hell, Corey thought. The Worm threw another stiff left but his heart wasn't in it and he left his ribs exposed. One thing boxers know is that it's the skeletal system that transmits the force, not the meat. Corey focused on his target and unloaded, fist, wrist bones, forearm, locked elbow, upper arm, and shoulder aligning right at the moment of impact, no flex in his joints, the weight of his body filling in behind the shot, mass times acceleration less the square root of the distance traveled, but that couldn't be right because you had to factor intent in there, somehow, and tonight he had a very heavy left.

The Worm grunted in surprise.

Corey spat blood at him again. "Come on, sucka," he said.

Anger flared in the Worm's eyes and he leaped at Corey, but just before he did he glanced in Aniri's direction.

Not happening, Corey thought, and instead of dancing away like a sane person would he ducked under the Worm's arms and threw a combination, boom boom, landed it in the same spot. The Worm came down on top of him. Corey felt the terrible strength of the hands that gripped him, trying to force him to the ground but he could feel the Worm favoring his right side. Corey twisted out of the Worm's grip and he saw his target again, hammered at it with his left. He didn't get as much into it this time but it was a question of accumulation now anyway. He broke free, backed away a few steps, bounced on the balls of his feet. He caught sight of the gray man out of the corner of his eye, there was a sick and hungry sheen to the sweat on the gray man's face. I still can't do anything about the gun, Corey thought, but he told himself not to think about that because he had no time. Aniri, who should have been hiding behind the Babalao, watched in horrified silence.

The Worm glanced her way again and Corey circled around to get between them. The Worm was crouched like a wounded bear. "He'll kill us both when this is over," Corey muttered. "You do know that, don't you." The Worm snarled by way of reply and he threw himself at Corey, exposing his damaged ribs once again. Corey ducked and threw his left but the Worm was spinning away, he'd been expecting that one and Corey felt the Worm's hand clutch the back of his neck. Corey tried to twist free but the Worm had him now, the larger man's weight crushing him down, forcing the air from his lungs, buckling his knees, taking him to the ground. But Corey Jackson hadn't done ten thousand back squats for nothing. With all of his remaining strength he levered himself back erect, driving the top of his skull into the Worm's face and then suddenly the weight was gone, he inhaled a big breath of clean air as the Worm reeled backward and went down. Corey straightened his back with some effort, the muscles complaining of the abuse.

"Finish him," the gray man said. "Finish him and I'll let her go."

Aniri was the first to move, she circled out around behind the Babalao and the Worm both, and then she was next to Corey, looking into his face, wiping the blood from his lips.

"No," she said.

Corey struggled to kick his brain into gear. "Babe," he said softly. "Please. Go now, just go, please."

"No," she said, shaking her head. "No more."

"Babe, listen to me. If you love me you gotta go, right now. I can't watch him kill you, I can't. Just go, please, baby . . ."

She shook her head.

The Worm rolled over onto his stomach.

"Your window of opportunity is closing," the gray man said, and he hefted his pistol.

The Babalao cleared his throat, they all turned to look at him, and then one by one they turned to see what he was looking at. A man loomed out of the darkness. He dragged a Chinese pimp by the back of his shirt collar. The pimp's face was unrecognizable. The guy dropped the pimp in between the gray man and the rest of them. "He belong to you?" he asked the gray man.

The Worm rolled over onto his back. "Saul Fowler," he said.

The gray man raised his gun.

Fowler stood and stared at the gray man. "It's yourself you should worry about," he said. "I found your little playpen."

The gray man cocked his chin. His face was a mask to scare little children, and their parents, too. "You're bluffing," he said.

"Am I really?" Fowler said. "Funny, O'Neill, but somehow I just can't picture you wearing a rubber. How much of your DNA they gonna find down in that floor drain? Because you know they're gonna look."

"Well, then, I don't have any time to waste, do I?" He raised the gun and pointed it at Fowler.

The Babalao cleared his throat. "You can't kill us all," he said. "This ends tonight."

The gray man glanced his way.

"You have less time than you think," Fowler said. "You got a buddy in the precinct? Actually, I don't think he likes you much. Guy named Scanlon. Works vice."

"What about him."

"You shoulda taken better care of him. I told Scanlon about the cash box you guys keep back at Los Paraíso. Yeah, I found it, the first night I was there. You know what I used to do for a living, don't you. That's how the Worm knew to call me a thief, back that first day I ran into him, because he got a heads-up from you. The cops in the precinct gave a heads-up to you and Josh Whelen. Probably the same guys that gave you the MO on the serial killer they been looking for. Bet you figured, two more bodies, who's gonna care? Anyhow, that's how your guys were on to me so quick. So you gotta know how hard it was for me to leave your money alone. And since I showed up you been too shy to show your face and they piled up too much dough to fit in the box. The dumb bastards got the rest of it in a Key Food shopping bag. I was in there the other night. I skimmed some but I left most of it alone. I figure Scanlon will take the money in the bag, and maybe about half what's in the cash box. Gotta leave some for evidence, Scanlon's a good enough cop to know that. You shoulda seen his face when I told him how much you had there."

"Nice try, fucko. I been running this thing for two years, almost. What Scanlon's gonna get his hands on ain't nothing. Once I get . . ."

A siren sounded in the distance. "Once you get where? They're *hitting your house right now. Scanlon didn't survive this long by being stupid. Once he and his boys figured out how much money is out there in the wind, they went crazy. They're hitting your house, they're hitting every building you own, they're gonna take down every single place you ever showed your face. You got nothing left, time they're done with you, you won't even have a pension anymore. It's over. I hope your old lady has someplace to stay tonight."*

The gray man stopped breathing. He looked away, off toward the projects, and his gun arm began to sink. The Babalao inched closer to the gray man but he was still too far away. Aniri dug her fingers into Corey Jackson's shoulders, pinning him to the spot where he stood.

"You know what they do to cops in prison, Frank."

The gray man turned back and stared at Fowler.

"That ain't even the worst part," Fowler said.

The gray man waited, expressionless.

Fowler gestured at the pimp. "This loser and his pal back by the pedestrian walkway both belong to Peter Kwok. I know you heard a him. He's gonna figure that makes this whole thing rightfully his. And that means you been stealing his money for two years now. And Peter Kwok is a very angry man. He's gonna burn your house down, man, he's gonna kill everyone you care about."

The gray man closed his eyes.

"Twelve grand a month," he said. "You believe that?"

The sirens were getting closer.

Fowler reached into his pocket, groped for a moment, fished out a hotel key, and tossed it to the Babalao. "Get them out of here," he said. The Babalao caught the key, then walked over and tried to hustle Corey and Aniri into motion but Aniri wouldn't move.

"What about your poor wife?" she said. "What's going to happen to her?"

The gray man moved then, he looked over in the direction of Avenue D where cop lights strobed the open spaces between the buildings, then he raised the gun barrel, pressed it underneath his chin. His face clenched like a fist, he inhaled one more time, and then he pulled the trigger. Corey was right, the .32 slug was too small to punch an exit wound through the gray man's skull but it bounced around inside, changing the shape of the gray man's head, for a moment he looked less like a man, more like a water balloon with a face painted on it, and then he pitched over on his back in the dirt of the park, eyes open, dead, his cartoon face staring up at the empty sky.

"Now can we go?" the Babalao said.

Fowler looked at Aniri. "I wasn't kidding about Kwok," he said. "You need to get off the street. Why don't you guys wait for me at the hotel." The Babalao managed to move Aniri, then, and soon the three of them were lost in the shadows.

"Vale," the Worm said.

"Yeah."

"Help me."

"Why."

The Worm struggled to his hands and knees. "You help me, I help you. I got a crash pad right over there in the projects," he said. "You got blood all over your pants."

Fowler sighed. "All right," he said. "Come on."

Coda

THERE ARE, I suppose, as many New York cities as there are people who live there, but I had sort of forgotten about the one you see late at night from the high floors of a midtown hotel. Manhattan lay far below my feet, twinkling and shining like a rich lady's jewelry box. This was the city that tourists paid money to see, to me it looked like a sort of zombie Disneyland, empty spaces and silent, motionless rides standing in mocking testimony that I was outside once again, looking in. The cruelest thing about it was the fact that I had come so close, or I thought I had, but in the end one more woman had decided that I was not what she had in mind after all. Maybe I was feeding the dragon, I don't know, but as I stood there in the hotel hallway looking out the window I knew in my gut that the correct dose of Percocet would knock this shit right out of me, that it would render me insensate enough to go on about my sham of a life without caring whether or not anyone gave a shit if I lived or died. The major difficulty with that mode of treatment is that it puts you on a track that will very shortly resemble free fall, and when you reach that bottom, you have only one option left if you can't stand the pain, and it is a rather permanent solution. And even knowing all that, it's a terrible pull to know that Eden, however transitory, is only a phone call away. I couldn't say yea or nay, though, because I had things to do, and the first thing involved the two kids who were, hopefully, holed up in my hotel room.

I knocked softly.

Aniri opened the door.

Wow, man, when she was up that close I could see why the kid from Alabama had fallen for her so hard.

She held a finger to her lips. "He's asleep," she said, but she stood back and motioned me inside. He lay on the hotel bed on his back, eyes closed and his breath rattling in his throat. It looked like his nose was broken and his upper lip was swollen. Aniri took my hand and sat me down in a chair by the window, and then she sat down across from me. "Did you see him?" she said softly, her eyes shining. "Did you see?" He'd stood up between her and a gun, he was probably the first guy who'd ever cared enough to do that, and she looked like she'd love him forever for it.

"I did." It was hard not to feel a little better, looking at her with her face all lit up. "But now you guys have got to get out of town."

A shadow passed through her eyes, a cloud across the sun. "I heard what you said. Peter . . . What was his name?"

"Peter Kwok."

"Will he really think I belong to him now?"

"Without question."

"Corey was on the phone earlier," she said. "There's a bus we can take to South Carolina, the day after tomorrow."

"No need to wait for that," I told her, and I fished the claim ticket for the Corolla out of my pocket. "Take this car. It ain't pretty but it will get you where you need to go. It's downstairs in the hotel garage."

She held the ticket in an open hand. "Why? Why give us your car?"

"Because at least one good thing has to come out of all this."

She stared at me for a long moment. I found it tough to breathe. "My ancestors were not like the people over here," she said. "Everybody in New York comes from somewhere else, but where I was born, people lived in the same little villages since the beginning of time. I think they knew some things that the rest of us have forgotten. That guy who was with us last night, did you notice him?"

"Guy in a suit? Looked like a lawyer?"

"Him," she said. "He's a Babalao." She must have noticed the blank look on my face. "A priest. From my part of the world. He says there are forces that we don't understand. But there are ways . . . The Babalao and I, we asked for help." She stared at me a moment longer. "The spirit he called up is named Oshun. The first woman. You may have felt her shadow."

I felt like I'd been punched in the gut.

"He said that's why you were brought to us last night."

"What else did he say?"

She hesitated. "He said that sometimes Oshun can seem cruel."

"Yeah, I get that."

She acted like she didn't hear me. "Does it make me crazy, believing in that?"

"You'll have to ask me some other day," I told her. "When I've had enough coffee. And more sleep." Because if she was crazy, I was, too.

"When Corey and I went to the Babalao," she said, "I knew there would be a price to pay. I can see in your face that you're the one who had to pay it, and I apologize for that. But ask yourself this, Saul Fowler. How many men do you know who've been touched by a goddess and lived to talk about it?"

I stood up. "Don't let him talk you into staying in the city."

She shook her head. "We already decided. We're gone. But I'm going to send my son to you. Look for him, say, twenty years from tonight. His name is Saul Fowler Jackson."

"That's an awful thing to do to a poor defenseless kid. Name him after your boy over there. Goober Jackson. How old is your son?"

"You're terrible." She grinned, though, and then she glanced over her shoulder where her man lay sleeping on the bed. "We haven't made him yet. But don't forget."

"Twenty years from tonight." I had to smile, in spite of everything. Some women can do that to you.

She walked me to the door. "You take care." She said it like she meant it, which felt pretty nice.

Maybe she was crazy.

Who could tell?

I NEVER FOUND out what happened to Hector; the last time I saw him Klaudia was wrapped around him, and she is beyond my reach. I'm still looking, not that I could do anything much for him. Spring for the services of a decent barber, maybe. Not knowing all of his last name has not helped my cause, and dealing with the city can be beyond maddening. I put the word out through Luisa that Hector Samisomethingorother had a rich uncle who wanted to make a contribution, but so far, nothing. A friend of mine told me that so long as someone says your name once in a while you are never truly dead, so most nights after I turn out the lights, I try to quiet my mind and then I say,

"Hector, five, maybe six, bowl haircut . . ." I don't know if it does either of us any good.

Sam Gelman, as he is now known, kept his gig at Los Paraíso. I don't think he really needs it anymore, but I suppose it keeps him grounded. When he isn't there he spends all his time at NYU, blazing new paths through thickets of abstract reasoning where few men go. I don't know that I have ever done a single constructive thing for him, not since the day I walked him across town, except perhaps to temper his enthusiasm for violently colored shirts. He makes me smile, though, and like Hector, he's got guts. I look in on him now and then.

I am in regular contact with Tommy, and I think his protege William has made me his pet project. If emotional maturity counts for anything, I'm like, fourteen, I guess, and he's nineteen going on sixty, so we make a good match. William keeps me in touch with what I have to do, should I wish to remain sane. Connection comes from such unexpected sources, and through it I am tied to life in ways I have never before experienced.

Who knew?

There was one last thing I felt like I had to do, from a certain perspective I suppose it was the sort of grand, useless gesture that addicts are good at, but there you are. It cost me about four grand to set up. The money didn't bother me at the time because I was still thinking of it as Mac's, but the begging that went along with it was much more distasteful. Mac initially hated the idea, and he didn't want any part of it. I eventually managed to guilt him into it. He was in town for the memorials anyway, he was a prime candidate, and he had the chops to pull it off. The limo guy was no problem, to him it was a straight money deal, five hundred bucks and I had one white stretch for the night. The club I picked out was a joint called Ballroom Ballroom, the place was way uptown but it was in a nice space and I figured, with a name like that, what I wanted had to be right up their alley. I met the music director on a Monday in the early afternoon, he and a couple of other guys were in there cleaning up the wreckage from Sunday night. The guy gave me attitude from the very start, maybe it was because I couldn't quit staring at his kewpie doll haircut. "We don't do bat mitzvahs," he kept saying. We were standing right next to the bar, I kept begging and he kept saying no. I told him my whole sad story, some of which was even true, and he just kept shaking his head. Finally the guy behind the bar walked around to where we were standing.

"We'll do it," he said.

The music director rolled his eyes. "Antonio . . ."

Antonio the bartender was a short and slight Hispanic guy but he wasn't going to be pushed around. He stepped up to the music director. "It'll be fine. We're doing it."

The music guy threw up his hands, literally, and walked away mumbling to himself. Antonio turned to me. "Come Sunday night," he told me. "Come early, say around nine o'clock. We get a lot of Spanish on Sundays anyhow. It'll be fine."

"You don't know how much I appreciate this," I told him. "How much do I . . ."

He shook his head. "Just take care of the band."

I really wanted to give him something. "Are you sure . . ."

He misunderstood me. "Of course I'm sure. They're musicians, all they really want is an audience. I'll speak to them first. You just tell them what you want them to play, and leave a nice tip."

The dress guy was the worst. I think he was afraid of me, and that never helps. I'm not sure he'd seen many guys like me in his shop. "Oh my gooowad," he kept saying. "By Sunday? And you don't even know her size?"

"No, but I figured you could go down Tenth Street and Avenue C, where she lives and . . ."

"Tenth and C? Oh my gooowad, that's a haarible block, haarible! I'd have to fit her, and then tailor the dress, it can't be done. And what if she hates it? You just . . . picked one out, like you were buying a bag of potato chips!"

"Why overthink it? She'll love it."

"You're nuts." His hands were two fluttering birds. "And I'm overbooked as it is. I'd love to help you, really . . ." He was like a tree in the fall, shaking and losing bits of himself all over. I took him by the shoulder, led him over to his sewing machine and sat him down. He didn't resist, and I thought he'd be more comfortable there. I sat down in his client chair.

"You're in business to make money," I told him.

"Yesss, but . . ."

"Can I try to explain why I need this?"

He gathered himself, I watched him do it. He rearranged himself on his chair, clapped his knees together and folded his hands in his lap. Then, when he was ready, he nodded.

"I met a lady," I told him.

"Common problem," he said. "Good luck with her."

"Not that kind of lady. She's Cuban. During the Korean War, she was a dancer. A professional. I wanna guess she was about nineteen or twenty, then. She showed me a picture. She was breathtaking. Back then." So much for the easy part.

"So she's, what, seventy now?" he said, his voice quiet.

Arithmetic again. "I don't know. Old. But have you ever been in a situation where you thought you knew what was going on, and then someone comes along and says something to you, something that makes it possible for you to see things completely differently?"

He nodded.

"It was like that." I wasn't sure how to tell the rest of it. It was one of those things that made a cracked kind of sense when you were just feeling for it but then when you tried to put it into words, you sounded like you were out of your mind. Even to yourself.

Even I thought I was losing it.

"So you want to repay a kindness," the dress guy said. "I can understand that. But surely something a bit more practical. Rent money, for example, or . . ."

"You know what, that's not exactly it." This was where the story started to get too much air under it, but there was no other way, so I sighed and jumped in. "When the Spanish brought African slaves to what became Cuba, the Africans brought their traditions with them. And when they got Christianized, okay, the goddess Oshun became Our Lady of Charity. I don't know if she's exactly a goddess. Probably not. A spirit, maybe, although that doesn't quite feel right, either . . ."

"A saint," the guy said.

I had him.

"I never believed in any of this shit," I told him. "I always thought, if you can't measure it, that means it ain't there. Black and white, cause and effect, mechanical universe."

He was shaking his head. "That's so five hundred years ago."

"So I'm told. Luisa . . ."

"Your dancer?"

"My dancer. She said . . . that Our Lady of Charity, or Oshun, or whoever, would sometimes, ah . . . look through a person's eyes. Speak with that person's voice. Feel with that person's emotions. Shadowing, she called it." I didn't buy it, not then and not now, but goddamn, it explained so much of what I'd been seeing. Frank Porter's mother, who'd made him take care of the Batshit-mobile, the office manager at Whelen and Ives, who'd pointed me at the Hotel Los Paraíso, the teller at the Bajun Bank, and on, and on. It just felt to me like I'd been led by the hand, all the way through.

And Klaudia.

It wasn't her. When I got to Klaudia's the next morning she had a big duffel bag open in the middle of her floor, most of her stuff packed away. "Are you okay?"

Stupid question, really. She didn't look okay. She was wearing a giant, shapeless brown sweater that effectively masked her features from her knees to her shoulders, and her blond hair hung like curtains on either side of her face, leaving barely enough space to peer out. "No," she said, and when she glanced at me her face, what I could see of it, flared red. "I was hoping I would miss you."

"Are you in there?" I asked her. "I can barely see you . . ."

"No," she said. "I know who you're looking for. She isn't here. I'm sorry, Mr. Fowler. I'm sorry for what I did to you, how I acted. It wasn't right."

"I thought . . ."

"I'm going to go visit my aunt in California. I'll call you when I, um, when I . . ." It was a lie and we both knew it. "I told you once that I didn't know what had come over me. I still don't. But it's gone now." She glanced at me, reddening. "Please . . ."

There was more, but it didn't change anything. Maybe Oshun or Our Lady of Charity had been looking out through Klaudia's eyes, but if that was true, she had departed, and that was that.

"If you were Christian," the dress guy said, "you'd say that God speaks to us through other people. Just saying."

"Yeah, maybe, but I am not a Christian. Listen, between you and me, I know this is all a misunderstanding. All of it. Oshun, the Yoruban spirit, is a misunderstanding, okay, a workable theory, trying to explain observable phenomena, nothing more. Our Lady of Charity is no different."

The dress guy sat there all smug, looking like he knew something I didn't. "But?"

"Yeah, but. What I think is this. For myself, at the very least, I think I need to make some kind of gesture. Something concrete. Something that says, 'I saw you. I felt you.' Something that nobody else would ever do." I pointed at the dress, the one I had picked out like a bag of chips off the rack. "This dress is my gesture."

He nodded. "All right."

Yeah, for two grand it was all right. I paid him half up front, went back with the other half when he was done. "You were right," he told me, misty-eyed. "She is beautiful."

So on Sunday night I sat at the bar in Ballroom Ballroom drinking lousy coffee, and it turned out the dress guy was right. I gave my high sign to the band leader when Mac and Luisa swept into the room. He nodded to me, gave them time for a drink at their table, and then he and his band kicked into a slow and old-fashioned Latin symphony of swirling dream and lost love that the kids in Ballroom Ballroom had probably never heard before.

Mac stood up, held out his hand.

Luisa was glowing, but so was Mac. I think I finally got him, that night. He was just an actor, under it all, and without a role and an audience he was empty and lost. The other dancers, all younger, gave way as Mac led her onto the floor. She saw me then, way back in my dark corner, I know she did, and again I got that funny little quarter smile, that sidelong knowing glance, and a nod to go with it.

So I don't much think the goonas forgive my sins, but I suspect that at least one among them is a woman, and that she understands.

And then Luisa and Mac tore that place up.

I left them to it.

Outside, I saw the white limo double-parked up by the corner, the driver leaning on the hood smoking a cigarette. I walked up to shake his hand and say thanks, thinking, as I did so, how different my life would have been if, in place of learning to do what I do, I had learned to dance, instead.

But we can't all be dancers.

I'll tell you one more thing I learned that night. I won't say that I figured it out, it was more like I woke up to it. But if I ever do drive the Batshitmobile up to the coast of Labrador, it will be for fishing, nothing more. If I cannot find what I need in New York City, I won't find it anywhere.

I do wonder who she was, the one with that smile I saw looking at me through Klaudia's eyes, I wonder where she went after that night at Los Paraíso, and I wonder if I'll ever see her again. Some dark nights, if I go up on the roof of my building and stare up into the sky, I think I feel something there, something just beyond my capacity to comprehend, but when I come back downstairs, it fades.

It's probably nothing.

Chalk it up to a family history of mental illness, or to my overheated imagination, or to the primitive need to believe in easy explanations. After all, the girl did tell me, that very first time I met her, that she didn't understand what had come over her, that she had been transformed by her friend's death, and maybe that's all it ever was. Maybe the sorrow and the rage she felt had activated some long-dormant gene, maybe a seed buried deep in her DNA from some distant savage ancestor had come alive long enough for her to help me hunt a murderer and avenge the death of an innocent, and then when the thing was finished it faded back into sleep. I do know that Klaudia Livatov turned into a pale imitation of the woman I had known, one that closely resembled Reiman's and Ms. Branch's memories of a frightened schoolgirl. I didn't tell her that I'd hang on to the cell so that she'd have my number if she ever changed her mind, I meant to, but in the moment, I couldn't think.

Maybe it was better that way. I really didn't need to see the embarrassment flame across her face when she looked my way. Let her go, some inner voice told me. Let her go and be what she needs to be.

Gelman told me I was looking at the whole thing the wrong way. I'd told him about Klaudia's transformation, and about the odd sensation I'd had, of being led, somehow, and that I thought maybe it was just a case of estrogen poisoning or something but I'd kept getting this funny look from the women I kept running into, and how could that be, man, when I didn't know them and they didn't know each other and now it was gone . . . Gelman had known exactly what I was talking about, even if I did not. "Yeah, so," he said, looking at me like I was an idiot.

"What do you mean, yeah, so?"

"Life is more complicated than we think it is," Gelman said, shrugging. "The universe is not a collection of inanimate objects. It's alive, and you and I are part of it. Whoever it was you saw in those women's eyes isn't gone, nothing is ever really gone. She's out there, somewhere. You'll run into her again someday." He paused, staring at me with those sad eyes, leaving me to wonder again how a shy and sheltered kid had gotten so goddamn smart. "It's the only explanation that makes any sense," he said. "If you think about it long enough, you'll see I'm right."

Maybe.

I'm holding on to the phone anyway just in case she decides to call me one day, but with each passing hour that star dims just a little more. I'll tell you something, though, once or twice I thought I caught her watching me through some other woman's eyes. I don't know if it's real or if I only want it so much that I make it feel like it is, but I swear I saw a woman just the other day looking at me through a bus window, she had that funny, queer little smile, that look that tells of longing, and maybe a touch of regret, but then the bus took off and she was gone.

Whoever she was. A goddess, maybe, or a spirit. Or maybe just a lady of charity.

Call it what you want.

If you liked *Shadow of a Thief*, keep reading
for a sneak peek at another gripping mystery
by Norman Green

THE LAST GIG

Available wherever e-books are sold!

Chapter One

THE THINGS A girl's gotta do to turn a buck . . .

Alessandra Martillo leaned across the pool table and lined up her shot. Black hair fell forward across her face and hung down over one eye. She knew Marty Stiles, the fat dude at the bar, was staring at the gap in her V-neck sweater, but she also knew that he couldn't help himself. Her single unobscured eye flicked once in his direction, then back down at the table as she struck the cue ball softly. It rolled half the length of the table, knocked the last striped ball into a corner pocket, then caromed off the end bumper and rolled to a stop about a foot and a half behind the eight ball. She straightened back up, ignored Marty, tapped her stick on the other corner pocket. Her opponent, relegated to observer status since four shots after the break, stepped forward and laid a folded twenty on the table. "Forget it," he said. "You're out of my league."

She shook her hair back out of her face and winked at him. "If that's the way you feel about it, baby." The guy walked off shaking his head.

She walked around the table and sank the rest of the balls. Now that her game was over, she hammered them home one by one, almost violently. No one had yet come forward with the price of the next game. Stiles didn't reach into his pocket, either. Marty never played anything, anywhere, unless he had an edge. Besides, when Al was dressed for the club, the guy could never think straight; all he could do was waste his time admiring her ass.

She knew she was no cover girl, but she was tall, dark, lean, fine enough in her own way. If you wanted a Barbie doll, she wasn't for you, and she was comfortable with that. She was more like the kind of broad who could pitch a shutout against your softball team, hit one out herself, then drink you under the table after the game. There were certain guys who went crazy for that, and Marty Stiles was one of them. She knew it: when she stared at him she could turn his guts to water. Every time she wore a pair of low-rise jeans his tongue would hang out so far you could put a knot in it and call it a tie. He'd had it bad for her for a while. He'd given her his best shot: laid off the sauce, dropped about thirty pounds, got into some new clothes, sprang for a fifty-dollar haircut . . . But when he made his move, she laughed at him.

Not a chance, she told him.

He hadn't taken defeat easily. He had a certain kind of fat guy charm, she had to admit it, and he certainly had the green, but she wasn't interested. Angered and insulted, for a while he'd told everyone who would listen that she was a rug-muncher. She hadn't minded that, but when he began speculating, aloud, how unnatural it was for a Puerto Rican chick like her to be so cold, she'd had a short and pointed conversation with the man.

She watched a new victim come forward—guy looked like an off-duty cop, young, big guns, Republican haircut. Looked like the kind of guy who let his size win most of his arguments. He approached the table, quarters in his hand. "May I have the plea sure?" he asked her. She looked at him, nodded, and he stuck the coins into the slot. The balls grumbled down into the tray beneath the table.

"Carlo," he said, holding out his hand. "You mind if I rack?"

"Alessandra," she said, and she shook his hand. "And I'm feeling so good tonight, I'm gonna let you break. How about that?"

"Beautiful thing," he said.

He got lucky, sank a ball off the break, then two more in quick succession before faltering. "Left you tough," he told her, backing away. "I don't think you have a move."

She chuckled softly, chalked the end of her stick, and then she ran the table on him. Carlo leaned against a column and watched in silence until it was over. "Twenty bucks," he said, reaching into his pocket. "That the standard bet?"

She shook her head. "Don't want you feeling like you been hustled."

"No, no," Carlo said. "Call it a lesson. You do this for a living?"

"Strictly amateur," she said, watching him. Her habit of making direct eye contact, together with her looks, intimidated a lot of men. Not this one, though.

"Listen," he said. "If I buy you a drink, will you show me how you drew the cue ball back on that last corner shot? I thought you were gonna scratch for sure."

She looked past him, caught a glimpse of Marty Stiles over at the bar, a sour look on his face as he downed a shot and picked up the beer chaser. She knew what Marty really wanted. He really wanted her to tell the guy to get lost, that she was taken, in love, going steady, head over heels crazy with this pudgy gentleman who—

"Cutty on the rocks," she said.

Carlo pulled a wad of bills out of his pocket, peeled off a twenty, and laid it on the table. "Right back," he said.

SHE FELT MARTY's eyes on her as she walked out of the place with Carlo about an hour later. Carlo's car was parked in two spots on the far side of the lot. She couldn't really blame him, it was a yellow Lamborghini Murcielago, a two-seat Italian sports car that optioned out for just north of three hundred grand, and it would be criminal, not to mention expensive, to find it with a ding from some meathead flinging his pickup door open.

"You like it?" he asked her.

"I love it," she told him. It was the truth.

"Climb in," he said. He put his hand on her butt and caressed her over to the passenger side door. "Let me take you for a ride."

They didn't get halfway across the lot before Marty Stiles stepped out from between two cars and stood directly in their path.

"Who is this guy?" Carlo said.

"Beats me," she said.

No one moved for about twenty seconds. Then Carlo blipped his throttle once. Twelve cylinders and five hundred and seventy-two horses murmured their impatience. Marty seemed to think it over for another ten seconds, then took a single step back, gave them just enough room to squeak by.

Carlo eased the car forward.

They passed by Stiles, his bellied shirt the only part of him visible, a hand-width away. He thumped his fist down on the car's roof as it passed.

Carlo stomped the brake. Marty backed away, groping for something under his jacket.

Carlo was cool, Al had to give him that. He didn't pop out of the car like an enraged prairie dog, he opened the door slowly and climbed out calmly. Marty walked unsteadily backward.

Carlo followed him five or six steps. "Exactly what," he said, his voice pitched low and hard, "is your fucking problem?"

Up ahead, a Pontiac GTO pulled up to the front door of the joint and stopped. The driver and his young female passenger got out, paused to watched the unfolding drama. "You oughta watch where the hell you're going," Marty snarled. "You almost ran over my foot!"

"You fat piece of shit." Carlo took another step in Marty's direction. "I am gonna—"

He was barely six feet away when Al made her move. Gripping the windowsill and the seat-back hard, she jackknifed her legs up out of the footwell, and, butt in the air, knees in her face, she levered herself over into the driver's seat. Nice, she thought. But it's a damn good thing this baby isn't a quarter of an inch shorter . . . She didn't bother to close the driver's-side door, she just tapped the magnesium shift paddle, eased on the throttle, let the door close itself. The V-12 murmured sweet lies in her ear as she pulled away slowly. She could just make out Carlo's shout, looked in the mirror, saw him running madly after her, saw Marty Stiles, red-faced, bent over laughing in the background. She toyed with Carlo, kept the Lambo just out of his reach, slid past the GTO, past the long, pink, phallic club awning where the Pontiac's occupants stood watching in amusement. She eased on the gas a little more when she hit the street, left Carlo standing there, hands on knees, sucking wind.

Aw, come on, Al, an inner voice whispered. The guy had his hand all over your ass, you owe him . . . She toggled off the traction control, stood on the gas. The engine bellowed in finest Italian operatic tradition; the Lambo spun madly. She did not have to fight it, it was now a living thing, a coconspirator, something you did not steer, you pled with it, you urged it with your knees and your hips, you let it feel your desire . . . The acceleration pressed her back into the seat as the car exploded down the street. Carlo dived for the safety of the ditch on the far side of the sidewalk as Alessandra and her new friend ripped off two beautiful tire-shredding donuts right where he'd been standing.

And then she rocketed away.

God, it was almost like the thing breathed for her, as though she could feel the air pouring over her painted skin, feel the soles of her shoes sliding on the pavement.

You shouldn't have done that, she thought, and the car slowed.

It was pointless, she thought, and stupid. The Lambo took the next corner calmly, almost quietly.

Oh, please, the inner voice said. What's the point of stealing a supercar if you can't behave like Supergirl, if only for a minute or so? Pete, the tow driver, was parked up on the next block. With intense regret, she slid up behind the big flatbed. It was already tilted down to the ground, Pete standing behind it with a cable in his hand. He was an older guy, gray ponytail and goatee, couple days' growth of beard, balding on the top.

Good-bye, doll, she thought, and she caressed the steering wheel. I'm really sorry to walk out on you this way, but it never would have worked. I can't afford you, honey, you're way too hot for me. I know, I know, it's a lame and tired excuse, but it's the truth.

It wasn't you, baby. It was me.

She opened the door and climbed out. "Hook it up, Petey baby, and let's get the hell out of here."

Just then Pete's phone went off, and she could hear Marty Stiles's voice shouting, right on the edge of panic. "Mayday! Mayday!" he yelled. "The mark jacked that GTO and he's headed in your direction!" In the distance she heard the basso profundo roar of an American V-8, with cop sirens singing soprano harmony in the background.

Here we go, she thought, and she cracked her knuckles. Here we go . . . "Hook that mother, Petey, get that bitch onto the truck and she's ours. I'll deal with this guy . . ."

IT WAS ALL over by the time Stiles got there. Alessandra leaned her butt against the fender of the cruiser, her arms crossed in front. She watched Stiles by the flashing lights of the police car and the ambulance. He horsed himself out of his car, looked at her and shook his head, but he kept his distance. She knew he was standing over there trying to figure a way to make this all her fault. It's your job, she told him silently, you're the guy who's supposed to give the mark the standard speech: "Nothing personal, my man, but you don't make the payments, Lambo takes their car back, so just chill, no point in anybody going to jail over this . . ."

The yellow Lamborghini sat up high on the flatbed. A blue-uniformed policeman watched two EMTs who were trying to attend to the Lambo's driver, but the guy couldn't hold still, he was down on his knees in the street, puking. He held his shaking right arm awkwardly away from his body. The cop's partner was over behind the cruiser, talking to Pete, who pitched his voice loud enough for her to hear.

"Well, Officer, she pulls up in the car, right, I get it hooked up, then we hear this yoyo one block over, he musta seen my flashers. So he comes screaming up, right, jumps out, but he don't care about the car anymore, he goes right for Martillo. He's gotta be twice her size, right, he makes a grab for her, I'm wondering how much of a pussy I am for not jumping in, then I hear this funny noise, sounds like when you bite a piece of celery, right, then the guy's fucking screaming. I mean, he's not yelling like a man, he's screaming like my wife after I track dog shit on the carpet. He had a piece, right, but when he tries to pull it out, she kicks him on the outside of his knee, he goes down, she takes the piece and tosses it under the truck. Which is where it still is. Whole thing took maybe ten seconds."

"She wasn't armed?"

"No, sir. I seen the whole thing. She done it just like I told you."

Another cruiser rolled up behind the tow. More lights, Al thought. Just in case someone wants to see us from the freakin' moon. Two cops got out, walked right past her, over to where the EMTs were trying to splint the Lambo driver's broken fingers. She shook her head. I do all the freakin' work, she thought, and what do I get? I get to stand here and wait while the big boys figure things out.

Same old shit.

Stiles stood over by his car. She ignored him, watched the EMTs. She knew he was staring, but the man just couldn't help himself.

Chapter Two

MARTY STILES, ELBOWS on the table, watched the dancer at the other end of the stage. She didn't look half bad, at least not from that distance. Be careful, he thought. You've had too much to drink tonight to be able to think regular . . . He didn't look at Daniel Caughlan, the man sitting next to him. "I'd love to do it for you," he said. "Problem is, Al is the best man I got. I put her full time on this, I gotta hire another broad for the office, then I gotta find another guy to do what Al does out in the field. You know what I'm sayin'? So it ain't like I just gotta replace the one guy. An' I don't know where I would get somebody else like her. This business takes a special kinda person. Al has a real feel for it." He finally glanced in Caughlan's direction. Fucking guy, Marty thought, he's watching me like a cat watching a parakeet.

"I'll make it worth your trouble," Caughlan said.

Marty Stiles shivered. He had known Daniel "Mickey" Caughlan for years. Stiles had been a rookie cop when he'd first run across the guy. Caughlan had been one of the few to survive the immolation of the Irish gangs that had once haunted the neighborhood of

Hell's Kitchen on Manhattan's west side. He had been just another body back then, just another face. Perhaps smarter and without question luckier than his betters, he had survived, left alone at the reins of something called Pennsylvania Transfer Corporation when his silent partners all wound up dead or serving long prison sentences. The last of them, Patrick Donleavy, had disappeared without a trace. Donleavy had been Caughlan's friend and patron, but Rudolph Giuliani, then a prominent DA making his bones on the backs of the mobsters in New York City, had been hard on Donleavy's trail, and if Donleavy had fallen, Caughlan would have been next. After Donleavy's disappearance, the hounds had snapped at Caughlan's heels for the next six months or so, but the trail was cold, and eventually they wandered off to seek other amusements. Stiles had no direct evidence of what may have happened to Donleavy, but he knew what his gut told him. What he did know for a fact was that in the years since, Caughlan, using the ruthless tactics taught to him by Donleavy and his compatriots, had built Pennsylvania Transfer into a major interstate shipping firm.

Caughlan stared back at him, his face blank. "Look," he said, "I got a situation and I gotta do something about it, Marty, but I can't have you stomping around in my life with those big feet of yours. No offense, but you got the finesse of a hippopotamus with a bad case of hemorrhoids. I've heard about your girl Alessandra, and she's the one I want. Don't worry, you'll be working this, too. There are some elements to this that are gonna require your special talents. You got the contacts and you got the moves. And there might be some serious money in it."

Stiles could hardly hear him over the noise of the music and the shouted conversations going on around them. That's why he picked this place, Marty thought, his stomach turning over. The

FBI could have a bug stuck right up Caughlan's ass, but they still couldn't hear a word, not over the roar in this place. Whatever Caughlan wants done, it can't be anything good. He thought for a second or two, wondering how bad he wanted Mickey Caughlan's money.

Caughlan put a hand on Stiles's shoulder, sending a chill all the way through him. Stiles tore his eyes away from the dancer, shifted in his seat, and took a long look at Mickey Caughlan. "How serious?"

Caughlan shrugged. "I'm thinking we're probably talking low six figures here."

Marty's eyes went wide. "No shit."

"Watch the girl, there." Caughlan gestured with his chin. "I think she likes you."

Stiles turned back to the stage. The dancer was still a long way off, but there was another one standing right next to him. Late twenties, he figured, blue eyes, dirty-blond hair, heavy breasts bursting out of a sequined bra. As he turned in her direction, he felt Caughlan press a folded piece of paper into his right hand. Glancing at it, he was astonished to see a hundred-dollar bill materialize in his fist. "Ben Franklin," he said to the girl. "My favorite president."

"Mine, too," she told him. She leaned up close, stuck her hand in his crotch. She whispered in his ear. "You like to dance, baby? Dead Benny always makes me feel like dancing." She massaged his growing erection through his pants.

Marty could hear a trace of the woman's Slavic origins. "Me, too," he told her. "But I prolly need some lessons."

She reached across with her other hand, plucked the bill out of his grasp, gave him one final squeeze. "Past the men's room door," she told him. "Go through the blue doorway. First room on the right. When you finish your business here, I'll be waiting for you." She leaned up close again, touched the tip of her tongue to his eyebrow, then released him. She stepped back slowly, turned her back, and walked away.

Marty swallowed, then looked back at Caughlan. "She come courtesy of you?" he said.

"Not me," Caughlan said. "Seen her coming, though. Man, I love this place."

"You kidding? You didn't pay her off?"

"All right," Caughlan said. "Maybe I tipped her on the way in. Maybe I told her about this lonesome and generous businessman I was meeting here tonight."

Stiles's head swam. "Just what is it you want me to do, Mickey?"

Caughlan glanced past Stiles at the departing blonde. "All right," he said again. "Listen up. Six, seven months ago, one of my trucks picked up a container off a ship down in Port Newark. No big deal, we do that all the time. According to the bill of lading, the thing was supposed to be a load of blue jeans headed for some discounter in Chicago. Okay? So the truck gets hijacked. We find it down by the river in Jersey City a couple days later. Container is empty, except for the driver; poor bastard was inside, deader than last year's Christmas goose."

"I didn't hear nothing about it," Marty said. "It musta not made the papers."

Caughlan shook his head. "We kept it quiet," he said. "There was some brown goo on the floor of the container."

"Goo?"

"Corn syrup, like. Thick and oily."

"Yeah." Marty Stiles felt the hair on the back of his neck rising. "What was it?"

"Chemist I sent it to said it was opium base," Caughlan said. "Stuff is like crude oil. Couple steps away from gasoline, but still damned expensive. You get me?"

"Yeah, I get you. What'd you do about it?"

Caughlan shook his head. "Nothing. Stuck our heads back in the sand. Hoped it would all go away."

Stiles stared at him. "For real, man. What did you do?"

"We waited. Figured whoever belonged to that shit would come looking for it, but they never showed."

"So you're off the hook."

"I don't think so. I got a tip, there's a secret grand jury looking into Penn Transfer. And into me."

"Over this? Over dope?"

"Don't know for sure," Caughlan said. "But I wouldn't want to bet against it."

I don't want to ask this question, Marty thought, but I have to, because Caughlan knows I should ask it. "You into dope? You get a piece of what moves through Port Newark?"

For a second, Caughlan looked like what Marty knew him to be: hard, cold, merciless. Then he looked away, caught a waitress's eye, waved his empty glass. He looked back at Stiles. "You and I go way back, Marty," he said. "You know I never been a altar boy. Joint like this one, maybe the cops think it's a brothel, and maybe it is, but I ask you: man can't get drunk and get his ashes hauled, what's the use in living? I ask you, where's the harm done? But the drug trade burns everyone it touches. I always kept my distance."

"So? You think someone's setting you up?"

"No. I think someone's using Penn Transfer to move their shit. I think they figure when the cops finally tumble to it, I'll be the one that swings, not them."

Marty nodded. What cop would bother looking past a man like Caughlan? "Smart," he said.

Caughlan leaned over and whispered in Stiles's ear. "Hundred large," he said, "you find out who's doing it. Buck and a half, you give me the score on the grand jury, too. A deuce if you get it all done before the end of the month."

It was too much money to even consider passing up, even if he was gonna have to walk through a few dark places to get it. "All right," he said. "But how do you want to work this? What is it that you want Al for?"

"I don't wanna tell you how to do your job," Caughlan said. "If I knew how to handle this, it'd be done already. But I figure you probably know every crooked cop and scumbag lawyer in Jersey. You chase the grand jury angle. Let Martillo loose, let her chase it from the other end."

Clever, Marty thought. Once I start turning over rocks, things will start to happen. Caughlan thinks it's someone close to him, and figures he'll have Al watching his back. "There's one problem with all of this," he said.

"Yeah? What's that?"

"Al. Al's the problem. She ain't great at following instructions. Matter of fact, she's prolly the single most annoying female I ever met. The bitch could find a white cat in a snowstorm, but she could never explain how she knew where to look. You get her going on this, she's gonna go where her nose tells her to go. You hear what I'm saying? You got some closets you don't want her looking in, that's your tough luck, she's gonna do what she wants to do. You better think about that before you pull the trigger here."

"I can handle her," Caughlan said. "Besides, I got too much at risk to worry about a few indiscretions coming to light."

Stiles watched the dancer. Caughlan thinks he knows Al, he thought, but the guy has no idea, not if he thinks he can handle her. Unless he figures he can just bury her once she gets to be too much of a pain in his ass. And good luck with that . . . But I might be putting Al in a tough spot with this, Stiles thought. His stomach rolled once, but the thought of two hundred grand in his bank account had a wonderfully restorative effect. "We need to talk money. I can't afford to go on spec. I'm gonna need fifty large up front and a guaranteed hundred, minimum, when we're done."

Caughlan stared at him for a moment. "Agreed," he said. "Set up a meeting—you, me, and Martillo. We can go over the details there."

"Okay," Stiles said.

Caughlan got off his stool. "The lady's waiting for you," he said. "Enjoy yourself, but watch that girl, she bites."

"She what? What did you say?"

Caughlan nodded. "Something wrong with her head. She bites. She'll want to blow you, but don't you let her. You knock her down and give it to her proper."

About the Author

NORMAN GREEN IS the author of seven crime novels. Born in Massachusetts, he now lives in New Jersey with his wife.

Discover great authors, exclusive offers, and more at hc.com.